M000201832

THE PRIVILEGE OF
THE DEAD

MILES NELSON

WORKING STIFF PRESS
www.MilesNelsonAuthor.com

The Privilege of The Dead

A Novel

Copyright 2018 by Miles Nelson

All rights reserved

ISBN-13: 9781732640504 (Paperback edition)

ISBN-10: 1732640505 (Paperback edition)

Printed in the United States of America

No part of this book may be used or reproduced in any manner whatsoever without the written permission of the author, except in the case of brief quotations embodied in critical articles or reviews.

The Privilege of the Dead is a work of fiction, and is entirely the product of the author's imagination. Apart from brief references to various real bars, restaurants, hotels, or other retail businesses visited by the characters, any similarity to actual persons, corporations, events, or situations is entirely coincidental.

Back cover author photo by Bonnie Boumiea

Back cover main photo Dreamstime

All other photos, artwork, and design by Miles Nelson

WORKING STIFF PRESS
www.MilesNelsonAuthor.com

For my wife Bonnie.
Thanks for supporting the dream and sharing the journey.

1

I t was my head cold that saved us.

Brenda was staying with me for a four-day weekend and I'd had the bad timing to pick up a cold from somewhere earlier in the week. By Saturday the worst of it was over, but I'd still taken some cold medicine to clear up my head and help me sleep. The sleeping part didn't work out too well, and by about midnight I'd decided to move into the guest room. I wanted to spare Brenda the annoying sounds of all my throat-clearing so at least she could get a few winks.

Fragments of dreams came and went as I tossed and turned. The room was very warm and soon felt stuffy, so I opened the window a third of the way and enjoyed the freshness of the cool air. Though cold for mid-December, there was little wind, and no arctic blast came rushing in. I left the window open slightly and got back into bed in hopes of better rest and more dreams.

Sound sleep eluded me, and at one point I reached over to the nightstand for my water bottle and took a drink. The glowing numbers of the alarm clock showed just a few minutes past three. As I set the bottle down, a sound from outside caught my ear. A stick breaking maybe, or something falling to the frozen leaves in the wooded strip that bordered my back yard and made up part of the boundary of the neighborhood. Nothing shocking necessarily, as I knew there were deer in the area, ground hogs, dogs—could be any of them. I was wide awake, so I slid out of bed and knelt by the window to look and listen.

The house was a twin. As I faced out the back window my connecting neighbor was to the right, while the narrow side yard and my other neighbor's fence with her house beyond was over to the left. The wooded strip that bordered the back yards of all the homes in this part of the neighborhood was about twenty feet deep, and beyond that was a sidewalk along a busy township road. The slope that my house sat on was steep enough that you could walk in the front door on the main level and then out though the basement door into the back yard.

As I listened at the window I heard something again, and it wasn't deer and it wasn't a groundhog, not unless it spoke English. The voices were quiet, but because the night was so still, I was sure I could hear bits of muffled conversation. The voices were accompanied by other sounds of twigs breaking and leaves crunching. I realized that there were people out there, somewhere in the trees in my back yard, at three in the morning.

I moved closer to the screen to look down. The deck off the main floor just below obscured my view of much of the small back yard, but between the outer edge of the deck and the wooded area along the rear, I could still see a patch of moonlit grass. As I tried to better gauge where the voices had come from, I saw several dark figures emerge from the tree line. At least three, or maybe four—it was hard to tell.

My first thought was that for some reason they were cutting through the yard from the sidewalk on the other side of the trees and into the community, but they didn't go up the side yard towards my street. Instead, they moved diagonally towards the back of my house, going under the deck and out of sight. Once under the deck, I knew they would be within feet of both the basement window and the sliding glass door.

I heard a few more snatches of conversation down below, and decided that whoever they were, they must now be at the basement slider. Then I heard a sound that I remembered from long ago when my family had spent years fixing up an old Victorian house at the Jersey

Shore. The sound of glass being cut was a unique, high-pitched scratching. Somebody was down in the back yard using a glass cutter on the door.

My mind raced, and I tried to make sense of what was happening. *Who the hell were these guys? And why?* I wasn't anybody. Not rich or famous. And anyway, most break-ins happened during the day when the owners were away. *Was I still dreaming?* I went to move and for a moment my legs didn't respond to the instructions from my brain. I heard the scratching again and that shook me free and into action. There would be time to try to make sense of it later. I invested fifteen seconds in pulling on my jeans, grabbed a small flashlight from the nightstand, and went quickly down the short hall to the master bedroom, shrouding the beam of the flashlight with my hand.

As I entered the master bedroom, I rapped lightly on the door to wake Brenda up.

"Hey—are you awake? I need you to wake up." Her bedside lamp came on and I could see that she was sitting up, confused and questioning. I knelt by the empty side of the bed.

"I'm up—I'm awake," she said. "I heard you in the other room. What's going on?"

"Shhh—listen. I need you to listen to me carefully and I don't have time to repeat myself."

She nodded.

"I heard voices in the back yard just now and I think some men are trying to break in. They're trying to get through the slider downstairs. I have no idea why. Push that lamp down now—less light—less light." She reached over and pushed the gooseneck way down. "My phone's down on the charger—is yours up here?"

She reacted quickly, grabbing her iPhone from the nightstand. "Yes, got it." She was on her feet and came around to my side of the bed.

She watched as I reached between the mattress and the box spring, felt around a bit, and pulled out three heavy objects, plopping them all on top of the comforter. A Beretta 92F automatic, one spare magazine, and a Ruger .357 magnum revolver. I took another small flashlight from the floor beside the bed, and added that to the collection.

I grabbed her shoulders and faced her straight on.

"Okay, I don't know what's happening but it's happening. I want you to go into the closet, call 911 and tell them what I told you—I heard people in the back yard and I think they're trying to break in. Take this." I handed her the revolver. "You shot this at the range that one time and you liked it, remember? No safety—you just pull the trigger and you have five shots. Please don't shoot me."

She nodded, accepting the gun and also the flashlight. I switched the flashlight on, folding her hand around it to muffle most of the light and pointing it down to the floor.

Picking up the Beretta, I pulled back the slide and let it fly forward, chambering the first round and noting carefully in the low light that I saw the shiny brass go into the chamber. I flicked the safety on and shoved it partway into my right rear pocket, a makeshift holster. The Beretta was a fine machine. I had fired at least a thousand rounds through it at the range and had never had a single jam or any other kind of malfunction. It was essentially the civilian version of the standard US Military sidearm—the M9—which I had first used during my basic training more than thirty years before, and in numerous firefights after that. My pistol was factory stock except for the hard rubber grips I'd added and the little dots of a bright white modeling paint I had dabbed on to the sights. There were fifteen rounds in the gun now and fifteen more in the spare magazine, which I scooped up and shoved into the left rear pocket of my jeans.

"Do what I said now—in the closet, call 911, pile some clothes around you and keep the flashlight off but handy." As I spoke I circled the bed and switched off the lamp, my own flashlight on now and held low.

"I'm going downstairs to see if I can scare them off. I'm hoping they never get in. I'll knock on the hallway wall when I come back up, got it? Right on the other side of the closet."

She was starting to dial the phone while moving into the closet. "Why do you have to go down there? Are you sure you need to?"

It was a fair question. Whoever these people were, I had to keep them away from her at all costs. In the condensed clarity of that moment, I knew like I had known few things before that I needed to do whatever I could to keep them from getting up the stairs.

"I want to stop them from getting in at all. I hope if I turn on the basement light that'll scare them away from the door. Make that call— we'll be okay." I gave her a quick hug. "I'll be right back—don't shoot me."

I heard what sounded like the 911 operator answering as I closed her in the walk-in closet and went back out of the room. Out in the hallway, I shoved the little flashlight into my hip pocket and drew the Beretta, sweeping the safety off with my thumb.

I paused for a few seconds at the top of the stairs. The house was silent. I started down as quickly but as lightly as possible, careful to avoid the creaky spot at the left end of the fourth stair down. As I approached the landing, I paused and listened again. I needed to get to the basement before they got through that glass door. Enough moon-light was coming down the hall that I could see around the empty living room and foyer at the bottom of the stairs. Everything looked in order. I stepped from the carpeted landing out onto the hardwood floor and turned to face down the hallway towards the rear of the house. I paused again to listen.

It was then that I heard what sounded like muffled conversation roughly below me on the basement stairs. I gritted my teeth and cursed silently to myself. I was too late to try to keep them out of the house. I went back up the stairs as quietly as I could, carefully avoiding the creaky step. In the hallway just off the top of the stairs, I flattened myself into a small alcove, hoping it would provide a measure of concealment from anyone coming up.

With my night vision intact, the end of the hallway and the top of the stairs were fairly well lit by the moonlight coming in through the guest room window off to the right. I froze and listened. Whoever they were, they were now on the first floor. I could hear a few whispers and then some footsteps in the hallway below. At least three men. And then

I heard a slightly different sound—someone had stepped from the hardwood hallway floor onto the carpeted landing.

I concentrated to control my breathing. I moved the Beretta to my left hand just long enough to wipe my right hand on my jeans. I tensed and released my leg muscles just to make sure I could move when needed. I checked that the hammer was back on the Beretta and that the safety was in the off position. I remembered a gunfight mantra that an instructor had taught me years ago: *In a fight—front sight. In a fight—front sight.* I heard footsteps coming up the stairs, and then time slowed down to tenths-of-a-second increments.

I heard the creak of someone reaching that fourth step from the top. I took a breath and stepped out from the alcove, pistol first in a two-handed grip. Someone was right there, a dark man-sized shape, just one or two steps down. I fired immediately, it seemed at the time into his head or upper chest. The muzzle was almost touching him, and the blast illuminated a startled face. I fired several more times and he let out a gurgling scream and fell away, tumbling down the stairwell and into one or two more people below. As he fell back, I stepped further out to center myself at the top of the stairs and let the lead fly downwards, trying to fire into whatever was upright and just putting that white dot onto the dark shapes below. Another shape fell. Two, three? I heard screams, yells, and crashes. In the low light and with all the bright flashes it was hard to tell how many of them there were. As they tumbled down onto one another, I kept firing at the shapes until the slide locked back on my empty gun. I didn't see anyone left who appeared to be still standing; just a big jumble all over the landing below and partway up the stairs. In there somewhere I thought I had heard one or more gunshots from something other than the Beretta, but I wasn't aware of having been hit.

I paused for a few seconds and took several deep breaths. I shook myself just to make sure that my brain was still in control of my body. My ears were ringing from the gunshots in the small space. Practice and training paid off as I released the empty magazine, and let it drop free to tumble down into the stairwell, replaced quickly with the full spare from my rear pocket. A quick flick of the lever with my right thumb and the slide flew forward, chambering the first cartridge. Fifteen rounds fired and now fifteen more ready. It couldn't have been more than thirty or forty seconds since I'd fired the first shot.

All pretense at quiet was gone, and I realized there must still be at least one person alive downstairs because I heard some kind of frantic yelling and someone running back towards the rear of the house. *Could there be two?* I bounded down the stairs, trying to avoid the bodies. Near the landing, my foot caught on someone and I tripped and fell on my ass. I heard a loud grunt and felt someone struggling under me. I slammed my elbow back into their chest and heard a yell. My body was partially lifted as the struggling continued, and then I felt a sudden, searing pain in my thigh.

"Fuck! You fucking stabbed me!"

I twisted around to bring up the gun, grabbing a fistful of hair with my left hand. I smashed the gun down, with a thud and a crack of breaking bone or teeth, and then fired downwards. In the instant of the bright flash I saw a distorted mess of a face and felt a splatter of something warm and wet. The body under me jerked once and then was still. I righted myself on the landing, my bare feet on the cold hardwood floor. My thigh hurt but it wasn't unbearable. I rubbed the area for a second and found it wet, but was relieved to not feel a knife still sticking out anywhere.

A sound to my left brought me back to the immediate business at hand. Framed against the moonlit door dead ahead down the hallway and at the rear of the house, someone was struggling to open the sliding glass door out to the deck, clawing at the latch mechanism.

With a few steps, I closed most of the distance down the hallway just as the figure turned my way, his back now against the door. I caught a glimpse in the moonlight of something shiny in his right hand. He jerked his hand up and fired wildly in my direction. I dropped to one knee. Three, four, maybe more shots whizzed around and mostly found homes in wood or sheetrock, but one bit into my left side. I felt a tug and then a sharp hot pain. I heard the gun clicking and realized that his revolver must be empty. I managed a decent two-handed shooting position and did my best to line up the white front sight dot on his center mass. I fired and kept firing, seven or eight times at least, before willing my trigger finger to stop. He jerked and spasmed as the jacketed nine-millimeter bullets tore into his chest and abdomen. One shot went either past or through him, partially shattering the glass door, and his body arched back through the wreckage. The double panes held in place enough to support him, bent over backwards, half in and half out. I watched briefly as he seemed to reach an arm towards the star-filled sky. With a final convulsion he was still, a grotesque, bloody statue in the moonlight.

I stood up, panting, and leaned against the wall. I felt my side where the bullet had hit. Wetness again, and painful as hell, but it seemed to be just a graze. I figured there were three dead bodies in the stairwell and now this guy stuck in the glass door. But then I heard something else. In the kitchen, which opened up to the right, someone was breathing heavy and fast. *Man, still more? Five?*

On the right wall, just before it gave way into the room, I felt for the main kitchen light switch that controlled the recessed ceiling cans. I moved the dimmer slide almost to the bottom and then flicked the switch up, turning the lights on. I stepped forward immediately, turned to the right to face into the kitchen and dropped to one knee with my gun up and ready to fire. The kitchen was now bathed in soft light.

A wobbly voice from across the room yelled something that sounded like "Don't shoot me!"

And there he was—the fifth guy. Despite the winter clothes, I could tell he was skinny and about my height, and he was backed up against the refrigerator. He had a pistol in his right hand, but it was pointed down at the floor. He was shaking and panting, almost hyperventilating. He was clearly terrified, and squinting in the sudden light.

"Please—please don't shoot. I was just supposed to drive..." He seemed to realize that he was still holding the gun. He opened his hand and let it drop to the floor. It clattered on the tile. He held both hands up with palms out.

"How many of you?" I said as forcefully as I could get out and ended up spitting out a raspy yell. I was fighting my own rushing breaths and my own shakes. "How many of you are there?" I was standing now and had moved a few feet closer. I pointed at him, then to the guy in the window. "You, him, the stairs—how fucking many?"

"Five, five, there are five of us." He was hyperventilating and barely able to get words out. "I was driving, and that's Joe there..." He pointed to the dead guy hanging through the window. "And Tony..."

And then I shot him in the chest and kept firing until the slide locked back for the second time. One shot went too far to the right and took out the microwave, but the other five or six ripped into his torso. He danced against the refrigerator and then slid to the floor. One of his legs kicked a few times, and then he was still. I thought I saw holes in the refrigerator door. It briefly occurred to me at that moment that I really hoped he was telling the truth about the five count, because I was now out of ammo.

I walked towards him, setting the empty Beretta on the sideboard. He was dead and still. The house seemed quiet aside from the ringing in my ears. I bent to pick up his gun, which looked like an old Smith & Wesson thirty-eight, but stopped myself mid-scoop, thinking of something better. I straightened and went quickly but stiffly across into the den, where I reached up to the corner of the big oak bookcase and grabbed the Walther PPK/s that I kept up there. I had just enough strength to pull back the slide and let it fly home, the gun now ready to fire.

I did a quick loop back through the kitchen, dining room, living room, and up the hall again, smacking light switches on as I went, the Walther's muzzle leading the way at all times. I took a peek into the laundry room, which looked clear, and noted that the door to the garage was still locked. I looked down the basement stairs and listened for a moment but didn't go down there. I figured the cops would arrive soon and they could earn their keep by clearing that part of the house.

I was coming down from an adrenaline high and my wounds were tired of being ignored. I was fighting a sudden wave of exhaustion and nausea. The house stank of gunpowder, blood, urine, and worse things released by bodies torn by violent death.

Brenda! I grabbed my phone from the charger at the end of the breakfast bar and called her. She answered quickly and breathlessly, almost yelling into the phone.

"Dean—what's going on? Are you okay?

"Yes, I'm..."

"Are you okay?"

"I'm okay, yes—yes. But stay up there. There's a bunch of bodies down here..." But I could already hear her running down the short hallway above me. I put my back against the wall opposite the landing and slid to the floor, dropping the phone and the Walther at my side. The light at the top of the stairs came on. I heard one scream followed by gagging and cursing. As she came down the stairs, I heard words that would have made a drunken trucker blush.

At the landing she stepped carefully around the tangle of dead limbs. She held her hands to the sides of her head as though trying to block it all out. It reminded me of that famous abstract painting of someone screaming.

"Jesus Christ—what is going on? Who are these people? What the..."

In the insanity of that blood-soaked early morning moment, I had to laugh out loud. It came out more like a painful groan.

She looked across at me, and, with a gasp, took the few steps and threw her arms around me.

And then we heard the sirens.

2

The house was soon flooded with police. Uniforms, plain clothes, two who identified themselves as county detectives, and a few more who looked like state troopers. They checked the basement carefully along with the rest of the house, the yard, and most of the neighborhood. They marveled at the mess of bodies, looked at me, and talked amongst themselves. They measured and photographed everything and everyone. There was plenty of mouth-holding and at least one person who ran out the front door to throw up in the yard. While the EMTs worked on me, I had just a few minutes to give the rough story to a group of cops and to Brenda at the same time, who at that point really didn't know much more than they did. I summarized what little I knew as well as I could.

Numerous questions were asked and I did my best to answer.

"The guy in the kitchen," one officer asked, "did he fire at you?"

"No, I didn't let him," I said. "He pointed a gun at me and I shot first. He had a revolver. It should still be there on the floor."

"And the only weapon you fired was the Beretta?" another asked. "Is that right?"

"Yeah, I emptied two mags," I said. "Then I grabbed the Walther, but it was all over. I called upstairs for Brenda. Then we heard sirens."

And no, I had never been in a gang or in prison. I was as much at a loss as they were. My best guess was that these guys had somehow come to the wrong house, looking for someone else and loaded for bear. No, I wasn't an undercover cop. Yes, I had been in the navy, long ago.

The questioning stopped when the EMTs insisted on taking me out the door to a stretcher. The township police told us they had someone who would come out and board up both sliding glass doors, so we made sure they had a house key and they let me go to the hospital. Brenda grabbed a few things and rode in the ambulance with me.

————

A gunshot and a stabbing were a big deal at our local emergency room and several doctors were rousted out of bed for the occasion. Thankfully, my wounds, while serious, weren't life-threatening. The guy who had managed to knife me on the landing couldn't have had much steam left in him at the time, because that wound was only about an inch deep. It hurt like hell before they juiced me up, but due to the way the knife had gone in, lined up with the muscle as opposed to cutting across at right angles, the damage was minimal. I was told that it should heal quickly.

The bullet wound was examined and treated very carefully, and there as well, I had been damn lucky. For the first time I was glad to have some love handles. The surgeon said the bullet had been small —probably a twenty-two. It had gone through my left side, mostly through fat, and just far enough in that it had a clear entrance and exit. Three quarters of an inch farther away from my center and it would have been a graze or even a miss. Several doctors concurred that it was an ideal bullet wound to have, should you need to have one at all.

At one point, when they had me propped up on my right side, I felt hands touching parts of my back, and heard two of the doctors talking.

"That looks like an old bullet wound," one said. "Look, there's another there."

"And look here," another said, "And here. I count four—yeah, four. Could they be something else?"

Both doctors came around the table and into my view. I could just make out the names on their plastic tags. I had a good guess at what they were going to say.

"Have you ever been shot?" Dr. Ward asked. "I mean, before today? You have marks on your back that look like old bullet wounds."

"Yes," I said. "Navy special ops, long time ago. Those holes are what made me get out. Ninety-two—no—ninety-three, bunch of us got shot up. That was another bad night. You can check my records."

"That's fine," he said, "we'll leave that to the police. Just so you understand that we'll have to report it to them."

"Sure," I said, "I understand. I've got nothing to hide. Thanks for patching me up."

Other than a few bruises and an angry carpet-burn from my fall on the landing, that was about it. Nothing life-threatening and mostly a matter of cleaning up, stitching up, and guarding against infection. I would be sore and stiff for a while. One of the nurses told me as they all packed up that I looked like I'd been through hell. I replied with something I figured that I'd earned the right to say.

"You should see the other five guys."

———

Close to dawn, I was moved into a private room, and the doctors and nurses left us alone at last. Brenda sat on the edge of the bed and held my hand.

"How are you doing?" I asked.

"How am I doing?" she said. "How are you doing? What the hell happened? I don't even know what to think. Are you sure you didn't know those people?"

"Bee, I'm telling you—you know as much about it as I do. What I told the police is the truth. I have no idea who they are—were—whatever. It has to be some kinda mistake."

I shook my head, completely spent.

"They must have broken into the wrong house. That's all it could be."

"Could they have known you when you were in the army?"

"Navy, but no, that was a long time ago and I wasn't anybody anyway. They're just punks from some gang probably."

"I know, I know," she said. "I know you're right. It's just so crazy. How do you feel? I mean, you killed those people. Don't you want to cry or throw up or something? Are you in shock?"

I let out a slight laugh at that but I was too tired and doped up to come up with very much. I shook my head slowly.

"No, Bee, I'm not in shock. And it's not funny. It's just that—I just can't feel much for those guys right now. I mean, I wish it hadn't happened, sure, but they broke in and didn't leave me any choice. I just reacted, that's all. I care a lot more about you and me."

"It's just so insane," she said, "I'd say it was some terrible dream except here we are in the hospital." She swept her hand over the room. We both sat in silence for a moment. "Well, I can see you're falling asleep, so I'll let you. I'm brain-dead anyway."

She began to walk away from the bed before turning and coming back to kiss my forehead.

"I'm sorry," she said. "I mean it. You saved our lives and I'm glad you're okay. Thank you. You try to sleep. I'll be right over here."

She went across to the armchair and I watched her as she made up a foot rest out of her rolled-up coat and a little side table. She settled into the chair and tucked a blanket in all around herself, adding a pillow that the nurse had given her. She looked safe and comfortable enough that I finally let myself surrender to the Demerol River for a ride into a medicated dreamland.

It seemed like my cold was gone.

3

A nurse bustling around, poking me here and there and checking my vitals woke us both up at mid-morning and Brenda went off to find the cafeteria. The nurse told me that I was doing well but they wanted me to stay at least another night. Considering my injuries and considering that it had all happened not twelve hours earlier, that seemed like a reasonable plan.

After a surprisingly good hospital breakfast, several hours were occupied with both Brenda and I being interviewed by local and county detectives, both together and separately. They showed us pictures of the five men, cleaned up, but still very dead. I had no idea who any of them were and neither did Brenda.

We were clearly treated as victims though we both had a feeling that there was a bit of disbelief in the air. I got a sense that they were trying hard to accept that this really could have happened. The hospital was abuzz.

Dr. Ward checked in on me and pronounced everything to be "So far, so good." By early afternoon we were left alone again and able to snooze for a while. It was after that, and after Brenda had found us some fresh coffee, that several of the detectives returned with a knock at the door. They filed back in and the county detective pulled a chair up to the bed. I remembered that his name was Saracen, and that he was the officer in charge of the investigation.

"We hear you're doing pretty well, Mr. Boudreau, considering. Glad to hear that. We found their car, parked in a plaza just down the road. Looks like, based on the New Jersey registration and the IDs we found on the bodies, they must have driven over from somewhere in North Jersey. That means the FBI is going to get involved. I don't see anything that looks like it would interest them very much, but be aware that they might come to see you.

"So, based on where the car was parked, these guys probably walked along the rear of the plaza, then out to the tree line until they cut through that strip along your neighborhood. That's probably when you first heard them. You were lucky in many ways, Mr. Boudreau. To have been in that back room, to have had the window open, and to have been awake for a start. And while we generally prefer that citizens don't shoot each other, in this case, it was good that you were armed and that you were able to respond effectively to the threat. It looks like all five of them came in armed but only two fired their weapons. One of the men in the stairwell put several shots into the ceiling at the top of the stairs, and then of course the man at the glass door. That was the one that hit you." He paused, looking at his notepad and seemed to puzzle over something there. "You fired an even thirty shots from the Beretta, in the dark, with a reload, and with only five or six not landing in one of those men. That was some damn fine shooting. A lot of pros train for years and still can't shoot like that."

He paused to let that set a moment before looking up from his notes. "So, you did, what, ten years in the navy before your honorable discharge. And you were wounded during that time—Dr. Ward told me about your scars. Could you flesh that out a little for us?"

"It was just under eleven years," I said. "I got out after I was wounded. It wasn't life-threatening thanks to my vest, but it was a long recovery and I'd had enough."

"Iraq?" Detective Saracen asked.

"That's where most of us were around that time," I said, "but I can't say more than that. It was classified back then and may still be.

You can check my record with the DOD. I've got nothing to hide except for what might be classified."

"I get that," he said. "I doubt we need to bother with that. Is it safe to say that, in the course of your military career, you have had advanced weapons training and at least some combat experience?"

"Yes," I said. "That is safe to say. Aside from that, I've been a gun owner and target shooter pretty much since I was old enough. Since I got out, I go to the range once or twice a month. I try not to get too rusty."

The detective broke into a slight smile and nodded before continuing.

"I don't think you need to worry too much about being rusty, Mr. Boudreau. And do you normally have guns all around the house?"

"You better believe I will from now on," I said. I realized immediately that I had let my irritation with the question show.

"Look, I don't have guns all over the house. It's pretty much like one on each floor. I rotate one or two under the bed, usually the Beretta. I keep a forty-five auto under my desk in the basement, because I spend so much time there, and then I like to be able to get to one on the main floor. That's the Walther. I don't have kids and I don't have people over with kids. Brenda's my only regular guest these days. She knows where they are and how to use them if she has to."

"Okay. I hear you," Saracen said. "The 911 call from Miss Patterson appears to bear out your version of what happened." He gestured towards Brenda when she was mentioned. "The call was recording everything until it appears to have been disconnected when you called her from your own phone. The local officers were inside your house about two minutes after that."

He rustled pages on his notepad, looking back at some older scribblings.

"I'm sorry that my notes aren't very clear yet on this. Tell me again please what the nature of your relationship is."

"I guess girlfriend is an okay word, right?" I said. I looked over at Brenda, who nodded her approval. "We've both worked for the same company for years, or rather, Brenda still does. I was laid off in June just as part of a big re-org. I used to travel a lot for work and I met her in our Detroit office. We've been doing the long-distance thing for about two years now."

"And that company is something called BEQ, is that right? What is that exactly?"

"Right, BEQ. Benson, Ellis, and Quentin," I said. "It's one of the world's biggest pharmaceutical companies, among other things. We are, or were, in different areas of data processing."

"So you're not presently employed there, or anywhere in fact, that right?"

"That's right," I replied. "Between my severance and my savings, I haven't had to rush out right away to find a job, but I will need to get on that soon. I can't afford to retire."

He turned to face Brenda.

"Are you in agreement with all of that, Miss Patterson?"

"Yes, that's pretty much it. I come out a few times a year, or Dean comes out to me, or we meet somewhere. I would have flown home tomorrow, but I'll stay around now for at least a week or two."

The detective put the cap back on his pen and put it in his breast pocket. "Thanks for filling that in. Well—a lot of people have been up all night and we're glad that both of you are okay. It hasn't even been twenty-four hours and we have work to do, but unless you turn out to be some kind of secret mob boss or drug lord—or you, Miss Patterson, for that matter," he turned again to nod towards Brenda, "our operating theory is some kind of mistaken identity. It sounds crazy but that's what we have so far. Like I said, lots of work still to do."

He stood up.

"I urge you both to consult with an attorney, though that's not to suggest that I think you'll be charged with anything. If this is really all as it seems, I just have never seen a more clear-cut case of justifiable homicide. Mind you, I'm just a detective. The county DA is going to have to make that call. It wouldn't hurt for you to educate yourself on the state Castle Law.

"Well, look—thanks for your time and cooperation. You know we have a job to do. We'll leave you in peace for the day and I'm sure we'll be in touch again soon. More questions may pop up."

On their way out, Brenda filled them in on which local hotel she had arranged for us until the house could be cleaned up. One of the officers volunteered to give her a ride over to the house so she could pack up a few things and pick up my car. She had already gotten approval from her manager back home for a few weeks off, whatever was needed, so planned to set up housekeeping in the hotel while things settled down.

4

The whole family was milling about in the side yard outside the house. I wasn't sure exactly who was there, but I knew it was family. I also knew that it was the big old guest house in Cape May, though the yard and the other houses looked more like we were in typical ranch-house suburbia. There were at least two, maybe three, weathered picnic tables in the yard and people walking here and there—almost like a yard sale. A car passed by slowly and we all turned to watch it pass—a large dark sedan. I turned back to the yard and for a minute I thought it was the yard of a rental house we'd had for one summer on Block Island when I was a little kid, but then I realized we were back at the Jersey Shore.

My father came across the yard to meet me at one of the tables. He was wearing dark jeans with one of his favorite chamois shirts neatly tucked in. He had the usual felt-tip pen along with a mechanical pencil, framed by a few of the notecards he always carried, all poking out of the left shirt pocket. On the table were several piles of letters, bills, and flyers, as though the mail had been collecting for some time. I touched one of the piles and found that the paper was warm from the sun. It felt like late spring or early summer. A beautiful day. My father gestured to the piles on the table and told me that he had to go away and wanted *me to take care of things while he was gone. I asked him how long he would be away.*

"I don't know. A few days. Maybe a few weeks. I have to take care of some things."

I had the feeling that he wanted to say more but couldn't for some reason. He looked at me and I realized that his eyes were welling up, and then mine were too. A warm breeze came through the yard and a dog barked, though I hadn't noticed any dog before that point. The dog appeared from behind my father and barked again towards the road. We all turned to see another car passing slowly, as if checking us out and deciding whether or not to stop. As the car passed I knew it was my old Ford Galaxy, but then it became my father's favorite Volkswagen bus, complete with fishing rods strapped to the roof racks.

The car faded from view as it drove away. I turned back to the yard and my father was gone.

I walked to the house and went in; it was a maze of dark and dusty rooms. I realized that I was in a mansion that had belonged to one of my great uncles. I walked through, passing various people whose faces were all too dark for me to recognize. A cat was sitting on a chair in a small room and watched me walk by. I knew she was one of my old cats though she didn't look like any cat I had ever had.

Down a narrow hallway was a large rectangular object. It seemed familiar to me, but I couldn't tell what it was. I walked towards it, but the hallway kept getting longer. Eventually I was close enough to see that it was a refrigerator. I knew then that I was in my kitchen and that the refrigerator door had several holes in it. Something was dripping out of the holes and, after watching for a moment, I realized it was blood. It was pouring down the front of the refrigerator and forming a puddle at the base. I saw a shape in the puddle that grew larger. I was frozen in place as the shape grew into a man rising to his feet. He took a step towards me; it was the young man I had killed in the kitchen. He reached out for me, just a few feet away now. He took another step towards me and I saw a face full of rage. Finally I was able to move, and I turned to run, slipping in the blood puddle and falling hard to the floor.

Hitting the bloody kitchen floor smacked me into consciousness and I bolted upright, gasping for breath. I looked around, panting, and realized that I was in my hospital room. Brenda ran up and threw her arms around me. The fresh floral scent of her long, red hair was a powerful sedative and my breathing began to slow.

"You're dreaming, Dean, just dreaming. It's okay. A nightmare." Her voice was soothing. "You kept asking someone where they were going. Was it the yard and the big house again? With your father?"

"Yeah, yes, it was. But this time one of them was in it. The dead guys, I mean—the last one in the kitchen. And there were bullet holes in the refrigerator and blood everywhere." I held her tight, aware that I probably wasn't making much sense.

"I think there are bullet holes in the refrigerator, actually," she said.

"Ah, shit. All right," I said, sitting up straight and wiping my face with my t-shirt. "You got the hotel, right? Help me bust outta here today."

5

Brenda took great care of me. She changed bandages, ran errands, and made follow-up appointments. We took turns waking each other up with nightmares and other strange dreams. We talked a lot, drank a lot, and ate out almost every night. My wounds healed well and quickly. We celebrated a warm but low-key Christmas in our hotel suite, complete with a table-top LED tree and champagne. Despite this, I felt that something was bothering her. I sensed a growing reticence.

I finally brought it up one evening after dinner. She told me that she was fine, but thought that she needed to head back home to Detroit to take some time alone to process everything. I told her that I completely understood, and I did.

"It has nothing at all to do with blame, or even with you," she said. "It isn't that. I mean, you saved my life. I don't blame you for anything. It's just that so much happened so fast, I just need to figure out how to think about it. Like…where to put it."

"I get that," I said. "I really do. I'm not sure either what exactly to think about it. It's all very surreal to me too."

We hugged, hard.

"I'm so sorry you had to go through all that," I said. "Take whatever time you need, but I really hope this isn't the end of us. It would be too hard for me to find someone else as great for me as you are."

———

After the police had finished with the house they set me up with a special cleaning crew that handled crime scenes. They cleaned up the various pools of blood and the bits of brain and who knew what that had stuck to the walls here and there. After that, I was able to get my regular contractor to spend a few days in the house. His crew filled in holes and replaced sheetrock, touched up paint, replaced carpeting and glass doors. I took the opportunity to upgrade the refrigerator and the microwave to newer models without bullet holes.

I hired an electrical contractor to install a home security system, which was an idea I'd been kicking around for a while. Better late than never, I told myself.

Lastly, Brenda arranged for a cleaning crew to do a thorough house-cleaning.

———

After almost three weeks in the hotel, the house was ready. We entered with some hesitation, looking carefully at where the bodies had been and where the blood had splashed, where bullets had slammed into wood. The workers had done well and the house smelled clean and fresh. We familiarized ourselves with the new security system and were glad to be home.

Brenda was able to stay two more days with me before she had to head back to Detroit and get back to work. During the drive to the airport I assured her that I understood her need for space and time. We promised to keep in touch and to see how things went.

"I'm sorry this wasn't exactly a fun visit," I said. We stood outside the terminal, sharing an embrace and light kisses. "What with all the gunfire and nightmares and everything. I'll try to do better next time, okay?"

"That shouldn't be too hard," she said. She laughed and shook her head. "But don't worry, nobody will ever hear me say that you don't know how to show a girl an exciting time!"

6

Shortly after the hospital stay, I had engaged an attorney and made sure he was present for the follow-up police interviews. The FBI did end up sending a few agents to talk with me, but it was perfunctory. It appeared that they were checking off the necessary boxes and otherwise were happy to let the county detectives take the lead. It took almost a month in all, but in the end, I was notified that there would be no charges filed against me. I was told this during my last meeting with the same county detective who had led the investigation. Detective Saracen had put in almost thirty years on the force and I had come to know him as a fair and reasonable man. My instinct was to trust him.

"Because of informants in place, and ongoing investigations," Saracen said, "I have to fuzz out some details, but I can give you the gist of it.

"What it comes down to, in the end, is an incredible case of mistaken identity. The five guys were from the Jersey City area. Apparently, they were some kind of gang or mob 'wannabees' trying to make names. We figure that whoever the leader was, he hatched a plan to show initiative and get in good with the big boss by getting rid of some guy who was causing trouble. That would be the guy who isn't you, and that's where the mistaken identity came in. Our people were able to confirm that the real target did in fact live in the suburbs north of Philadelphia, like you, but nowhere near your neighborhood. That person had the same house number, on a similarly named street in a similarly named town. Looks like someone was in charge of looking up the directions and screwed it up royally. The others fell in line."

"So they had the right house number," I said, "and the right state, and that's all. Must have really been my lucky day."

"I know, Mr. Boudreau," he said, "definitely an absurd situation. There's another thing we learned, through a federal informant, and this is something you'll want to hear. This 'boss', whoever that is, was decidedly not impressed with what his five bungling junior associates did. We understand that he has issued a clear prohibition on any level of retaliation. Like a memo coming down from the CEO. You wouldn't know this, but it makes perfect sense in their world. You see, organized crime likes things kept quiet. They don't like headlines or the kind of attention that comes with shooting up a quiet middle-class neighborhood as part of some kind of turf war. As a matter of fact, the feds actually have this guy on tape saying he was glad that you took care of these guys in a final way.

"We at the county level, are in agreement with the feds about one thing. That is, that we're pretty comfortable that you aren't in any further danger. It's in keeping with how these people operate. They don't want any more attention than they've already gotten regarding this matter."

"Pretty comfortable?" I said. "Should I be comfortable about that?"

"I'm sorry for my choice of words, Mr. Boudreau, but yes, we believe that you should be. We don't think you have anything to worry about.

"Look, that was a hell of a mess that you and Miss Patterson went through, and we've looked at it every which way, inside and out, facing east and facing west. Everything I've seen keeps telling me that you're a level-headed guy. A cool customer. So it's in that spirit that I say this, and this is strictly off the record. I see that you have a concealed carry permit in good standing. Do you carry a gun very often?"

"No," I said. "Very rarely, actually, like maybe just when I go down into the city and I think I'll be there after dark."

"Well, given that you already have the permit, why not use it for a while, a few months maybe? You know, if only to make yourself feel more secure.

"Now, that off-the-record comment doesn't change what I said—you'll be fine. This is over."

He ended our meeting by thanking me for my cooperation and telling me that I was welcome to stop by the township station at my convenience to pick up the Beretta, the Walther, and the Ruger.

"Try not to shoot anyone for a while, Mr. Boudreau, if at all possible." And he actually winked.

"I'll do my best, detective."

7

Newspapers all over the country had covered 'the invasion' completely, and later added follow-up stories during the investigation and again when the decision was made not to file any charges. It was front page news for local papers and for the Philadelphia Inquirer, and second or third page in other major cities. I was cornered by reporters just a few times and gave brief comments, sticking to the basic story with no embellishment.

It was only a few weeks after that night that the gun companies started to contact me for endorsement deals. Along with that came all the magazines. More than I had ever known existed wanted to do a story and to put me on the cover. American Hand Gunner, Combat Handguns, Home Defense Illustrated—all of them. One publication was working on a special edition called *Famous Gunfights* and wanted to talk to me about a piece of that action. Several companies that manufactured ammunition wanted me to hawk their products. A company that made firearm accessories wanted to pay me to be on the cover of their new holster catalog despite the fact that I hadn't used a holster at any time during the big night. The company that most wanted to be my friend was Beretta, and, to be fair, I felt I owed them my friendship. Ruger wanted an endorsement deal and didn't care that neither Brenda nor I had fired the Ruger that night.

Being unemployed, and realizing that my 'fifteen minutes' probably wouldn't last very long, I went back to the attorney and we reviewed all the offers carefully.

The biggest fish of all was, of course, the NRA. To them, I was the ultimate poster child for gun ownership and armed home defense. I was about as far from the gun-nut stereotype as anybody could get. I didn't own a pickup truck or a John Deere cap. I didn't hunt, smoke, or chew tobacco. I spoke excellent English with a slightly upper-crust accent and had been a registered Democrat for years. They came after me like a starving dog snapping at a T-bone steak.

We had a series of meetings and eventually came to an agreement for various appearances and endorsements. Part of the deal was that Brenda's real name and particulars would be kept out of it and she wouldn't do any interviews. And they would provide legal representation for both of us, if ever needed, for any issues that might arise related to the incident. My favorite part was the several hundred-thousand dollars that I would be paid, courtesy of a group of wealthy life-members. The NRA set me up with a ghost writer and we churned out a slim volume covering the big event, fleshed out with lots of background on other home invasions and similar gunfights. An unidentified buyer—with a Hollywood address presumably—snatched up the movie rights. That got me another large chunk of cash.

I spent several months doing as many appearances and endorsements as I could. I posed for pictures and signed catalogs at gun shows. I was given all sorts of free products and was asked to test or review others. The money poured in at a high enough rate to mostly compensate for any whittling away of my dignity.

There was a strange moment at a Valley Forge gun show one Sunday. I was signing a copy of *The Greatest Gunfights* for someone who thanked me profusely.

"What's it like," he asked me, "to be one of the world's greatest gunfighters?"

I knew he meant well, but the question threw me off for a moment. I didn't see myself that way at all.

"Hey thanks, man," I said, "but I don't know about all that. I'm just a regular guy. I did my best and it worked out. Hey—check out the Beretta booth down on the left there. Do what I did and get yourself one of those 92Fs."

He nodded excitedly and hastened off towards Beretta.

———

All the fuss died down within a few months and my bank account was pleasingly swollen. My wounds had completely healed up and I was back in good physical shape, but mentally exhausted. With a clear calendar and a pocket full of cash, I planned a much-needed trip out to Seattle to hang out with my old friend Tommy. It had been way too long and we had lots to catch up on.

8

"So that's it. That's about how it went down. It was a hard night but here I am to tell you about it." I raised my glass to Tommy and to the Seattle skyline spread out before us to the south. He'd heard about everything that had happened, and we'd talked on the phone, but this was the first time I'd been out to relate the in-person version. It was late afternoon, but it had already been a long day. Flying in from Philly earlier, it had been good to see him waiting for me just outside security. Though he was a full inch taller than my six feet, Tommy and I were alike enough in looks that an observer might well have thought that it was my brother picking me up. We had chatted away during the ride from the airport to his house, and had come right out to the deck.

He took a sip, nodding in acknowledgement. "Yeah, that is some heavy shit. There could be parts of that story that I wouldn't believe if it weren't coming from you."

"What parts, exactly?"

"Just the part about how Brenda actually checked into a hotel with you," Tommy said. "I'm fine with the rest of it. The coolness under pressure, the superhuman shooting, the instant recovery—no problem there."

"Very funny T—you had me there for a few." We laughed, and I poured us each another several splashes. "And by the way, it wasn't exactly an instant recovery. I was sore for weeks. Really lucky I had Brenda for a while before she had to go back to work. Would've been a lot harder without her."

"How is Brenda? She handle it okay?"

"Oh, she's solid as a rock. I mean, she was terrified—shaken. Well, we both were of course, but she recovered. She's taking some time to herself, but we keep in touch. I really hope it's not over, but I can't blame her. That was a lot to expect someone to just shake off."

"She sounds great. I hope it works out for you guys," Tommy said. "Be nice to meet her one day. She still have that wild hair and all those legs?"

"Oh yeah," I said. I remembered that I'd sent him a picture. "That sounds like her. Lots of red hair and freckles. Put a thick wool sweater on her and she'd be at home pulling pints of Guinness in a Dublin pub. I hope you meet her too, she's really cool. We've talked about her moving in, but now I don't know. We'll see what happens, I guess. Not much choice about it."

We sat in silence for a few minutes, enjoying the view. It had been an unusually warm late March day and the afternoon breezes were growing cooler. His house was in one of the hilly neighborhoods north of the Space Needle and the downtown area. It had great views south to the city and beyond to Mt. Rainier. My favorite feature was the small teak deck he had added, which nicely accommodated a few Adirondack chairs and a barbecue grill. For me, it was a very peaceful and therapeutic spot. Better than any shrink's couch.

A few years after going through high school as best buds back in New Jersey, we'd enlisted in the navy together. It was more right for Tommy than it was for me, but I had stayed with it and after four years we had both been recruited into one of the Special Operations groups. That had suited me better, and was much more interesting. We had spent some time in the dirt and seen more than our share of action. Eventually, a mission had gone south and I had caught a bunch of bullets. Tommy had also been shot, but his wounds were minor. My body armor had saved my life, and I had a full, but long recovery. After that, Tommy had stayed in and made a career out of it. For me, it was off into the corporate world.

Tommy's travels, my corporate career, marriages, child-rearing in Tommy's case, and whatever else popped up had made it hard for us to get together very often. Much later, we had met up when he had come east for a high-school reunion, and we'd been glad to reconnect. That had been about ten years ago and our friendship had re-kindled easily. I tried to make it out west at least once a year. After the big gunfight and all the craziness of the last few months, settling down on the deck with my old friend and a good bottle of bourbon was like sinking into a hot tub after a cold, hard, dirty day.

"After it all happened," I said, "my doctor, and the police, Brenda —everybody either suggested or insisted that I talk to someone. A therapist, psychologist, you know. There was actually a county program that offered sessions at no charge, so I figured why not, couldn't hurt. Brenda went to something similar too, after she got back to Michigan."

"Did it hurt?" Tommy asked. Always the joker.

"No, it was fine. I went three, no—four times. Nice man and he really tried to help except that there didn't seem to be much to help with. I mean, it was good to talk it out with someone who had no dog in the fight. Not sure how to put it but… I think in a way he was upset that I wasn't upset. Does that make any sense?"

"Yeah, yeah, it makes a lot of sense," Tommy said. "But you have to understand that for most people, most normal people anyway, having to kill someone is very traumatic. Many people don't recover from it at all, and many mostly do but are haunted by it for years or even for the rest of their lives. Maybe your therapist didn't have any experience with veterans. Maybe he couldn't relate to the idea that you've been through it all before. You told him, right? I mean, in a general way."

"Yeah I told him. He was a good guy but I think you might be on to something. He's probably never dealt with combat vets before. I guess I was a weirdo even back then. It never did bother me as much as I think it should have." I said. "But anyway, that was different. We were on missions. We had the government stamp."

"Yeah," Tommy said, "more and more I don't know about that government stamp. But you're right, we were following orders. That's a big something."

"I don't know how you've done it for so long," I said, "but don't shortchange yourself, T. That last time, we really came through—we saved all those people in that camp. I'll never forget that crazy day. It was like slow-motion special effects except that it really happened. You did that. I hope you feel good about it."

"I do, I do," Tommy said, "The best, dumbest thing I've ever done and I have the scars to prove it. But I haven't forgotten the cost either. I helped write letters to four families after that day."

He swirled the ice in his glass, watching the cubes spin, but he was far away somewhere for a minute. I wondered if ghosts were swirling around him. The whiskey was sitting on the deck between us and I pushed it towards him with my foot. He reached for it.

"How many has it been?" I asked. "Or do you even know?"

"Twenty-six," was his immediate reply. "Four that day with you, four before that, and eighteen more since you got out. But that was mostly long ago and definitely far away. Over the river and through the woods, you know. Except the woods were usually sandy and hot and there weren't any trees. I've been more of a trainer for years now."

"Did it—or does it—bother you?" I asked. "Are you haunted?"

"You mean other than by several college billing offices? No," he said. "Okay, I'm sorry. Serious topic. No, it—they—don't bother me. I mean, the first one did, probably the first three or four. I remember throwing up and having nightmares. But then you accept that you're doing what you have to do, and you learn to put it all on a shelf some-where up high. Different things help different people, like doing your duty, following orders, protecting the country, covering your buddies— all of that. Like you said, the government stamp. But I'll tell ya, man— nothing makes it more sort of 'acceptable' than when they're shooting at you or hunting you. Anybody shoots at me—I'll light them up and go to Taco Bell for lunch right after."

He sat up and turned towards me.

"Five armed men break into your house—with Brenda there—and you did those fuckers up. Maybe you feel bad about it, maybe not. Maybe you'll start to, that'd just make you normal. It's okay with me if you don't ever feel bad about it. They got what they asked for."

I laughed at that and we clinked our glasses. I knew he was right. I stood up and went over to the deck rail, looking south. I took in the view for a minute and realized that Tommy was humming a song that I recognized as one of his favorites from way back when. I came back and sat down again.

"I gotta tell you something, something I haven't told anyone else. Not Brenda, not the cops."

"Shoot. Oops—I mean don't shoot. I guess I should be careful not to tell you to shoot."

"Come on, man, be serious for a minute," I said. "Trying to say something here. Actually, that's what he said—the last guy."

Tommy quieted and cocked his head. "What are you saying? You mean the guy in the kitchen? He tried to shoot at you."

"No, actually he dropped his gun. He was terrified, almost crying. He dropped his gun and then I shot him six times."

"All right, all right—so let's keep that between us," Tommy said. "But that doesn't change the overall equation. He was still one of five guys—five guys, all armed—who busted into your house in the middle of the night. Don't you dare hang yourself on a hook about that shit. They weren't there to deliver flowers. Besides, much neater package the way it all ended up. Would've been a sticky mess if one of them had lived. You did the right thing. I forthwith and henceforth absolve you of all sins related to killing those men."

"Thanks, I appreciate that," I said. I had to shake my head and laugh. He was right again. Much neater package the way it happened. All wrapped up with a bow on it.

"There's one thing though," I said. "I had a minute—no—it seemed like a minute but really it was probably five seconds, who knows. Maybe three. For a few seconds it wasn't him there. It was the fucking asshole director at work who fired me. It was the jerk in the Mercedes who cut me off on the turnpike last summer. And, oh man, it was that idiot woman at the McCain rally years ago who insisted Obama was an Arab. It was all of them. People who fuck with their cell phone in a restaurant. That guy in my kitchen took the bullets, but part of me was paying off everyone who ever pissed me off. And you know what?"

I paused and looked at Tommy, not really having meant to ask a question but still giving him a chance to answer. He did.

"Yeah, I know what. It felt good, didn't it?"

"Yes! Yes—dammit—it felt good," I said. "At the time, I only had those few seconds before I had to move on and get Brenda, but I felt that. It's like I sent a lifetime of payback flying out of the barrel at twelve-hundred feet per second. And it was exhilarating. It all came rushing back—that feeling from years ago. You know the high."

"Yeah I do. Hey—you're okay," Tommy said. "I've been there and I know what you mean. You didn't ask for that situation but there you were. You did what you had to do. And yeah, what you're saying is, part of it is, that you were in a rare and crazy circumstance where you had the opportunity to kill people with relatively no repercussions. I mean, how many ordinary people experience that?

"Now, it wouldn't do to make a habit of killing everyone who pisses you off."

"Yeah, I guess you're right about that," I said. We both laughed out loud.

"Of course," Tommy said, "maybe we could arrange for some more assholes to break into your house in the middle of the night, like people who park facing the wrong way. I'd really like that one."

"Hmmm, that is an interesting one," I said. I made a show of stretching to look along the street below to see how his neighbors were parked. "I like that one too. People who... wow, the possibilities are endless."

"Oh shit," Tommy said, "I think we've both gone off the deep end. But it is fun to think about, isn't it? A fantasy. Like winning the Powerball."

I refreshed our drinks and noted with mild alarm that the bottle of Knob Creek was approaching an unfortunate state of emptiness. I had known that state well myself on many occasions. I noted also that the sun had started to set, reflecting orange light off the downtown skyscrapers. I could see the twin round towers of a hotel I had stayed at a few times when out here on the company's dime. The distant mountain had retreated into the evening mist. It had gotten chilly. I was up again, leaning against the deck rail. I'd always been fascinated with Seattle. To me it had the nitty-gritty feel of a big city, like New York, Chicago, or Philadelphia, but also the nautical flavor of a town by the sea. Fog and foghorns in the night, ferries and fish markets. And of course, six coffee shops on every block. There was no excuse to not be fully-caffeinated in Seattle.

Tommy came over to the rail and stood beside me. We both watched the mist roll in over the bay.

"We should go get some dinner soon," he said. "But one thing before we move entirely off this happy topic. Since I'm already planning to charge you two hundred dollars an hour for your therapy. Something to think about, maybe just think about and forget about, I don't know. But something. With all this that's happened to you now, after your long diversion into the corporate world, you may have just found something that you're really good at. Or come back to it. You're a natural at the bad stuff, is what I'm trying to say."

I'd been listening carefully to the words of my best friend. I took them in and tossed them around for a few seconds.

"Yeah, maybe you're right. Strange how things happen," I said. "Now if only I could find someone to pay me for it. Other than the government I mean. Been there already."

We tapped our glasses together and laughed again. Middle-aged men. Best friends letting a touch of the inner delinquent shine through. Aided and abetted by good Kentucky Bourbon.

"You know," Tommy said, "speaking of getting paid for it, I could probably get you in with Blackstone. You need a job, right? They'd love to get you."

"Thanks," I said, "I do need to get a job, but I don't think that's for me. I mean, I'm not knocking the guys that signed up with them, but if I'm going to be a mercenary I'd rather work for myself."

"I hear you," Tommy said. "I've been saying no to them for years. Not really my thing either. You remember Chandler, right? He's been with them for ten years or more. He says the money's really good and there aren't as many rules."

"Yeah, I remember him," I said. "We called him Ajax because he was so abrasive. Then after a couple of kids he mellowed out some, and we started calling him Soft Scrub."

"Steve too," Tommy said. "Remember that guy? 'Stevie the K'. Nobody could pronounce his last name. Chandler got him in. Mostly about the money for him, I think. That's the part that tempts me the most. I wouldn't mind the chance to make some real money. Divorces and colleges are expensive."

I waved my hand over the city before us.

"Isn't there a Capitol Grille down there somewhere? Let's find it. My treat."

9

W e located the Capital Grille, and over an obscenely expensive steak dinner I filled Tommy in on the events of the past few months that we hadn't yet discussed. All the magazine ads, catalogs, appearances at gun shows—the NRA. Also, the circumstances of my separation from my long-time employer, BEQ.

"It's just so stunning the way it ended," I said. "More than twenty years and then the phone rings and that's it. We'll send a box for your laptop. It wasn't my manager, she went off on vacation and left the dirty work to her boss. That's a human booby prize for you—Vince Gallo is his name. A blood-sucking pencil pusher. We called him The Ogre. Funny—I didn't make that up even. A bunch of us were at a company thing out in St. Louis one time and I heard two of the managers that report to him refer to him that way. He's like one of the company hatchet men—always looking to go down another list and can somebody. I really think he liked it. I wasn't too surprised when he got around to me."

"I've never worked in the corporate world," Tommy said. "Why does that happen? I mean, surely they don't really just fire people without good reason."

"No, not really, you're right," I said. "But 'good reason' is certainly open to interpretation. All the big companies do it. I saw it on the news the other day, another big company—Infotech—got rid of several thousand Americans in the past six months, while at the same time opening a new center in Manila and hiring thousands of locals there. The president talks all the time about bringing back manufacturing jobs, but the same thing goes on every day with white-collar jobs too. Ten people on a team work together and make ten widgets a month. In order to increase profits and executive bonuses you lay off two people and the remaining eight then work harder and manage to make the same ten widgets. They do so well that you demand they now make twelve widgets. After a while someone realizes that you can lay off two more people—Americans, mind you—and hire four hungry young college grads in India or the Philippines for the same or even less money. They call it 'smart-shoring'."

"Yeah, I heard that Infotech story too. I've been reading for years about jobs going overseas," Tommy said. "But I thought it was mostly the factories, like clothes, shoes, electronics—that kind of thing. Assembling stuff."

"It's both, but the manufacturing part gets all the press. Take me for example—early fifties, twenty years in, and then 'your position has been eliminated.' Only thing is, six months later they start hiring for the same work, but now the position is strictly 'off-shore'. You see? Even if I was willing to make a lot less, they couldn't hire me. Came down from the boardroom that this or that position must be off-shored. Happens every day. They literally won't even interview me for the position because I'm an American living in the States. Of course they have other ways of putting it, but the fact is the fact."

"That's amazing," Tommy said, shaking his head. "But I have no doubt it's happening. Do people still go postal? That was a thing back in the eighties with the postal service. Seems like we need some people to go postal on Fortune 500 CEOs."

"I agree. I'll put that on my to-do list. Maybe that'll be my niche. Sorry I'm blabbing, T. As you can tell, it really pisses me off. The guy who canned me, that prick. I'd really like to bump into him in a dark alley someday. The thing that really gets me is that I was within days of completing a really big project. I'd worked hard on it for a year or more. Sure as I'm sitting here, one of Vince's favorite pals will be put in charge just in time to take the credit."

"And what about your manager?" Tommy said. "Where do you think she is in all this?"

"Donna? She's just covering her ass," I said. "I don't think she really cares about anything other than looking just good enough to her boss to keep him off her back. She's just quietly content with being part of the problem and getting a nice bonus.

"Shit man, I sound like a bitter old fart, don't I? I'll stop—Sorry.

"Anyway, I'll have to do a lot of thinking and get a job sooner or later. I have some breathing room, so I'll use it and see what comes up. Maybe one day I'll thank The Ogre for giving me a new start. At this point, I'm open to anything that keeps me out of the corporate world. And if I manage to hang on to Brenda, it would be great to get her out too. We'll just go sit on a tropical beach somewhere."

"Roger that—put me down for that idea in spades," Tommy said. "I've been thinking of retirement for more than a while now. I'm aching to get out but can't swing it quite yet—need to beef up the nest egg first. All I need is a truck full of rum and a palm tree to sit under. Sort of like a tall ship and a star to steer her by except, you know, different."

We sat for a while and the waiter poured more coffee. I savored the last bite of my crème brulee.

"Do you ever see Kate?" Tommy asked. "Down at the shore maybe? I haven't heard from her since that last reunion. I hear about her every once in a while from Mary. I'm sort of an informal godfather to her, you know. She's a real sweetie. Reminds me of my own daughters. You were lucky to get to work with her."

Kate had been the other best friend for both of us while we were growing up and going through school. She and Tommy and I had been so close that some of our other friends had called us "the triplets".

I knew that Tommy had dated Kate's cousin Theresa for a short while many years ago. They'd managed to stay in touch after their breakup and even after her subsequent marriage and the birth of a daughter, Mary. When Theresa and her husband were killed in a huge pile-up on the New York Thruway one winter, and Kate and her family had stepped in to care for the orphaned girl, Tommy had made it clear that Mary could always count on him to help out in any way. I knew that the relationship between Tommy and Mary had been a long-distance one, but I also knew it to be a warm and caring one. She had told me once at work that she got a big kick out of calling Tommy "Godfather". Despite the fact that Tommy, Kate, and I didn't get to see each other very often, Mary had acted as a bit of insoluble glue connecting the old friends together.

"I haven't seen Kate in a long time," I said. "Same as you, I've heard more about Kate from Mary than I've heard from Kate for the past few years. And you're right that Mary's a sweetie. You must know her husband Evan too, right?"

"Not really," Tommy said. "I've spoken with him on the phone once, but haven't ever really met him. I did rate a wedding invitation, but I was overseas at the time. I guess that means I haven't seen Mary in the flesh since before that. Sheesh—how time flies."

"Yeah, it sure does," I said. "Of course, since I was canned, I don't hear much from Mary anymore. You know what? I think the last time I saw Kate was at the service for my brother. That must have been almost exactly two years ago."

"I'm sorry I couldn't make that," Tommy said. "I was stuck over-seas that whole month. I haven't asked you how you're doing with that."

"Oh, that's alright. Don't worry about it," I said. "I know you couldn't be there. It's hard, you know, but I'm okay. The hardest thing was just that he was so young. Heart-attack at forty-four—that came out of the blue. He was laid off too, you know. That's what did it. He took it really personally and went into a rut that he couldn't get out of. Vodka and painkillers didn't help."

"Now he wasn't BEQ also, was he?" Tommy asked.

"No, no. He had about fifteen years with Betacon but they've been doing the same thing. He just couldn't take the idea of being replaced by some college kid in Mumbai. He couldn't get out from under it. Same shit I was just telling you about. Different company, same shit. Now you know why this stuff gets me so worked up. It really makes me want to smash some heads.

"I'm sorry again. You asked about Kate and you got all that. That's the last time I saw her, but we do an occasional email back and forth. I think she's doing fine up in Boston or wherever she is. Pretty sure she had some rich older relatives. I think we're all good. It's just life getting in the way.

"Anyway," Tommy said, "I wish we could all get together somewhere. You know, bullshit about old times and where we all went astray. You, me, and Kate."

"Yeah, I agree," I said. "We should try to do that soon."

"Once upon a time there was a tavern…" he sang out quietly. I recognized the old tune immediately, being at least as sentimental as he was. I joined him for the next line. "Where we used to raise a glass or two…"

Other diners were looking at us. I motioned for the check.

10

F unerals, like weddings, have a way of bringing friends and family together for unexpected reunions. Less than a month after my visit to Tommy out in Seattle, he got his wish for three old friends to get together.

Mary and Evan Flores, husband and wife, both friends and former co-workers of mine, had died the week before in a horrible murder-suicide situation. Younger than me by about twenty years, they had met each other at BEQ not long after being hired around the same time. For several months I was one of the more senior people assigned to help them get oriented and up to speed. They were rising stars and they were good people.

Mary was the much younger cousin of my old friend Kate, and my understanding was that someone in Kate's family had helped her get in the door with BEQ.

We'd become friends and had met several times after work for dinner or drinks. After they'd moved on to their own separate teams within the department, we'd kept in touch. They'd sought my advice on numerous occasions and I'd always been happy to help out. We'd drifted apart after a time but had always been glad to catch up when-ever our paths crossed.

Just a few weeks before, there had been another round of layoffs, and Mary and Evan had both been shown the door. The story was, not unexpectedly, that several departments were being reorganized as the company moved to more 'off-shore resources'. I knew personally that it could be quite a gut-punch to be suddenly canned without warning. Mary and Evan were apparently devastated. I wasn't surprised to hear that it was Director Vince Gallo who had done the firing.

I'd been largely out of the communication chain since getting laid off, but still heard snippets from mutual friends. Mary had gotten a promotion, Evan had joined a new team, they had just closed on a new and bigger house, they were excited about starting a family, etc. I had also heard that Evan had struggled for years with what was frequently called a 'chemical imbalance'. As far as I could discern he had been able to control it with medication, but was still subject to the occasional serious mood swing.

From what I was able to put together, it sounded like the stress of committing to the new house followed immediately by both of them losing their jobs had pushed him over the edge. During some kind of heated exchange, Evan had gone into a violent rage. He shot Mary dead and then, shattered and overcome with grief presumably, had turned the gun on himself.

———

The news had immediately begun to spread amongst both current and former employees, and concerned friends. I had gotten several calls. One of the first calls I got was from Kate. She had been Mary's second-cousin, though due to the great age difference, Mary had always referred to her as 'Aunt Kate'.

"We're shattered," Kate said. "Elliot and I, and my aunt and uncle. I can hardly think right now. Please tell me you'll meet me at the service. I know that you knew Mary and Evan both. I'm going to need someone to lean on."

"Of course, Kate," I said, "I'll be there. Will your husband be with you?"

"No, Elliot's too sick to travel," Kate said, "and so's my uncle. It'll be me and my Aunt Martha. We're both just sick to death over all this."

Kate told me that the service was being planned for a church in Cape May, with a reception afterwards at the historic Congress Hall Hotel. We made general plans to meet, and she promised to send me further details soon.

One of the next calls I got was from Tommy. He explained that Kate had already called him and told him all about Mary and Evan, and that he intended to fly in for the service. I knew that he had treasured his relationship with Mary. As we talked, I heard two distinct qualities in his voice. The first was something I could not recall hearing from him before—an intense and genuine grief. The second was something that I had heard in his voice many times—a tightly controlled rage. I knew that there was an explosion in there somewhere. We talked for quite a while, exchanging memories of Mary. I did my best to give him a description of Evan, who he had never met. Our occasional laughs were separated by silences longer than we were accustomed to sharing.

So it would be a reunion of sorts. Just like Tommy had mused about back in Seattle. I would meet his late flight at the Philadelphia airport, we would spend the night at my house, then off to Exit Zero of the Parkway and over the bridge into Cape May in time for the service.

We didn't get to see Kate or meet her aunt until we were all exiting the church at the end of the short service. Tommy and I waited on the sidewalk until they were able to mingle towards us. Kate looked the same as she had when I'd last seen her at the service for my brother. She was again wearing black.

She was with a lovely and elegant older woman with a distinct facial resemblance. The woman who Kate introduced as her Aunt Martha was also wearing black. They were two striking ladies, though the strain of the past week was evident. They were both perfectly made up and composed, but clearly had been crying recently and probably not sleeping much. They both clutched handkerchiefs.

Martha Phillips hugged both Tommy and I tightly. Kate did the same, and we offered our condolences to the two ladies.

"Thank you both for coming today," Martha said. "I've been hearing about the two of you for much of Kate's life, so it's good to finally meet you. And we appreciate the support."

"Of course, Mrs. Phillips," Tommy said "And please let us know if there's anything we can do to help. Anything at all."

"Thank you, Tom," Martha said, "We certainly will. In fact, there may be something, but that can wait. Thank you. I understand that you were a special part of Mary's life. We've all lost someone wonderful."

A man in a nearby group of people caught Martha's attention with a wave.

"Will you all excuse me, please?" she said. "I'm going to join the Gordons for the walk over to the reception. That'll give the three of you a chance to catch up and I'll see you over there."

She hugged all three of us before moving away down the sidewalk, leaving us to our own short walk through the historic center of town. We strolled under the great old shade trees, and past the colorfully painted Victorian houses, mostly in silence. The dappled sunlight painted the small front lawns and the grey slate panels of the hundred-year old walkway. We arrived at Congress Hall within fifteen minutes and found our way to the designated reception room.

After less than an hour of awkward mingling and tearful reminiscing, Tommy and I couldn't wait to make ourselves scarce. Exchanging a coded wink and a nod, we slipped out and down the hall for a drink in the nearby Brown Room Bar. We were elated when Kate soon joined us there.

"My aunt is pretty wiped out. She says she's going to stay here a little longer, and that we should go on to lunch without her. I'll meet up with her later at our hotel. She asked me to pass on her wish to see you both again soon under happier circumstances."

11

After another very short walk, once again passing an array of Victorian mansions, we settled in for lunch in the dining room of the elegant Virginia Hotel, which turned out to be where Kate and her aunt were staying. The servers laid out an extensive and skillfully prepared buffet, which we enjoyed with a fine cabernet, followed by strong coffee. The delicious meal was a welcome respite from the somber tone of the day. After a few awkward starts, we eventually began to gab away like the old friends that we were, and it was clear that Kate in particular was glad to have a break from the crying and mourning. It was also clear that she was very tired and worn from the whirlwind week.

She had heard about my recent 'adventure' on the news and had followed all the reports. She was interested to hear my account of it all, and I obliged with a much-less gory version than the one I had initially related to Tommy. Kate was very concerned about how Brenda had taken all of it and I reassured her that she was fine.

Kate filled us in on the news that her husband Elliot had suffered a serious stroke the year before and was on a long road to recovery. To hear her tell it, she and other relatives were certain that it had been largely brought on by Elliot being shunted out of his position at

BEQ in favor of 'new blood'. I wasn't surprised to hear her say that the 'new blood' in question had turned out to be a crony of the same guy who'd been handling most of the recent layoffs—my own included.

We eventually got back around to the topic of Mary and Evan. I described my time of first working with Mary, and then Evan, shortly after.

"I've always assumed," I said, "that Elliot helped them get into BEQ, right? He must have been very proud of them."

"Well, yes, Elliot," Kate said, "but there's another family connection that helped."

Before she could elaborate, or I could ask a follow-up question, there was a series of interruptions as Kate settled the check, restrooms were visited, and we started to gather ourselves to leave.

Out on Jackson Street in front of the restaurant, we all hugged again, and Kate took a minute to dab at her eyes with a tissue. She caught her breath and forced a smile.

"Thanks," she said, "I really needed that. Part of me feels bad about coming out and enjoying an afternoon with you two, but it's been good. I'm really out of steam though, and still in shock over all of this. I didn't get to everything I wanted to say today but I really need to get back to my aunt. What would you think of coming up to Rhode Island to hang out for a few days? Dean—you know Block Island, right? Wasn't that a vacation place for your family?"

"Yeah, that's right. It's been one of my favorite places all my life. I've even taken Brenda there. Come to think of it, how is it that we've never gotten together there?"

"I don't know," she replied, "bad timing I guess, but there's still time to fix things. My aunt has a house with plenty of room." She looked at Tommy and then at me. "I know at least one of you is unemployed at the moment."

Her small laugh seemed strained, and I had the impression that the dark cloud was returning. Tommy was the first to answer.

"I can't this time, Kate. It was all I could do to be able to get out east for this. I've got to get back tomorrow and finish up a project.

After that I can take time off again. Maybe next time for me. You go, Dean. You guys get together and fill me in after."

"I guess there isn't much reason that I can't come," I said. "So sure —why not? Any trip up there is a good thing. Count me in."

Kate took out a small notepad and we all made sure we had current contact information.

"Sure you can't join us for dinner?" I said. "With your aunt too, if you like."

Tommy nodded in agreement.

"Thanks guys. Really—thank you for coming and the invitation. I'll take a rain check for today, but let's not let so much time go by again."

She hugged us both once more, and then Tommy and I set off in search of where we'd parked the car. We had agreed during the ride south earlier, that if Kate wasn't available for dinner, we would just head on back to my house in Pennsylvania, since Tommy had an early flight back to Seattle the next day. In short order we had retrieved the car and were cruising up the Garden State Parkway at a good clip.

"Seems like she's holding back something," Tommy said. "Or maybe that's just the spook in me. What do you think?"

"Well, she did say she wanted to talk more, but I agree with you." I shrugged. "People grieve in different ways. You and I are the weirdos in that area. Maybe she's just more affected than she's comfortable showing."

"To us even?" he asked. "No, maybe you're right. Anyway, you should go for that visit and see what's up, if anything. Call me after and tell me about it."

I hit the switch and opened the sunroof. We enjoyed the music of the wind and the warmth of the afternoon sun.

"I don't care much for this corporate world you guys have lived in," Tommy said. "Seems pretty fucked up to me. I mean, I thought I was the one with the bloody job."

"That's funny, T," I replied. "But you're right; the corporate world can suck the life right out of you until you're like, some kind of withered raisin. A lifeless shell. They squeeze every drop they can out of you then move on to the next sucker who needs a job. That's the old Fortune 500 for you. The people at the top move us around like pawns. Cheap little plastic checkers. Then they go home with their big bonus. I tell you, more and more I'd like to grab a few of them and slit their fucking throats."

"Well, I'm going to," Tommy said.

"What?" I said. "What are you talking about?"

"If I've been hearing things right," Tommy said, "the same guy that fired you and those other people last year is the one who just fired Mary and Evan. Is that right? And it sounds like Kate believes he had a hand in pushing her husband out too."

"That's right. Good old Senior Director Vince Gallo. He's not the only one, just he's the one that I hear about in my circle. There are plenty of pricks to go around. If you remember what Kate said at lunch, even though Elliot was a VP, she's sure as shit that Gallo engineered his departure. Probably with the help of his old bud John Campbell, another VP. They're shaping their part of the company into whatever they want it to be. This thing with Mary and Evan has his prints all over it."

"Okay then," Tommy said. "I'm going to hunt him down and kill him. You can help, or you can stay out of the way. Either way, dead man walking. Nobody fucks with my friends that much and gets away with it. Mary was a sweet girl with her life in front of her. I just keep thinking about my own daughters."

"Whoa, hang on a minute," I said. "Don't worry T—I'm on your wavelength, but let's think about this. We're all pretty raw right now, and you know as well as anyone that's a good time to step back and take a breath."

We had been in the car for almost three hours by the time I turned off the old Bethlehem Pike on to the local road that led to my community. Tommy had seemed lost in thought for a while.

"You're right. Let's keep cool, but we need to talk about it some more later, or better yet, after your weekend with Kate. I'm interested to see what's going on there, if anything. Maybe nothing. It bugs me that this guy, these people, get away with all this shit. I mean it. Really pisses me off. This will not go unpunished."

"Okay, okay, and agreed all the way. We'll revisit after my trip," I said. I realized with mild chagrin that corporate-speak nonsense like 'revisit', 'circle back', and 'deeper dive' would probably be with me forever. "Let's inventory the liquor cabinet and talk about dinner."

12

I t was five-thirty on a Wednesday. Vince Gallo had just wrapped up his fifth and final meeting for the day and was about to shut down his laptop, when his personal cell phone rang. The phone display told him that it was John Campbell calling. He and John went back more than forty years and they had been through a lot together. John was a Senior Vice President of Data Processing, and was Vince's boss. At least that's what Vince allowed him to believe.

He pressed the button to answer the call.

"Hey, what's up?" Vince said. "I know why you're calling. I couldn't believe those latest overtime figures. Maybe we've cut too many people after all."

"No, that's not why I'm calling," John said. "Haven't you heard?"

"I don't know—heard what?" Vince said. "What are you talking about?"

"Two of the people we just let go," John said, "you know, the married couple—Evan Flores and his wife Mary. They're both dead."

"Holy shit, I had no idea," Vince said. "What happened? Some kind of accident?"

"No accident," John said. "What I hear is that he flipped out and killed his wife. Then blew his own brains out. If the press gets hold of this, it isn't going to look good."

"I know, shit. They were nice people," Vince said, "but there was no way we were going to meet goal without those cuts."

"Jesus Christ," John said, "do me a favor, if anyone asks you about it, don't put it that way. Keep that between us. I'll talk to HR about what we can do. Maybe start a scholarship fund in their name or something rosy like that. That'll make the family happy."

"Right, right," Vince said. "That's a good idea. And we'll certainly send flowers to the families. Or a plant. I hear plants are the thing these days. And let's put any further cuts on hold until at least year-end."

"Agreed," John said. "Alright, well, I wanted to make sure you were aware. You should call a team meeting and we both better come up with something that sounds sincere. How are things otherwise? How's the month looking?"

"Looking really good for the month," Vince said. "Gloria will do the distribution by the end of next week. I think you'll be pleased."

"Good," John said, "I'll watch for that. Let me know when that meeting is. I gotta go—running the tavern for my parents again tonight."

Vince set down the phone and spent a full minute gazing out his third-floor window at the row of pine trees that stood along the far edge of the parking lot. They'd grown so tall. Within a few years he wouldn't be able see over them to the giant datacenter building at the rear of the complex. The goose that was laying the golden eggs.

Dammit, he thought to himself. Why can't these weak people keep their shit together and just move on?

13

Crossing the Hudson on the Tappan-Zee Bridge at four in the morning was something I had done numerous times in the past and it was always both strange and exhilarating. The huge, flood-lit bridge, almost completely empty, with New York City itself just barely visible to the south was like a scene from some post-apocalyptic movie. Then past White Plains, down towards I-95 and on east into New England.

A long drive was always a good time to think. I thought about Mary and Evan and tried to figure a way to be less furious about all that, without much success. I spent twenty miles or more thinking about what misery Vince Gallo had inflicted on me and others. I imagined the medieval horrors I wished I could bring down upon him.

I vividly remembered the sunny Tuesday morning early in the prior June when I had just started my work day. I had refreshed my coffee and was starting to process emails from the night before when his instant message popped up on my screen. I remember the unpleasant sensation that always came over me whenever I knew that I would have to interact with him. I figured at the time that he probably wanted me to spend hours putting together some report that would likely have a 99 percent similarity to something I had already given him three times. Instead though, after calling him, I learned that my position had been eliminated, effective immediately. Within fifteen minutes, an HR person had sent me a pile of paperwork and I had been disconnected from the company network. Twenty years of service ended with no fanfare and I joined a club of millions of cast-offs.

Re-living that morning in my mind as I drove brought back the tight feeling in my gut that had come over me at the time like a sudden wave. I remembered his voice as he asked me to drop my company credit card in the box when I mailed in my laptop. I wondered how Mary had felt just a week or two ago when she had gone through a similar conversation. My thoughts naturally progressed to all the other people I knew that had been laid off by Gallo and others like him. All the people I didn't know too. Lives upended, plans smashed, years of hard work and contributions tossed carelessly into the trash. All in the interest of some tiny improvement to the bottom line and larger executive bonuses.

I remembered what Tommy had said he wanted to do and I thought long and hard about it. I knew Tommy well enough to know that he didn't joke about killing people. He had done enough of it in reality and didn't see it as material for jokes. I did understand that it was possible for him to change his mind.

But I wouldn't. Yes, I decided, it was time for a punch-back.

Long before my night drive ended and I pulled in to the ferry parking lot, in my mind I arrived at the conclusion that I would track down and kill Gallo myself. Nothing short of putting him into an early grave would suffice.

Of course, I would need to make an arrangement with Tommy and somehow coordinate with him so that we didn't trip over each other, but I knew that it had to happen. Who knows, I thought to myself, maybe we could somehow work together on an attack plan. I smiled in the dark at the silly idea that maybe there was a way that we could both kill him.

I worked on clearing my mind of negative energy, and after a while, I was able to turn to more pleasant thoughts and began to embrace the therapeutic qualities of the night drive. I thought of old favorite songs, incorrectly remembering the words over and over until the right ones finally burst through. I cracked the rear window and let the bracing air fill the car as I flew past Stamford, New Haven, and New London. In Mystic I stopped at a favorite breakfast spot where the waitress always asked if I wanted my coffee 'regulah'. After breakfast, it was just a few miles to the Rhode Island state line and then down along the coast road to Pt. Judith and the ferry dock.

The ferry over to Block Island, as always, left on time, and shortly we were past the outer breakwater and headed south towards the island, already a shape in the distance. The snack bar opened. I bought a coffee and looked over the latest Block Island Times, which billed itself as 'The East Coast's most informative fish wrap'.

As we got closer to the island and the Clay Head bluffs came into view, I went outside to lean against the starboard rail and breathe the salt air. The long night drive had given way to a crisp and clear April morning. It was going to be a warm and beautiful day, though still cool out here on the water.

I had stood here by this rail and watched this island come into view so many times and it was always like coming upon a treasure. As the gentle arc of Crescent Beach drew near, the ghosts of my mother, father, and brother came and stood with me. Their presence was comforting. They brought a warm cocoon, sheltering me briefly from the gusts of cold sea air. I wasn't too surprised to see them in this moment. With them beside me, we looked back into the past at the grouping of little red rental cottages that had stood above that part of the beach for decades. Many happy summers had been spent there. The red cottages were long gone now, and soon too, after a while, were the ghosts. I was jolted back to the present by the loudspeaker blaring out the usual demand that all drivers make their way down to their cars.

Within another ten minutes we were docked, and I drove off the boat into the little town. The town was generally called 'town', though it appeared on many maps as a place called 'Old Harbor'. That was a very old term for the island's only real town that would have made no sense originally. It had come into common use in the 1800s to differentiate it from the newer grouping of docks and boating facilities that had been built up in the southern part of Great Salt Pond, called 'New Harbor'.

Two minutes up Spring Street I pulled up to The 1776 Inn and checked into my room, which was a comfortable suite that Brenda and I had enjoyed the year before. I called Kate to confirm my arrival and told her I would see her at her aunt's house at two. I was excited to be seeing Kate again so soon and to find out what she had on her mind. Having only spent a moment with her at the service, I was also looking forward to seeing the elegant Martha Phillips again.

I had a few hours to kill and I had been up most of the night. I set the alarm on my phone, kicked off my shoes, and stretched out on the antique sofa for a short nap. A light wind whistling by outside and the faint sound of distant surf carried me off into slumber.

14

I was familiar with the island and found the house with no trouble, pulling up a few minutes early. The place fit right in with my imagined ideal picture of a big Block Island house on this part of the island. It was indeed large—easily five bedrooms or more. What looked like a great room with huge windows looked out over a deck and an expanse of lawn. On a clear day you would have been able to see Montauk Point and Long Island in the distance to the west. It was a classic island house covered in cedar shakes worn grey by time and weather. The white trim all around looked fresh and well-maintained. The yard was the closely cropped and somewhat mangy grass common to the area and was bounded on three sides by the low stone walls that had divided island properties for centuries. There was a Range Rover and Kate's Audi already in the driveway, pulled up close to the house.

Kate appeared in the driveway and rushed to me, enveloping me in her arms. We shared the big hug of old friends who had recently been brought back together through sadness and loss.

Martha Phillips came out of the house to join us and greeted me with her own big hug. I was struck by the two of them together. They could have posed for one of the preppy family-gathering layouts in any number of New England-style clothing and accessory catalogs. No longer in their black dresses, both Martha and Kate wore faded but pressed jeans and sweaters over white oxford shirts. They were both slim and lightly tanned, sharing the windswept radiance and good looks that were expected of wealthy New Englanders. The redness in their eyes was the only clue to the recent trauma the family had endured. Martha made me feel welcome right away as she ushered us inside to lunch.

Armed with sandwiches and side dishes we sat around a huge barn-wood table that was awash in sunlight pouring through the glass doors to the deck. We chatted about our family experiences on the island. As it turned out, Martha and her husband Ben owned several homes on the island, the others being seasonal rentals that otherwise sat empty apart from the occasional big family gathering or other special event. Kate and I had been close friends in the past and had always enjoyed catching up, but I was realizing how little we knew of each other in terms of the past few decades. Both she and Martha asked about me in such a way that I felt that they really cared.

"I was married for about two years in my mid-thirties," I said. "You might remember Laurie. It was a good relationship, but we shouldn't have gotten married. Probably should have flipped a coin for the cats and gone our separate ways. I see her on occasion and we're fine.

"After the navy, I started with BEQ and was with them for just about twenty years. You pretty much know the rest of my story as far as that goes. I would probably still tell anyone that it's a good company overall, but that it's infected with some really bad people."

"But Brenda, right, Dean?" Kate asked, "That's something good that came from your time with BEQ."

"Yes, you're right," I said. "I met her in my travels, and that is a good thing."

They were both good, natural listeners and hadn't said much. I realized that while this was such a pleasant afternoon and good company, we had been chatting away and I still didn't know why I'd been asked there. As Kate cleared away the remnants of lunch and poured coffee, Martha asked a question.

"I understand that you became quite famous recently, though I gather that you might rather not have. Is that right? How are you doing with all that?"

"I'm okay with it," I said. "I mean, I think about it sometimes, but I don't dwell on it. It was a fairly black and white situation. The fact that they had the wrong house and all that, is either a tragic or a tragically funny detail, depending on how you look at it. I got tired fast of all the 'great gunfighter' kind of talk. Anyway, my fifteen minutes didn't last long unless you happen to frequent gun shows. I did make some good money off the whole mess, including the book and then the movie rights. Though I don't know how anyone can make a movie out of a two-minute gunfight."

Kate interrupted. "Come on now, ever hear of The O.K. Corral? How many movies have been made about that?"

We all laughed together and I had to nod in agreement.

"You're right," I said. "That's funny. Maybe Tom Cruise will star in it."

"No way," Kate said, "with your Hollywood looks, there's no way they'd hire anyone but you to star in it. Teenage girls will be waiting in line to buy tickets."

"Thanks, but I doubt it will ever come to that," I said. "But really, the only thing that upsets me about it is that Brenda had to go through it with me. I'm lucky to have her. Well, that is, I hope I have her. She's taking some time off. I can't blame her."

We sat in silence for a few minutes, enjoying the coffee. The sun was lower in the sky though still sending its warmth into the room.

"All right, ladies," I said. "Thank you for lunch, and it's a beautiful afternoon, but you did ask me here to talk about something, right?"

"I'm sorry, Dean," Martha said. "You're right. I've been enjoying your company and am maybe hesitant to bring up something unpleasant." She paused, and it seemed to me that she was gathering something up from inside.

"Vince Gallo." And to the extent that it was possible for such a lovely and elegant lady to spit out words, she spat them out like they had gone bad last week. I tried to decide whether it was pain or anger that dominated her eyes, concluding that it was an even mix. "Someone that I'm afraid we've been hearing too much about lately."

"Yes, unfortunately I've known him for some years, though I wish I never had. He's been one of the worst parts of my life. And now, well, you know. This thing with Mary. I wouldn't try to describe what I'd like to do to him in such fine company."

"Oh, go ahead," said Martha. "We both hate that fucking man. Don't sugarcoat it on our account."

Kate blushed and stifled a gasp, but also nodded in agreement.

I recoiled at the language but almost immediately had to laugh. "I knew you reminded me of my mother somewhat, Martha, but now you really do, and it's a compliment! But yes, I couldn't have put it better. He made my work-life at BEQ hell before finally canning me. Just really a terrible person." I shook my head and silently told my guts to go easy on the anger that threatened to bubble up inside.

"If we can set aside for the time being what we all wish might happen to him, or what we might like to do to him for that matter," Martha said, "let me fill you in on some other things. We'll come back to Mr. Gallo later." She held up her coffee cup. "Something stronger? Sherry?"

I made a show of consulting my watch for at least a half-second before countering, "Brandy?"

Kate served her aunt a glass of sherry and gave me a double brandy in a snifter. She sat back with her own snifter.

"You know that our darling Mary was Kate's second cousin," said Martha. "Though she thought of Kate as her aunt, and that label mostly stuck. She was also, of course, my granddaughter. The only child of my own late daughter and only child, Theresa. She was raised mostly by me with lots of help from Kate. My only sibling—Kate's mother—and her husband both passed fairly young. They were only in their early fifties. My sister, my daughter Theresa, and now Mary too, and Evan. All gone before their time. Our small family has had more than its share of losses. I would suspect that we were cursed except that I know we've been blessed in so many other ways."

Martha paused, holding what looked like a silk handkerchief to her eyes. She looked over at Kate.

"When Mary started with BEQ," Kate said, "and soon got together with Evan, they were both concerned about any suggestion of favoritism or any special 'hand up'. They chose to not advertise her family connections. You knew about her relationship to me, but most didn't."

I sat back, sipping my brandy and taking this all in.

"Hand up? I don't understand," I said. "You just said 'connections'. You've never worked for BEQ. I know Elliot was a VP, so it was about him then, right? What am I missing? I thought you started to say something at lunch last week but we were interrupted."

Martha leaned in. "Dean, I'm sorry, we hadn't intended to be dramatic and cause you all this confusion. I'll clear it all up, but let me ask you—can you remember the original founders of BEQ, back in the late forties?"

"I don't think I know all three first names, but I know that those were the three men who started it, Benson, Ellis, and Quentin. John—no—Josh Benson was CEO when I started over twenty years ago. And Frank Ellis cashed out at some point before I came along. I guess I don't know anything about Quentin."

"Quentin was my maiden name, Dean," Martha said. "Bernard Quentin was my father. He ran the company finances for years as it grew and went public, and served as CEO before Josh. He took my husband, Ben Phillips, under his wing and Ben eventually became chief financial officer. Ben retired long ago. I was on the board for years and we've always been major stockholders."

This was all a lot to take in. The world was getting smaller this afternoon. People I knew or had known were more connected than I ever would have guessed.

"Okay, so let me get this straight," I said. "Your father was one of the founders of BEQ, your husband was CFO, and you spent years on the board. And Kate, you haven't worked for BEQ but your husband did for years, and he was a VP. Mary was your cousin-slash-niece. So I guess we're all a big happy family. Except, where does Vince Gallo come in?"

Martha seemed to be trying to think of the best place to start a convoluted story.

"Several years back, after my husband's second heart attack, he mostly retreated from public life and I took over something he'd been working on. I should add that my husband had always fancied himself in charge of finding and rooting out anything rotten at BEQ. It was his particular passion, like a corporate Elliot Ness. He hated corruption and hated the idea of anyone tainting the company's good name. I think he also carried that responsibility in part to honor my father.

"Well, I took over a project that he'd begun, and I started to quietly investigate what looked like some substantial embezzling going on related to the new datacenters. This was all strictly back-channel with no public accusations. That last part of it was very important to my husband—nothing could go public. BEQ has always been conservatively run and we've always been proud of our reputation. I brought Kate in early and we worked on it together off and on, almost like a hobby, but an important one."

"You know I'm an accountant, Dean, right?" Kate said. "Which generally makes people's eye's glaze over, but you may not know that my specialty is forensic accounting. Digging into old records and finding where the money's all buried. Who hid what and where is it now. We handle a lot of wealthy people's divorces. There's always money hidden somewhere."

"And I paid for a few confidential investigators out of my own pocket to keep things quiet," Martha said. "One of my husband's old legal friends led us to one man in particular, a Mr. Barnes, who has been very helpful and has brought us reams of material."

"So," I said, "I gather this investigation must have led you to Vince Gallo before long. That's where this is going, right? Why am I not surprised at that?"

"Yes it did," Martha said. "He isn't the highest ranking person but he seems to be a sort of ringleader in terms of this whole affair. Gallo reports to John Campbell, who is a senior VP. Those two go way back to their boyhoods in Connecticut. As a matter of fact, back at that time, Ben and I knew their parents. That was the first time our family ever crossed paths with them.

She hesitated a minute before continuing. "It really pains me to even think about this now, but the boys were involved in a terrible accident and two people were killed. As a favor to the Campbells—our neighbors at the time in Westport—we used our position and our friendship with the local judge and the police chief to make it all go away. Payments were made—you know. It was not one of our best moments. I think there's a file on it included in all the material that Mr. Barnes gave us. So then, years later, Ben helped them get jobs at BEQ. That's one of the worst aspects to this. It's one of the things that upsets Ben the most. Like he planted a bad seed decades ago and now it's a twisted, evil vine that we need to somehow chop down."

I was shaking my head. "What a story. I can see how your husband could feel that way. I've met Campbell a few times. He's a really cold fish and a perfect match for Vince. But what I don't get is that I've always thought BEQ was such a tightly run ship. I'm having a hard time believing that anyone could steal enough money to make it all worthwhile. And these guys aren't exactly low paid. Did this Mr. Barnes get you details on what they were doing?"

"Yes, he did," Martha said, "and I agree, I would never have thought it possible. And it makes me very sad, not the least for what's happening to my husband's company. I know your history, Dean, you worked with the operations teams for years. You must know that when the Atlanta datacenter was built, there was so much concern about the centralization of computing equipment that a separate budgeting and bill-paying process was spun off as part of an effort to allow the data-center teams to react more efficiently to changes." She sipped her sherry and shook her head. "Look, I'm not current on the technological aspects and that never was my thing, but the point is that money flowed more freely through the datacenters. Purchasing was faster, bill paying, construction, all of that. Gallo and Campbell found a way to exploit that relative laxness."

"Apparently it came down to the BardLogic servers," Kate said.

"When the datacenter was created in Atlanta, with the backup facility in Montana, there were huge contracts with BardLogic. We're talking almost ten million dollars a year or more initially, less after that, but still a lot of money. So those bills come in, and because of the process in place and the critical nature of the datacenters to worldwide operations, they got swept into the queue and paid much more quickly, and, frankly, looked at less closely than would be the case in other parts of the company."

"Okay, so lots of companies have BardLogic servers, how did Vince and John exploit that?"

"Well, the thing is that those servers didn't really work out," Martha said. "There hadn't been enough vetting and they turned out to just not be the right fit, though I'm not the one to say exactly why. The phase-out began less than a year after they were installed, in both Atlanta and Montana. And there must have been some screw up after that whereby BEQ was still billed, and the bill was still paid. And without putting us all to sleep with the banking details, Vince and his little team must have seen the temptation and figured out a way to keep the bills coming in and the checks going out, and the money went, well, who knows where the money went."

"And it sounds like you trust this investigator you hired, is that right?"

"We came into the whole thing slowly, but yes," said Kate. "Mr. Barnes came highly recommended by one of my uncle's old friends. Former military, NYPD, and then a private agency going way back. He must have had lots of connections because he gave us piles of information. I've picked through most of it, and once I got past the craziness of the whole idea, it all started to add up. We're convinced." She gestured to her aunt, who nodded in return. "Vince Gallo and John Campbell have embezzled hundreds of thousands of dollars—probably millions—and it's still going on. They have a few people in key positions that make it all possible. Looks like a half-dozen or so people in all, including one former BEQ person actually working at BardLogic."

"Oh my God," I said. "That has to be Gloria Parsons. One of

Vince's favorites. She left the company to go to BardLogic. That must be her. A horrible person—fits perfectly."

"Yes, I think you're right," Martha said. "That name sounds familiar. So, we just never came up with enough to prove anything. One reason is that much of Mr. Barnes' information was obtained, well, what the hell, illegally. As good as Mr. Barnes has been for us, his methods were apparently never designed to lead to official prosecution. So maybe that was a mistake on my part, but it's water under the bridge at this point."

"But why is that?" I said. "Why is it water under the bridge? Isn't there enough to drop it all on the New Jersey Attorney General's desk? Or the FBI?"

"Here's the thing, Dean," said Kate. "We're both out of steam on this. I've got to take Elliot somewhere quiet and focus on his recovery and then, who knows. I can't deal with this crap anymore. In a few weeks we're headed to our house outside Paris. There's a private clinic nearby that we think can really help him. And Martha..." She looked at her aunt and trailed off.

"My husband had his third heart attack a few months ago," Martha said, "and this was probably his last. His mind is still sharp but other problems are piling up and we don't know how long he has. He's haunted by this business. I think he sees it as his last problem to be solved. Now we're stuck again and it's very frustrating. In any case, I need to focus on Ben and enjoying what time we may still have together. And I don't want to be the daughter who sullied the name of my father's great company. We want this cancer to stop and we want Vince Gallo and the others to go away as quietly as possible. It would be nice if they were somehow punished, but that's looking less and less likely. The main thing is that it has to stop. But, like Kate said, we just can't deal with it anymore. Kate thought of you some time ago because you know Vince and the others involved. You know BEQ—the structure, the culture, the locations—and she trusts your discretion. Having spent the afternoon with you today, so do I. And I'll admit it, we thought you might have your own motivation to bring them all down.

"There's another young man who's worked for my husband for

years. His name's David. He's former military, like you. We thought at first that he'd be a good choice to take this on, except that he was wounded in Iraq and now has some physical challenges that make travel difficult for him."

"Look, none of this is your problem of course," Kate said, "but Martha and I need to pass this on to someone else who cares. Someone we can trust." She paused for a moment, formulating her next thoughts. "These people are either going to quietly get away with this, or somebody is going to do something to stop it. Would you consider, if we financed everything, picking up the effort of at least going through all the files and seeing where that might lead? Maybe we need a new investigator. Maybe we need someone else, like some kind of tough guy to scare them off. Maybe that's crazy, I don't know. And you could use some work, right?"

"It's true that I'm out of work, but I've never been any kind of investigator," I said. "What about this Mr. Barnes? Is he finished with whatever he was looking into?"

"Oh, I'm sorry!" Kate said. Her hand had flown up to cover her mouth as though she'd just remembered something. "Yes, you could say that he's finished. Did you hear about that big office fire in Arlington about three weeks ago? It was actually late on—yes, it was a Friday night. A dozen or so people who had been working late in the building were killed, including Mr. Barnes and two of his staff. Their entire office was destroyed."

Kate pointed across the room to a bankers box under a side table. "Fortunately, he had just shipped updated files to us, along with a few thumb drives."

I sat back and took a sip of the brandy. I scratched my head a few times. "I'm sorry if I keep summing up the obvious, but this is all coming at me fast. So Mr. Barnes is dead and you believe that box over there to be the only record of his investigation. On a silver platter is a term that seems like it might fit. Is that about the size of it?"

"Well, now that you put it that way," Kate said, "yes, that's pretty much the size of it. It does seem a little strange. Before the fire, the plan had been that Mr. Barnes was going to make a few recommendations as to how to proceed. I think one of the ideas would have been to get a high-level prosecutor involved, but then, as I mentioned, it looks like so much of the material we have is compromised and wouldn't be of much use in court."

"And ideally," I said, "you'd like someone you trust to pick up that box and bring the whole thing to some sort of quiet resolution. Am I still on track?"

They both nodded.

"Well, I'm a confident guy and I'm smarter than most people I've met, but I'm no detective. I was just thinking maybe we could find a way to scare them off or threaten them somehow. I don't know. My head's jumping back and forth between 'let me think about it' and 'when do I start?'"

"I get it," Kate said. "It's a lot to think about. The thing is, we just can't deal with it anymore. We hate the idea of those people getting away with everything. And now there's this thing with Mary." She went quiet and dabbed her eyes with a tissue. "Part of me blames this Gallo for that."

"Oh, I blame him, Kate," I said. "You better believe it. I don't have to stretch very far at all to make that connection."

We sat in silence for a minute.

"Can I take that box of files," I said, "look through it, and think about this? Get back to you in a few days? Also, I need to know that it's okay for me to discuss this with Tommy. Martha, you met Tommy last week. He's in shock about what happened with Mary and Evan just as we all are—and feeling the anger towards Gallo too. I trust him completely. He'll know what to do.

"Of course, Dean," Martha said. "That sounds fine. And there isn't any wrong answer. This isn't your problem of course, but we do appreciate any help."

Almost out the door with the box, I had a thought and turned around to address both ladies again.

"You know, when I clarified that you would like all this to come to some kind of quiet resolution—let me ask you something. And I'm not suggesting anything, but do you care what kind of a resolution?"

"Quiet would be good," said Kate. "It would be great if it all just went away. It crossed our minds to just pay them off, but then that would just be good money after bad. And certainly not any kind of justice."

Her aunt nodded in agreement.

I thought about that for a moment, looking back and forth between the two of them. I knew that it wasn't the time or the place to bring up what Tommy and I had both decided to do to Vince Gallo. I also knew that justice was something that could be hard to come by, though usually was something worth striving towards.

'Yes, you're right," I said. "I can see that. Some form of justice would be nice, but we may have to take what we can get."

We exchanged parting pleasantries, hugged goodbye, and I went out to my car.

15

K ate watched from the screen door and gave a wave as Dean drove away. Her Aunt Martha came up behind her and put a hand on her shoulder. Kate wiped her eyes on her sleeve.

"That is one of my oldest and best friends," she said. "I hope we didn't come on too strong. I don't want him to think I've lost it."

"His affection for you was very apparent," Martha said. "And if there's another thing I can see about that man, he can take care of himself."

Kate nodded at her aunt and they shared a long hug.

"I just...I don't like feeling that I'm trying to manipulate my friends."

"I don't think you are," Martha said. "I think you—we—explained ourselves and asked for help. He's capable of saying no if that's what he decides. Maybe Ben will feel good enough to talk to him. And David. It would be good for those two to talk. They have a lot in common, after all. Things we can only imagine."

Kate nodded again and looked straight at her aunt.

"I'll say this—if he helps us out with this, he and Tommy, one or both of them. I want them to be very well paid. Very well."

Martha hugged her niece again.

"Yes, of course, dear. I agree, and I'll make sure your uncle does too. They will be very well paid."

16

Instead of going back the way I'd come out, I continued around the southwest part of the island, then back past the old island cemetery and towards town. I parked along the road and walked out onto the beach, going barefoot. My head was just short of spinning with the afternoon's information overload, but the sand, sun, and surf helped. For a few minutes I let myself be flooded with memories of playing on this beach as a kid. Hours on end, with just a plastic shovel and bucket, sand, and ocean. Not a cell phone or video game anywhere in sight.

Looking towards the mainland off to my left, I saw a ferry coming from Pt. Judith, the same one I had come in on just hours before. I sat and watched it getting larger and closer, crossing from my left to my right until it passed the breakwater and tied up at the dock. I knew that it would probably carry light traffic today, but on any summer weekend each ferry would disgorge a load of people into the little town. They would all be looking for lunch, or fudge, or a sweatshirt shop, or maybe they'd be on their way to a rental house. The shop and restaurant owners undoubtedly got sick of the onslaught, but they knew which side of their bread was buttered.

On the way back into town I stopped briefly at the grocery store for a few snacks and then at the Red Bird for a bottle of Johnny Walker Black. Back at the inn, I commandeered a small carafe of coffee from the kitchen crew before settling down in my room with the bankers box. I separated the contents into several stacks and began to read.

It was all there, arranged very neatly in twenty or so file folders. Everything Kate and Martha had described but in much greater detail. There were copies of elaborate bills from BardLogic and other vendors, receipts, sections of spreadsheets and of bank statements, and enough details related to datacenter purchasing to knock out a team of CPAs. There were files on each individual involved, along with a hand-drawn organizational chart describing the overall scheme. The individual files contained a smattering of personal bank account records. There was a handwritten note—from Mr. Barnes himself, presumably —to the effect that both Vince Gallo and John Campbell had recently bought the same model of office safe and managed to charge it to the company. I shook my head at that. Those guys had brass balls.

Mr. Barnes, or one of his people, must have done some traveling and surveillance, because each of the individual files included a few recent photos of the principal, along with a basic write-up including address, bank balances, credit information, living situation, and family. For each person there was a page or two of general notes that covered how they got to work, who went to weekly bowling, where Campbell's young mistress lived, and other personal minutia.

One folder was light blue, while all the others were the standard manila. The contents of this folder told the story, sketched out roughly by Martha earlier, about the young Vince and John getting into trouble long ago. There was a police report along with several follow-up notes from different officers. There were copies of articles from several Connecticut papers. There was a copy of a grainy photo of Gallo and Campbell together, maybe forty years ago, back when they both had hair. With some imagination I could see the older men that I had known. The story was a sordid one indeed.

After a night of partying, Vince and John had been driving very fast down a dark road near Westport, with Vince at the wheel. They had blown through a stop sign and t-boned an old pick-up truck driven by the owner of a local landscaping business. The landscaper and his young daughter were killed while Vince and John both had minor injuries. Mr. Barnes' summation of what happened next was a tale that has been told many times. Spoiled kids commit a terrible crime and are obviously guilty, wealthy parents and friends pull strings to get test results quashed and witnesses silenced. Payments are made, poor family clams up and moves away. Spoiled kids go on to successful and entitled lives. The kind of thing that happens every day, handled through hushed meetings and tacit understandings.

The last item in the file was a page of notes on a meeting with the landscaper's widow. The investigator had managed to track her down and she had consented to an interview during which she had confirmed the gist of the story. There was an interesting addendum to the effect that she had accepted an 'interview fee' of fifty-thousand dollars. No doubt, I thought to myself, there was a direct line from that payment to Martha Phillip's regrets over the handling of the matter long ago.

I closed the file but held it in my lap, tapping it with my fingers as I leaned back on the old sofa.

Vince and John had actually killed innocent people—and gotten away with it. Very interesting. And potentially useful.

I stood up, stretching to loosen myself and get free of the sofa's powerful pull. It was getting late and I was hungry. For the second time that day I needed to switch mental gears. I dropped three ice cubes into a glass, covered them with scotch, and stepped out onto the small deck. The night had moved in quietly and brought a mist along with it, circling the light at the top of the inn with an amber halo. After a few swallows of scotch and a last look around, I freshened up and headed out for the five-minute walk into town.

17

A s I passed the historic old Manisses Hotel I was pleased to see that the hotel's restaurant—one of the island's finest— was open for business. As expected for a late Thursday night, the place was mostly empty, with just a handful of lingering diners and staff starting to refill salt shakers and sugar bowls. After confirming with the hostess that the kitchen was still open and promising not to dawdle, I accepted a menu and went straight into the empty bar. It was a gorgeous space with rough stone walls and lots of dark mahogany. Soft accent lights lit the highly-polished bar and trim. I remembered that one of the last times I had been there, maybe five years before, had been with my mother. I had taken her there knowing that it would be a perfect place for her to have her Manhattan and feel elegant and sophisticated for a while. I took a seat at the near end of the bar.

The bartender emerged from the kitchen at the other end and came over to me; a friendly young guy, maybe thirty or so and all in bartender black. I spoke before he could.

"Hey, I was just hoping to grab a late bite if I can, but I won't hold you up too long."

"Yeah, that's fine man, no problem. I'll be here for a while. Always the last person cleaning up anyway. What are you drinking? You a wine drinker?"

"I drink about anything depending on the occasion, but I was thinking wine for now, sure."

"Oh great. You have good timing," he said. "Our wine dealer was in today and left more sample bottles than we're ever going to add to the list. The owner told me to try them and pour them out liberally to good customers. What do you say we toast to the storm that didn't come?"

"Sounds like an excellent plan. If your kitchen can throw a steak on the broiler for me, how about a big red?"

He nodded, and after I elaborated a bit on my order, went off to the kitchen and shouted instructions at someone. He came back out and skillfully opened a bottle of wine, pouring a little into each of two balloon glasses. It turned out to be an excellent Sonoma County Zinfandel. It was hearty and delicious with the characteristic Zinfandel peppery spice and just a hint of oak. We both marveled at the first sip and grinned like kids who had stolen a fresh baked pie. He filled our glasses and then spent some time cleaning up around the bar before coming back over.

"I thought you looked familiar," he said, "but I had to think about it for a while before it came to me. I've met you before."

"Really? Are you sure I'm not just one of those people who looks familiar? Because those guys are all around these days."

"No, no, now I'm sure," he said. "I remember your voice too. It was a camping and gun show at the Pittsburgh Civic Center. You signed my Beretta catalog. You're that guy."

"Oh jeez," I said. I covered my face with my hands. "You're on to me. I hope this doesn't mean you're going to take the wine away."

"Oh, no way. That just means we open an even better bottle. You did good, man—that was some horrendous shit."

I was relieved to see that he looked around first and then spoke more quietly than before. He knew without my having to ask that the topic should be kept between ourselves. We shared a small conspiracy.

"What's a nice Block Island guy like you doing at a Pittsburgh gun show?" I said. "Seems incongruous."

"Actually, it's kind of the other way around," he said. "I'm former army. Two tours in Iraqistan and got out without getting shot. Family's around Pittsburgh. Long history of hunting and target shooting. A girlfriend turned me on to this place a few years ago and we've worked here off and on since."

"You still with her?" I asked.

"Yeah, we're still on but she's planning to spend the summer in Spain. I'm hoping she comes back. I'm actually out for the summer myself. The regular guy will be coming back next month and he'll get this job back. Not sure yet what I'll do, but it's cool. With luck I'll find something else here on the island."

"So not off to Spain with your girl?"

"No," he said. "She's doing that with her sister, so if I don't get anything here, I'll probably head back to Pittsburgh and look for something there."

"Well," I said, "here's to storms that don't come, bullets that miss, and women that don't run away." I raised my glass in a toast.

"And what brings you here?" he asked, after a sip of the wine. "Are you doing a book signing at Island Bound?"

"Oh no," I said. "People here don't want to hear that bloody story. No, I've been here off and on since I was an infant. Not every year but as often as I can. I came up this weekend to visit a friend. Not sure yet, but it looks like a business opportunity may be rearing its strange head."

"Well, that sounds like a good thing," he said. "I hope it works out. Hey—I'm available and mobile for a few months if you need any help. Really. Keep me in mind."

"I sure will," I told him. "I'm living proof that you never know what life's going to deal out to you."

We raised our glasses again and then someone yelled from the kitchen. He disappeared for a few minutes, returning with my dinner and refilling my glass. I dug in gratefully while he busied himself with more bar work. As I watched him work I was struck by how much he reminded me of my younger self. He was probably thirty but looked mature for his age. My instincts told me to like him.

He checked on me now and then and after a while cleared the remnants of my dinner away. I noticed that I seemed to be the last customer in the place and the staff had been thinning out as well. I reached into my hip pocket and pulled out a thick wad of bills, plopping the pile on the bar. A small shiny object rolled free from the pile and I caught it with my hand, but not before he'd seen it.

"Whoa—that's cool. Looked like a bullet. May I?"

"Sure, it's a silly thing the NRA gave me. It's just a dummy." I handed it over to him. Any soldier would have known that it was a perfectly proportioned forty-five caliber cartridge. Any jeweler would have known that the bullet part was solid sterling silver and the case was gold plated, engraved with my initials—DB.

"Beautiful little thing," he said as he handed it back. "But you didn't use a forty-five, did you?"

"No, you're right. I have a few, and I love 'em, but that night was all about the Beretta. The night of the nine-millimeter it was. I grabbed a Walther PPK/s when the Beretta went dry but it was all over at that point."

Noting that I had brought money out he produced a check and I handed over some bills. He made change at the register and brought it back.

"Been great meeting you and chatting. I know your name's Dean Boudreau—mine's Damien. Damien Stevens." We shook hands. "Join me for a quick brandy? We have a great Armagnac. Really special. Sound okay?"

I nodded in surrender and he poured out two substantial doses into small round glasses. I sipped the amber liquid and it was warm and luxurious. The taste afforded me a brief trip to an old stone patio on a warm night in the rolling hills of the French countryside.

My new friend Damien thanked me again and took his glass back to the kitchen, leaving me alone in the restaurant. I enjoyed the brandy and the surroundings for a few minutes more, then put on my jacket to leave after tucking a crisp fifty under the empty glass. I started towards the door but had another thought and turned back, digging in my pocket. I moved the glass off the fifty and set the bullet on top instead.

Crazy, sure, I thought as I moved to the door, but hell, it would make his day. He'd remember me forever as the vigilante drifter or some such.

I exited to a wide landscaped pathway where a half-dozen wrought iron tables were arranged in linear fashion, a few on either side. There would have been dinner or cocktail service out here in the warm summer months. Past the tables the path narrowed, bordered by gnarled old trees and bushes. The road was just above to one side and maybe twenty feet away, though quiet at almost midnight on this off-season night. There was a light breeze that moved the fog slowly along the ground. I heard a ship's bell somewhere in the harbor down the hill. I stood and enjoyed the atmosphere and the cool sea air.

Looking at the tables lined up along the path, I thought again of that night years before when I had brought my mother here for dinner. It had been such a warm and pleasant evening that we had brought the second half of our cocktails out here to wait for the hostess to call us. The whole scene flooded back to me in vivid color. Just before we had been called to our table, she had said something to me then that I had thought odd at the time.

"I'll always be with you, honey, don't ever forget that. You're part of my greatest treasure."

Thinking about it again, it made more sense to me now. After years of watching one of her brothers waste away from Alzheimer's disease, I wondered if she had suspected that she herself would soon be in the terrible grip of that affliction.

I lowered my head to wipe my eyes, and then turned as a car came up the hill from town and sped past, high beams ablaze through the border of trees. My vivid picture of that night had been wiped away and I was alone again with the night and the fog.

I stretched and inhaled the cool air greedily. After a last look around I turned and walked past the restaurant door and started up the hill towards the inn.

18

I was awakened the next morning by my phone buzzing on the nightstand. A text from Kate suggested I meet her in town for breakfast.

It was a gorgeous sunny morning with a crystal blue sky, though the world was still damp from the foggy night. Ernie's was busy as always and mostly with locals since the first ferry from the mainland wouldn't be in yet for another hour or two. I found Kate out on the rear deck, with its view of the harbor and the ferry docks. She looked cozy and comfortable in a thick Block Island sweatshirt under a light windbreaker. She was alone with just a coffee and I sat down to join her. One of the waitresses came by and we ordered. She brought my coffee right away.

"We laid a lot on you all at once yesterday," Kate said. "I'm sorry to have ambushed you like that. You must think we're pretty batty. After you left the house, my aunt and I were concerned that we'd pushed it on you like it was your problem."

"Oh no, I didn't take it that way. And please tell Martha that I'm fine. You were no more batty than most revenge-seeking rich ladies."

Kate laughed and had to catch herself from spitting coffee out onto the table. After straightening up, she looked around at the other tables before speaking again.

"Maybe if he's well enough you'll get to meet with my uncle. His assistant David too—he's a really good guy. It could be good to get their perspectives on this whole thing. I bet they'd be leaning in the direction of getting a mercenary or someone like that. God—I sound like a criminal."

"No, not at all," I said. "Anyway, you don't look like one. But let's keep this all very quiet. Who knows about all this aside from you and Martha? Her husband and this guy David obviously."

"That's right, and now you. And you said you wanted to talk it all over with Tommy."

"Yeah, Tommy. He'll be the man. This is right up his alley. I'll go out to see him after this trip. He'll be anxious to hear what you wanted to talk to us about."

"There's another thing, Dean. This is awkward because I really don't want to offend you. I don't want you to be just 'hired help'. You're one of my few oldest friends and I'd rather think of you even as family. The thing is that my aunt and uncle are very wealthy. It's fair that you know that if you take this on and bring it to some kind of conclusion, there will be a large, shall we say…bonus involved. Who knows, you might decide not to look for a job after all."

"Well," I replied, "I will need money sooner or later. Seems like whatever it is that we end up doing, there could be some serious expenses involved. Money could really grease the wheels."

"Right, and Martha already has the money set aside. We can wire it or deliver it wherever needed. It would be small change to her."

Breakfast arrived and we changed to lighter topics. Kate told me that Martha was flying off the island later in the morning to take care of some business and spend time with her husband in Providence. She'd enjoyed seeing me again and hoped that I would come visit whenever I could.

As we ate we shared island memories and found them to be surprisingly similar. We had both played on the beach, ridden bikes, and picked blackberries. We had both bought penny candy at the Star

Department store and had both had our favorite flavors at the ice cream counter in the King's Spa drugstore. My family had rented cottages by the week and her family had enjoyed fancier digs.

After breakfast we walked through town and browsed the shops for a while before Kate announced that she needed to run some errands and take care of things back at the house. We made arrangements to meet at the National Hotel for dinner and she drove off in her aunt's Range Rover.

I spent most of the day touring around the island and visiting the favorite spots that I tried to check in on each time I was there. Later in the afternoon I did the easy hike through the Rodman's Hollow Nature Preserve, ending up at the bluffs that largely made up the southern edge of the island. I was rewarded by dramatic vistas of rocky beaches far below and the open ocean beyond. That area of the water just offshore down below where I stood had always been known as Black Rock, though I didn't recall having ever actually spotted the huge dark boulder that was supposedly visible at low tide. I had never seen it, though everyone knew it was out there and very dangerous to watercraft.

In town I bought a thick hoodie sweatshirt and then settled into one of the Adirondack chairs on the sunny lawn outside the inn. I chatted with a few other guests and enjoyed the sun and the beautiful ocean view. After they left, I dozed in and out until it was time to freshen up and meet Kate at the National.

———

We met at the appointed time in the hotel lobby and a hostess led us to a table in a quiet corner of the dining room. Over a cocktail and then a fine dinner we shared more island memories and filled each other in on the small adventures of our lives. We talked politics and the world, family, movies, and books. Through no conscious effort we steered clear of the main topic at hand until after coffee had been served.

I had noticed when we had arrived that Kate's shoulder bag was really what looked like a man's messenger bag. She pulled it up to her lap and fished around inside, producing a much smaller lady's handbag which she set aside on the table. She then set the messenger bag on the extra chair between us. It was a casual style of bag but clearly one of good quality canvas with brown leather trim. She gestured to the bag as she spoke.

"Like I said at breakfast, please don't be offended by this, Dean—we're friends first and foremost in my mind, and I trust you completely. Before that office fire that, well, ended our relationship with Mr. Barnes, we'd been planning to make the next payment due him. Our arrangement was always very confidential, and part of that was that my aunt always paid him in cash—literally. It made sense for all concerned. This is that last payment that would have gone to him. We appreciate that you came up here at my request and you also mentioned that you wanted to go out to see Tommy and run this all by him. Those things cost money. Please let my aunt and uncle cover your expenses."

I pulled the bag over to my lap and looked inside, seeing a dozen or more thick bundles of currency. I replaced the flap and set the bag back on the chair. I began to speak, trying to come up with the appropriate protestation, but she cut me off decisively.

"No protests, please. We really had this ready for that last payment and it's all, you know, off the books so to speak. Don't give me any trouble about it."

"All right—you're the boss," I said. "But remember one of the first things you said—friends first. And you're never going to have to pay me to help you."

We were interrupted by the waiter refreshing our coffee. As soon as he left, Kate leaned in.

"I know," she replied. "I really do. But the money's here, so take it and use it. After you decide what you plan to do, if anything, I can move whatever money you need to whatever bank account you like. I realize you can't use a pile of cash for everything."

We got our things together and vacated the table. I slung the messenger bag across my shoulder as we went out to Water Street. The Range Rover was parked nearby.

"I'm headed off-island early tomorrow," Kate said, "but I want you to keep in touch. Can I give you a lift?"

"No, I'm fine, thanks. I can use the fresh air. I need to walk and think. I'll get in touch with you soon."

We said goodbye, hugging tightly before she drove off.

————

I enjoyed the night-time views of the old harbor town on my short walk back to the inn. One of the ferries, the 'Carol Jean' it looked like, was docked for the night, all tucked in under the floodlights. The old Ballard's Restaurant was dark, having not yet opened for the season. I remembered that Ballard's was one of the favorite places my parents liked to slip out to for an adult dinner on the occasional summer nights when they could get an island babysitter. Walking by the Manisses I saw that they were almost empty and near closing up for the night. I walked on up the hill.

Back in my room at the inn, with shoes off and a glass of Johnny Walker in hand, I again opened the messenger bag. I took the neat bundles of bills out and arranged them on the coffee table. There was sixty-thousand dollars in seventeen neatly strapped bundles. Looked like five thousand each in fifties and twenties, with the bulk of it—fifty thousand—in hundreds. I guessed that must have been something agreed upon with Mr. Barnes.

I sat back on the sofa and thought about the events of the past thirty-six hours. I sipped the scotch and let my mind wander farther back through the past few months. A hell of a lot was happening, and I needed to be careful not to get run over.

19

For the second morning in a row I was awakened by a text from Kate.

It was eight o'clock on a Saturday and the message asked me to call her as soon as possible. She answered immediately.

"Hey, good morning," I said. "What's up? I thought you were headed off-island this morning."

"I am, but I'm a little delayed," Kate said. "The plane is waiting for me. I just spoke with Martha though, and there's a development. My Uncle Ben is apparently feeling very good this morning and is demanding to meet with you. I mean, he's making that demand of Martha, but of course you're entitled to say no if you like. She filled him in on our meeting and now he's wanting some say in this matter. What do you think? Are you up for that?"

"Yeah, Kate, I can do that. I'm up for it, if you and your aunt are sure that he is."

"Great, thanks so much, Dean. Can you get to the airport by ten? The flight to Providence is very short and we'll have a car meet us. You can be back on the island in time for happy hour at the Beachead."

I told her I'd meet her at the airport just before ten and set about getting dressed and grabbing a quick breakfast.

———

I parked at the small island airport and easily located Kate. We loaded into a four-seater private plane and took off promptly. Within forty-five minutes we were driving away from the Providence airport towards the Phillips's main house along the water south of the city. As we drove up, I wasn't surprised to see a long winding driveway leading up to what most people would call a mansion. Martha greeted us and embraced me warmly.

"I know that you and Kate have spoken several times," she said, "but I would also like to apologize for what must have seemed like some kind of hard sell the other day."

"Thank you, but please don't give it another thought," I replied. "I realize what an emotional time this is for your family. Nothing that was said offended me in any way."

"Well, thank you," Martha said. She ushered us inside. "I'll add diplomacy to the list of your obvious skills. And thank you for coming on such short notice. It had occurred to me that my husband might want to meet with you, but I had no idea he'd be chomping at the bit. He's in bed, you know, but feeling relatively good today. What we discussed during our lunch the other day is very important to him. I would say that it haunts him as unfinished business. He remembers you, or more accurately, he remembers Kate talking about you over the years. I'm sorry, but be forewarned that you might be in for another hard sell. He's a tough old bird, but I think you should be able to hold your own. Kate, will you take Dean up?"

Kate led me up an ornately-carved staircase that curved up to the wide hallway above. There was dark wood everywhere, and I had the feeling of being in an old English manor house.

I followed her down the hall and through a massive oak door that would have been at home in the medieval section of a history museum. We entered a large suite of rooms that had been partially converted into a well-equipped hospital unit. The hospital bed was neatly made up with clean sheets and was empty. A uniformed nurse across the room got our attention with a wave and we started towards an elderly man seated in a reclined armchair next to the fireplace. A burning fire crackled away.

Ben Phillips was still a very sleek man with a thick crop of silver hair that was neatly combed and parted. He was dressed in black sweatpants and sweatshirt and had a blanket loosely draped over his shoulders and mid-section. Our approach seemed to wake him up and he beamed at Kate, who took his hands and kissed his cheek. They spoke quietly for a few moments before he seemed to notice me standing behind her. He gestured to me to come closer and reached out a hand. I was surprised by the strength of his grip.

"Every once in a while I surprise everyone by having a bit of pep. Today seems to be one of those times. All indications are, that again today, I'm not dead yet. I'm Ben Phillips and I believe you're Kate's friend of many years, Dean. Is that right? There was another friend that Kate was close with also. Tom, I think it was, if memory serves."

"It's a pleasure to meet you, Mr. Phillips, and yes, I am Dean. Tommy is our other old friend. We've known Kate since grade school back in New Jersey."

"Wonderful," Ben Phillips said with a wide smile. "Thank you for coming and I hope you will forgive me if I ramble a bit. I don't get much practice talking with visitors these days. We have today, as many old songs go. Please sit with me for a little while. I get tired quickly so I won't keep you long."

I pulled a chair up close to his and sat down. Kate brought me a cup of coffee from somewhere across the room and then left us, saying she'd return in a little while. I could see the nurse bustling around in an adjoining room. For the time being, I was alone with Ben Phillips.

"I was one of the 'captains of industry' for quite some time," he said. "Now I watch movies and eat a lot of ice cream. Everyone takes great care of me. My wife tries to keep me informed as much as she can, and she never gets mad at having to repeat things over and over. My mind is still in pretty good shape, but you know, memory goes for everyone eventually. I hope I give up the ghost before I don't remember people."

He allowed himself a small laugh at that and coughed into a handkerchief. He gestured towards his side table and I handed him his glass of water. He sipped gratefully.

"I call my nurse Rachel. That isn't her name but she doesn't seem to mind. She tells me it's okay because at least I always call her the same wrong name. Maybe it's one of my last games."

He laughed at that with some delight and I joined him.

"I've had the best of what life can offer," he said. "And I have no right to many complaints. One thing that I failed to deal with before my health got so bad is this situation that my wife told you about. I just wasn't ever able to handle it in any effective way. By the time we really knew what was going on, well—it was too late to do much about it. Makes me both sad and furious. You worked for the company, didn't you?"

"Yes sir, for twenty years, give or take," I said. "I was laid off last summer by the man who seems to be at the head of this embezzling racket—Gallo. From what I've heard so far, I know all or most of the people involved. Terrible people in general. All of them. The dregs of humanity. Gallo is also the same man who let your granddaughter Mary go the other week. I'm so sorry about that Mr. Phillips. She and her husband Evan were friends of mine."

Ben Phillips was looking at the fireplace, seemingly mesmerized by the flames. He turned to look back towards me.

"Thank you Dean. Kate told me that both you and your friend Tom have known Mary over the years. We've all lost someone very special. This whole thing with constantly laying people off for such short-sighted reasons really makes me sick. We didn't do that in my day with the company. Martha and I have worn out the phone lines with the board of directors trying to put a stop to that, but haven't gotten anywhere. Some of them agree with us, but they're in the minority. I wish there was something I could do to persuade the others but I don't think there is at this point. I understand that some jackass coined the term 'smart-shoring'—as though that makes it all more acceptable."

"I share your feelings about the smart-shoring Mr. Phillips. It was done to me personally, along with a number of my friends. Please don't lose hope about that just yet. I'm working on a few ideas of my own about that."

He looked at me and nodded slowly, appearing to be in deep thought.

"I'm having a recollection of a time many years ago when you helped my dear Kate out of a jam with some man that was bothering her. Yes, I remember now. The man spent time in the hospital and then walked with a cane after that."

"Oh my gosh," I said. "I probably should deny that, but at this point, what the heck. We must have been eighteen or nineteen, I guess. Just out of high school. There was an older college guy who had it in his head that he had some right to own Kate and wouldn't leave her alone. She was really afraid of him, I remember that clearly. Tommy and I had a talk with him and that did the trick."

"Do you always refer to throwing someone out of an apartment window as 'having a talk'?"

We both laughed again at that, though a part of me understood that it was a terrible thing to laugh at.

"Well, you know," I said, "it was only the third floor and he did land in some hedges."

"That's funny," he said. "Though I hope you didn't make a habit of it. Before you arrived today my wife filled me in on many things. She told me about what happened to you a few months ago. That sounds like something out of a pulp fiction book. I understand that you pulled off quite a feat."

"Yes, it was a hell of a night. Pulp fiction is as good a way as any to describe it. It certainly was unreal."

"A lifetime ago," Ben Phillips said, "the young man who became me spent some time in North Korea. One night I had to come up behind a man and slit his throat. I've never been able to forget the metallic smell of all that blood. It was everywhere. I remember that I almost threw up right there. A week or two after that I was on a patrol with three other men when we were attacked by at least two or three times as many North Koreans. We got away with just a few injuries, but only after I had killed two of them up close. I wish those memories would leave me but I don't think they ever will. Were you in the service?"

"Navy, yes. Regular service and then Special Operations. I know that metallic smell well and I assume I'll never forget it either."

"And this friend of yours, Tom, was he also in the service?"

"Yes, actually he still is," I said. "We went in together and spent much of our time together. After this one mission, well, after a while I got tired of being shot, and got out. I started with BEQ shortly after. Tommy made a career of it and has done well, but he's looking to retire when he can find the way out. He's seen and been through enough."

"I understand completely," Phillips said. "How about you? What do you want? I think I could make a call and get you a different job with BEQ if you wanted that."

"Thanks, Mr. Phillips, I suppose you could. I appreciate the thought but I've had enough of the corporate world. I have some money but not enough to retire. I'll have to do something eventually."

He nodded in understanding and looked around stiffly, perhaps confirming that we were still alone.

"I can see that Kate trusts you, and your friend, totally. It's that trust that has led me to want to meet with you. My gut tells me that I can trust you also. Is that correct?"

"We've always had a special bond, that's true," I said. "The three of us. And yes, you can trust me, Mr. Phillips."

He leaned in and lowered his voice.

"When I was that young man all those years ago back in Korea, I was attacked. At that time, I was able to fight back. Now, my family and business have been attacked and I'm no longer able to fight back myself. Those people, this Gallo character, Campbell—all of them. I hate them. What they've done to my company and now to my family. If I were that young man again, with my big old army knife and my M1 rifle, I'd give them what they deserve. I would kill them myself. Then I could lie down and fade away in peace."

He fell silent and closed his eyes. I could see that the conversation and the concentration had drained him. He held up a finger for a brief time-out. After a long moment he opened his eyes again.

"Dean, my young friend, I'm afraid I've let my emotions get the better of me. Kate will be back any minute to shoo me back to bed, so I'll get to it. I'm old and sick and don't have the energy for any fighting. Now, you and this friend of yours, who wants to retire, you still have it. You've helped Kate, this family, in the past and you have my thanks. If you could see your way to helping us again, with this dirty business, I could use one of the last things I have left—money—to help you out. Find a way to stop this embezzling as quietly as possible. If some harm comes to these people in the process, so much the better. Now, I'd like you to meet someone who has become sort of a right hand to me. David's a fine young man. Hand me that intercom gadget there, please."

He pointed to a small device on the side table and I handed it to him. After he pressed a button, I heard a voice that sounded like that of his wife. He pressed another button and spoke into the thing.

"I'm fine, dear, just enjoying my chat with Mr. Boudreau. Would you ask David to join us please?"

In less than a minute there was a double knock at the door and a man came in and walked towards us. I could see immediately that he was ex-military. He was tall and slim, and despite a slight limp, appeared to be very fit. His thick blond hair was cut very short, and he was casually dressed in khakis and a dark blue polo shirt. Retired military with a preppy flair, I thought to myself. As he approached and held out his right hand to me, I noticed that his left was in fact a very life-like prosthesis.

"David Elzey," he said. "It's good to meet you Dean. I've heard a lot about you. Heard and read, that is. A navy man, and then some."

"Pleased to meet you as well," I said. "Army?"

"That's right," he said, "75th Rangers, Fort Benning. Six years out and been with the family here for about five."

"Dean," Ben Phillips said, "I wanted you to meet David because he will represent me in this matter from here on in. If you and your friend Tom are inclined to help us, that is. Whatever it is that you do, I don't want it to be hindered in any way by my condition.

"David has been with me for years and has my complete trust.

Please consider that he speaks for me and my family at all times. He doesn't like to talk about his Silver Star and three Purple Hearts, but he humors me when I mention them."

I watched as David made a face as though hearing a joke for the hundredth time, and saw that the face turned quickly into a broad smile. Having a few medals stashed away somewhere myself, I understood the complicated emotions that went along with them for many people.

At that moment, as if summoned, Kate came back into the room. Phillips reached out to put his arm on mine as she approached and locked eyes with me. I leaned in to hear his whisper.

"Please consider what we talked about. I take care of those who help my family. Talk to David about whatever you need."

I nodded my understanding. Kate came up and fussed over her uncle, fixing his blanket and adjusting the chair.

"It was an honor to meet you, Mr. Phillips," I said. "I hope you're with us and comfortable for a long time to come."

"Thanks for sitting and listening to me," he said. And then he spoke to Kate. "I'll be ready for my nap soon but let me have just a few minutes with David first."

"Sure, Uncle Ben," Kate said. "We'll be just outside."

As we started to move away, David touched my arm and spoke directly to me.

"And could I have just a few minutes also, before you leave?"

"Of course," I said. "I'll be right outside the door with Kate."

I waved at Ben Phillips. He lifted a hand in a slight return wave, cocked his head to one side and gave me a wink. I smiled back at him and walked out with Kate, closing the door behind us.

———

"Well, it seems like you hit it off with my uncle," Kate said.

"He's a very interesting man," I said, "no doubt about that. I'm glad I didn't have to go up against him in the business world."

"And you met Elzey also," Kate said. "What's your impression?"

"David? I only just met him," I said, "but he seems like a solid guy. Certainly your uncle puts a lot of stock in him. I'll say this—what he's been through—it takes a lot to get through that. He's made it through some stuff. I think I like him."

David Elzey came out after a few minutes and joined us on the landing.

"He's ready for you now, Kate. Is this a good time for me to borrow Dean for just a few minutes?"

Kate agreed to that and went back inside the suite to her uncle. David led me down the ornate hallway into a small office and gestured to a chair.

"I know you and Kate go way back," he said, "and I don't need to insinuate myself into that in any way. It's just that Ben—Mr. Phillips— would like to insulate her and his wife from any further exposure to this matter at hand. That's why he asked me to serve as an intermediary."

"That's fine with me," I said. "Frankly, it's been strange and some- what uncomfortable talking about it with them. Which isn't to say that they aren't pretty tough. I'm glad you're here. What do you do for them?"

"I handle security for all the properties," he said, "which is mostly routine but keeps me busy. I studied accounting after I got out, so I help out with the investments, though that's mostly Kate's area. If anyone needs a driver or an errand done, I do that. Pretty much what- ever's needed. Mr. and Mrs. Phillips took me in after the army and helped me get back on my feet. With this job, medical bills, whatever I needed. They go way back with my parents and they wanted to help. By the way, Mr. Phillips calls me David, but most people call me Elzey. Been that way since I was a kid."

"Elzey it is then," I said.

"I was in the room," Elzey said, "when Martha filled Ben in on the meeting with you on the island the other day, so I have an idea of what was discussed and how. What was your take on it? What I mean is, what was your sense about what they were asking for?"

"They mentioned that they thought this investigator—this Mr.

Barnes—would probably have either hired some kind of mercenary or recommended that they do so. Possibly somehow to put a scare into these people. Though it wasn't verbalized, I must say I got the impression that Martha wouldn't mind at all if Gallo and his crew would fall down a steep flight of stairs. Maybe I imagined that, except that I just got a much clearer idea along those lines from Mr. Phillips."

Elzey nodded in agreement.

"Let me flesh out something a little bit for you," he said. "It will be no news to you that Mr. Phillips is extremely wealthy. Money is thick in the air around here. You can see that. But this is not at all about money for him. These people—this Gallo guy, and Campbell, the others in their little crew—have been stealing money, yes, but that isn't what this is about for Mr. Phillips.

"It's really about three things. First, he sees these people as having assaulted the honor of his company and the memory of Martha's father. Second, he feels that his family has been attacked. For example the funeral you just attended and Elliot Bannerman's stroke."

"I get that," I said. "That's in line with what I've heard from Kate and her aunt. What's the last reason?"

"The last reason," Elzey said, "is intertwined with the first two, but frankly may be the biggest for Mr. Phillips. He is a dying man who wants to get right with the universe for bringing these guys up and helping them get where they are. He wants to fix his karma. To do the right thing. My new-age words of course, not his, but I think he'd agree with the gist of what I'm telling you.

"I just thought it might help you to have that background. Now, you know BEQ, and I understand that you know most of these people involved. What's your thought on this idea of hiring some mercenary to help these guys fall down some stairs?"

"That is some harsh punishment," I said. "But I'd say they deserve every bit of it. At least two of them have killed and gotten away with it. Gallo sure stabbed me in the back personally. And the points you just spelled out. So yeah, I could look the other way for that. For a mercenary."

"And just hypothetically," he said, "what if the mercenary was you? Or you and your friend Tommy?"

I took a deep breath and thought for a moment before answering him.

"I had a feeling you were going to say that. It's funny, it was only a few weeks ago that Tommy and I were talking about working for Blackstone. Not really considering it—just talking about it. We both know people that signed up. You ever think about that yourself?"

He held up his prosthetic left arm, reminding me.

"Fair question, but this pretty much takes me out of the running. It's the best that money can buy but still not good enough for real action. And if you're wondering, yes, I would take this on myself for this family if I could see it through. Mr. Phillips and I talked about it at length, but what we kept coming back to is that I'm just not the right person for the job. Not with this, not anymore. So the question stands —how about you?"

"Well, yeah, so that's the question," I said. "The funny thing is that Tommy and I have already talked about it. We both knew Kate's cousin Mary. Tommy was like a godfather to her. I know he'd like to burn Gallo to the ground for his own reasons, and so would I for mine. You only get to kick the dog so many times before he turns around and bites, you know?"

"Mr. Phillips," he said "has asked me to move six million dollars into a new account for this. That money is at your disposal if you take this on. Completely at your disposal. Certainly there will be some expenses. Travel, lodging, payoffs—whatever. If there was any money left over, well, he wouldn't be expecting any of it back."

"You know," I said, "I've been through a few shootouts, and my hearing may not be what it once was, but I think I just heard you say something about six million dollars."

Elzey laughed out loud.

"I know what you mean about the shootouts," he said. "My ears are still ringing. But yes, you heard me correctly."

"Shit man, that's a lot of money," I said. "Give me a week to look at this and talk it over with my friend Tommy. If I'm in this, it'll be with him as my partner. I'll get back to you."

After giving me a folded piece of paper with his information, Elzey took me back out into the hallway where we found Kate waiting for us.

"I'm sorry I went over my time, Kate," he said. "Thanks for waiting for me. Dean, it was great meeting you and I thank you for your time. I look forward to hearing from you soon."

We both said goodbye to him, and Kate took my arm as we descended the stairs.

Downstairs in the foyer we were met by Martha, who hugged me again and thanked me for visiting.

"I'm going to sit with Ben for a while and read to him while he still feels up to it. Please keep in touch with Kate and do come visit us again out on the island. Any time at all."

———

Kate and I piled into a recent-year Jaguar sedan that must have belonged to her aunt or uncle, and she drove me to the airport where her family's plane was waiting to take me back over to the island. We chatted during the drive but she didn't ask for any specifics about my discussion with her uncle, or about my time with Elzey. It occurred to me that she might know full well what was in the air, but had decided to not let that unpleasant reality be a part of our friendship. If that was the case, I thought, all that was fine with me. If I would go down this dirt road, there would be no operational need to have Kate be a part of it any further.

———

Within an hour after leaving the Phillip's house outside Providence, I deplaned at the Block Island airport and drove into town. After parking on Water Street, I walked out onto the jetty by Ballard's and called Tommy on my cell. He answered on the third ring.

"Hey T, after the service last week, that thing that you said you really wanted to do, you weren't kidding by any chance, were you?"

"Come on," he said, "you know me better than that. You know I don't kid about things like that."

"Yeah, I know, sorry," I said. "Just checking. I decided that I wanted to do the same thing, and I don't kid about that either."

"Well we don't have to fight over it," Tommy said. "I can do it. You can do it. As long as it gets done."

"Here's the thing though," I said, "There have been some developments out here. I think I've stumbled on a way that we can get that thing done, and help out some really good friends of ours in the process, all while dramatically enhancing our retirement funds. Maybe even throw in some justice. I see a way to get that truckload of rum, the beach with the palm tree, even a driveway to park the truck in. Only thing is, we're going to have to behave very badly to earn the ticket."

"This is all very interesting," Tommy said. "And those possibilities sound very exciting. Behaving very badly is, after all, what I do for a living. Are you coming out west to fill me in? The deck awaits."

"I'll be home late tomorrow," I said. "Give me a few days to pack up and take care of some things and then I think I'll drive out. Been wanting to check Mount Rushmore off my list anyway."

20

I t was the cool dawn of a summer morning and a surf caster was just off the beach, casting a long rod in a powerful, graceful arc. I walked towards him, stopping to sit on a driftwood log to watch.

The tide was coming in, pushing a mist towards shore. The fisherman turned and waved to me. I knew that he was very good at what he was doing and I was glad that he didn't seem to mind my watching.

After a while he reeled in his line and started to walk towards me. As he got closer I saw that he was my father, as he had looked in his last few years. The surrounding air got warmer as he approached.

"Hi, Dean, I'm so glad you're here," he said, as he came across the sand to me. "Those stripers are out there, I know it. Maybe you'll bring me luck."

The air seemed to have an electric charge. I could feel a tingling sensation all over my skin but at the same time I felt safe and at peace.

"Hi, Dad. I'm glad you're getting to do some fishing. That's nice. I've really missed you."

"And I you, son, and I you, every day, or whatever a day is now. Dean, I saw some men near you. They're gone now, but they seemed angry."

"They're angry because I killed them. They thought I was someone else and they tried to kill me."

"You killed all five of these men?"

"Yes, in two minutes. It's the only impossible thing I've ever done."

He looked off across the ocean as my tears fell to the sand. I felt a warm pressure on my shoulder and I looked up to see that he was beside me with his hand on my shoulder.

"That must have been very difficult."

"That's the problem, Dad. I found it very easy."

We stood together for a moment, just listening to the wind and the sea.

"It's all right, son, you did what you had to do. We can't always see what our lot is. There's more to be done but you have everything you need. You've already done the impossible."

The waves crashed loudly and I saw that they were bringing the mist in with them.

"Dad, was it hard to die?'

"No, not really. Like so many things we fear, the anticipation is worse than the thing. I no longer have to fear death, which is a small recompense. A privilege we earn through dying."

I nodded in agreement with the good sense of that.

"Well, I'd better get back out there; the stripers are running and the blues too. Good seeing you, son. I'm so proud of you. Follow your heart. No compass or advice from another will ever serve you better."

He started to walk away. He was maybe twenty feet up the beach when he paused and turned back to wave and yell something to me.

"I'll try to catch one for you!"

I lifted my hand in a farewell as he continued up the beach and then waded out into the surf. I sat and watched for a while as he cast his line. The mist continued in, pushed by the waves, and it got harder and harder to see him. Eventually he was gone and I was alone on the beach.

———

I awoke with the smell of the ocean still in my nostrils. I sat in bed for a few minutes before rising, pondering the dream and the weekend. What was it he had said again? "I'll try to catch one for you."

I had the feeling that in one way or another I'd been visited by both of my parents. I wondered if there was some kind of warning there, or perhaps just a signpost along a strange and curvy road.

I showered, dressed, and went out to the dining room for breakfast. There was a ferry to catch and a long drive home after that.

21

The next morning, at home in the Pennsylvania suburbs, I began to prepare for a course of action that was far from set. I had a lot of thinking to do still and had yet to run it all by Tommy. I hoped it wouldn't take much convincing to get him to sign on and help me formulate a plan. There was some chance that he would just say I was nuts, but I didn't think that likely. In any case, it was good to be prepared. I planned for at least a few weeks on the road, with options for several months.

To stay as flexible as possible, I decided to supplement the cash that Kate had given me with some of my own money. Fortunately, I was pretty well cashed up. Over several days, I visited different branches of my bank, cashing checks along the way. I kept the amounts between five and eight thousand each time in order not to raise any eyebrows. I made friendly comments about taking a long cross-country vacation. Between that money and some more that I already had in a small safe in the house, I ended up with a personal traveling bankroll of thirty-thousand dollars on top of the sixty that Kate had given me.

Each morning I subjected myself to an hour-long workout that started with a short early run and then moved to the weights. It had been a few years since my last Krav-Maga lesson, but I dusted off a set of instructional DVDs and did my best to follow along and get back what I could. I knew that a DVD was no substitute for professional training and sparring, but something was better than nothing. It was my fervent hope to avoid any sort of physical altercations. I had no interest at all in any so-called 'fair fights'.

I spent an afternoon going through my basement arsenal, picking out a few key items. Though the Beretta had served me well in my recent adventure, I opted for one of my forty-five autos as the main assault weapon. It was a combat customized model that the NRA had given me as part of their thanks for my promotional work. Months before, I had been in contact with the actual gunsmith who finished the piece and he had hooked me up with a spare barrel that was threaded on the protruding end, along with a matching coupler. All with a smile and a wink. With that special coupler and a few evenings bent over a friend's metal lathe, I had built a basic but highly effective suppressor.

After a coat of flat-black metal stain for the suppressor and the addition of a laser site, I had a super-accurate and reliable assault pistol that any Navy Seal would have approved of. It had only an eight-round magazine, but there again, I wasn't planning to get into any firefights with armed opponents.

I tested the rig in the basement by firing into a stack of magazines and found it to be very quiet. The red-hatted Ladies Who Lunch could have been having tea upstairs in the kitchen and wouldn't have noticed anything amiss.

As company for the forty-five, I set out a Walther P22 automatic. It was only twenty-two caliber but was small and light, as well as accurate and fast handling. A hundred rounds of hyper-velocity hollow points completed the package.

I packed both pistols into a hard-sided and lockable case, along with spare magazines, holsters, and cleaning equipment. I put the ammo supply into a separate locked box. I knew that traveling with the two locked boxes secured in the trunk of my Lexus would have me in compliance with laws governing the transport of firearms across state lines. I was confident that once in Washington State with Tommy, he would know how best to handle things from there.

The home-made and therefore highly illegal suppressor was inconspicuously nestled amongst a pile of tools in a canvas bag in the spare-tire well.

I corresponded with Tommy via email to let him know when I would be starting on the cross-country drive. He confirmed that he would be available off and on after I got there.

I emailed both Elzey and Kate, separately, to let them know that I was headed out west to meet with Tommy and would be in touch in the near future.

I arranged with my neighbor to check on the house now and then. Judy was a professor at one of the Pennsylvania state colleges but was a wine-country California Girl at heart. We had a reciprocal arrangement through which I would sometimes watch her house and she would watch mine. We always paid each other off with bottles of artfully fermented grape juice. I left a fine Napa Cabernet out on the counter for her with a note promising more to come.

I packed up a duffel bag for the trunk and my backpack for easy storage and quick reach in the car. The more than ninety thousand dollars in cash was spread out between the duffel, the backpack, and the spare tire compartment. I had several thousand at the ready in my pants pocket. It was my intent to liberally draw on the supply of smaller bills in my travels and for lesser expenses. I had an almost three thousand-mile drive before me and I intended to make the best of it. I'd always wanted to drive cross country, and this potential 'mission' was as good an excuse as any. I was hoping that good champagne was still available in the heartland.

With a final check all around, I closed up the house and headed out for the turnpike. I was westward bound on the last Sunday of April, towards sunsets and potentially profitable adventures.

22

Tommy set down the last of the files as I drained the last of my coffee. It had been a long morning and afternoon of poring over all the information in the bankers box. Three rounds through the material had been fueled by as many pots of coffee and some Chinese takeout. It was time for a break.

Tommy rubbed his eyes. He looked at me and uttered one of his favorite expressions.

"Let's have a drink."

He gestured to the papers spread across the dining room table. "This is some heavy shit. We have a lot to think about and a lot to talk about, not necessarily in that order."

I held up the bottle of Woodford Reserve bourbon and cocked my head towards the deck.

"Capital idea!" he said. "Let me piss for the sixteenth time today and I'll meet you out there."

I cleared away the food containers, grabbed glasses and ice, and settled on the deck. Tommy joined me after a few minutes and I poured us each a generous triple.

We enjoyed the warm spring air for a while before Tommy spoke.

"I suggest that we start by just throwing it out on the table. Just you and me here. Let's just get it out with no filters."

"Sounds good," I said. "I've obviously had more time than you to think about it but I want to hear your thoughts."

"I'll start then," Tommy said. "First, let's set aside for the moment what we would both like to do to your friend Gallo. After that, it seems to me that the embezzling at the core of this whole mess is well-researched and not in question as far as I can tell. Looks like there's a ton of evidence for that so I'm willing to accept it at face value and go from there. My next thought is, that isn't my problem and it isn't your problem. Just another group of assholes stealing from a big, rich company. That's a problem for the company or for law enforcement. If Kate's aunt and uncle don't want to go public for whatever reason, that's their business, but then these people may just keep doing what they're doing and getting away with it. So far so good?"

"Yeah, I agree," I said. "There's an embezzling racket going on for sure. They want it stopped. Stamped out."

"And," Tommy said, "they don't want the publicity that would come with taking this to the feds or the cops."

"Well, yes," I said, "but they also have a lot of concerns about the way much of the evidence was gathered. They think that if this went through the legal route it would be a lot of heat and publicity with no convictions."

"Right," Tommy said. "Certainly the embezzling would be stopped and all involved would be fired, but also no convictions and tons of publicity. Let's talk about other angles. What other sins have these people committed?"

"Well you have that old accident that killed the landscaper and his daughter. Circumstantial perhaps, but this isn't a court of law. Vince and John killed those two and got away with it. Next you have the epidemic of firing good people. I'm a big boy and I can take it, but with Mary and Evan it certainly led to tragedy. I get that Evan had issues, but I hold Vince—and by extension John Campbell—responsible for what happened to them. Everyone knew how hard those guys worked. There was no reason for them to be treated like that. Vince and John may just as well have pulled the trigger is the way I see it, and I know that Kate and her family feel the same way. I never knew any of Evan's family, but whoever they are, they've also lost a son or brother."

I walked over to the deck rail to look out at the city. It was a clear enough day that Mt. Rainier was visible to the south. It seemed almost to loom over the city though its peak was at least forty miles away. I knew that locals would have said that 'the mountain was out today'.

"Yeah, I agree on that," Tommy said. "That case seems pretty clear. No doubt that kind of shit happens all the time in the normal course of the affairs of the privileged. We go to jail, they go to Yale. Old story."

"You said it, T. The last thing is that John Campbell, probably insti-gated by Vince Gallo, maneuvered to get Kate's husband Elliot pushed out of his position and into early retirement. Kate is convinced that's what precipitated Elliot's stroke and threw their lives into a spin. He's only in his fifties and he's going to have a long struggle just to get back to eighty percent. That's a bitch for both of them."

We sat for quite a while after that, just taking in the day as it shifted into evening. Tommy went inside to get us some more ice, which we then covered with bourbon. A car went by on the street below with windows open and radio blasting. We both recognized the tune from a concert we'd been to with Kate many years ago as teenagers. We exchanged a look and a smile.

I picked up the conversation again.

"Just so you know, I'm aware that I'm very biased when it comes to talking about big companies firing people just to increase profits and bonuses. I know that's what crushed my brother. Should it have? Prob-ably not, but it did. And of course, it happened to me too. I'm not as fragile as he was but it still pisses me off. It's a punch in the face that we didn't deserve. It upsets your life.

"I'm also aware that sometimes I rant about other shit companies do. Like those recent stories about airlines yanking paying customers off flights because they screwed up and sold more tickets than the plane has seats. I got so pissed off about one of those stories the other week, I actually called my congressman and senators. I shit you not, I really did. These big companies just get away with so much and the politicians just endlessly wink at it. I am so fucking sick of it."

Tommy nodded but didn't add anything.

"I'm not just raving, T; here's my point. Maybe this is a chance for us—or maybe even just me—to punch them back. Punch them in the gut with a high-velocity lead fist. Wouldn't that feel good?"

"It would, yes," Tommy said. "But it wouldn't really make a dent. We could kill off this gang or beat the shit out of them and it might feel really good, but it wouldn't have any effect on corporate America's bad behavior. After everything I've heard about this Gallo character, I have no doubt that he deserves a long dip in boiling oil. But let's hold off on the idea of an attack on corporate executives in general, and keep to the matter at hand. How did Kate and this Elzey guy come at you about all this? What was their angle?"

"Tough and tougher. My take on it is that this Mr. Barnes must have been a highly competent character but from the dark side of the street. Kate mentioned to me that he may have been planning to suggest that they hire a mercenary of some sort. Scare them off, kill them, we don't really know what he would have done. I'll tell you though, Kate's aunt is one tough lady. I mean if the mob was all WASPs in Vineyard Vines sweaters, she would make a good boss of bosses. I think she's really grown to hate Vince and John for the reasons we've discussed, and blames them for a lot of pain. And her husband Ben, too. He's in his final act now but he must have been someone not to mess with. He was infantry in Korea and saw combat. I got the impression that if he were twenty years younger he'd be going after those guys himself, spraying hot lead from the hip. To answer your question, I think the whole family would be very happy if Vince and his gang were pushed off a cliff, though the ladies didn't really ask for anything like that outright. When I met with Ben Phillips and his man Elzey, they were quite a bit more forward. Ben Phillips wishes he could kill Gallo and Campbell himself but he's obviously not up to it.

His guy Elzey would be happy to do the job but he doesn't think he's capable of it. He did leave an arm somewhere in Iraq, after all. So in their mind, that's where Kate's trusted old combat-tested buddies come in. Enter stage left, Tommy and Dean. Gunfighters and saviors."

"Wow. Okay, well, that's pretty much what I thought you'd say," Tommy said. "Are we nuts to even be thinking about this, or what? I mean, doesn't this bother you at all? Not all of these people have killed someone. The others just look like thieves."

"We may be nuts, yeah," I said, "but no, it doesn't bother me much. Probably because of my hatred of Vince Gallo. At a minimum I'm going to take care of him for both of us, but I wish I could kill him several times. I'd like to kill him and then dig him up after the funeral and kill him again. Drive a stake right through where his heart isn't. He deserves it. John Campbell too. Though with John I only need to kill him once. And for the others, to borrow an old term—collateral damage. They bought their tickets on the Gallo train. I just want to make them get off a few stops early. And also, T, I don't know about you, but three million bucks would buy me a big fat slice of forgiving myself."

"What the hell," Tommy said, "you didn't say anything about any three million clams!"

"Sorry, man," I said. "I was saving that for the right moment just to get you riled up. Actually, it's three for each of us. Three times two. Elzey told me that Ben Phillips had him set six million dollars aside for this situation. He made it very clear to me that anything left over after expenses was mine. And by mine, I mean you and me. A fifty-fifty split. That would go a long way towards our retirement. Remember I told you I thought I found a way to get us to the rum and the palm trees?"

Tommy whistled through his teeth and shook his head, but didn't add anything.

Just then we were interrupted by a single loud 'caw' as a large black bird swooped down to land on the south railing right in front of us. I was startled enough that I jumped and spilled booze on my lap. Tommy laughed at me.

"Is that a raven?" I asked. I thought Tommy might know his local birds. "Maybe this is an omen."

"I think it's a basic crow," Tommy said. "Crows have that classic long 'caw' sound. Ravens make a more staccato sound—almost like barking, but bird-barking. And ravens are bigger. They're both in the area."

"All right, so this may not be an evil portent then?"

"Well, it could be," Tommy said. "But bear in mind that aside from death or doom, crows can also signify change. And whatever happens, change is in the air."

The crow visited with us for a while, exchanging loud calls with another bird high up in a nearby tree. After a few minutes he turned and flew off to rendezvous with his friend. As he burst into flight his shiny feathers reflected the arriving sunset in a quick flash of color.

"I put in for my retirement last week," Tommy said. "So that's one big change. Thirty-two years is enough. It's been a twisted path since that idealistic young guy joined the navy. To see the world or to get out of New Jersey, or whatever the hell my reason was back then. Maybe you remember why we joined but I forget. Anyway, it doesn't matter now."

He sipped at his drink and found the glass to be empty. I reached over with the bottle and poured.

"The last time we talked about this," he said, "I was flippant about it. You know me—that's how I deal. You're that way too. But the truth is, I have done some terrible shit. That's for sure. I like to believe it was all for the greater good but I don't really know anymore. One thing leads to another and again and then again and eventually you don't even remember where you started. I've killed a lot of men who I think were mostly bad guys—whatever that means—but they probably didn't think so. Their wives probably didn't think so. By no stretch was it always clear.

"A while ago I was about to say that I wasn't any kind of mercenary, but I stopped myself when I realized that maybe I have been just that. A good one maybe? Working for the good guys? Who is that these days? Don't get me wrong—I really hope it's us and I think it usually is. But I'm tired of it. I've served my time and left pieces of my soul all over the unfriendly map. My retirement should go through within five or six months. I have to wrap up a few projects, help train some people, and then I'm out. I'll have a decent pension but nothing to jump up and down about.

"So here's the thing. I'll help you with this, but not to protect this BEQ company from publicity and not to help these rich people with their guilt. I have enough of that on my own. That's for damn sure. For the Gallo guy, that's personal for both of us, but the rest of it—no, I'll do it for the money, plain and simple. I'm going to retire and I want to do it in style. After this, who knows, I might even want to leave the country. Would be nice to set my daughters up with some savings too. Pay off their college loans. Also, I don't want you to go off half-cocked and fuck this up. Just because you made the covers of all the gun magazines doesn't mean you're some super commando now."

He jabbed a finger at me with at least part of a smile.

"One thing though. I still have a job, at least for a while, and you don't. To do this we're going to need my contacts and my access. You're the one who's going to have to travel around and do the legwork. I'll be support and communications. Command and control."

"Agreed," I said. "That's the way I figured it had to work. You stay right here but I'm going to need a lot of help. Equal shares of whatever we get."

"And as to your ranting about corporate layoffs and off-shoring and all that," Tommy said, "I hear you. That stuff really pisses me off too. But let's focus on this one thing and get it done right. If we make it through this, we can talk about the other thing. Like you said, maybe there's a way we can punch them in the gut. Send a message. One thing at a time though, okay?"

"Yes, okay," I said. "One thing at a time."

"All right, sounds good then," Tommy said. "I can take the next few days off. Let's start working on a plan tomorrow. One thing I know is, we're going to need a good pile of expense money up front, a hundred large easily. That won't be a problem, will it?"

"No, I don't think the money will be any problem," I said. "Kate already gave me sixty in cash when we were on the island and I brought that out with me in the car. I have another thirty grand of my own with me also, just in case. I don't mind using that if we need to. Elzey takes over from here as my main contact, and he can move whatever money we need when I ask for it.

"One minor thing I've been thinking about—with all your connections, do you know any hackers? You know, who might do some work for us for a monetary consideration?"

"Sure, some really good ones," he said. "One right here in Seattle. If I asked nicely, she'd probably take on some side work. Why?"

"Well, just an idea really, but, when I first met with Kate and Martha last week we talked a lot about money having been embezzled from BEQ, possibly millions but certainly hundreds of thousands. Whatever we may do about it will be strictly extra-legal. Nobody is expecting to recover any of that money. That's not what this is about. The way I see it, whatever money we might be able to recover—if any —is ours to keep. Maybe none, but in any case, nobody is going to worry about it. If you know a hacker who can pull off half of what they do in the movies, we'll be in like Flynn."

"The person I'm thinking of has done banking work before. She'll know what to do and she'll give me the straight dope. We can set up a meet when it's time."

We sat in silence for a while before Tommy spoke again.

"So we'll do this then. We'll do it and we'll walk away with some good money. We'll take the memory of what we did and bury it deep. Maybe you'll be able to afford that island house you've always talked about. Maybe I really will move to Costa Rica and drink rum on the beach. We'll do it and then afterwards it won't have happened. That's it. It won't have happened.

"A toast to the mission then. A toast to Operation Pale Horse."

"Pale Horse," I said, "I like it. Where did that come from?"

"Well, operations need to have a code name," Tommy explained. "Overlord, Desert Storm, and Thunderball have all been used already. Anyway, Pale Horse just seemed to fit."

"An excellent choice," I said. "Operation Pale Horse it shall be."
We clinked our glasses together and drank deep.

A memory came to me just then of something I had read long ago
while doing research for a morbid high school paper.

*And when the forth seal was broken, I looked and beheld a pale horse.
And his name that sat on him was Death, and Hell followed with him.*

23

W e started after breakfast the next morning.

I agreed with Tommy that the first thing we needed to do was to clearly identify the mission parameters.

"First of all," Tommy said, "I took the liberty of calling a friend in DC yesterday. He made some calls for me and checked into this office fire in Arlington and this Mr. Barnes. As far as he can tell it's all on the up and up. The Arlington police aren't talking about any kind of foul play. They say it looks like the fire started in some low-bid wiring and spread from there. And he says this Barnes guy was much respected in the community. What I got back is that Barnes specialized in expensive jobs for rich folks avoiding publicity and he was one of the best. So, I guess that starts us off with good info from him."

"Good," I said. "I'm glad you did that, thanks. That whole thing was very odd at first glance, but you know, some things are just odd."

"Yep, you can say that again," Tommy said. After a pause he tapped one of the piles of file folders that we had spread out over the table.

"I see five people in on this whole thing, you agree?"

"Yes, five," I said. "The gang of five. I've known all of them for a minimum of a few years and it adds up. They would cover the right positions to pull this thing off. Given the craziness of the whole setup, that is. Here, let me show you."

I grabbed my legal pad and moved around the table to a chair next to Tommy, pushing some folders aside as I sat down. I had drawn a quick stick-figure diagram.

"So here's John Campbell at the top of the food chain. His title is Senior VP, Data Processing. He would be in a position to have final approval of the datacenter expenses, at least at a certain granular level. Nobody above him would need to see, or would care, for that matter, what type of server was being used or what type of cabling had been installed. He's at corporate headquarters in Ridgewood, New Jersey.

"Next we have Vince Gallo. His title is Senior Director, Data Processing. He reports to John, though they're old buds. If I had to guess, I'd say that this whole thing probably started with Vince and then he brought John in as his partner. Vince got his start as an engineer and eventually moved into management. Knowing these people, it just makes sense that he would be the one to cook this up. He's based out of an office in Roswell, which is northern suburbs of Atlanta.

"Mark Sonetto is a director who reports to Vince. Mark is based in the Chicago area out west of O'Hare, but is one of the people in charge of day-to-day activities in the datacenters in Atlanta and Montana. He and Vince together would be able to doctor equipment lists and financial reports to constantly show that these non-existent servers are being used for vital operations. Then they send it all up to John for the VP sign-off.

"Michael Sanchez reports to Vince and would probably help with the covering paperwork. He works with payables and all the reporting related to that. He would have all the access he needs to approve reports and payments in Vince's name. I knew him back when he was starting out in programming. He did a good job of kissing asses to work his way up. He used to be a decent person, so I'm guessing he just got caught up in all this through Vince.

"Last but not least is Gloria Parsons. What a gem. She and Michael are both long-time Vince hangers-on, but she left almost two years ago to work at BardLogic. She's got to be the agent-in-place who somehow makes sure that BEQ still gets billed for the servers they don't have. She's a world-class asshole, but smart as hell. In any case, same as Michael, I'm sure she just went with the flow on this. Vince has got to be the puppeteer.

"So that's the rogue's gallery. That's them. Here's my thought though—I was up most of the night going over this. The more I think about it, the more I think a decapitation strike would do it. If we take out the top three—John, Vince, and Mark—I really think that Michael and Gloria would just quietly go away. Count their money and go away, that is. Humpty-Dumpty would break apart and there wouldn't be any way to put him back together again."

"Then just to play devil's advocate," Tommy said, "what about one or both of them going to the police? Or even before they got to that, what are they going to think when the other three turn up dead? Wouldn't they freak out?"

"Fair to bring up and I have thought of it," I said. "I can see them freaking out, sure, but not going to the police. I mean, what are they going to say? They're concerned that the other members of their white-collar theft ring are turning up dead? I don't think so."

"Don't dismiss it," Tommy said. "It could be more like, hey, I was down with skimming this money, but I didn't sign up to be killed. And by the way, let's not forget the possibility that if you take out person one, let's just say that's Vince, then maybe person two, whether Mark or John, would look around and get paranoid. Go to ground, leave the country, throw themselves on the mercy of the cops—who knows."

"You're right, T," I said. "We shouldn't dismiss any of those possibilities. But hang on, that's one of the things I've been pondering. Most of the week actually.

"I'll elaborate, but just briefly, I think I see a way to have Mark killed in a robbery. A random violent street crime. People would be shocked but nobody would make any connection to this embezzling or to BEQ."

"We can't go hiring thugs, if that's what you're thinking," Tommy said.

"No, you're right of course and I know that," I said. "I'm getting there, hear me out. Mark's about our age. Recently divorced, no kids, probably makes about one-fifty. He's always been a flashy guy. He drives a Corvette and probably wears a gold chain. If he were in the mob he'd be one of the young lions with the slicked hair and the Armani suit. Actually he does have the slicked hair but I don't know about the suit. Anyway, there's a point to this. He's always worn a gold Rolex President. That's the solid gold one. Much fancier than my little 'ole stainless Submariner. Easily a ten-thousand dollar watch and very gaudy. He was always getting ribbed that one day he was going to get mugged for that watch.

"So you probably know what I'm thinking. If Mark were gunned down or got his head bashed in with a tire-iron and someone stole that watch, there would be a whole lot of people who would say 'I knew that was going to happen someday,' or 'well, I told him to stop flashing that damn watch'!"

"Hmmm—yes, I see," Tommy said. "I think that idea could fly. So, you do Mark first and everyone just thinks it's a violent mugging."

"That's right," I said. "Now keep rolling with me. Mark gets killed by an unknown mugger, who of course gets away scot free—that part is very important to me. Then, a few weeks later, Vince dies in a tragic accident. I still have to figure that one out. That leaves John Campbell. Is he wondering about the coincidence of Mark and Vince dying within a few weeks? Quite possibly. But, if Mark's mugging story is plausible, and the explanation for Vince's accident is plausible, then I figure that even if he's on edge, he doesn't really have anything to go on. Surely not enough to make him liquidate assets and disappear to Singapore at that point. And surely not enough to make him throw away his high-paid respectable life and run to the police in disgrace.

"So, a few more weeks go by and then we make John meet with an accident also. Or better yet, I saw in his file that he helps his parents run a tavern. Like a neighborhood pub, in Paterson, New Jersey. Maybe there could be an armed robbery."

I got up to move around the room and stretch a bit. Tommy went into the kitchen to start up another pot of coffee. I joined him there and leaned against the counter.

"Going with your idea so far," Tommy said, "Mark has a fatal mugging, few weeks later Vince dies in an accident, then another few weeks and John buys it when someone robs his bar. I guess that's when those other two are sweating bullets. I sure would be by that time if I were in their shoes. It wouldn't be a leap for them to believe that their number was up next."

"Yeah, you're right," I said. "But we can only guess what they would do. I still don't see them going to the cops. I think it's more likely that they quietly freak out and stay behind locked doors, hoping it's all a coincidence. But what if we sent them a message? Like a note telling them to take their money, resign, and go far away."

"They might hightail it," Tommy said, "but the problem with that is that then they have some real proof that there actually is a conspiracy going on and someone really is out there killing them. That could push them over the edge and towards the police."

"Yeah, you're right again," I said. "Dumb idea, sorry. Better not to confirm what they may not even be thinking of. Dammit. Sure would be nice if they all lived in the same area and had regular meetings, wouldn't it? Then we could just have a nice gas line explosion or something like that. Get them all in one fell swoop."

"Let's keep it in mind and stay flexible," Tommy said. "For the time being I propose that we operate under the hypothesis that those last two will be suspicious to some extent, but will keep their heads down.

"There is something we can do, particularly since we have plenty of expense money to work with. We should be able to keep an eye on them. For the right pile of cash, I think I can get someone to tap their phones. Or land lines anyway, if they have them. We can set something up to see if they call each other and if so what they talk about. That'll cost us a chunk but we can do it for a limited period of time. I'll work on having that in place for a day or two before you take Gallo out."

"All right, I'm down with that plan," I said. "And based on how things unfold we adjust accordingly. So, it's Mark first then, with a mugging outside of Chicago. Then I'll head to Atlanta, watch Vince for a while and work out a plan. Maybe we can come up with a way to make that look like an accident. Otherwise, I don't know. Robbery probably. As long as it doesn't look like there's any connection to BEQ, the embezzling, or Mark's recent mishap. Lastly, it's Campbell up in North Jersey and maybe we can exploit the family tavern thing. And all the while we keep tabs on Michael and Gloria. You know, there's another tidbit in the John Campbell file that I'm sure you must have noticed too, T. Those two guys who hang out in the tavern when it's Campbell's night to run the joint. I'd have to look up their names, but they're Gambino family associates, according to Mr. Barnes. His note on that says that he didn't see any indication of a business relationship, more just like old friends of Campbell's from the neighborhood. Maybe that's something else we could exploit."

"Hmmm, yes, I did read that," Tommy said. "The bar belongs to Campbell's parents but he runs the place for them on most weekends and handles the business side. Yeah, maybe that's something we can use. Respectable executive closing down the tavern late at night with two known tough guys hanging around. Good thought, I like it. Could really be something there.

"So then, if all this plays out remotely like we're talking about, with the three of them six feet underground and the other two scared but quiet, where do we stand?"

"Well, then," I said, "I think we've achieved our goal. The embezzling is shut down hard. The Chicago police will be looking into a mugging. The Atlanta police will be looking into some terrible accident or house fire—whatever. And police in New Jersey will be looking into a robbery gone bad that looks like it could have mob connections. I suppose it's possible that someone high up at BEQ could wonder if there was some kind of connection to these sudden deaths. But as long as they look like completely different crimes or accidents, I don't see any reason that these three jurisdictions would call each other up and start talking conspiracy. I think it's more likely that the CEO starts a scholarship fund or something like that. There would be an announcement about how tragedy has struck the wonderful staff of our great company this year, blah, blah, blah.

"Worse comes to worse, somebody does make a connection and

gets the ball rolling on an investigation. Like if the CEO happens to be friends with the FBI director and convinces him there's something to it. In that case, well, again, the embezzlement has been stopped but we have a chance that word of an investigation gets out, so we bungled that part. That would be too bad but we can't entirely prevent it. What I really want to prevent is us getting caught.

"And as for the money, if we manage to recover any, nobody can say anything about it as long as we only take money that's obviously dirty and hidden away somewhere. I mean, we don't want to make Mrs. Gallo suspicious by cleaning out the household account the night I off her husband. But if we happen to find some Cayman Islands account with a million dollars in it—that's fair game. If she does know about that she can't say anything to anybody. Those files had bank account information for each of these people. Let's take another really close look to see if there's anything on any offshore accounts. And if we find anything at all, maybe that's where your hacker friend can dig deeper."

We'd walked out onto the deck with our coffee. It was early afternoon and another beautiful spring day. I could tell that Tommy had gone fully into mission planning mode.

"I think you've summed it up as well as we can at this point," he said. "What cash do we have available right now?"

I went into the house for a minute and returned with a canvas bag, handing it to him.

"There's fifty in hundreds. I have most of another ten in smaller bills that I can use for travel or whatever. And I have that thirty of my own. I'll ask Elzey for what, another fifty? Seventy?"

"Ask him for another eighty," Tommy said. "I'd rather have more than we need handy then to have to wait for another installment. Let's keep a tally of whatever we hand out. Have him get it ready to move but wait for us to give him an account number. We'll open an account at a bank I know where we'll be able to get whatever cash we need without attracting attention. We can't do that until we've got your new identity. That's the first call I'll make later today to get that ball rolling. That'll eat up ten or fifteen of this."

I looked at him wide-eyed but didn't say anything.

"Hey, you want to get away with this, right? I know I do," Tommy said. "We can't have you traveling all over the country doing this shit as yourself."

I held up my hands in surrender to his wisdom and good sense.

"We need to do all this," he said, "get away with it, and then have nobody looking at us. You see, getting away with murder is really quite simple if you think about it. All you need to do is to not be the person they're looking for. Easy as pie."

24

"I hope you're going to elaborate on that," I said. "My new identity. But first, how exactly does one get away with murder?"

"There are many ways," Tommy said. "Only a little more than half of all murders in this country are solved. That ranges by area, of course. Some cities have a clearance rate as high as eighty or ninety percent. So lots of people get away with murder, and most of them are a lot more stupid than you or me.

"Overwhelmingly, most murders are committed by someone who knows the victim, right? Someone very close. Someone's been rejected or humiliated, caught their wife cheating, tired of being raped by the stepfather, tired of being overshadowed by the successful older brother, all of that shit. Spouses and other close family members kill each other in the heat of an argument. Sorry to mention it, but Mary and Evan are an example of that. That stuff happens when you live, eat, and sleep together.

"Then of course you have the business partner. Who benefits? Or the nephew who gets tired of waiting for his inheritance while his sick old uncle hangs on in the expensive nursing home, eating up his assets. One day he holds a pillow over the old guy's face. That's why the police always start right off by asking themselves who would've wanted this person dead and/or who might benefit from their death.

"And to anyone thinking about doing away with their wife, I say don't do it, because the grieving husband will never get away from being the prime suspect. That one is hard to get away with. Same with the other way around."

"But with these people, we don't have any personal connection at all, and there's no reason for us to show up on any kind of list of people who might benefit."

"Right," Tommy said, "you got it. I never had any connection to any of them. You worked with some of them a year ago, but then so did hundreds of other people. Any connection to you is really thin. We just need to make sure that none of this looks like corporate revenge or whatever you want to call it. Because then the police might start to look at current and former co-workers or people who were fired recently. Let's keep it from even going there.

"That's why serial killers are so hard to catch—because they have no connection to their victims. See, if you want to kill someone you know, like your wife or your partner, for whatever your motive is, then you're constrained by their movements and habits. Which way do they walk to their car after work? What jogging path do they take through the woods every morning? Which night is it that they meet their friends at the bar and then walk through that big parking lot?

"But a serial or random killer doesn't care about any of that. They pick a time and a place, like a highway overpass, a path through the woods, or the underground parking lot at the mall. Kill whoever's in that place at the right time and then get the hell outta there. Barring stupid mistakes, you're likely to get away with something like that.

"So my point in all this is that we need to not have Dean Boudreau in any of these places at any time near when these crimes or these terrible accidents occur. You'll obviously need to be there, but you'll be someone else. You'll do a few small things to alter your appearance a little, maybe some fake glasses, hair dye, some different clothes. It doesn't need to be a lot and I'll help you with it. The gist is that if you were to somehow show up on some security camera footage nobody is going to have that gut feeling that they know you or that they've seen you before. We want you to be as unremarkable as possible. Just people-watch when you're out around town. You'd be amazed at how few people will remember your face if you wear a bright red hat. They remember the bright red hat."

"Please don't ask me to wear a bright red hat," I said. "But I get your point. That all jibes with things I've read and heard over the years. What about the ID? How does that work? What do we need to do to start that?"

"In the business," Tommy said, "we have what we call a 'travel kit'. It's a driver's license, social security card, two or three credit cards, and a few other cards depending on the locality, like store discount cards or a library card. Because we sometimes need that in a hurry, a lot of the prep work is done already and we just need to fill in the blanks, such as physical description and nationality, and add pictures.

"I should step back for a minute and give you a little background. You might remember this but I'll refresh your memory anyway. In the military, and certainly where I am now, you get to know plenty of people who are very good at what they do but don't mind making a little extra money on the side. They're good people and patriotic Americans, but if they know you and they don't think you're doing anything treasonous, they'll help you out. Like if you have the newest issue pistol. You want the silencer that goes with it but strictly off-book. You don't want the hassle of all that federal paperwork. Well, your friend in the armory might be able to lose the records for one for say, five hundred or so. Happens all the time. I've helped people in ways that I've been able to on plenty of occasions and there are people who would be glad just to return a favor. They're accustomed to me working on things I can't talk about and they know better than to ask."

"Yeah, I remember a lot of that," I said. "It was very common and pretty much just understood."

"Right," Tommy said, "and where I am, we also outsource some work, like for the ID kit and other paperwork. Or like with Sophia, the hacker I told you about. She's a civilian who got fired from Microsoft.

I'll see if I can set up a meeting with her for the next day or so. I helped her out in the past and she'll probably be glad to help me. Between the people on the inside and on the outside, I think we can get whatever we need."

"We've got a lot of work to do," I said, "and I'm glad you know what you're doing. I think we might actually have to earn our money."

"If we're going to do this," said Tommy, "let's do it right and get away with it. I know there's going to be some improvisation here and there, but wherever we can plan something out, we need to be spot-on."

"How long do you think our prep is going to take? Before I can head out on the road as whoever I am?"

"Maybe two weeks," Tommy said. "Or about that, as long at the ID gets done as quickly as it usually does and any banking goes smoothly. Also, I want you to spend a few days with a friend of mine—Travis— who does hand to hand combat and weapons training. That's another call I need to make. He has his own gym right across town. You'll like it. He's a great guy and I know he reads all those magazines that you were on the cover of. He'll be thrilled to meet you. He'll help you dust off your old training and show you some new stuff. You'll be sore as hell after but you'll thank me."

"I'll do it if you say so, boss," I said. "Does he know Krav-Maga? I was trying to brush up last week but I could use some help with that. Of course, I really hope I don't get involved in any hand to hand. It's my plan to shoot 'em from across the room."

"Agreed, absolutely," Tommy said. "Always best to catch the mark unawares and shoot them from across the room whenever possible. Three days training is only going to be worth so much, but if things go south and someone pulls a knife on you, or punches you, it won't hurt to be ready. Travis does teach Krav-Maga, so you'll be off to a good start. And I already know that you know your way around a gun better than most by far."

25

The first thing I did was to take another close look at the files on Vince Gallo and John Campbell for anything related to money or bank accounts. I found plenty of information on normal household accounts with balances suitable for two professional men at the high end of middle class, but nothing more interesting than that.

I was starting to put the files back in order when I remembered that there was a thumb drive at the bottom of the bankers box that I hadn't yet looked through. I grabbed my laptop, connected the drive, and started to browse through the folders.

Most of the material was just a copy of the paper documents that we'd already studied. In a folder labeled 'Banking' I found sub-folders for each of the five principals. Again, most of the information duplicated the paper copies but I found one document that I hadn't seen before. It was a memo from Mr. Barnes or one of his people to the effect that the only evidence they had found of any off-shore banking was an account that Vince Gallo held at the First National Bank of Nassau. No information was provided as to the balance.

The Bahamas. That was interesting. That had to be the hiding place for whatever Vince had stolen. But there was no sign of accounts for

Campbell or the others. I printed out the memo for Tommy to look at later.

I put together a communication to Elzey, giving him a quick update and asking for the additional expense money. I uploaded it to a secure lockbox that he had set up.

> *E -*
>
> *T and I accept the mission. Operation to begin in approximately three weeks and to be completed within about two months.*
> *You may inform family in vaguest terms but no questions now or after. Use your judgement about what to tell them.*
> *Need additional 80K for expenses. Will forward destination bank account number in day or two.*
> *Will commence checking lockbox every day by 10:00 a.m. ET when possible. Please do the same.*
> *Thx – D*

I sent another email to my neighbor back home in Pennsylvania, telling her that my trip was likely to be extended. I knew that she didn't have any travel plans of her own coming up, so I hoped it wouldn't be a problem. I promised to bring her back an assorted case of hearty reds from Washington State.

I checked my own online banking, making sure all household bills were up to date and would be paid automatically if needed.

I spent another hour looking at videos and reading blog entries about using various simple techniques to alter appearance so as not to be noticed or remembered on the street. I took lots of mental notes.

I set all the notes and files aside both physically and mentally. I sat back in the armchair and allowed myself a few quiet moments to relax and clear my mind before dinner.

26

D inner was at a nautical-themed place alongside the harbor with a view of Lake Union. The décor was wonderfully tacky and the food was excellent for both of us. I was thrilled to find that they had a special of braised short ribs with root vegetables, while Tommy enjoyed a seafood combination platter that looked as though it could serve a small family. We shared a fine Amador County Shiraz and chatted mostly about non-violent topics. I did my best to describe Block Island to Tommy and I think he got it for the most part, having visited both Nantucket and Provincetown himself in his youth. We agreed that it would be nice to join Kate there together sometime in the future.

I went back and forth in my mind for a while about whether or not to mention my recent series of strange dreams. In the end, I decided that lots of people had strange dreams and there wasn't any relevance. While I knew that Tommy trusted me absolutely, I also knew that it wasn't the best time for either of us to have any doubts about my state of mind.

The restaurant had a large gravel patio area outside along the docks where there were rows of Adirondack chairs and a brick fire pit. After dinner, we invested a substantial chunk of expense money in a pair of double brandies and carried them outside. I noted that my twenty to the bartender had made them seem more like triples, which suited us just fine. Outside, we were able to commandeer two chairs where we could sit off by ourselves and out of earshot of anyone else.

"I set up a meet with Sophia for tomorrow at a coffee shop just down the road from the house," Tommy said. "My hacker friend. You can give her a general idea of whatever it is you have in mind. It would be normal to have her on some small retainer against future work. I'd say three thousand would be a good start. I've worked with her before, she'll be happy with that, with the potential for more."

"Also tomorrow, I'll take you over and introduce you to Travis so you know what to expect and how to get there. The day after tomorrow, I've got to go to San Diego for three or four days. I'll get a ride to SEATAC, so don't worry about that. That will be a good time for you to start with Travis.

"I took the liberty of setting up another appointment for you. There's a lady I know just down the hill who runs a small salon. Her name is Sharon. She isn't going to do anything drastic to your lovely hair, so don't worry. A slightly different style and a few color highlights I think would be good. I've worked with her before and she knows what to do and she knows not to ask questions. Pay the normal fee and then slide her a C-note. As soon as you leave there, go to one of the big chain drugstores and get a set of passport photos. We'll add them to a package of cash that you're going to give to Travis. He'll get that to the guy who's doing your ID."

"All right, well, it seems like you've really gotten things in motion then," I said. "Hacker, salon and then pictures tomorrow. Get pictures along with money for the ID man to Travis on Friday. What about Travis himself? What do I give him?"

"Give him three even," Tommy said, but then paused. "You know what, make it five. I'll talk to him about spending some time with you on basic street tradecraft. Blending in, tailing, quick disguise. Stuff we talked about. He'll know what to do. He's rush-trained many an operator, officially and not so much. He'll take good care of you. Now, let's talk about armament. What did you bring from home?"

"I have a Wilson Custom forty-five with a suppressor and a laser site. It's a fine machine."

Tommy gave me a curious look.

"Suppressor? You make that yourself? I'm impressed."

"Yes, I did," I said. "It's probably not as fine as the official stuff you're used to, but it's solid and works great. You can check it out and tell me what you think. On that note, I also brought my Walther P22 but I don't have a suppressor for that. Do you think we can get our hands on one?"

"I have a P22 also," Tommy said. "And I have the matching Gemtech. You can take it. I'd like it back if at all possible but don't go out on a limb. I can always get another. How about something pocket-sized as an extra backup? I have an undocumented Ruger LCP that you can take. Fits in a pocket and packs a mean punch. If you have to use it just wipe it down and throw it into a lake."

We sat in silence for a minute, our glasses long empty. I looked around and realized that we were the last customers out on the patio.

Tommy stood up and stretched.

"Let's pack it in. Long day tomorrow and lots to do."

———

During the short drive back up the hill to Tommy's house we worked out a rough outline of what we wanted to say to Sophia the Hacker at our morning coffee meeting.

Before going to bed I quickly checked my emails and saw that Elzey had acknowledged my message. I made a mental note to check the lockbox after my morning errands. I set my phone alarm and turned out the light in hopes of a sound sleep.

27

I t was early and the coffee shop was sparsely populated. Tommy spotted Sophia sitting at a corner table for four. She closed her laptop as we approached and Tommy made the introduction.

My first impression was that she must have been sent over by central casting, what with the faded jeans, hoodie sweatshirt, and the glint of a nose ring. When she pulled the hood away, revealing a bright-eyed and lovely face and releasing a cascade of shiny copper hair, it occurred to me that maybe she was one of those many people who weren't entirely comfortable with their abundance of good looks. In any case, she was polite and very well-spoken. I remembered Tommy telling me that she had double master's degrees in computer engineering and programming.

I took orders and went to the counter, leaving the two of them to catch up. I figured this would give Tommy a few minutes to tell her about me and make sure she was comfortable. A good five minutes later I returned to the table and handed over the drinks.

Sophia watched me as I sat down and sipped my coffee. I set my folded newspaper on the table just in front of me.

"So is this a job interview?" she asked.

"Well, I guess it could be," I said. "I know you and Tommy have worked together in the past and he speaks highly of you. Whatever you've worked on together, official or not, is none of my business. I'll take it on faith that you have a level of trust in each other. I'll also assume that if you weren't interested in any work then you wouldn't be sitting here with us."

She nodded.

"We're working on something," I said, "and I have a feeling that we might be able to make use of your skills at one or more points. It might be quick and simple. It might grow a little bit. I can pay pretty well."

"Dean and I go back to grade school," Tommy said to her. "You can take whatever he says as if it came from me. We signed on to a project—privately—for another very old friend of ours. It has to do with breaking up a corporate embezzling ring but you can call it whatever you want. I took this on for a little extra money myself, thinking of retirement in a few months. We both got involved for the money, plus, as I said, helping a friend."

"I have an idea," I said, "just an idea at the moment, that this, aaah, this case, may lead down a certain path. There may be an opportunity for us to recover some money under circumstances where nobody else is going to be able to say anything about it. I don't know it for sure and I could be just plain wrong, but I think it's a real possibility. If that doesn't materialize, we could probably still use you for some basic data gathering.

"If it does go where I think it may and we find where the money's hidden—that's a bunch of big 'ifs' mind you—it could be substantial."

"I'm still here listening," Sophia said. "When do you think you'll know more about whether or not the money angle is going to pan out?"

"I think we should know within a few weeks," I said. "Maybe days —not sure yet. Seems to me that first I need to know if you're willing to work with us on this. If not, no hard feelings."

"I'm not a thief," Sophia said, with what I thought was a small hint of indignation.

"We know that, Sophia," Tommy said. "And neither are either of us. All Dean is saying is that, in the course of other activities—which we don't need to talk about—there's just a chance that we could recover some stolen money. But that's a peripheral thing that might happen."

I looked at Tommy and, after a quick look around the room, he nodded slightly in a signal to me that we were unobserved. I slipped a business-size envelope out of my folded newspaper and pushed it across to Sophia. This time Tommy's nod was to her, telling her to go ahead and look inside.

After her own look around, she opened the flap of the envelope and looked inside. Her eyes widened a bit but she said nothing.

"That's three to start," I said. "Against another three when the project is done in maybe two months at which time you'll be off the hook. I need a secure way for either of us to be able to contact you. We'll need a response within a half day or so. I'll expect you to tell me straight if there's something you can't do or if you want to suggest a viable alternative. I can't imagine why we would ask you for more than a few days of work, all told, unless that money recovery thing starts to look promising. If it does, we can discuss and agree to further terms."

Her face seemed to brighten at that possibility. She looked at Tommy, then at me, then at the envelope in front of her, then back to me again. She held up a finger for patience.

"Who else is in on this? Just you two?"

"Just us," Tommy said. "We'll be getting help here and there but just transactional. You've been around, Sophia, you know the community. You're the only one who knows about the money. Dean's a civilian and this is strictly side work for me. Totally off-book."

"And when you mentioned the money," she said, looking at me, "you used the term 'substantial'. What are you thinking of?"

"What's 'missing'," I said, "is probably at least several hundred thousand. Could easily be twice that or even over a million, but really that's just an educated guess. Inadequately educated at the moment."

"I'm guessing," she said, "that the main reason I'm here is that you think this money is somewhere in an offshore bank account."

"Yes, that's exactly correct," I said. "Maybe more than one account. We'll need other help but that's the biggie."

We sipped our coffee and gave her a moment to think. She looked around and then leaned in towards us.

"I only work from home. I don't travel. I need another three in cash in thirty days, and another three in sixty days. Ten weeks from today I'm off the hook regardless of your status, unless we re-negotiate. Legitimate expenses are additional, though that shouldn't be much. That will give you forty hours. If I go over that, we'll need to renegotiate. If you agree and we walk away from this table, this envelope is mine no matter what happens."

Tommy and I looked at each other and did two lousy jobs at trying not to smile. I got the sense that he really liked this young lady. I got the sense that I did too. He gave his answer with a nod to both of us.

"I can live with that," I said. "What do we get from you?"

"You'll get my cell phone number and I'll also set up a secure online bulletin board where we can post messages. I'll respond to you within two hours, not so fast if it's the middle of the night. Give me whatever you have on the banking and I'll start looking into it. Looking at the two of you, I know not to ask for specifics on what exactly this project is, so I won't. For example, I won't ask you why you think nobody is going to be looking for this money. It'll be your job to make damn sure that's accurate. If I need information from you and you manage to provide it, such as a banking password, I won't ask how you got it."

"I think we have a deal then," I said.

"Just one last thing," Sophia said. She circled her finger in the air to indicate the three of us. "Any money we recover, a thousand, a hundred thousand, a million—whatever—gets split three ways. Agreed?"

I saw no point in telling her that Tommy and I already thought of any recovered money as icing on the cake. At that point, while I had high hopes for a big payday, I had no way of knowing whether that would really happen. Again, Tommy nodded to me.

"Agreed," I said. "Three-way split of whatever. We'll do what we can to make sure that 'whatever' is as big as can be."

We exchanged email addresses and phone numbers, agreeing to

minimal communications until she got the bulletin board up and running. I gave her a note I'd prepared with everything I thought that might prove helpful to her in tracking down any offshore accounts that might exist for Vince Gallo or John Campbell. Full names and addresses, spouses' names, and the name of the Bahamian bank where we believed Gallo had an account. I mentioned the closeness of the relationship between the two men and my thought that if one had a secret account, the other would likely have an account at the same bank.

Sophia promised to send us both information on the bulletin board as soon as it was up and running, and with that, we all shook hands and said our goodbyes. Tommy and I set off walking back to his house.

"That is one tough young broad," I said. "She has it together more than most of us. I think you made a good choice there."

"Yeah, she's good," Tommy said. "If what we're asking her to do can be done, she'll get it done. Either way, there won't be any bullshit."

28

Back at the house, Tommy went off to pack and organize for his trip. I had some toast and coffee on the deck before I had to walk back down the hill to the hair salon. Tommy's friend Sharon did a fine job and my new style didn't really reflect any drastic change. I thought I looked a little bit younger but that may just have been wishful thinking. I think the gist of the effort was that I looked a little bit like *not me*. Someone who knew me already might be thrown off for a minute. They wouldn't immediately connect me to me.

Just down the block from the salon was a major chain drugstore. I was pleased to see that there was no wait when I went in to take care of the photos needed for my new ID. I was out of there twenty minutes after walking in.

It was late morning when we drove over together to meet Travis. He was a tough-looking, lean, cylinder of a man. All muscle and hardness, but with a big smile and a bigger laugh. I had no doubt that he could tell me a funny joke and then break my neck with one hand while I was doubled over in laughter. I felt comfortable with him right away even though I foresaw hard workouts and muscle aches for the next few days. It was clear that he and Tommy had a close relationship. I gave the two of them a few minutes to catch up while I looked around his place. I could tell from the pictures on the wall next to his office that he must be well versed in a number of different martial arts, included Israeli Krav-Maga.

I gave him the envelope with his money, as well as the other envelope for the ID man, and we agreed to meet there the next morning at nine. Travis made it clear to me that he was looking forward to grilling me about my home invasion and expected vivid detail.

————

As we left Travis' place, Tommy announced that he needed to spend a few hours in his home office to prepare for his trip. We agreed to meet later for dinner and I dropped him off. I drove downtown, where I parked for some strolling and shopping.

I'd always been one of those strange men that likes to shop, and a virtually unlimited budget added an element of fun. In and out of a number of stores and enclosed shopping arcades, I picked up several outfits in styles that I wouldn't normally have gravitated to. All nice clothes, but like the haircut, just a little bit unlike Dean.

While I walked around the downtown area, I tried to pay attention to what was memorable about the people I passed and what wasn't. Like Tommy had said, if I saw someone with a loud colorful hat, I found it very difficult to remember their face just a minute later. I watched a man walk along the sidewalk with a limp, and I realized that I had to concentrate more than usual to remember anything else at all about him. When I passed a person wearing glasses that was the main thing that struck me about their face. It made me think about the old Superman TV show with George Reeves playing Clark Kent and his heroic alter ego. Back then I was always amazed that nobody recognized Kent as Superman even though the extent of his disguise was a fake pair of glasses. Now I understood—you noticed the glasses more than anything else.

I was deep in the spy game when my phone rang. It was Tommy and he was getting hungry. Since he was going to be away for a few days and knowing that we had a generous expense account, he had made a reservation at the revolving SkyCity restaurant at the top of the space needle.

There were plenty of empty tables when we arrived, so we felt no guilt in asking to enjoy our cocktails for a while before ordering. Befitting the surroundings and the magnificent city view, we ordered a round of classics. For me, a dry bourbon Manhattan, up with a twist. Tommy went with a Bombay martini, also straight up and with two olives. We toasted to Operation Pale Horse and to the panoramic evening view of the city and its environs. We sat quietly for a few minutes before Tommy spoke.

"Anything at all from Brenda lately?"

"We've emailed back and forth regularly," I said. "Once or twice a month maybe. I wrote to her the other day from North Dakota but haven't heard back yet. I've got a feeling that it's over. Don't get me wrong—I don't need it to be. Or want it to be. But that's my prediction."

"I'm sorry about that," Tommy said. "I never told you, but that was my personal prediction too. I hope I'm wrong, I mean, if that's what you want. What you guys went through would change most people. It may be that she just needs to have a clean slate and not be reminded of that night. For her, you would be about the biggest possible reminder.

"You know, I can't say for sure, but I've always thought that was one of the big things that made Becky get tired of me and want out. I came home from that one trip pretty banged up and ended up telling her that I'd had to kill three men. I really don't think it was ever the same after that."

"I guess I believe you," I said, "but that's lousy. You can't blame soldiers for having to do that."

"You're right," Tommy said, "you can't. But some people still do. Anyway, I could be wrong, but that's what I've always believed. I think it was a factor. So I wouldn't be surprised if it was the same for Brenda. Doesn't mean she's a bad person."

"No, it doesn't, you're right," I said. "I agree. One thing I've always tried to do, but I think I've been really bad at, is to look for the silver lining in any seemingly bad situation. When I was going through divorce, I remember thinking, 'Well, at least I'm single again!'"

"There you go," Tommy said. "That's the right spirit. So, I have a car picking me up early tomorrow and I should be back by Friday. I'll get a ride back to the house, so don't worry about that. You have a few days with Travis and you have nights free to work out your trip and your plans. Don't forget to relax on the deck while I'm away. It's very important to take quiet time before a mission to clear the head. We can take time over the weekend for shop talk. Hopefully your new ID will be ready by the time I get back.

"Oh, another thing. I made a few calls today and I think we might have a good car for you to use. You'll like it if we can get it. It's an '04 Marauder that's in great shape. My mechanic bought it as a junker and fixed it up. He's wavering on what to do with it but I think he'd part with it if the offer was good enough. I'll let you know what I find out."

The waiter arrived and took our order. I let Tommy pick a fine bottle from the wine list. The lights of the city twinkled below as far as the eye could see.

"Do you ever have nightmares?" I asked. "You know, about things you've done. Ghosts coming back to haunt you."

"All the time," he said. "I've made peace with them. I think I'd worry more if things didn't bother me, at least subconsciously. You having nightmares?"

"Yeah, not every night," I said. "But regularly. About last December, but also about this whole thing. It's not cold feet—I'm good with it. It's just that the reality is pushing the fantasy out of the picture. I am excited about it though, don't worry about that."

I looked around to see who was close to us and then leaned in.

"We can get away with this, right?"

"Yes, you can," Tommy said. "We can. Because you won't be who you are and you won't be where you'll be. You'll drift in and out like a ghost who isn't there."

29

The next three days were dominated by my training sessions with Travis. He was tough but not abusive. He helped me get back as close as possible to where I was when I'd mustered out, even though my body was now more than twenty years older. It helped that I was still in pretty good shape overall. We touched on all manner of fighting situations. How to attack someone with a knife and various ideas for how to respond to such an attack. How to use an improvised weapon, such as a tree branch or some other blunt instrument. A lot of what we went over was material that I'd covered in the past, but I found his refresher to be both exciting and encouraging.

I got sore all over, as expected, but the exercise felt good and the fighting lessons added to my confidence.

He grilled me on the details of my home invasion. He wanted to know about the weapons I'd used as well as any that the five men had used. He used my descriptions of that night's action to discuss what could have gone differently if any of the men had been more able or I had been less so. We agreed that the night had been an astounding example of an imbalance of situational competency.

On the third day we spent some time in the shooting range reviewing the pair of pistols I'd brought with me from home and firing them extensively. While he respected that I was reasonably skilled, I was still glad for his expert assessment of my abilities. As with the hand to hand, I was glad to find that the firearms practice and discussion further bolstered my confidence.

Each evening I spent some time looking over maps and notes and kicking around different ideas. I dipped into Mr. Barnes' files several times and realized that I was starting to memorize them.

Early each morning and again late at night I checked the lockbox for any messages or updates from Elzey. I passed on to him the bank account information as soon as Tommy got that to me and he responded that he would move the requested money as soon as possible.

On Thursday evening, as though ordered up by the God of Relationships, I got the email from Brenda that I'd been expecting. As we had always done with each other, she got right to the point. Thanks for the good times and let's stay in touch, but she was getting back together with a guy from her past before me. She'd worked hard to move on from the horror of the home invasion, and, though I was a great guy, I was also a big reminder of that night. Just like Tommy had predicted she would be thinking.

"Oh well," I said, closing my laptop. "That settles that."

It was late for the first drink of the day though still mostly light outside. I poured myself a bourbon on the rocks and took it out to the deck. I reflected on my status, suddenly clearer.

I was free of romantic entanglements, which also meant that I was available for new ones.

I was mildly famous, at least in certain circles.

I was planning to kill people I hated and who needed killing, and if that fell into place, I would be very richly rewarded for it.

It took a few glasses of Maker's Mark to shift Brenda from my present to my past, but it worked.

The next day was Friday and I was expecting Tommy. Like a little kid excited about Dad coming home from a business trip, I was looking forward to his return. Maybe, I thought, he'll bring me a present.

30

I was up early the next day for a brisk walk. My reward was a stop at a cozy corner café that served a hearty breakfast. On the walk back up the hill to Tommy's house, my phone vibrated.

"I'll be home by noon," Tommy said, "and I have exciting news. I was able to get the car I told you about. I'm bringing it home. I'll see you in a few hours."

Two hours later I was sitting outside on the front step, enjoying the day and waiting for Tommy, when a newish Volkswagen Beetle pulled up and stopped right in front. I watched as a tall young woman got out. She came around the car and started towards the house, her face breaking into a broad smile as she approached. She was dressed casually in jeans and a button-down shirt, with long fine hair pulled back into a pony tail. I figured she must be about twenty-five. Southern California surfer girl, I thought to myself. Cleaned up for an appointment. She spoke to me as she approached the steps.

"Hey you, I was hoping you'd be here."

"Well then, I'm really glad to be here."

She laughed out loud as her smile became distinctly mischievous.

Various lecherous thoughts were just starting to form in my brain when a horn honk caused us both to look back at the street, where a slate-blue Mercury Marauder had pulled up behind the Beetle.

"Oh, that must be my dad," the woman said. She waved at the car as Tommy started to get out and then turned back to me. "And you must be Dean. Dad told me you were visiting."

I hoped that my face wasn't too red as Tommy came up and joined us at the bottom of the steps, picking up his daughter in a bear hug. Seeing the two of them together, the family resemblance was clear. She shared her father's tall, athletic frame, along with the blonde hair, blue eyes, and prominent cheek bones common to those with northern European ancestry. Though Tommy had always loved to joke that I was the good looking one, he was himself a very handsome man. His daughter had benefited from his DNA. She came to me and gave me a hug of my own as soon as she was released.

"I'm sorry if I confused you," she said. "I must look a lot different from the last time you saw me. What, ten or fifteen years at least, right? I'm Julie."

"Julie, right," I said. "And your sister is Gayle. Yeah, must be something like fifteen years. You've changed a little."

"I'm sorry, Dean," Tommy said, "I should have called to warn you. Julie needed to stop by to pick something up. Can you join us for lunch, honey?"

"Not today, Dad," she said. "I need every minute to work on my paper. Call me next week and we'll make a date."

"Okay," Tommy said. "Hang on a minute, I'll go get those files."

Tommy ran up the steps and into the house, leaving me alone with his daughter.

"I'm working on my masters," she said, "and he's helping me with a paper. 'Utilization of Naval Forces in Land-Based Conflict in the Twentieth Century'. I know my working title is terrible, but that's what I'm working on. I'll admit that having an expert in the family influenced my choice of topic."

Before I could think of an appropriate response to that, Tommy came back out of the house and handed her a thick folder.

"I answered as many questions as I could," he said. "And there's a copy of a paper I wrote a long time ago in there too. You might get some material out of that. Let me know what else you need."

"I will. Thanks, Dad."

She gave Tommy a hug and a peck on the cheek, and then gave me a quick hug as well.

"I'm sorry I have to run," she said, "but it was good seeing you again. If you're still here next week, maybe we can all have dinner."

"Thanks, Julie," I said, "and it was really very nice to see you too. I'm not sure if I'll be here that long, but if not, I'll hope for next time. If you see your mother, please tell her I said hello. Your sister Gayle too."

As she turned and walked back to her car, Tommy called after her.

"Tell your mother I said hi, and see if you can get your sister to come for dinner next week too. Call me."

With a nod and a wave, she got in the car and drove away.

"They have both been such good students," he said. "I try to help however I can. She's doing this paper on naval history and I guess I should be honored. Just seems like such a dry topic, but then, maybe I'm biased. I've had my fill of naval history."

"You must be very proud," I said. "She seems like a fine young lady. You and your ex have done well."

"Thanks, probably Becky more than me," he said. "But I might have done a few things right. They both volunteer a lot too, you know. They do that Habitat stuff—like when you go fix up a house after a hurricane or something. I've been thinking of joining them next time, maybe, as long as it isn't 'churchy'."

"You're surprising me," I said. "I always thought you were so much better at destroying things."

"Yeah, you might be right," Tommy said. "I've sure as shit done my share of that."

We both laughed out loud.

"Well, come on," Tommy said, "let me show you around this car."

The Marauder was, in essence, a beefed up and somewhat sporty version of the police favorite, the Ford Crown Victoria. It had a powerful 302-V8 and would be a good highway car. It was large enough and comfortable enough to live out of for weeks.

Tommy got his duffle bag and briefcase out of the spacious trunk and we checked the whole car out together. It was as clean as a show-car, both inside and out.

"Here, let me show you something," Tommy said. He motioned me back to look into the trunk. "Look at this."

Deep in the main trunk space, towards the front of the car, was an upper shelf that was two-thirds occupied by the spare tire. To the left of the tire as we were looking into the trunk was an empty area that was almost big enough for a case of beer. Tommy reached up to the trunk ceiling above that space and felt for something. I heard a click and saw a panel come down and slide out. Tommy was grinning from ear to ear. My few seconds of initial confusion gave way to the realization that we were looking at a sort of secret shelf or compartment that had been added to the upper rear of the trunk.

"It isn't huge," Tommy said, "but it's big enough for a stash of money and a few guns. Ammo. Not a lot more. Nobody's going to find it unless they really get in there with a flashlight. Here, you try it."

I watched him as he gave the shelf a little push. It retracted up and away and we heard a slight click as it locked back into place.

I reached in and felt around a bit until I found a rubber button. I pressed it and the shelf came out again. I could see that it was lined with dark grey foam in the style of an egg crate. I jiggled the shelf this way and that and found it to be surprisingly tight and solid. Whoever had added it had done a very professional job.

"Oh, that is cool," I said. "That could be really handy. Very cool. Now show me where the switches are for the forward machine guns and the ejector seat."

"Sorry to disappoint you," Tommy said. "I couldn't get them added in time, but let me show you one or two other things and then let's get some lunch."

We went through the rest of the car fairly quickly. It was mostly standard aside from the secret compartment in the trunk and one or two other added features. Within twenty minutes we had locked up the house and were on our way to one of Tommy's favorite dockside pubs.

With burgers and beers in front of us, we worked on catching each other up.

Tommy had heard from his ID contact that my papers were ready to pick up. He would drive over and take care of that later. He told me that while he didn't yet know the name, he knew that the new fictional ID would be an employee of the same shell company to which the Mercury was registered. Standard procedure in his circle, as he explained.

Elzey's transfer of the additional money had gone through to the designated bank account. Tommy would work on getting some of that in cash the next day. Between Travis, Sophia, the ID man, and now the car, we were already down a little over thirty thousand.

"But that's a good chunk of the expenditures out of the way already," Tommy said. "We'll owe more installments to Sophia of course, and I'll need as much as ten if I can get any taps or traces done. You'll need a big pile with you for moving around easily and paying cash.

"With your ID kit, you're going to have two bank cards. They'll both be live. You use them just like a credit card but actually it'll be a declining balance setup that draws on the bank account I opened. I suggest just picking one of them, say the VISA card, and use it normally but sparingly. Keep track of what you spend so we know if we need to plow more money into that account. I'll start it off with a balance of ten thousand. What you should do ideally, like if you need to use the card for a hotel room for example, is to go ahead and hand it over, but then pay cash when you check out. The same for anything where they want a card up front. Okay to use the card but try to pay cash if you can. Whatever it takes to be least remembered or noticed.

"Pack up your real ID and cards or what have you and stash them into that trunk compartment. If things fall apart and you need to disappear, just jettison the new ID and become yourself again. If that happens just pay cash as much as you can and make your way back here. If it's worse than that, call me and we'll figure it out. Hopefully everything will go well and afterwards the false-you will just cease to exist, along with the bank and credit card accounts. You know what— leave me one of your own cards and I'll make sure it gets used a few times around here while you're away. Same for your cell phone and laptop. I'm just going to put your car in the garage and nobody has to know whether it's here or not. We'll get you a burner phone and a clean new laptop for your trip. Destroy them when you're done."

31

"David Somerset—all right, that has an elegant ring to it. I like it."

"That's good," Tommy said, "because that's who you are for the foreseeable future. Month or two—whatever. It can be nice to be somebody different. I've done it quite a few times."

"Yeah, it's an interesting prospect," I said. "To be somebody new, with a fresh start. Maybe I'll try dancing."

Tommy laughed out loud at that idea.

"Okay, you're right," I said. "Forget the dancing idea. I'll settle for getting away with murder. That sounds a hell of a lot easier than dancing—for me anyway."

There was a Washington State driver's license, a beat-up social security card, the two credit cards we had discussed earlier, a library card, and a small assortment of membership and shopper's loyalty cards. There were several business cards showing me to be an employee of a company I had never heard of.

After he'd shown me the ID package, we broke out the good Kentucky bourbon and settled into the deck chairs. It was a seasonally cool evening. The neighborhood was quiet and there was no sign of the crows or ravens.

"The ID will stand up to a basic check—like a traffic stop. If anyone digs much further, like for example you get arrested, at a certain point they'll get a standard flag indicating that you're an undercover federal agent. Just a standard thing—there won't be any connection to me or my team."

"You mean like a 'get out of jail free' card?"

"No, nothing quite like that. More like professional courtesy. I'm on the job and I can't talk about it, etc. Please let me go and this didn't happen. It won't stand up to a whole lot of scrutiny.

"Look, here's the thing. You need to not let anything like that happen. Don't attract attention and don't get into any trouble. If you do get into any trouble, try to settle it yourself quietly. If you need help and you're in a position to call me, we'll figure it out. Just try to fly under the radar if you can. And remember, like I said at lunch, if you need to, just jettison and revert. That's where the cash could come in handy."

"Got it," I said. "David Somerset will fly under the radar and will not get into any trouble. I will move across the country like a ghost from the plains to the alleys. A digital specter riding a razor's edge."

Tommy looked at me.

"Somehow I don't think that David Somerset will win the Pulitzer Prize for poetry. Anyway, remember to be The Four Cs—cool, careful, and quiet."

"But that's two Cs and one Q."

"I know, I know," Tommy said. "I tried to make that up, but it didn't quite come together. It's something like that. I'm not the wordsmith that you are. You get the point though, right?"

"Yes, T," I replied. "I get the point loud and clear and it all makes good sense. I do pay attention to you, after all."

"Here's one more thing that might come in handy," Tommy said. He pulled a small envelope from his shirt pocket and handed it to me. "I paid an extra grand for a fallback option."

Opening the envelope, I saw that it contained only a Nevada driver's license in the name of David Scofield. It had my picture on it.

"Keep that one filed away unless you really need to do something as someone other than David Somerset. It's actually a valid license, so you can use it to book a flight or something else where you might need to show ID. If you use it, keep Sophia informed. She'll be able to make changes or to wipe it out of the system."

"Fantastic," I said. "That could really come in handy." I gathered the ID materials all together into a bundle and set them aside.

"By the way," I said, "I did finally hear back from Brenda and it's pretty much just like you thought. She needs to move on and I guess I'm too big a part of what she needs to move on from."

"I'm sorry," Tommy replied. "Really I am. That's a shame. But I can't say I'm surprised. It all makes sense. This may be too early, but cheers. Here's to being a free agent. That's not so bad, right?"

"You're right. That's the way I have to look at it. And tough shit if I don't, because that sure is the way it is. Anyway, just wanted to let you know that. I do always prefer things to be settled, so that's something. To new beginnings and all that rot."

Tommy made a halfhearted gesture of raising his glass but seemed lost in thought.

"Do you think we were screwed up way back when?" he said. "Like when we were teenagers? Seemed like we had pretty good families and all that. Who could have known how life would unfold? Did you ever think that you might kill someone?"

"No," I said. "I don't remember thinking about that. I mean, not in any real way. Of course I had all the usual fantasies that you did. You know—killing everyone that pissed me off, that sort of thing. I think we were pretty normal."

"Yeah, maybe you're right," Tommy said. "Maybe we're not so strange. Hey, you remember when we used to go out to that big quarry by the canal and shoot at cans and whatever else we found? Those were the days, weren't they? The other day in San Diego I tagged along to a shooting range with a navy friend and it reminded me of that."

"Yeah, those were good times," I said. "I remember the time we took Jeff and Dave out there and you guys all wanted to know what it felt like to be shot at. Remember that? You all lay down below that long hill and I shot at the top of it with that Ruger twenty-two. Like pretend trench warfare. We were nuts. Good thing nobody was hit. Your mother would have been pissed."

"Good thing you were a crack shot even back then," Tommy said. "We were nuts all right. I think we probably still are. But soon we're going to be rich. Rich nuts. Rum-drinking, beach-sitting, rich nuts. I want to find the beach where the steel drum band is playing and everyone is happy and laughing. Like in the vacation resort commercials."

"I've looked for that beach," I said. "It isn't real. That beach is only in the movies and those commercials. But let's keep looking anyway."

32

The next morning we got an early start with breakfast at a local diner. We agreed that if we could get a few more things taken care of, that there was no reason I shouldn't start driving east in the next day or two. We decided to try for Monday. We were ahead of schedule.

After breakfast Tommy went off to do banking and to pick up the burner phone for my trip. He told me that the phone would be all configured so all I had to do was to program in a few numbers.

I went shopping and bought a new laptop, which I handed off to Sophia at a brief coffee shop meeting. She would get it all set up and ready to go and would get it back to me the next day. She told me that she'd been able to confirm that both Vince Gallo and John Campbell did indeed have numbered accounts at the Bahamian bank. She hadn't been able to determine balances, but she did tell me the information I'd need to get out of them in order to transfer any money. It appeared that customers of this bank had some leeway in terms of what type of security they wanted. For Vince's account, I would need three pieces of information—an eight-digit number with no zeros, a one-word color, and a one-word animal name. For John's account, I would only need the number and the color.

I gave Sophia the pertinent information about the bank account that Tommy had opened at his friendly bank. That account, which presently held only the latest money transferred in from Elzey, would be the destination for any monies liberated from the Bahamian bank after Sophia finished bouncing transfers around the world. She told me in a nutshell that there would be several points in the transfer process where a digital 'trapdoor' would slam shut the instant that the money left an account, deleting the source account and any trace of the transfer. I paid for her fancy coffee and told her to keep up the good work.

Meeting up with Tommy back at the house, I spent some time familiarizing myself with the new phone and programming numbers. Tommy came into the guestroom and dumped a small pile of items onto the bed.

"Here's that Gemtech suppressor for your Walther," he said, handing me what felt like a heavy metal cylinder wrapped in a piece of old flannel. "It's my own, so I know it works well. Of course I don't have to tell you that a twenty-two is faster than the speed of sound, so you're still going to have that crack. At least it won't sound so much like a gunshot.

"And these are a bonus from a friend of mine. They're standard Nevada license plates, but they aren't registered to anything right now. If you need to use them, contact Sophia and tell her what make and color of car and all that. She'll create records that'll pass a basic police check. They can be reused or throw them into that lake. One cool thing is that they're coated with a special reflective lacquer. They look normal to the eye but blurry to the point of being unreadable to any digital camera. So basically they won't be any help to someone poring over surveillance footage. Pretty cool, huh? They're from Nevada because that's the state that she was able to hack into. She found a back door or something like that."

"Wow, this is great," I said. "Christmas in May. And what's that? X-ray glasses?"

Tommy picked up a small case which looked a lot like it had come with a pair of high-end sunglasses or eyeglasses. He opened the case to reveal what looked like a series of small vials.

"Remember those combat medic kits we used to carry? I took a few things out that I didn't think you'd need and I repurposed this little case. These are self-contained morphine injectors, very similar to the old ones you would have trained on. If someone is shot, one of these in the leg should make the pain bearable. Two or three will likely knock them out or kill them, since, as you know, morphine can inhibit respiration. Point is, if someone is injured but you need to communicate with them, one dose should calm them down but they should still be lucid. There's a little instruction card at the bottom of the case. And by the way, if you need to use this, make sure it's for the other guy."

He picked up the last item, a box about the size of a hardcover book.

"I was thinking this might come in handy for your surveillance in Atlanta, but you decide. It's a small digital camera that you set up and leave somewhere, like pointing at a doorway, for example. You can set it to take a picture every few seconds for an hour, two hours, whatever. And you can tell it when to start and stop doing that. The best part of it is that you can snag the data from the camera remotely with the control unit from within about a hundred feet. It's called a burst transmission. You drive by the camera and trigger the download while still leaving the camera in place. Then later you can review it all on your laptop. I've already asked Sophia to load the software. Oh, and there's a directional microphone that's very sensitive. It'll pick up sound in about a ten or fifteen-foot cone from fifty feet away."

"Really good. Wow," I said. "That'll save me a lot of money in donuts. I won't have to do a stakeout in the car across the street from the house."

———

We hit the grocery store and the liquor store together and then grilled steaks out on the deck to the tune of an excellent Santa Barbara Pinot Noir and then switched to a Sonoma Cab when it came time to actually sit down and eat. We talked about old times and times yet to come. We told corny jokes and laughed at them more than they deserved. We mused about long days on sunny islands with good rum and interesting women.

"I'll meet with Sophia again tomorrow to pick up that laptop," I said. "After I get packed up, and final checks, I guess I'll hit the road early Monday before the traffic rush. The car is ready, I should have good comm, plenty of cash, ammo, and about as good a plan as we can get. To Chicago I'll go."

————

Sunday was a leisurely but dedicated day. I met with Sophia and picked up the new laptop. She gave me details on a new secure mailbox she had set up for just the three of us and I double checked that I had good contact information for her, and vice versa.

"I don't know what you're doing," she said, "but good luck and be careful. Keep in touch and let's make some money."

The day was capped by another fine dinner at the top of the Space Needle and a not-too-late night out on the deck.

————

I set off in the pre-dawn light of Monday morning. Eastward towards Chicago—The City of Big Shoulders, where I planned a rendezvous with someone I used to know and work with. A rendezvous that he didn't yet know about and wouldn't enjoy.

He would meet the pale horse, once, and only briefly. I had no idea what would flash before his eyes.

Traffic was pleasantly light on I-90 as I drove off into the rising sun.

33

Three days out from Seattle I was sitting at a bar about thirty miles inside of Minnesota. I had made my goal for the day of getting past Fargo and not much more. Continuing down the interstate into The Land of Ten Thousand Lakes, I decided to make camp for the night when I found an exit that showed a few signs of life.

I took a room at a roadside motel called The Buffalo Inn.

When I checked in, the desk clerk had seemed like a nice guy. At the time I hadn't seen the need to bring him down by pointing out that there weren't any buffalo in North America and there never had been. What most of us thought of as buffalo were actually bison. Since I was trying to follow Tommy's instructions not to be noticed, I kept to myself the fact that you would have to go to Africa or Asia to see a real buffalo.

The Buffalo Inn had a colorful neon sign in the shape of a bison and there was a life-size fake bison standing in front of the office. Fiberglass was my guess.

The room was clean and the bed was comfortable enough. The surrounding area was largely desolate but I had noticed a roadhouse sort of a place a few miles back. I doubled back there hoping to catch the kitchen before it closed for the night.

I made it just in time, and dinner was fine for the occasion. Grilled pork chop, a baked potato, and something closely resembling broccoli. All washed down with a huge glass of some house wine that was good enough to not spit out.

By the time dishes were cleared away and I had a glass of bourbon in front of me there were just a few late drinkers left. One of those had apparently taken on a mission to keep the jukebox going, which was fine with me. I'd always found country music to be somewhat comical, but it did seem like the right place and the right time for it, so I took it in stride.

At one point, an energetic twenty-something who wanted a fresh pitcher of beer came up to the bar near where I was sitting and drummed loudly on the surface. I knew that was a common thing people with nervous energy did, but I didn't like it. I amused myself for a minute imagining coming up behind him and slamming his face repeatedly onto the surface of the bar. I smiled at the mental picture. That might teach him to be less irritating in public.

I was halfway through that first whiskey when I heard the distinctive sound of a high performance Ford V8 pulling up outside. A minute later an unescorted woman walked in as I heard the Ford peel out and drive away. She trailed a small roller bag behind her. She wore faded jeans like she was an ad for faded jeans. Not the kind with the strange 'whiskering' that people pay extra for, but the kind of fade earned through long years of wear and weather. Vintage Guess maybe, or perhaps just Levi's. Whatever they were, they'd been invented for the likes of her. There was a pair of low brown boots, and up above was a white t-shirt and a loose and lightweight flannel over that. The flannel overshirt was open down to the middle with the front tails loosely tied in a manner I had seen before on casually dressed but stylish women. Her dirty blonde hair hung in a shoulder-length blunt cut that looked perfectly untended.

The bar was one of those places where you could expect everyone inside to turn and look at whoever came in. The newcomer shrugged that off smoothly, as she did again when everybody came back for the double-take.

She did a slow scan of the room and did her own double-take when she saw me, her face, somewhat pained, letting a hint of a smile break through. She started across the room towards me and the bar.

It took me a few seconds to recognize her and then I recalled that I had bumped into her at a gas stop earlier in the day, somewhere back in the vast expanse of North Dakota.

We had chatted casually while operating gas pumps and then again inside the associated convenience store while fixing coffee. Her traveling companion had apparently been off in the restroom and then later messing around with the car.

I remembered that something must have clicked between us during those few unguarded moments because she had opened right up to me with minimal polite prompting.

I wondered briefly what it was about me that gave her the impression that I was that safe. Was my aging face giving me an air of respectability? I decided it must be the highlights and new style inflicted upon me by Tommy's salon friend.

In the few minutes we'd had to talk I learned that she lived with a sister in St. Louis but had been out in Portland for a few weeks visiting friends. She was now on her way home to St. Louis where she planned to help her sister expand a small local cleaning business.

It wasn't hard to pick up on the fact that she was not happy with the guy she was with, and I'd asked her about it.

She told me that the bus she'd been on had broken down in a small town just short of the North Dakota border. She had met the guy in the truck stop there and had thought that he seemed very nice. After some breakfast and conversation, she had felt comfortable enough with him to accept his offer of a lift to Minneapolis. She admitted to me that his souped-up Mustang had sweetened the deal a bit. My impression from her was that he had shown himself to be a jerk almost right away.

"Hello again," she said. She parked her roller bag and then parked herself on the stool next to mine. "Come here often?"

"I was kinda hoping never again," I said. I motioned for the bartender. "But I might be open to second thoughts."

She laughed and ordered a beer. I ordered another round for myself.

She was pretty in a way that reminded me of that bubbly blonde that all the football players were trying to score with in one of those exaggerated teen dramas. Her looks weren't faded, I thought, but more like well-seasoned by a real life where not everything had been simple or easy. I guessed that she must have been early to mid-forties and wore every moment well.

"Me David," I said, "and you... Jenny?"

"Good for you," she said. "You get a point for that."

I gestured to her luggage.

"So, did you just get passenger dumped? He get tired of you already?"

"Yeah, I think so," she said. "The last straw must have been when I made it clear that no, we weren't going to spend the night together. God, did I ever misjudge that one. One of the dumbest things I've done in a long time. I need to find somewhere to stay, then I'll get a cab to a bus station in the morning and I'll be fine."

"Well, at least that's done with," I said. "If you're crazy enough to accept a ride from yet another strange man, I'd be happy to drop you at my hotel. The rooms are clean and there's a fiberglass bison. I don't know the area, but maybe there's a bus station around somewhere. I could take you there in the morning if you're okay with an early start."

"Thanks, I'll probably take you up on that. You're certainly an improvement over Glen. What a jerk."

The bartender announced last call so we ordered another round and I paid the bill. Several other people settled up and left. At that point there was just one other couple in the place aside from us and they were caught up in each other. It looked like the only remaining staff was the bartender. He was busily cleaning up and restocking and was back and forth between the bar and the kitchen.

And then I heard that Ford V8 pull up outside again.

Jenny looked at me with her mouth opening into a silent curse and we both turned to look at the door as Glen came in. The other couple didn't pay much attention to him and the bartender was in the back. Glen looked our way and came right over. He was a slim, wiry guy with a cowboy look to him, but built up. He made me think of a high-school athlete who'd kept in shape while trying not to grow up. He gave off the cocky air of someone who needed a big smack.

"She's with me buddy," he said, then turned to Jenny and roughly grabbed her arm.

She slapped his hand away.

"Glen, come on," Jenny said. "Thanks for the lift but just leave me alone! I don't even know you."

Oh shit, I thought to myself. What now? Tommy wouldn't like me getting involved in this. On the other hand, he would put this guy on the floor in two seconds. I spoke to his back.

"Hey, man, how about just leaving her alone? Seems to me she's not interested."

"You go fuck yourself," he said, spinning around to face me. "I told you she's with me."

As he faced me he made a deliberate move to lift up his shirt, showing me that he had a sheathed knife stuck in his belt. Looked like a small but vicious double-edged dagger. Probably a Gerber boot knife or something similar. I smelled alcohol on his breath.

"Hey—no problem," I said. I held up both hands, palms out. "I'm just passing through, having a drink. I'll stay out of it."

"Good plan, asshole," he said. He sneered at me before turning back to argue with Jenny.

I moved two stools away and sipped the bourbon. The other couple across the room were still in each other's faces and I could hear the bartender banging things around in the kitchen.

I overheard the guy tell Jenny something to the effect that he was going to the can and then they would be leaving together. I stood up and made like I was counting bills for a tip as he passed by me on the way across to the restrooms. I looked over at Jenny who immediately gave me a pained look and began to say something.

I cut her off with a finger to my lips and a nod towards the restrooms. I stepped closer and pointed to the watch on her wrist. I twisted the bezel on my watch to zero it and start a count.

"Finish your beer and act like everything's fine. In exactly fifteen minutes grab your stuff and go outside like you're waiting for a ride.

Fifteen minutes. Don't be alarmed if you hear his car start up. You'll be okay. Just keep cool."

She hesitated a bit but nodded. I saw her look at her watch to note the time.

I had been to the restroom earlier and I knew that the men's was adjacent to the ladies' room in a short hallway that went towards the rear of the building. Past the restrooms was a small utility area and then the rear emergency exit. It was unseasonably warm for this part of the country and the emergency door was propped open with an old wooden crate.

I left the bar through the main entrance out to the parking lot. I noted what must have been Glen's Mustang. It was a bright yellow Cobra, maybe ten years old, and looked to be well cared-for. I walked around it to the side of the building where the door was still propped open. I looked at my watch. Two minutes. I stepped over the crate and went inside.

I entered the men's room and saw the back of Glen as he stood at one of the two urinals. He looked over his shoulder and shook his head.

I stepped over to the other urinal and spoke loudly, adding a bit of fake drunkenness to my voice as I pretended to fumble with my zipper.

"Hey, I'm sorry about butting in out there, man. She's a good catch though—good luck with that."

"Fuck you again. You and that dumb bitch."

I heard the automatic flush as he stepped back slightly to zip up. I took one quick step back and another to the side so that I was halfway behind him. Shoving my open hand up to above his collar so that the webbing between my thumb and index finger was centered on the back of his neck, I slammed his head forward as hard as I could. There was a loud crack as his nose and forehead impacted the tile wall above the plumbing. As he stumbled back in a daze I saw that one of the tiles had shattered and I figured his nose was probably in a similar state.

He tried to say something that I couldn't make out as he lifted his hands to his damaged face. I didn't see blood yet but his nose was already turning purple.

I grabbed a handful of shirt at his chest and slammed him backwards into the stalls. This time the back of his head took the brunt as it smacked into the steel support between the two doors. That put him out cold immediately, and he slid to the floor in a heap.

I took a peek into the hallway but didn't see anybody. Glen hadn't had time to make a sound and nobody was coming running. I gathered him up with some effort and hoisted him over my shoulder into a sloppy firemen's carry. Finding the hallway still clear, I took him out and through the emergency exit door as quietly as possible. I was careful to make sure that the door was still propped open.

I carried him over to the Mustang and dumped him face up across the hood. Walking around the car I could see the few other cars along the front of the building. No change and no activity. There was the Mercury that I was driving and two others, one for the romantic couple and one for the bartender.

I went back over to Glen where he lay across the hood. I found the keys in one of his pockets and used the fob to unlock the doors. I drew his knife out of the sheath and stood over him for a minute, figuring I hadn't yet done enough damage to him. After pondering a few options, I had a different thought. I used the knife to cut off a handful of Glen's shirt. I used that to wipe the knife for prints and then dropped it into the nearby dumpster. I checked my watch. Eight minutes.

Using the fingers of my left hand, I felt through his shirt to locate his left collarbone. I made my right hand into a hammer-fist and slammed it down onto his upper chest, hearing a distinct cracking sound as the collarbone broke in several places. I knew that he was lucky at that moment to be unconscious, but that he wouldn't feel so lucky later. I lifted him again and dumped him into his passenger seat. Climbing into the driver's seat, I started the car and drove out onto the road.

A vast cornfield began within a few hundred feet and then almost immediately I saw a dirt road cutting into it on the right. I steered the Mustang down the dirt road and followed along as it curved to the left. I turned off the car, got out, and walked back far enough to confirm that it wouldn't be seen from the road. Back at the car, I used the piece of Glen's shirt to wipe down any parts I had touched. Wiping his key set carefully, I tossed it away into the corn. I checked on Glen and found him to still be in a deep sleep. Checking my watch, I ran up the dirt road and then on the main road back towards the bar. I was glad that I'd been exercising recently.

I got to the bar's parking lot just in time to see the door open. Jenny appeared with her roller in tow and saw me approaching. I gestured towards the big Mercury and pressed the remote button to open the trunk, where I stowed her bag.

"What happened?" she said. "I heard the car. Was that you?"

I nodded to her and gestured to her to get into the car. I waited until we were driving down the road before speaking.

"Yes. I moved his car and he's in it, taking a nap out in the corn-field. He's going to be all right but really pissed when he wakes up. Let's get my bag from the hotel and move a little further on down the road. Just to make sure we don't have any more trouble."

Jenny nodded, clearly in shock about the whole situation. We drove the few miles to The Buffalo Inn in silence.

We pulled into the parking lot and parked near my room. Jenny asked if she could use the bathroom to freshen up before we drove. I asked her not to take too long and propped myself up at the head of the bed to relax for a few minutes, suddenly realizing how tired I was. I heard her lock the bathroom door and I thought that was smart. I heard the shower come on and I let my eyes close. Sitting down felt good and closing my eyes felt better.

34

I heard a church bell ringing in the distance, and I got out of bed to walk towards the sound. The night air was a warm, thick fog that danced back and forth in the wind like a heavy curtain. In between gusts I could see that the ground was covered with grass and I realized that I was stepping amongst graves in a cemetery.

A few shafts of moonlight managed to cut through the fog and illuminate a row of headstones enough for me to read the names carved there. I saw Ball, Dodge, and Littlefield, telling me that I was in the old Block Island cemetery.

Suddenly I heard children calling to me and then it was a bright sunny afternoon and I too, was a small child. We ran up and down the paths, laughing and shrieking. I saw a young girl's ponytail bobbing up and down as she ran ahead of me, looking back and laughing, teasing me about something. After a minute I heard a woman yelling as if to call the children home at dinnertime and then once more I was alone with the foggy night. I heard the bell toll again, eight times, and I walked on.

As I walked, the grass path narrowed as rows of gravestones on either side appeared to close in, funneling me forward to some point ahead in the murk.

I heard the soft voice of Martha Phillips repeating the story of the car accident forty years before. Then the voice became that of Ben Phillips, telling me again about the man he had killed with the knife in Korea and describing the smell of blood. Their voices faded away into silence and my pace quickened.

More shafts of moonlight allowed me to read the stones to my left and I saw that all of them were carved with nothing but the name 'Gallo'. I turned to read the stones on my right and saw that they too all read 'Gallo'.

I looked up as a voice from somewhere overhead began to speak. It was a woman's voice and seemed to be calling my name from somewhere off in the distance.

I stopped walking as the rows of gravestones on either side came to an end and the fog parted. I looked down and saw that I was standing on the edge of a freshly dug grave that looked bottomless. There was a plain granite slab planted at the head of the grave and I could see that there was writing on it. I strained for a moment to read and was able to see that the word carved into the stone was 'Boudreau'.

I felt the empty grave drawing me in. The church bell rang and I fell forward and down.

As I tumbled downward into the dark pit I tried to yell but couldn't hear myself. I flailed away with my arms, trying to grasp the roots and dirt that flew by on either side. I heard the woman's voice again and felt a hand grab me by the shoulder, arresting my fall and jolting me out of the darkness.

35

"**D**avid, wake up! I think you were having a nightmare."

The woman's voice sounded vaguely familiar.

"Right, right," I said, rubbing my eyes. "Jenny. Thanks. Yes, a nightmare. I have them sometimes. I seem to be haunted. I guess I fell asleep. What time is it?"

She laughed and pointed to the watch on my wrist.

"Shit—it's almost five," I said. "Your asshole friend will be waking up pretty pissed off, if he hasn't already. We shouldn't still be here."

"I'm sorry," she said. "When I came out of the bathroom you were sound asleep. I knew you wanted to get going but I figured you could have a few minutes. Then I sat down in the chair and fell asleep myself. You yelled in your dream and woke me up. Sorry."

"It's okay—not your fault, but best we get on down the road in case he's still interested in you. We'll get coffee and breakfast somewhere."

I threw cold water on my face and we gathered our few things quickly. I cracked the door and had a look around, noting no activity in the area. The fiberglass bison glistened under a floodlight mounted on the wall above the hotel office. We left the room, closing the door behind us, and went out to the Mercury.

———

It was close to daylight as we started down the road headed east. My plan was to get at least twenty or thirty miles behind us and then stop at the busiest truck stop we could find for coffee, food, and gas.

In ten minutes of driving I had only seen one other car, which passed us headed in the opposite direction towards Fargo behind us to the west. Then I saw something in the rearview mirror. A spot way behind us was getting closer and starting to take shape. I cursed to myself as I realized that it was a yellow Mustang. I figured it had to be him, awake, sore, and very unhappy. He must have had some kind of key finder or maybe a spare set that I'd missed. I was impressed with his determination.

The yellow spot got larger, maybe a half mile back. I accelerated past eighty, then on through to ninety.

I looked over at Jenny and saw that she was leaning against her window and appeared to be asleep. I stretched my arm around to feel for my backpack to make sure I could grab the forty-five auto in a hurry if I needed it. The silencer was in the trunk with the rest of the armory, but I didn't think there would be any need for that out here in the middle of nowhere.

The Mustang was coming up on us fast. My speedometer read a solid ninety-five so I figured he must be doing better than a hundred as he worked to close the gap. Very reckless, I thought to myself. He must be in a rage. He came up fast like he was going to ram us and then backed off. And then he did that again. He was toying with me.

The road had been very straight for several miles, but up ahead I could just make out what looked like a substantial curve to the left; almost like a bank turn at a racetrack, but flatter. We'd been driving through a landscape made up primarily of cleared farmland, but as we got closer to the curve I could see that just off to the right of it was a thick line of sturdy old trees. Part of someone's property line maybe, or perhaps defining a rocky area not suitable for plowing and planting. The trees looked to be less than a hundred feet from the road. I checked my mirror and saw that Glen had backed off again after one of his rushes. I started to formulate an idea that I thought just might work.

I dropped back to about eighty-five to let him get closer, then accelerated quickly as we came up to the curve. The big Mercury was about at its road-holding limit but I knew that both the tires and the road conditions were as good as they could get.

Just starting into the beginning of the curve, I saw that he'd taken the bait and was zooming up fast to ride my rear bumper again. With my left hand at the nine o'clock position on the steering wheel, I adjusted my grip so my index and middle fingers were firmly planted on the little rubber pressure switch that Tommy's mechanic friend had added. As I held steady into the left curve at just north of ninety, I stole a glance in the mirror. The Mustang couldn't have been more than ten feet off my rear bumper.

We were halfway through the curve and the line of trees was just off the road to the right.

I pressed the switch.

36

The little rubber switch was in fact a normally-open relay switch. When I pressed it, the low-voltage relay circuit closed, sending its signal down a thin wire to close a higher-voltage switch that was in turn connected to the Mercury's brake light circuit. The result was that even though I hadn't applied the brakes and wasn't slowing down, the brake lights instantly came on full-force, as though I had stomped on the pedal. The whole thing worked perfectly and had the desired effect.

Riding my bumper at high speed, Glen thought I'd braked hard. Not having even the fraction of a second needed to process the fact that I was actually not slowing down, he did what was probably the only thing he could have done. He tried to brake himself and jerked his wheel to the right to get away from me and into the field.

Had it been a clean, flat, open field, the outcome might have been better for him. As it happened, the slight bank of the road along with a substantial ditch just outside it, caused the Mustang to go airborne, tumble end-over-end a few times, and then smash into the row of trees. The violence of the crash caused something to happen that I knew to be more common to action films than to real life.

The car exploded into flames and blew apart.

As the curve to the left ended and the road straightened out, I was able to see the burning stand of trees in the rearview mirror. Black smoke from the gasoline fire reached into the morning sky. I didn't need a science book to know that there was no chance that anyone could have survived that mess. I felt a pang of regret for having harmed those gnarled old trees and I made a mental note to sell my stock in Ford.

A cough from my passenger brought me out of my reverie.

"Where are we? How long have I been asleep?"

"Not even a half hour," I said. "Everything's quiet—hardly seen any other cars at all since we left. I don't think we'll have to worry about Glen ever again."

She sighed with relief, smiled, stretched, and looked around. Fortunately she either didn't glance in the mirror or didn't notice the flames fading into the distance behind us. No need to bother her with that. Water under the bridge.

"Let's keep our eye out for a good looking exit," I said. "I'm starving all of a sudden and I wouldn't mind some coffee. How about you? I think it's going to be a beautiful day."

37

O ver our truck-stop breakfast, we agreed that I would drop her at the Greyhound station attached to the huge Mall of America, in Bloomington, just outside Minneapolis. From there she would have an easy shot to St. Louis, where her sister was waiting for her. She told me more about their plans to expand her sister's already successful small business by buying another franchise. They were trying to save up the funds for that. She asked about me and I explained that I was a contractor traveling cross-country to finalize several accounts.

"It sounds like you've got a good plan and the right attitude," I said. "If your sister is anything like you, you guys will be successful. What kind of money are you talking about? I mean for the franchise. I hope I'm not out of line for asking."

"Oh no, that's fine," she said. "Ships that pass in the night and all that. We're trying to save up eight thousand. That would cover the franchise and some new equipment. We're patient. We'll get there."

"I bet you will," I said.

I paid the bill and we hit the highway again, headed for the largest mall in the country. Four hours later, I took the exit and parked outside the mall bus station. I pulled my backpack into the front seat and rummaged around in the main compartment, finding the overstuffed bag near the bottom by feel.

"The other day I stopped at one of those big casinos in Montana," I said. "Seems like a long time ago but I guess it wasn't. Anyway, I had a really good afternoon there and I want you to have something."

I pulled two packets from the backpack and handed them to her. Her eyes widened in shock as she examined the money.

"That's ten thousand," I said. "Consider me an investor. If you make it big someday you can buy me lunch and we'll be even."

"What? I can't take this, are you crazy? That's a lot of money. But no, I can't take this from you."

She tried to hand the bundles back to me but I held up my hands.

"Oh, come on, I just won it," I said, "and more. Besides, I'll just spend it on whiskey and overpriced hotel rooms. You can really use it and I don't need it. Take it, but remember, you owe me lunch someday."

She wiped away what might have been a tear and dropped her hand on the seat as though the money was printed on lead.

"Okay, okay, crazy man," she said. "But it'll have to be a pretty damn nice lunch. Let me run into the restroom and freshen up and then I'll say goodbye and you can be on your way."

She tucked the packets into her shoulder bag and went off to the ladies' room. I got out of the car and leaned against it next to her roller.

She was back within a few minutes and was indeed looking fresher. Her teeth glistened and her lips were glossy. She had brushed her hair and touched up her make-up. She stood close to me and handed me a folded piece of paper.

"Thank you, mysterious Mr. David Somerset. Thank you very much. You must be some sort of angel. I hope you'll look me up one day and take me up on that lunch. That's my number and also my sister's information. She'll always be able to find me."

She moved in closer and I prepared to welcome a peck on the cheek but that isn't what happened.

She kissed me all right, but hard and deep, like she knew what she was doing and doing what she wanted to do.

The kiss must have lasted ten or fifteen seconds, but time slowed down to make it seem much longer. I had been around the block quite a few times but I knew then and there that I would remember that kiss for a long time to come, and probably forever.

We separated and she punctuated the kiss with the peck on the cheek that I'd originally expected. I must have had a 'wow' look on my face which she repaid with a schoolgirl giggle. I gathered myself in an effort to come up with something intelligent to say.

"Wow. That was nice. Mango?"

"That's right," she said. "Mango coconut. But lip gloss doesn't count as lunch. So there, now you can drift back up to the high plains or wherever it is you came from and you can go wherever it is you're going."

"Well, then. Have a safe trip and best of luck with your sister and building your business empire. I'll try to look you up when I finish taking care of some things. Keep in touch. Oh, and Jenny—don't change your number."

"Anytime, anyplace," she said.

"Yeah, sounds good," I said. "Another time, another place."

I left the station and walked through the parking structure to the Mercury, trying to clear my head and shake off the pull of a thousand wonderful thoughts. If I lived through the next weeks and months, there would be time for this and other diversions.

For now, I thought to myself, I had roads to roll down. I had people to see and scores to settle.

I had graves to fill.

38

It was late afternoon when I began to penetrate the western suburbs of Chicago. The small city of Deer Valley was my target. Right along I-90 and less than ten miles west of O'Hare, Deer Valley was home to one of BEQ's largest offices and was where Mark Sonetto worked. He would have a small office on one of the top floors, near the computer operations center that the company called the Control Center.

Years before, on one of my several visits to that location for training on some new process, Mark had invited me and another guy to join him for a regular get-together with friends of his from BEQ and other companies. I remembered that he did that every Thursday night. It was an unusual routine in that it was later in the evening on a 'school night'. Most of them would go home for dinner with their families and then come back out to meet for a few hours. I could only assume that they met on Thursdays in order to not interfere with everyone's family weekend activities. I remembered Mark's routine and hoped that he still kept to it.

The designated meeting place was one of the expense-account steakhouses that sat on the periphery of the Woodfield Mall, just a few miles from the office. Because of the way that Mark approached the mall area, and because he was always concerned about his car getting dinged, he would park way out on the outer edge of the main mall parking lot. He had shown us that night how we then just had to walk across a narrow grass strip to get to the rear of the restaurant parking lot. He felt that his system of parking was much easier than trying to negotiate the complicated Mall Boulevard that allowed access to the front of the restaurant.

I had timed my arrival in order to be able to observe on this Thursday night.

I had a few hours before I needed to be in place for my surveillance, so I checked into a nearby hotel. After a long, hot shower, I found dinner at a chain restaurant close to the mall, and was in place to watch for Mark by six-thirty. I parked amongst a small cluster of cars farther out from the mall entrance than most, but not as far out as I was expecting Mark to park. From my vantage point in the Mercury, I had a good view of the edge of the lot where I hoped he would pull up. If needed, I had a pair of night-vision binoculars that Tommy had set me up with, at the ready on the passenger seat. I wouldn't need the night-vision feature at around seven on a May evening, but it might come in handy later when the party was breaking up. Mark was a tall slim man with dark slicked hair, so unless he had a new look, I hoped to be able to recognize him from a distance.

I rolled down the window and waited. Though I was in the middle of an unattractive mall parking lot, the warm spring air and light breeze was still very pleasant. I allowed myself to sit back and relax, though kept my eyes open and scanning lazily.

I thought about Mark and what I remembered about him. He had destroyed the promising career of one of my best work-friends. Pete, like me, had put in twenty years with the company until being moved to Mark's team like a game-piece. Mark hadn't wanted anything to do with him and had let him wither on the vine with very little to work on or to learn, until finally firing him and washing his hands of the matter. I knew that Mark had been divorced about a year ago, and the scuttlebutt had been that his wife had hired an attorney shortly after showing up at a Deer Valley urgent care with a cracked jaw. I suspected that if he hadn't worked for Vince Gallo and been a key part of this embezzling thing, he probably would have been shown the door.

It was about ten minutes after seven when I saw a recent-year cobalt-blue Corvette enter the lot from one of the side streets and pull over to the expected area. I lifted the binoculars and watched the car as the brake lights went out and then the driver's door opened.

Mark Sonetto stepped out, looking just as I remembered him. He glanced casually around the lot, and then closed the car door, locking it with his key fob. I watched as he stepped over the curb at the front of the car and crossed the grass strip to step down into the restaurant's rear lot. He walked around the side of the steakhouse towards the front lot where most people would have parked, disappearing from view. I felt my excitement building, even though I knew there wouldn't be any action until the following Thursday evening. Good, I thought to myself, the first little piece of my plan had fallen into place.

Figuring he'd be inside partying with his friends for at least two hours, I started the car and drove around to one of the mall entrances. I parked and went inside to kill some time strolling and browsing around the mall.

An hour later, with two fancy-label silk shirts from Nordstrom's, some new sunglasses, and with a cup of coffee inside me, I was in position again in the quiet rear lot with a view of Mark's car.

I didn't need the binoculars to see that it was a C7—or seventh generation—Corvette, so it couldn't have been more than two or three years old; probably the most technically advanced model Chevrolet had ever made and a thing of beauty. I knew that Mark was an asshole but I had to concede that he had good taste in automobiles. My thoughts briefly ran away with the idea of stealing it somehow, but I quickly dismissed that. That sort of reckless behavior would throw off the whole plan. I made a mental note to buy myself one instead. I could afford it now; I'd soon be able to afford my own collection.

I snapped myself out of my Corvette-reverie and refocused my attention on the rear parking lot of the restaurant and watching for Mark. I had no intention of interfering with him in any way. The plan for this night was just to confirm that he still kept his routine date at the steakhouse and to make a note of arrival and departure times.

It was almost nine-thirty when he reappeared. He reversed his earlier trip around the side of the restaurant and into the rear lot. I watched as he turned to respond to something apparently yelled from the side of the building out of my view. It looked like he yelled something back and waved, probably saying goodbye to another friend out towards the front. He then crossed the rear lot and the grassy strip, stepping down to his car. I noted with some amusement but no surprise that he swayed a little as he walked, doubtless the effects of a few strong drinks almost at the end of the work-week. Hmmm, I thought to myself. He pours it on strong—I can use that.

After digging his key fob out of his pocket, he opened the door, got in, and drove away. At no time had he appeared to look around the lot or otherwise pay much attention to his surroundings. Bad habit for him —situational awareness impaired by drink—useful for me. I realized that I was starting to look forward to bumping into him—and bumping into him hard.

I was thrilled with the information I had gathered but suddenly realized how dead tired I was. I reflected with some amazement on what a day it had been. It was only last night that Jenny had walked into that roadhouse in Bisonville. And it had been very early this morning that I had helped Glen to shuffle off his earthly burdens. A good day's work, all in all, but I was exhausted.

I left the mall and headed back towards my hotel, stopping at a small plaza along the way for some snacks and a bottle of scotch. I remembered with a smile that I had bumped up my hotel room to one with a whirlpool tub.

39

I had work to do but more than enough time to do it. With a full week to burn up, I figured I'd have plenty of time to prepare for the second Thursday night without any need for haste.

The first thing I did was to buy a stack of Chicago and suburban newspapers along with a few local tourist-oriented magazines. I pored through all of it, both to refresh my general memory of the area as well as to find out about any special events and activities that might be going on.

One thing I was looking for was a gun show. I had no need of guns, but I knew that those types of events were great for picking up an unimaginable array of items related to guns, hunting, camping, surviving, and spy-type stuff. I was in luck, finding an event in a town about twenty miles away. After I finished my reading, I drove over and paid my admission.

In my recent past I had spent plenty of time at gun shows and had always enjoyed wandering around and browsing. In this case I was looking for something in particular—a small, portable, closed-circuit camera detector. Tommy had sent me information about what features to look for.

There were two basic types of surveillance cameras, wired and wireless. Any device that claimed to be able to detect a wireless camera worked (if it worked at all), by detecting the transmissions sent between the camera and its receiver, somewhere in the area. Such a method would only be effective if and when the camera was turned on and active. Since a hard-wired camera did not emit any transmissions, the main method of detecting one of them was optical. Essentially, you looked for it. Devices designed to find that type of camera used either a laser or a powerful LED to shine a concentrated light as you panned the device around the room. The sensors in the unit would then watch for reflected light bounced back from a camera lens. My common sense told me that this optical method wouldn't be worth a hill of beans in the context of a huge mall parking lot. It was my hope that between a wireless camera detector and a careful visual search, I would be able to find most of the cameras around the mall parking lot and the rear of the restaurant.

I found one that looked promising and appeared to meet Tommy's qualifications. I paid the asking price in cash without quibbling and got the unit, a spare battery, and a nifty little carrying case.

At another booth I bought a Gerber Mk 1 fighting knife with a matching leather 'inside the pants' sheath. With a five-inch double-edged blade, the stiletto-style knife was one mean weapon. It wasn't meant to carve a turkey or to slice vegetables. It was designed to stab straight into a human body, slicing through anything in its path. I stopped off at the booth of the knife-sharpening guy who was always at these shows and gave him a few bucks to make sure that my new toy could shave the dry hairs from my arm.

I walked past one table that offered an assortment of gun magazine back issues, and saw at least two that had my face on the cover. I had to suppress my first instinct to cover my face and hurry away, instead finding myself amused by the fact that a few simple changes to my looks had made a difference. I bought one of the copies just for fun, noting that the salesperson was polite but otherwise uninterested in me.

I spent another hour browsing around the show, buying several items. One of them was a roll of thick, tough, tape with a rough finish. I planned to use it to wrap the hilt of the knife to improve the grip. At another booth I found a 'paperweight' that looked and felt remarkably like a classic old pair of brass knuckles. I was sure that it would serve as a good paperweight, but I had a different plan for it. On my way out of the show, I picked up some beef jerky that looked tasty.

———

On both the next day and the day after that, I surveyed the parking lot looking for cameras. I circled the lot in the Mercury several times, just like any shopper might. I parked in different places and used the binoculars, both in daylight and later, in the dark. I walked the lot several times, including the area around the restaurant. One of these times I did this dressed in common business casual office attire and held my cell phone to my head, pretending to have a long conversation while actually monitoring the wireless camera detector.

I used the information gathered to make a rough sketch of where I thought the cameras were. There was an array of them that clearly belonged to the mall and appeared to cover most of the rear parking area. They were mounted high up on some but not all of the light poles that dotted the lot. I wasn't surprised that there was also a camera high up on the rear corner of the restaurant that undoubtedly was meant to keep an eye on their own rear lot. I had no way of knowing if the coverage of that camera would extend across the grass strip to where Mark parked his car.

In the end, I identified just one of the mall cameras that I thought would likely have a good view of Mark's car. There were several others, including the one on the restaurant, that might be able to see his car, but probably not with a good direct view. I would need to rely to some extent on darkness and my ability to disappear with minimal trail left behind.

And I needed to find a large movable object that I could use to obstruct the view of that one camera.

40

The next day I went car shopping.

Specifically, I was looking for a large van. Using the auto section of the newspaper, I spent most of the day driving the area, passing car dealerships and giving them the once-over. I wanted an inconspicuous van in reliable condition, but more than that, I was looking for a certain type of seller. I bypassed the busy, modern, well-staffed and successful-looking dealerships. What I was looking for was more of a small-time neighborhood sort of place. The kind of quiet place where a cigar-chomping old-timer with nothing to do would be really glad to see me and be happy to make the kind of deal I was looking for. I had already dismissed the idea of a private seller, because to the average person, a car sale would be too much of an event. A big deal in their lives, and memorable.

I must have driven past and rejected a dozen dealerships before I came upon one that looked promising. It was by itself on a sleepy block back from the main drag. A row of ten or so vehicles, several vans included, stood in front of a white-washed cinderblock building. A large 'U-Pull It' junkyard spread out behind and to one side of the building. I saw a front-end loader back deep in the junkyard, no doubt moving piles of old car parts from one spot to another. The only other sign of life was a bony old man who was moving between the cars for sale, wiping dust off the windshields. It looked like a workable prospect.

I drove past and back towards the main business district nearer to the highway, where I parked the Mercury in a busy hotel lot. Entering the hotel from one of the side doors, as though attending a meeting or seminar, I exited through the main lobby where several cabs were waiting outside. The first cabby was happy for some business and I gave him directions back to the car dealer, where he dropped me ten minutes later.

In an abundance of caution, I had made a few minor changes to my appearance. One thing I had done was to put a small pebble into the middle of my left shoe, forcing me to have a slight but obvious limp. I carried an aluminum cane, going for the look of someone just recovering from an injury or a medical procedure. In truth I was glad for the cane as I walked towards the salesman because my left foot was taking a beating. I made a mental note to use a smaller pebble in the future. I carried a small cross-body messenger-type bag that contained not much other than money, the set of license plates Tommy had given me, and a Leatherman multi-tool. In my wallet I had the extra driver's license at the ready.

The salesman introduced himself as Clarence. I introduced myself as David.

He was glad to show me a ten-year old Ford Econoline that appeared to run well and be in good overall condition. He was also very receptive to my story about going through a divorce and wanting to keep things as quiet as possible. Wife was after my assets, lawyers were bastards, and so on. I thought his asking price of twelve-thousand was a bit high for the van, but had no intention of bargaining. I noticed that he gave me a bit of a strange but delighted look when I nodded acceptance of the price and gave no indication of a counteroffer.

Standing with him behind the van, I reached into my bag and pulled out a fat manila envelope.

"So what's that with tax? Shall we say the twelve plus another twelve hundred?"

I handed him the envelope, concerned that his mixture of shock and delight had rendered him mute.

"There's ten, and I owe you thirty-two hundred more, right?"

He nodded his agreement.

I pulled a thick wad of hundreds from a hip pocket and counted out thirty-two, handing that to him as well.

"Well, thank you sir," he said, handing me the keys. "You've got yourself a fine vehicle. Now, if you'll just step into my office we can take care of the paperwork in just a few minutes." He gestured towards the cinderblock building.

Inside, he made a copy of David Scofield's Nevada license. Since I was paying cash, there was no need for any credit check or banking paperwork. It was the simplest car buying experience I had ever had. I signed several forms as David Scofield and Clarence agreed to finish filling out several others that I didn't care about. I told him that I already had plates and would take care of the registration paperwork later that day. He told me that he might close early and take the rest of the day off.

Thirty-five minutes after arriving at the dealership, I drove the van off the lot, stopping just around the corner to text details to Sophia.

———

In a nearby Walmart, I bought a small roller bag, an assortment of towels, a stack of magazines, and some cleaning supplies and plastic bags. I also picked up a multi-pack of tight-fitting latex gloves and a set of heavy-duty adhesive Velcro strips.

Back in the van, I loaded the roller bag with some of the towels and the magazines, giving it heft and balance. If anyone were to observe me pulling the bag around, it wouldn't look so obviously empty. I drove the van to a far corner of the store parking lot, where I used the Leatherman to remove the license plate bolts, re-attaching the plates with the Velcro strips. This would allow me to quickly yank the plates off without tools.

From the store, I drove straight to O'Hare and parked in the long-term parking lot. I locked up the van and dragged the roller into the airport hoping to look like just another person planning to catch a plane. I moved around the airport and went between terminals, being careful to avoid contact with any of the secure areas. Eventually I found my way to the taxi stand outside of baggage-claim, and took a cab back to the hotel where I had left the Mercury. I loaded the roller bag into the trunk, to be available as a prop again when I went back to the airport to retrieve the van on Thursday.

41

The next morning I went to a grocery store and bought the largest Virginia ham I could find, along with a reusable canvas tote bag to carry it in.

I drove out to the nearby Busse Woods nature preserve, which offered hiking trails in varying degrees of difficulty. Managing to just fit the ham into my backpack, I set off on a hike. It was a quiet morning along the trails and there weren't many other hikers to be seen. I branched off onto a somewhat overgrown trail that took me around and down a hill to a small clearing that appeared to have not seen humans for a long time.

The hand-to-hand combat training I'd been through in my twenties had covered knife fighting, but throughout my service career I had never had occasion to use a bladed weapon in anger. This week would be my first time, and I knew that any practice would be better than no practice.

I had already wrapped the hilt of the Gerber with the thick tape from the gun show. The sticky and somewhat spongy wrapping provided a very positive and natural grip. I found that to be particularly helpful after pulling on a pair of the latex gloves. The tape more than made up for their somewhat slippery nature.

I wedged the ham between two heavy branches at about belly-height, and practiced stabbing it over and over. I tried a few different grips and several different angles of thrust until I found what seemed like the right approach. I tried it all over again after drenching the knife with water to approximate how it might handle if it was wet with blood. I was keenly aware that a grown man would probably try to fight back, unlike the ham. It was my plan to hit Mark fast and with enough force to immediately take any fight out of him, but I needed to be ready for complications.

After what I thought was enough practice, I left the ham for the enjoyment of any local carnivorous wildlife, and headed back up the path. I took a mildly strenuous hike along one of the main trails, relishing the clean, fresh air. I tossed the ham packaging and the canvas tote bag into a trash can back at the main parking area before driving away.

Late Wednesday afternoon in my hotel room, I turned off the lights and sat in an armchair. I ran through all my thoughts about Vince Gallo, Mark and the others, remembering and savoring every offense. Mark fit right in with Vince's little group, helping themselves get richer while they steamrolled over good, hard-working people.

Thinking of what they had gotten away with and the people that they'd hurt, I let my anger come to a simmer, and then to a low-boil. The next night I planned to draw on it like a concentrated energy force; anger compressed into rage and then focused like a laser beam into sudden action. I needed to be able to access that energy with strict discipline. I would have only a few minutes to act decisively and would have to be on it.

I felt the anger and pictured it. I named it and the name was 'Gallo and Co'. I gave it a color and a temperature. I packed it away to where I thought I could get to it when needed. Then I put the beast in a cage and slammed home the bolt.

Switching to twenty minutes of peaceful meditation, I sat still until rising gradually, refreshed and ready for what would need to be done the next day.

Using some of my ample supply of expense money, I treated

myself to a fine dinner at a nearby Ruth's Chris Steak House. Afterwards, I made it an early night back at the hotel, flipping channels and
sipping scotch. I was asleep by midnight.

42

Thursday dawned a perfect spring day. A light rain had moved through during the night and the morning sun had set to work drying up the few small puddles left behind in the hotel parking lot. The weather report had mentioned the possibility of another shower sometime later, but for the time being, it was a beautiful day.

I settled the hotel bill in cash and checked out. David Somerset was on the road again.

With most of the day to while away inconspicuously, I visited the nature preserve again, enjoying another dose of the tranquility and fresh air. I drove to a different mall in a neighboring town and wandered around there. I had lunch but otherwise didn't buy anything. I passed a movie theater, and on a whim, took in a matinee. The movie was forgettable but the theater was comfortable and the popcorn was a delicious treat.

By late afternoon, it was time for action.

I drove the Mercury east past the exit for O'Hare and parked it in the commuter lot of the Rosemont station for the Chicago Regional Rail. I knew that O'Hare was the last stop on the Blue Line from

Chicago, with Rosemont being one stop short of that. I then took the Blue Line westward to the last stop at O'Hare.

With roller bag in tow, I made my way through the airport and got the van out of hock at long term parking. I paid the exorbitant parking fee in cash.

I drove the van to the mall, parked, and again posed as a shopper, browsing for a while from store to store.

As my watch ticked around towards seven, I stood outside one of the lightly-trafficked rear mall entrances and acted as though I was talking on my cell phone. Though I was at a distance, this allowed me to look across and see the Corvette pull up and park in the usual area. I watched as a man who looked like Mark got out and walked to the restaurant.

There was an ominous darkness to the sky, punctuated by a few rumblings in the distance. Some rain would be great, I thought to myself. That would decrease the amount of people who might be walking around outside later and would limit visibility overall.

Back in the mall, after buying a large golf umbrella, I went out the main entrance to where I'd left the van. Driving around to the rear, I welcomed the first few raindrops as I parked in the spot I had chosen to block the surveillance camera's view of the Corvette.

It was twenty past seven. I pulled on a pair of gloves and settled back to watch and wait.

43

O pening his small pocket umbrella, Mark Sonetto gave a last wave to one of his friends as they parted ways in front of the restaurant. He turned the corner and followed along the side of the building towards the smaller rear lot and the big mall. He walked quickly in the rain, glad that at least it was still quite warm. The bartender had been pouring strong drinks inside, and he was feeling it.

Listening to several of his friends talk about their wives had made him miss his own ex-wife, and he was surprised by the intensity of the feeling. That one argument last year had gotten loud fast, and he had punched her. That had been the last straw for her and she had contacted an attorney.

He knew that the whole thing had been her fault, and she had pushed him into losing his temper. *She was a bitch*, he thought, but he still missed her. *Ah screw her.* With all his money, and his beautiful new car, he'd be able to find someone better.

As he traversed the restaurant's rear lot, he could see the Corvette sitting there in the adjacent mall lot, just across the grass strip. He saw that there was a van parked off to his left that hadn't been there when he'd arrived. As he approached the car and started to feel for his keys, he thought he heard someone call his name. He tilted the umbrella to get a better view of the van and realized that someone had gotten out and was calling to him again. The person was approaching and saying something about the Control Center.

Oh Christ, he thought to himself. *I can't even go out for a few drinks without those idiots tracking me down. What is it now? Some program's probably taking five minutes longer than normal to run. And now this joker in the rain, what's he saying? Jason somebody. Give me a break.*

44

Mark appeared along the side of the restaurant at a quarter past nine.

Exactly as I had witnessed a week before, he walked across the back lot with a bit of swaying, though this time no friend yelled out to him. There was a light rain falling and Mark was under a small umbrella. He stepped up to the grass strip, crossed it, and then down again to the Corvette. Sitting several spots away in the van, I could see that he looked over as if wondering why the van was parked out here.

I rolled down the window and yelled out to him.

"Mark?"

That got his attention and he looked up from under his umbrella. I got out of the van and started to walk towards him under my own umbrella.

"Mark Sonetto? Is that you?"

"Yeah, it's me," he yelled back. He watched my approach with either caution or irritation in his voice. Maybe both.

"It's me, Jason Cooper—from the Control Center," I said. "They sent me over to find you. There's an emergency in the computer room. Is your phone off?"

At that point I slowed as I rounded the rear of his car and came towards him. With the umbrella in my left hand, I held my right hand low and slightly behind me to conceal the brass knuckles. I came within a few steps as he was fumbling with the small umbrella, reaching for his phone.

"Here, I'll hold the umbrella," I said. He collapsed his own as I moved mine closer to cover him. "I'm not sure what it is, but Vince wants you to call him. I just transferred here by the way—been looking forward to meeting you."

I heard him say something that sounded like angry words about the Control Center management as he worked his phone free of its pocket. He didn't appear to have noticed that I was wearing gloves.

As he looked down at the phone, I took one step in and hammered a right uppercut into his jaw and the right side of his face. I felt the impact up through my own arm and into my shoulder. I had the sensation of having hit something hard that broke and gave way with an audible crack. His head snapped up and back with the force and he staggered backwards a few steps, dropping the phone and gasping for air. As he lifted both hands to his injured face, I hit him again in the solar plexus, spinning him towards the hood of his car and doubling him over almost parallel to the ground. I let the umbrella drop to the asphalt. The rain had increased and I heard a thunderclap. Perfect timing, I thought. Thank you, Mother Nature. Nobody in their right mind would be outside.

His face at this point was hovering about a foot above the hood of the car as he tried to recover from the attack. I let the brass knuckles slip from my gloved hand and drop to the ground. With both hands, I grabbed the upper back of his shirt and slammed his head as hard as I could into the Corvette's hood. He slid to the ground beside the left front fender with his back to me, moaning.

I took a quick look around and saw nobody in the area.

I reached to the small of my back and drew the Gerber. I took several deep breaths, stepped forward, and dropped to one knee beside him as he continued to gasp for air and try to right himself.

I gripped the knife as tightly as I could and stabbed him in the lower back. The slim, razor-sharp knife went in deep, meeting no resistance from his thin polo shirt and hitting no bones. He let out a low gurgling scream and straightened with the shock of the assault. I yanked the knife out and stabbed again, and then again. He twisted partly around towards me, his face contorted with a mixture of pain, shock, and confusion. He managed to get one word out.

"Why?"

I looked into his face, thinking the question to be a reasonable one. I wondered if he recognized me. If so, he must not have had enough life force left in him to express it.

"Haven't you heard?" I said. I moved my face close to his. "Your position has been eliminated. But don't worry—it's nothing personal."

I stabbed him again, hard and deep, jerking the knife from side to side before withdrawing it. In an effort to make the attack look less than professional, I gave him a few more quick and shallow stabs into his side, up higher around his ribs, and into one arm. Certainly he would be dead within minutes, and probably sooner. Leaving him there alive would be an unacceptable risk.

He melted to the ground, unconscious, and I helped him lay flat. After taking another quick look around, I did my best to drag and push him partly under the car and aligned with it. I set the knife down next to the brass knuckles and looked at my hands in the low light. As near as I could tell I had little or no blood on me, though a puddle of it was growing quickly under Mark.

I pulled my umbrella over and propped it against me for some partial protection from the rain. I dug quickly into one of my cargo pockets and pulled out two freezer bags, large and small, and a small towel. Snapping the towel open, I laid it flat on the wet pavement. I scooped up the brass knuckles and put them onto the towel along with the knife and sheath. I gathered the bundle up quickly and put it into the gallon-size bag, which I rolled up and shoved back into my cargo pocket. Turning back to Mark, I found no pulse on either his wrist or his carotid artery, so pronounced him dead. Finding the gold Rolex, I released the safety clasp and pulled the watch up around his hand and off. I quickly dipped it into the spreading blood puddle, sealed it into the smaller bag, and shoved that into my pocket to join the other. I found his wallet, pocketed the dozen or so bills it contained, and then tossed it under the car.

After pushing Mark's phone and car keys under his body, I walked back to the van. I put both plastic bags into a small storage bin under the passenger seat and tossed the umbrella into the cargo area. I used a tissue to peel off my latex gloves and set them aside on the floor. I started the van and drove around the mall, across the access road, and onto the highway.

The rainy Thursday night traffic was light as I drove towards Chicago and entered the city limits. I parked the van along Division Street near the Blue Line station for that area. The notorious Cabrini Green housing projects were long gone, but I figured that part of town would still be a pretty good bet to have the van taken over by some interested party. It would be gone by daylight.

Still in the van, I texted Sophia, asking her to delete any trace of the registration as well as the Scofield license. I pulled on a fresh pair of gloves and used the towels, bucket, and bleach I had gotten at Walmart to thoroughly clean the knife and the brass knuckles. I tossed the brass knuckles under one of the seats, done with them. The knife, in its sheath and stripped of the spongy tape, went into one of my cargo pockets. The gloves I had worn back at the mall went into a fresh plastic bag along with the tape from the knife. This bag went into one of my pockets, to be destroyed later.

I gathered the loose towels and bags into one plastic grocery bag and added the oversized sweatshirt I'd been wearing, pulling on a fresh one from my backpack. I wasn't worried about the bleach or the bucket. Those could very well be normal things that someone might have in the back of a van.

I did a final wipe-down of the interior for any prints. Steering wheel, shift lever, keys, umbrella—anything I'd touched. After a last look around I left the van with the keys in the ignition and the umbrella on the seat. Scanning the area and not seeing anyone nearby, I quickly removed the license plates and stowed them into my backpack.

It was raining lightly as I walked the half block to the Blue Line station. I dropped the shopping bag into a large public trash can. Just as I saw my train approaching, I took the watch from the small bag and dumped it over the side of the platform into the grassy area below. I figured that anyone finding it around here was likely to hock it. And if the police thought, as I hoped, that Mark was killed to rob him of his watch, they would certainly be checking pawn shops. The watch bag, along with the second pair of gloves, was added to the plastic bag in my pocket. Neither pair of gloves would have any blood on them, but both would have my real prints inside them. I would burn them later when I had a chance.

I didn't know what would happen to the van but I knew that it had no connection either to David Somerset or to Dean Boudreau.

I hoped that I had spread enough false breadcrumbs.

I rode the Blue Line train out of the city and back west towards O'Hare, getting off at the Rosemont station where I had left the Mercury. The station was quiet, with nobody else getting off the train. As I descended the cement steps from the platform, I used a tissue to toss the knife off into a small wooded area adjacent to the station.

After stowing the bag with the used gloves and tape into the Mercury's hidden trunk compartment, I left the station and pulled out onto the highway.

It was almost midnight before I entered Indiana. I pulled into a busy truck stop where, after gassing up, I allowed my body to shake free of the rigid control that I'd imposed on it for several hours. I yielded, vomiting into the grass along the side of the building and out of view of any other travelers. I felt better almost immediately but sat shaking for a few minutes more, trying to erase the sound of a knife going into a man's back. *One down*, I thought to myself, standing up and stretching—*but I'm sticking with guns from now on*. Tommy had told me that knife-work was horrible and he was right. I knew that I would likely be dreaming about rivers of blood later when I finally closed my eyes to sleep in some motel down the road. What I had done to Mark was indeed horrible, but causing him to meet that messy, violent end was a necessary part of the story I was trying to tell. I allowed myself to feel bad about it for just a very few minutes.

Rolling down the road again, with a Coke and some chips, I felt better still. An hour later, I got off at a busy exit where I checked out several motels before choosing one. The two crisp hundreds I pushed across the counter to the sleepy kid running the joint did the trick and he didn't bother me for ID or a credit card.

Inside the room, I poured a generous scotch and put the clothes I'd been wearing into a trash bag to be disposed of in some well-used dumpster the next day.

I fired up the laptop and sent a brief message to Tommy.

Phase One complete. No problems. Headed south. Stopped for the night in Indiana. Details when next we chat. – D

45

From my years of working under Vince Gallo as part of BEQ's data processing organization, I knew that he had a habit of working from his home office on Wednesdays, and frequently held evening meetings with various support people who worked late shifts.

While I was considering different action plans, one of my main working ideas was that I needed to use that day when he worked from home. Or the evening, probably. I remembered from some small talk at the beginning of a conference call that he had told the team about the fine job the workmen had done converting the space over his garage into an office. The Vince Gallo file that Mr. Barnes had provided had included a few pictures of the Gallo residence. Before I had left Seattle, I had committed the visuals to memory and also had used Google Earth to study the property and the surrounding area.

I planned to arrive in the Atlanta area in plenty of time to observe Vince for one or two Wednesdays to confirm that he still followed his routine. I hoped to use the digital camera Tommy had given me to help with that, but I would need to figure out a place and a way to plant it. I decided that it was time to check in with Tommy, and called him during a stop outside of Louisville, Kentucky. It was the first I'd actually spoken with him since Seattle.

"How're you holding up?" he said. "So far so good?"

"Yeah, I'm okay," I replied. "Lost lunch after, but fine, yes."

"That's good, so you're half normal after all. Good to know but don't let word get out about that."

We kept the rest of our brief conversation friendly and innocuous, agreeing to email later.

"Will you be available at five your time?"

"I'm working today," Tommy said. "Give me time to get home and settled in. Let's say seven to me, ten to you. That oughta give you time to make it to Bardstown and tour a bourbon distillery or two. Get us some fancy bottles while you're out there."

––––––––

I was checked in to a motel outside Bardstown, Kentucky, when I used the software that Sophia had installed on the new laptop to open a secure chat with Tommy. The software allowed us to have a real-time conversation as fast as we could type, but highly secure. He replied immediately to my first greeting and I filled him in roughly on the Chicago job. I told him that I planned to be in the Atlanta area sometime on Sunday.

> T – Let me know hotel when you can. I get copied on law enforcement summaries and bulletins from across the country that I usually delete. Will watch for Atlanta news and will pass on anything interesting.
>
> D – Thanks. Been a few years since I was down there. Will recon area and read all local papers. Will let you know any ideas as well.
>
> T – How is your money supply?
>
> D – Okay for now, still have over fifty, maybe fifty-five. Chicago expensive.

T – Have about the same here, maybe a little more. Techie needed another two to buy some special code from a friend. Says she has an idea that might help her figure out how to break into the bank accounts. I thought it sounded like a good investment. Let me know if you need more and I can overnight.

D – Roger that. Can always ask E for more if needed.

T – Right. Keep in touch. Remember, don't do anything too soon. Two weeks minimum, three better.

D – Got it. Will text hotel by Sunday. Over and out.

46

By nine-fifteen, Vince Gallo was halfway through his morning emails and ready for his second cup of coffee. He was about to get up when a little colored indicator popped up in the corner of his computer display telling him that he had a new instant message. He set his cup back down on the desk and clicked on the message, seeing that it was from Michael Sanchez, one of his team. An ass-kisser of the highest order, he thought to himself, but one who did a good job.

"Is Mark out today? I need some information from him. He appears offline."

Vince checked his own instant message contact list before typing his reply to Michael.

"I'm expecting him but I don't see him either. I'll see what I can find out and get back to you."

That's odd, he thought—almost eight-thirty in Deer Valley, and Mark's usually on by seven anyway.

He clicked on Larry Spencer's name in the messaging app. While Mark reported to Vince in Georgia, his office was just down the hall from Larry's in the Deer Valley building. Larry might know where Mark was. He replied right away to Vince's query.

"There's been an accident. I'll call you in a minute."

When Vince's desk phone rang, he snatched it up right away.

"What's going on Larry? Is Mark hurt?"

"I just got off the phone with his brother," Larry said, "and I still can't believe it. Mark is dead. The police are saying it looks like he was mugged and killed last night."

"Oh my god," Vince said. "Mugged? Really? Like, give me your wallet kind of thing? What else do you know? Where did this happen?"

"His brother said he was found right outside that big mall near the office here," Larry said. "He had a regular Thursday night thing with some friends at one of the restaurants over there. Remember that steak place I took you to last time you were out here? Looks like they took cash out of his wallet, but his new Corvette was just sitting there with the keys beside it."

"It was that watch, I bet," Vince said. "That gold Rolex. Was that missing?"

"I don't know, maybe," Larry said. "The brother told me that the police mentioned the car and the wallet. He brought up the watch because he thought it was odd that they hadn't mentioned that too. He told them about it but wasn't sure yet if it was missing."

"Did his brother say," Vince asked, "I mean, how he died?"

"Yeah," Larry said. "It's horrible. He was stabbed, but that's all I think they told him so far. Anyway, the police are still working the scene and it's early yet. It was raining most of the night so it's going to be tough. I'll check in with you later and let you know what else I find out."

"Okay, thanks, Larry," Vince said. "I'll watch for your call later."

Vince hung up the phone and immediately looked at his message app to see if John Campbell was online. He was. He got John on the phone in two rings and shared what he knew about Mark.

"We talked recently about wrapping things up," Vince said. "It seems that the decision has been made for us, agreed?"

"Agreed," John said. "There's no way to get someone to replace Mark and do what he's been doing with us. Will you talk to the others?"

"Yes," Vince said. "I meet weekly with Michael and Gloria and I'll start planning the wind-down with them. It'll take a few weeks to close out everything, but we'll start on it right away."

"Good," John said. "It's been good but it's gone on long enough. Time to get out."

After Vince ended the call and set the phone back on his desk, he sat quietly.

Was there any reason to think that this could be something other than a mugging? Was it possible that someone could be coming after them because of all this BardLogic mess? Law enforcement wouldn't bump someone off like that, and they weren't stealing from anyone else who would. He shook his head after a minute and laughed. No, that was crazy thinking. *Someone knifed him for that watch. Tragic, but that's all there is to it.*

47

W ith time to spare and just an easy day's drive to the Greater Atlanta area, I took Saturday off in rural Kentucky. Having read that Bardstown was a common launching point for parts of the famous Bourbon Trail, I picked up a local tourist guide and used it to locate and tour a number of bourbon whiskey distilleries. Naturally I had no choice but to pick up several bottles at each stop.

It had always been an understanding between Tommy and me that it was my responsibility to supply the libations for our chats out on his deck. He supplied the deck and I supplied the booze. After those stops along the Bourbon Trail, the trunk of the Mercury was home to a dozen bottles of the good stuff. If I managed to get the car and its contents back to Seattle, we would be all set for quite a few of our therapeutic sessions in those Adirondack chairs.

Anyone who had ever driven through Georgia would know that it was the land of peaches. During my dozen or so previous visits to Atlanta and the surrounding area, the degree to which almost everything was named after the favorite fruit never failed to amaze me. Peachtree Mall, Peachtree Boulevard, Peach Street, Peach Orchard Estates, Peachtree Plaza, and so on. Fortunately for me, I did like peaches.

Upon my arrival in the area on Sunday, I checked into a hotel that I had used in the past when staying on company business. On this occasion however, the money was flowing more freely, allowing me to take one of the nicest suites. Inexplicably, the word 'peach' was nowhere to be found either in the name of the hotel or in the name of the street outside. The hotel was, however, just down the street from the Peachtree Mall.

After a quick check-in, and a text to Tommy with hotel details, I went back out to drive around and explore the area, finding that I remembered more than I had expected. The hotel was in a leafy but also very built-up area called Dunwoody, north of Atlanta proper and just outside the beltway at the twelve o'clock position. The main BEQ office in the area was in Roswell, about fifteen miles farther north up a busy freeway that jutted out from the top of Atlanta. The Gallo house was in that area as well.

Staying in Dunwoody, I would have easy access to the freeway up towards Roswell, as well as to the beltway and several main routes south into Atlanta or away towards other parts of the state.

I stopped for an early dinner at a McCormick & Schmick restaurant that sat on a small man-made pond not more than a mile from my hotel. The restaurant was quiet and the outside deck more so, but I enjoyed the late afternoon heat and the view of the pond. I lingered over a cool, crisp, glass of New Zealand Sauvignon Blanc after the dishes had been cleared away.

On the way back to the hotel I stopped at a newsstand and bought a pile of newspapers and magazines. As I had done for Chicago and environs the week before, I wanted to refresh my general memory of the area and get informed about current events. Back in my room, I set the news pile aside to be attacked over coffee and breakfast in the morning.

After a call down to room service for a bottle of Moet & Chandon

Champagne, I lined up the laptop and my phone and set to the work of catching up on communications.

I checked the secured email box that Elzey had set up but found nothing new from him. I sent a brief message indicating that I was now in the Atlanta area and that things were on track.

I brought up Google Earth on the laptop and looked again at the Gallo residence and the surrounding area. It wasn't surprising to me that Vince had a huge house on a corner lot in a very upscale and wooded neighborhood. I noted though, that the house was on the edge of that upscale neighborhood, and within about two blocks of a small street that looked to be dedicated more to shops or restaurants—no doubt also upscale in their way. As I knew to be common in many neighborhoods, particularly in the south, there was a separate service alley that ran behind the Gallo house and the other homes on that street. That was where the trash truck would come, oil trucks would make their deliveries, and the air conditioning repair guy would park.

On one side of the Gallo house, to the right if I was looking at it from the street—Peach Valley Lane—was another huge McMansion. A twenty-foot wide wooded area separated the two homes, from close to the street back through to the service alley. The main house and yard was to the left of that wooded border. The detached garage building was to the left of that, separated from the house by a narrow walkway extending through to the back yard. Along the far left of the garage was another pathway that appeared to hug the building all the way back to the alley. Finally, at the outer left edge of the property ran the side street. This street—Cutler Street—was perpendicular both to Peach Valley Lane and to the service alley. The sidewalk along Cutler Street was separated from the property by what looked like some kind of fence lined inside with a row of narrow trees or hedges. I looked at that area carefully. I still needed to test out the time-lapse camera, but I considered that this narrow border at the side of the Gallo yard might offer a good spot to plant the thing.

I really needed to get up to that neighborhood for a drive by and a general recon. A satellite picture was good, but there was no substitute for being right there on the ground. For one thing, I didn't know how old the satellite picture was or what changes might have occurred in or around the property since it had been taken.

The next day was going to be a busy one.

I poured another glass of champagne and cranked up the AC. I dimmed the room lights and switched on the TV, hoping to find something stupid and funny.

48

The next day began very early, with a short but invigorating run around the area. My hotel was one of three well-known chains that shared a small man-made lake with several corporate office buildings. A landscaped pathway wound through the complex for the use of joggers, strollers, and dog walkers. The morning was cool, but the clear sky held the promise of a sunny and warm spring day.

I ordered up a room service breakfast with coffee for two and started on the stack of newsprint. The glossy magazines were similar to those published for most other major cities; advertisements for all the upscale malls and the new restaurant of the moment, a list of the ten best cosmetic surgeons, and all the biggest personal-injury law firms. The newspapers told the story of local political shenanigans and who had won the good citizen award. A little league team had earned the honor of going to some national championship in Cooperstown. Some vacuous teenager had been texting while driving and had driven into a black walnut tree and been killed. I was glad to read that the tree was only slightly damaged.

One small article in the Journal-Constitution that caught my eye had to do with the ongoing investigation into a violent home invasion that had occurred a few weeks earlier. The article was brief and focused more on some kind of law enforcement procedures than it did on details of the crime that had been committed. I tore it out and set it aside, thinking that Tommy might be able to glean some more information from either his news feed or his connections. If there was an opportunity to piggy-back on some kind of local crime spree, I wanted to know more.

After finishing my reading, I jotted down some directions to the Gallo house up in Roswell, and, still in my jogging outfit, got in the car and started driving.

Within a half hour I was in the neighborhood, and within a few minutes more had located the house. I drove through the neighborhood slowly, as though admiring the area or considering whether or not to buy. The Gallo property offered no great surprises relative to what I had already seen on Google Earth. There was the main house, roughly rectangular, with what looked like a detached two-car garage at the rear of the driveway to the left of the house.

Above the car-bay doors were three wide windows that spanned most of the upper level. These would serve to give the upstairs office an unobstructed view of the whole driveway and the street beyond, as well as the side of the main house.

I parked the car on a quiet side street a few blocks away where it looked like I could get out and start a jog unobserved.

I ran back into the neighborhood on Cutler Street, along the sidewalk that bordered the property. I jogged slowly, getting as much of a visual as possible through the wood fence and the row of tall hedges just inside it. It was easy to see that the fence, along with the hedges, would provide some privacy for the yard, but zero security. During my slow jog along the fence, and then during the reverse trip some minutes later, I was able to see through numerous gaps in the foliage to get a good picture of the driveway and the front of the garage. After making the left turn to go along past the front of the property, I was also able to get some good mental snapshots of that frontal view. On my return trip, I slowed to a stop along the side fence and did some stretches, as any jogger might routinely do. There was no one in the area but I kept up appearances as I rested my hands on the fence crossbeams and executed a number of leg and back stretches.

I could see that there was a narrow walkway that ran from the rear of the driveway back along the side of the garage farthest from the house. This appeared to go all the way back to the service alley. As I completed my last stretch, I noticed what I thought was a flash of something shiny up high, apparently on the wall above what looked like a side door from the garage into the narrow alley. Stealing a look, I realized that it was a pair of floodlights, not lit at this time of the day. I knew that there was likely to be a motion-sensor unit mounted above that door—just like I had installed outside my house in Pennsylvania.

That was something I would need to keep in mind.

I walked up to the corner of Cutler and Peach Valley, then back all the way to the alley. A casual observer would probably not notice that I was carefully pacing out the distances from the main street to the garage, the side door, and the alley.

After a glance down the alley, I resumed an easy pace for the few blocks back to the car.

49

It was almost exactly noon when I got back to the hotel. I unpacked the little camera kit and examined it more closely than I had previously. I noted that the batteries were fully charged in both the camera and the matching control unit. There was an instruction card along with some added notes from Tommy spelling out his version of quick set-up steps. His notes indicated that the camera charge should be good for at least twelve hours of intermittent pictures, depending on what settings I used. If I needed to capture more than that, I would have to retrieve the camera, charge it, and then place it again.

Showered and dressed, I took the camera, control unit, and laptop out to Sweetwater Creek State Park, which I knew from prior trips to the area.

It being a Tuesday in May, with school still in session, traffic at the park was very light. I hiked around several of the trails until I found a small clearing at a point where two trails met and then diverged. I decided that, with a liberal dose of imagination, the trail junction would serve as a reasonable stand-in for the rear of the Gallo driveway. I visualized the mouth of one trail as the door from the side of the main house. If someone came out of that 'door', and walked about twenty feet, they would reach an outcropping of rock that I imagined represented the door into the garage. A somewhat straight line of trees extending away from the rock pile would represent the front face of the garage. I made a mental note of the approximate height of several distinctive tree branches. My thought was that, when viewing the images later, I would have some reference for how high the viewing area extended above the ground. Specifically, I wondered, if the camera was positioned to observe traffic between the house and the garage, would the field of view include any portion of the large windows over the garage doors?

I walked into the woods, pacing off thirty-five feet from the imagined junction between the Gallo house and the garage. Finding a gnarled tree limb that was roughly horizontal and at about chest height, I set up the camera, using the detachable spike set that formed what amounted to a small tripod. The legs of that tripod—the 'spikes'— were sturdy and sharp enough to allow one or more of them to be jammed into a tree limb, fence post, or similar material. The camera unit itself was about the size of a deck of cards and was a mottled grey-green, not unlike a standard military camo pattern.

I walked another fifty feet away into the woods, visualizing that I was now at one of the street corners opposite and across from the house. From there I used the pocket controller, only slightly larger than the camera itself, to adjust the zoom on the camera. From the remote, I told the camera to record one image every five seconds, for a period of twenty minutes, and to begin doing so immediately.

Hearing some other park visitors approaching, I hurried back to the main trail, which I followed around at a leisurely pace, enjoying the woods and the fresh air.

After about a half-hour, I made my way back to the staged area. This time, I stayed on one of the trails at a point that I thought was about fifty feet from the camera. I pressed the appropriate button on the remote to initiate the burst transmission, and watched as various lights flickered. Within thirty seconds the unit displayed a message indicating that the transmission was complete, all images had been transferred successfully, and that the camera memory had been cleared.

I went back to the car, where I plugged the control unit into my laptop and watched as the software opened and a download occurred. Once that was complete, a video screen appeared and I was able to scroll through all the captured images of park visitors walking along the trails and past my imaginary garage. With my landmarks in mind, I had done a pretty good job of positioning the camera. It was good to know that, without there being an actual viewfinder, the little unit was still easy to aim as desired. That accuracy would come in handy when I put it into position the next morning with minimal time for adjustment.

I found that Tommy hadn't been kidding me when he told me that the microphone was very sensitive. With my first test, I had to turn the volume way down in order to not be distracted by the sounds of hikers crunching over leaves.

I practiced with the image software for a while, finding the speed controls, zoom, and freeze-frame to be both intuitive and effective. Satisfied that the system was working as expected, and that I would be able to operate it with some degree of competence, I shut it all down, collected the camera from the woods, and left the park.

As I drove, I thought about camera scheduling. I wanted the camera to help me confirm that Vince Gallo still kept his routine of working those long Wednesdays from home. I remembered him to be a punctual creature of habit. If he still was, my job would be that much easier.

I decided that I would set the camera to record a ninety-minute window in the early morning, and then again around lunch time, and then for a three-hour window encompassing dinner time and after. A total of six hours per day would permit recordings on two Wednesdays before a new charge was needed. I hoped that Tommy's battery estimate was accurate.

If I could get the camera to do that and then study the results for the next two weeks, I would have the information I needed. After that I could finalize the details of my plans for the third week.

Plans that Vince would find to be quite unpleasant.

50

The next morning also began with a very early jog. I was again up in the Gallo neighborhood along Peach Valley Lane.

I had parked amongst a few other cars, early commuters probably, in a small municipal lot adjacent to the retail area which was about two blocks outside of the neighborhood. The sun was half-risen and the light was still dim, dimmer still in the tree-lined confines of the neighborhood.

As I did a slow jog up Cutler Street and along the border of the property, I stopped roughly where I had the day before to stretch, grasping the fence in several places. I already had the pre-programmed camera in my hand, knowing that if anyone were to look out their window in the early morning, they might think I was just a jogger with a cell phone.

I picked out a spot on one of the horizontals that was right next to a vertical post and partly shielded by leaves. For my second stretch, I reached in a little further and jammed the camera spikes into place. With one more stretch, I twisted it slightly to better face the target area.

I finished my stretching routine and took off for an easy jog around the neighborhood. This time, I took one pass through the service alley, noting that several homes in the area appeared to be unoccupied. Between people working for a living and students getting ready for school, it was a time of day where just about any occupied home should be showing signs of life. The house directly across the alley from the rear of the Gallo house was not. I filed that observation away, thinking that an empty house there could help me get out of the area undetected when I needed to. I also noted that, while several motion-activated floodlights had come on behind homes at the other end of the alley, the last several homes on the near end didn't appear to have any. The Gallo home itself did, on the rear of the garage building, and on the side along Cutler Street. In any case, I would need to deal with several of them.

———

On the way back to the hotel, after breakfast at a busy diner, I stopped in at a mega-store that sold everything under the sun having to do with camping, shooting, and all things outdoorsy. A half hour later I left the store with a twenty-two caliber, match-grade air pistol that claimed to be capable of firing a jacketed pellet at six-hundred feet per second. While that was much slower than any bullet fired from a conventional firearm, it was fast enough to break human skin or to dispatch small game. I just needed it to be able to take out floodlights at up to a hundred feet. Having spent some time with a variety of pellet guns in the past, I was comfortable that this one, at almost five-hundred dollars, would be up to the task and in fact probably represented substantial overkill. I had a supply of pellets and CO_2 cartridges for it, as well as an accessory 4-power scope. I had bought a plain black gym bag that would be big enough for the pistol along with the detachable folding stock and the other supplies.

At a hardware store across the parking lot, I picked up a six-pack of industrial grade floodlight bulbs.

My last shopping stop was at a chain dollar store, where I picked up several items, including a roll of Necco Wafers from the candy section. I knew that the colorful candy disks made excellent improvised targets. Thin, brittle, and quarter-sized, they shattered nicely when hit with a pellet or bullet.

I drove out to the same park where I had tested the camera. It was another quiet day there and it didn't take me long to settle on an area where I could test out the pellet gun without being noticed and without scaring anyone.

I attached the scope and adjusted the windage and elevation settings to be what I thought was about right for eighty feet. I estimated that as the right distance for the floodlights that I intended to shoot out.

Opening the Necco wafers, I wedged a white one into the bark of a tree. Pacing off what I thought was close to eighty feet, I leaned against another tree and took careful aim, missing the wafer several times.

I walked back closer to the target to see where my pellets were hitting, then made adjustments to the scope and tried again. It was after my second round of adjustments that I was able to kill my first candy wafer. I went through the process several more times, along with much of the candy, before I was satisfied that I had the scope properly zeroed. I also moved closer to the target by twenty feet and then farther away by the same distance, noting how these moves affected my aim point. The end result was that the setup was closely zeroed at eighty feet, but I also knew that give or take twenty more feet, I would still be within an inch of zero.

For my second test, with the floodlight bulbs, I laid out a large plastic sheet to catch any broken glass, and lay the six bulbs across it. I shot at them from several distances, finding that they broke apart nicely when hit. I decided that when possible, I would aim for the widest part of the bulb stem in order to incur maximum damage to the inner filament.

I gathered up the plastic sheet carefully and stowed it into a garbage bag. As a responsible outdoorsman, I well knew that broken glass was no good to man or beast.

I then set about the task of making a simple suppressor for the pellet gun out of the other items from the dollar store. A pellet gun didn't make much sound relative to a real gun, but the one I had bought was more powerful than most, so I thought some effort would be prudent. It wasn't my intention to make anything very elaborate or of particularly high quality. I was hoping to lessen the volume of the report at least a little bit, and I only needed the thing to last for a half-dozen shots.

I dumped the contents from several water bottles and choose one with a neck that fit closely around the end of the gun barrel. I cut off and discarded the bottom of the bottle along with the screw cap. I stuffed the empty bottle with a handful of plastic Easter basket straw from the dollar store, packing it in only very lightly. I then fed the neck of the bottle over the end of the gun barrel and taped it in place, taking care to line up the bottle such that a pellet flying out of the muzzle wouldn't hit the inside walls of the plastic bottle. The intent was to have the pellet fly through the bottle and out the open end, obstructed only by the light filler of plastic straw. My hope was that the straw wouldn't throw off the trajectory of the high-velocity pellet, but would serve to muffle the blast of the compressed air bursting out behind the pellet.

It worked like a charm, easily halving the sound of the pellet gun as it was fired.

I tested the whole setup on several more Necco Wafers until I was satisfied that the plastic straw wasn't noticeably affecting the pellet trajectory.

I now had an effective tool to knock out a few floodlights as needed, hopefully without being noticed.

51

I drove through the Gallo neighborhood again that evening at nine. Pausing briefly at a stop sign across from the house, I used the remote control unit to trigger and receive the burst transmission from the concealed camera. Within thirty seconds I got the messages indicating that the operation had been successful and that the camera memory was now clear. Unless reprogrammed, the unit would sit idle until waking up to execute the same cycle again on the following Wednesday.

Back at the hotel I reviewed the images gathered, with the sound off, freezing frames and zooming in at numerous points. While the majority of the footage showed nothing going on in the Gallo driveway, there was good information sprinkled throughout.

At seven-twenty that morning, several images showed that Vince Gallo left the house through the side door and entered the garage, presumably to begin his work day. Shortly after, a woman left the house from the same door, accessed the garage via one of the large garage doors, and drove away in a new BMW. The files I had studied didn't indicate that Mrs. Gallo held a regular job, so I guessed that she was probably going to run errands or attend some appointment. The morning camera cycle didn't show any other activity.

The lunch-time camera cycle showed Vince going back over to the house for about forty-five minutes, and then returning to the garage. Just before that cycle ended, a landscaper's truck appeared in the driveway, which explained the strong scent of fresh-cut grass I had noticed when I had gone by for the transmission.

The evening camera cycle began at six o'clock and went on for three hours. Vince must have already been over in the main house for dinner at that point, because the first recorded activity showed him leaving the house for the garage at ten minutes to seven.

As the daylight faded, a low-power floodlight at the upper corner of the garage nearest the house came on to illuminate the short path from house to garage and the driveway in general.

At precisely eight-forty-five, Vince exited the garage, pulled the door closed, and went across to enter the house. The camera cycle ended shortly after that.

I watched the recording again with the sound off, and then twice more with the sound turned up high. Listening carefully while watching Mr. and Mrs. Gallo go back and forth, I was able to hear a distinctive electronic tone when the door to the house was opened that I didn't hear when the door to the garage was opened. It was the same one-second tone that my own home alarm system made when an alarmed door was opened while the house alarm system wasn't armed. I concluded that the house was equipped with an alarm system while the garage was not.

Aside from reinforcing what I had already suspected about Vince Gallo's Wednesday schedule, the footage gave me other useful information about the garage building and area in general.

The building was a two-car garage but generously sized and obviously designed to also accommodate some other useful space, such as a full-sized office, as was the case for the Gallo family. Two matching garage doors in a sort of barn-door style took up most of the frontage of the building, with the office windows above them. To the right of the garage doors, closest to the house, was the regular 'human door' that Vince had gone in and out of. I figured that this door would lead to a flight of stairs up to the office and whatever else was there above the car bays. Though it wasn't visible in the recorded images, I had already ascertained during my morning jogs that the garage also had a side door that opened onto the narrow path between the far side of the building and the fence that separated the property from the quiet Cutler Street that ran up the side.

If my plan was going to work, that side door was certainly the ticket.

———

Before going to bed, I checked my various email accounts and secure mailboxes.

There was a brief message from Kate thanking Tommy and me for our help and ordering us to be careful and safe.

There was a message from Sophia telling me that she had figured out how to determine the balances in the Bahamian bank accounts held by Vince and John. Vince's account held just over one and a half million dollars and John's held about half that. I thought to myself how interesting that was. Maybe John was spreading his money out to a greater degree, or maybe Vince was holding out on the others and keeping more for himself. In any case, the amounts were exciting. Her message also indicated that she was working on something that might help to determine the eight-digit numbers that were part of what was needed to access the accounts. I thanked her profusely and asked her to keep Tommy and me both informed.

There were two messages from Tommy.

The first one told me that he had been able to gather some very interesting information relative to the article I had seen in the Atlanta paper. Atlanta Metro police were investigating what they were calling a home invasion in an affluent neighborhood in the Buckhead suburb. The building in question had been a large detached garage with a residential apartment taking up the second floor.

The place had been set on fire, but investigators had been able to recover enough evidence to determine that two men had apparently been beaten to death and numerous valuables stolen. The nature of the crime, the makeup of the area, and certain details about the two victims indicated that the attack had been well planned and that robbery had likely been the motive.

Tommy's message ended with a suggestion that I consider trying to mimic the crime.

I paced the room for a few minutes, considering the idea.

I had been thinking along the lines of some kind of break-in or robbery that would cause Vince's death on his own property. The garage office idea had always been attractive to me, in part because that would allow me to avoid running into or having to harm Mrs. Gallo.

I knew that I could just shoot Vince in his driveway, but that would simply look like a hit, and would probably cause John Campbell to freak out.

No, an attack on him in his home office was the way to go. The idea to mimic the Buckhead crime was solid. I'd kill Vince, steal some things, and burn the place down. With solid execution and some luck, the police would suspect a connection to the earlier crime and the papers would echo that. I remembered seeing in the files that Vince had bought a safe. Hopefully it was up there in his office. Regardless of whether or not I was able to access it or get anything of value from it, it would look like a good target.

I sent a reply to Tommy asking him to see if he could get any further details about the crime from his law-enforcement sources. A detail held back per standard procedure perhaps. He would know, as I did, that it was common police practice for investigators to hold back key details of crimes in hopes of later weeding through suspects or eliminating any nuts that wanted to confess to a crime for their own demented reasons.

He replied back to me almost immediately that he agreed with the premise of the question, and that he had an idea of someone that he might be able to get that information from. He would get back to me the next day.

His second message related to the first job in Deer Valley, Illinois. All indications from officials in that area were that the killing of Mark

Sonetto was being treated by police in exactly the way we had intended. He had been attacked and killed in the rain apparently for his valuable watch, which had been taken. Police were operating under the theory that the killer was probably someone that Mark interacted with peripherally and had noticed the watch or had heard about it. Mall security cameras weren't much help due to the weather and also because of a large van that had blocked the camera that might potentially have had the best view of the crime scene.

I poured myself a generous nightcap of bourbon on the rocks and sat back in the suite's little living area to reflect on all that I had just learned.

Hopefully Vince and John were reading the same news reports about the Sonetto killing.

As to Atlanta, I thought I had an exciting possibility to work with.

If I could pull off a copycat job, it could provide some good cover and give me enough time to deal with John Campbell up in New Jersey. Eventually the Atlanta police would catch this crew and my mimicry would fall apart, but that was a problem for the long run. I didn't care about the long run.

In the long run, some of us would be dead, and some of us would have disappeared.

52

Debbi Gallo was jarred out of a deep sleep by a loud crash. Sitting up suddenly, she rubbed her eyes and looked at her bedside clock, seeing that it was just after two in the morning. She jumped out of bed and walked quickly down the hall to her husband's bedroom. She was sure the noise must have come from there.

"What happened?" she asked. "Are you okay?" She had opened the door to find that the light was on and her husband, in his pajamas, was picking up pieces of a broken lamp.

"Yeah," Vince said. "I had a nightmare. It scared me to death. I was trying to yell and trying to wake up, and I must have knocked the lamp off the nightstand."

His wife put her hand on his shoulder. She could tell that he was still breathing heavily and fast. She realized that she had almost never seen him scared.

"I can get that in the morning, honey," she said. "Try to relax and settle down. Do you want to tell me about it?"

"It was just silly, just a nightmare," he said. "I don't know where it came from. I don't even remember the last time I had one. I was being chased by someone who wanted to kill me, like some kind of hunter. I couldn't see him but I had the feeling that he knew me. You know that old movie about the crazy rich guy on the island who hunts shipwrecked men in the jungle? Like he gives them a head start and then comes after them? Something like that. That's what it felt like—like I was being hunted. Scared the shit out of me. Why would I have a dream like that?"

"I don't know, honey, that is really weird," she said. "You know what? It's probably because of what happened to Mark. That was so horrible, and you've probably been thinking about it a lot. That must be it."

"I guess you're probably right," he said. "Even if it's only subconscious. Yeah, you're right."

"Can I get you some tea?" she said. "Or would you rather have some scotch?"

"I think I need both," he said. "Thanks Deb. That really shook me up. Dammit."

After Debbi had brought the tea and a small glass of scotch up to her husband, and sat with him for a while longer, she wished him goodnight and went back down the hall to her room. She sat for a while with the light on, sipping her own hot cup of tea.

After Mark's death, they had decided to close out the BardLogic deal, and Vince was working on that with his people. It made her sad to think of all the money that they'd be giving up, but it made sense to cut their losses and end it quietly.

It had been about a year and a half ago that she and Vince, along with John Campbell and his wife Joanne, were vacationing together at a beach resort on the island of Grand Bahama. Joanne hadn't been feeling well and had gone back to the room for a nap, leaving the other three on the beach. Debbi had been dozing on her lounge chair when she overheard John and Vince talking about a problem with some company called BardLogic. They kept billing BEQ for some special equipment that BEQ no longer had. Debbi was about to yell at them playfully to stop talking shop, when she had another idea. At first, they had laughed at her, but the conversation had been started. And now, eighteen months and almost five million dollars later, Mark's death was bringing the whole thing to a close.

The setup with the BardLogic billing was only one of the special activities that began that day on Grand Bahama.

Vince had gotten drunk in the sun and had gone off to bed early. Joanne was still under the weather and had taken a sleeping pill. John and Debbi had a late dinner together and the wine flowed freely. There had been a walk on the beach and then nature had taken the course that it frequently did. A passionate interlude on a large beach towel laid out on the sand between two of the rental kayaks had left them both feeling satisfied in ways that neither of them had felt for some time.

Since then, they'd only been able to get together on a very few occasions, but they had both relished those moments. It was an occasional and fleeting pleasure, and Debbi had no illusions about it. She hoped to be free of Vince before she got much older; him and his two spoiled daughters from his first marriage. When that day finally came, she didn't see herself running into John's arms. She was looking forward to being free. Rich and free.

53

A s Thursday morning arrived in the Atlanta suburbs, my planning and preparations were on track.

The camera was still in place to record Vince's activities for a second Wednesday, and I looked forward to reviewing the data yield from that day. Once I had done that, and barring any unexpected changes or developments, I would make final plans for the third Wednesday evening. Vince Gallo's demise would be almost exactly three weeks after that of Mark Sonetto. With some luck, it would all look like a terrible coincidence, a loss for the families and a blow to the great institution of BEQ.

Apart from keeping up on communications, which I could do from anywhere, I didn't have much to do for most of a week. Lie low and stay out of trouble, yes, but I could also do that from anywhere. Since I was planning to pay cash for my hotel stay, it wouldn't be a bad idea to check out and do that before the bill got much larger. Going home would be problematic. It might look strange for me to be there for a few days and then suddenly go off again. Good-natured though any questions might be, I didn't need them at all.

I considered the idea of contacting Jenny in St. Louis, but eventually decided that, there as well, I would end up having to either make up stories or explain comings and goings that I'd rather not address. I would wait until the business at hand was all wrapped up before trying to see her again.

In the end, I settled on the historic coastal resort city of Savannah, and enjoyed a long weekend there. Somehow, I hadn't realized until I tried to get a hotel room that I'd arrived at the beginning of Memorial Day Weekend. In my case, however, because I had money to burn, that wasn't really a problem. I simply had to settle for the honeymoon suite.

I dined and drank lavishly, toured, swam, and sunbathed. I exercised early in the morning and walked the cobblestone streets at night. I resolved that if I needed to kill time again over the following weekend, I would come back to the Savannah area, but would try to get a room right on the beach. That would be the weekend after Memorial Day, so there ought to be a greater selection of rooms, at least for those with fat wallets.

By Monday evening, I was back in the Dunwoody area, north of Atlanta, checked into a different hotel. On the drive back from Savannah I had made several stops, shopping for odds and ends that I thought I might need in the near future.

Over the weekend I had kept up on communications with Tommy. It had taken a few days but he'd eventually been able to find out about the police investigation into the earlier crime, and one of those details that had been hushed up.

Cannon fuse. Available at many stores, online, and certainly at any gun show.

In the garage apartment attack and robbery, forensics had determined that a length of standard cannon fuse had been used to start the fire. Very clever, I thought to myself. A simple, cheap, and effective way to accomplish a delayed ignition.

The piece of cannon fuse I had bought earlier was ten feet long. At thirty seconds burn time per foot, that would give me five minutes to get clear. Longer than that, because it would likely take a few minutes for anyone to notice a fire.

I thought to myself, that's it then. That's the plan. And if I can't get clear in five minutes, I'm pretty well fucked anyway.

54

By late Wednesday night, I'd finished reviewing the image data from the second burst transmission.

The second day of surveilling Wednesday activities in the Gallo driveway had confirmed what I'd learned the week before. On Wednesdays, Vince Gallo worked a regular schedule in his home office. He went over to the main house for lunch. Later, after dinner in the house, he went back over to his office above the garage around seven and stayed there for two hours.

This time there was no sign of Mrs. Gallo going out to do errands and no sign of any landscapers.

———

The next day, I went through and around the Gallo neighborhood and the larger surrounding area, both driving and jogging. During my early morning jog, I was able to recover Tommy's remote camera in the same manner that I had used to place it. Back in the hotel room, I drew sketches and made notes. I compared everything to what I could see on Google Earth's satellite view. I modeled various possibilities of moving around the neighborhood until I felt that I had a reasonable plan to get in and then out of the garage. Indications were, incredibly, that the garage building wasn't alarmed, so I should be able to get through that side door quietly. I planned to check that door very carefully when I had it in view, and make adjustments as needed.

The upcoming Wednesday would be the day. I would enter Vince Gallo's garage during his dinner break and wait for him in his upstairs office. In order to liberate whatever money was in his Bahamian account, I needed to somehow encourage him to reveal to me an eight-digit number—unless Sophia somehow came up with it—a color, and the name of an animal. Then, I would deal with him harshly and with finality, and get the hell out of there.

I had the weekend off and I drove over to the seashore.

———

On the way into the Savannah area, I acted on an idea that had occurred to me the week before when I had first visited.

Stopping mid-morning in a nearly empty store parking lot, I cleared out the Mercury's hidden trunk compartment, transferring guns, ammo, and money to an overnight bag and then locked the compartment. I then dropped the car off at an auto body shop on the outskirts of Savannah. The place was shabby, but was large and busy and the staff seemed competent. For a premium on their usual price, they agreed to do a rush repaint job for me. The Mercury would go from dark blue to a pearlescent silver. I made a show of pointing out the large supply of bourbon still in the trunk.

"This stuff going to be okay here?" I said to the owner, as I shouldered my overnight bag.

"Yeah, no problem," he said. "I count ten bottles. I'll make sure your trunk isn't touched."

He was able to rent me a five-year-old Toyota Camry to take to the beach for a few days.

By Friday afternoon I was reclining comfortably on the beach of Tybee Island, just to the east of Savannah. I'd been able to find a clean and modern oceanfront hotel with a secured parking area for the Camry. There was warm sand, cool water, and a tiki bar.

———————

By Monday evening I was in a third hotel in Dunwoody, mentally and physically refreshed and ready to work. The Mercury had a new look and was sporting the Nevada license plates. I had contacted Sophia the day before and she'd quickly made the appropriate adjustments to the registration.

I had a message from Tommy indicating that he hadn't been able to do anything along the lines of tapping phones or otherwise intercepting calls. We would just have to keep our eyes open and our ears to the ground. He had confirmed with Sophia that she would be on the lookout for any unusual banking activity on the part of Michael and Gloria. A flurry of banking action might be one indicator that some-body was planning to make a run for it.

There was a message from Sophia, marked as urgent, asking me to give her a time that we could talk. Her message included instructions on how to use the scrambled voice-over-internet software on the laptop. I texted her, getting an immediate reply, and we agreed to start a conversation in a few minutes.

When we started the VOI call, Sophia's voice was clear enough, coming through the laptop's speakers, if with something of a robotic sound.

"So this should be secure then?" I asked.

"Yes, it's all scrambled," she said, "but I'll try not to take too long anyway. I've been working on something for a few days but I wasn't ready to tell you about it until today. Have I caught you before you do whatever you're planning to do that might get us into the Gallo account?"

"Yes," I said. "That'll be this Wednesday night. I was going to let you know when I need you to be on standby."

"Great," she said, "because I already figured out the number. All I need now is a one-word animal and a one-word color."

"You're shitting me, right?" I said. "That's great. You really figured out the number. How the hell did you do that?"

"Well, that's what you're paying me for," she said. "Seemed like a good investment of my time to put some effort into it. I was actually surprised at how easy it was. I was able to see that the user-password part of the bank's security software was in separate pieces. Like one for the number, another for the animal, and a third segment for the color. Almost like, if you get the first one, you get passed through to the second, and so on. It looked like the segments were probably written by different people. I could see how to isolate the number part, but not the other parts."

"Tommy told me that you'd needed money to buy some code from someone," I said.

"Right," she said. "I needed a subroutine that would allow me to copy out the code covering the number security part and then allow me to loop through it trying different number combinations. That way, I would be able to try different numbers in a controlled environment without worrying about triggering the 'three strikes' lockout. I knew who to buy it from rather than spending a week myself writing it. It worked great."

"That is fantastic," I said. "How many numbers did you have to run through before you got the right one?"

"Less than ten," she said.

I was both stunned and elated, and I could tell that she was in her element and having fun.

"Alright, I'm impressed," I said. "Tell me how you did it. And don't forget to tell me the number before we hang up."

"Okay," she said. "If you're anything like Tommy, you must know some basic things about codes. Most people use children's birthdays, the name of their first dog, their first license plate—something like that. In this case we needed eight single-digit numbers, and no zeros. So phone numbers, social security numbers, and zip-codes wouldn't be any good. Birthdays might work, as long as no zeros. I tried a few dates first, his birthday and one of the daughters but they didn't work. The date he got his degree wasn't it either.

"But then I started looking at his wife's name."

"Okay, sure, Debbi," I said.

"Right," Sophia said. "There was a picture of them in one of the files Tommy gave me, and I could see that she was clearly Asian. Korean, in fact, I found after some more digging. I found out that her maiden name had been 'Cha'. Also, I guess the Gallo family has a small sailboat, because the file had a picture of them on a dock next to it. Name of the boat was 'DEBBI CHA'. Isn't that sweet? So I was thinking about that name. Anything jump out at you about Debbi Cha?"

"I have Korean neighbors named Cha," I said, "so that might be a common name. But if you're getting at what I think, we still need to convert that to a number."

"Right," she said, "and for a non-professional, what's the most basic code there is?"

"I guess that would have to be a simple substitution," I said. "If you were sending a coded message to another person, you would use an agreed-upon key, like a book or a famous poem. But he's not sharing it with anyone. He would just want a slightly obscured way to hide the number while also having it be impossible for him to forget."

"I agree with all of that," she said. "What else do you see about Debbi Cha?"

I'd been scribbling notes as we talked. I'd written the alphabet in a line across my notepad. I scribbled and counted.

"I think I see it," I said. "The name 'Debbi Cha' only uses the first nine letters of the alphabet. So if I match the first nine letters to numbers one through nine, let's see…That's it, Debbi Cha would be 45229381. Are you kidding me—is that it?"

"There you go! I'll make a cypher expert out of you yet," she said. "Yes, my software loop tells me that's it. Now we just need you to come up with the animal and the color."

"Will you be able to do the same with the number for the other guy? Campbell?"

"I doubt it," she said. "We can try if we have a guess at the number, but for an eight-digit number in the decimal system, there would be a hundred-million possible combinations. I don't have the computing power for that, and anyway, I don't think we have the time. I can input as many guesses as I want, but we still have to come up with those guesses. We lucked out this time."

"Okay, I'll take what I can get," I said. "I'll try to get that animal and color. If I have any ideas about a number for Campbell, I'll let you know. Good work and thanks, Sophia. I owe you a giant Starbucks card."

We signed off after agreeing that she would be sitting with phone and computer ready starting at seven o'clock Atlanta time on Wednesday evening. I would text her between seven and nine, hopefully with the needed information.

On Tuesday morning, I checked out of my hotel in Dunwoody, moving to a quieter place off the beltway where I was able to use the 'crisp hundreds' routine to avoid having to show any identification to the bored young staffer. I recycled the embellishment that I was going through a messy divorce and was hiding from my wife. He seemed to enjoy the story and clearly enjoyed the big bills even more. I assured him that I would be on my way in the morning.

———

It was about two-thirty Wednesday morning when I managed to tear myself out of a nightmare, my heart pounding and sweat soaking the sheets.

I took a moment to remind myself where I was and why I was there. I worked to control my breathing and was gradually fully calm. I didn't remember much of the dream except that I had been trying to get away from some huge fire and had run into a dark stream which turned out to be a river of blood.

I'd slipped under the surface of the ghastly river and the sensation of drowning must have been what jolted me out of sleep, gasping for air.

I reached for the nightstand and looked at my watch. Dammit, I thought to myself—too late for another drink.

I rinsed my face in the bathroom sink and studied my reflection in the mirror. The recent dye job was still hiding any grey, but it peeked out around my face whenever I hadn't shaved for a few days. I considered myself lucky to have lived my life with a face that had turned many a head in my day, but my good DNA could only save me for so long. I knew that many people were prone to wrinkles just as many were prone to baldness, bad teeth, and brittle bones. I hadn't had to worry about any of those, but still, the stories of my life, good and bad, were starting to show themselves. Horror, joy, love, hate, loss—all of them were starting gradually to etch themselves onto my face. Slowly, thankfully, but relentlessly.

I thanked whatever gods might be that my father had been such a good-looking man, because there he was, looking back at me. He had emerged gradually over the past few years, sneaking into my features a little at a time, until now he couldn't be denied. I hoped that he would forgive the hairstyle.

In lieu of a stiff drink, a long hot shower served to relax me greatly. After the shower, I was amazed at how good it felt to get back into bed, and I was soon in the grasp of a deep sleep.

I awoke feeling more refreshed than I would have thought possible not many hours before.

I mentally reviewed my plans for the day over coffee, then showered again and dressed. I was out of the room within an hour, leaving no trace of who I was or why I had been there.

55

It was ten after six in the evening when I parked along a quiet side street three blocks removed from the row of homes along Peach Valley Lane. I slung both my backpack and the black gym bag containing the pellet gun over my shoulder and started to walk into the neighborhood.

Inside the community, I crossed the first street and turned right to continue along the sidewalk that fronted the homes sharing the service alley with Vince Gallo and his neighbors. It was still daylight but the shade from the huge old trees dominating the area kept me mostly out of the sun. If I encountered someone coming home from work or out for some pre-dinner exercise, I hoped that I would look like I myself was just getting back to my house or apartment for the evening.

As it happened, though I caught occasional glimpses of human forms inside windows here and there, and heard some music spill out when a back door was briefly opened, I didn't meet anybody at all.

Ten feet before the end of the block, I paused my stroll to do a quick visual check for anyone else out on the street. Seeing nobody, I ducked behind the hedges of the house whose back yard faced the utility alley roughly across from the back of the Gallo property. I moved along the side of the house, concealed in a narrow pathway by tall hedges and by several groupings of trees along the property. Neither the house nor the yard was decrepit in any way, but my several prior visits to the neighborhood had convinced me that it currently stood empty. It occurred to me that the owners might simply be away on vacation.

As I came to the rear corner of the house, I looked carefully across the back yard towards what part of the alley I could see, and found it to be clear. Crossing to the side of a large shed and passing it, I again carefully looked out. This time I had a much clearer view of the alley, and still found it to be empty. Just across the alley from where I was concealed was a thin strip of Gallo property and the expansive rear wall of their garage.

Still seeing no one in the area, I backed up towards the rear of the shed, where I set down the gym bag and took out the parts of the pellet gun. After attaching the modular shoulder stock and the makeshift suppressor, I waited for the covering sound of a loud passing car before I stepped partly out of concealment and started to shoot out floodlights.

56

By seven o'clock, Michael Sanchez had picked up Gloria Parsons at her apartment and they were headed up the freeway towards the Gallo house on Peach Valley Lane. Traffic was surprisingly light and they realized they would be a little early.

"I've been thinking of asking for a larger share of whatever the last payment is," Gloria said. "What do you think?"

"I think that's a good idea," Michael said. "I've been thinking about that myself. I mean, it's not like it could have been done without us. You more than anyone, really. I guess Vince and John think they're risking the most."

"Well, let's see how the conversation goes," Gloria said. "We can play it by ear. I'm glad it's ending anyway. I've been thinking of leaving BardLogic."

"I bet Vince could get you back in at BEQ," Michael said. He hated the idea that she might come back to work with them full time, but kept that thought to himself.

"Yeah, maybe," Gloria said. "He probably would, but a clean slate somewhere else is looking pretty good too. What do you have going on for the weekend?"

"Some friends are visiting from Jersey," Michael said. "We thought we'd take them to some touristy things. Maybe the Cyclorama, the World of Coca Cola. The underground is always fun."

"That sounds nice," Gloria said. "One thing about when friends visit is that it can be an excuse to get out and do things you wouldn't normally do. Long before you moved here, there used to be a Café du Monde in the underground. I miss that. Now you have to go to New Orleans. A friend of mine is visiting too. We'll probably just hang out. We're thinking dinner in Buckhead with some other friends."

They drove in silence for a while before pulling onto Peach Valley Lane.

"I hope this doesn't go too late tonight," Gloria said. "I recorded a Jimmy Buffet concert last week, and as soon as I get home I'm going to mix up a margarita and park on the couch."

57

The dinner dishes done and the counter wiped, Vince Gallo poured the last of a bottle of Valpolicello into one of his favorite juice glasses. The small glass made it all more authentic for him—a little bit of 'the old country'. One day he'd be one of those wise old guys, he thought to himself. White shirtsleeves with suspenders, and a little glass of wine or an espresso in the summer sun. Sitting at a table along the sidewalk of a small town, or maybe by the fountain in the town square. Everybody respected them and sought their counsel. He sipped the wine and let his thoughts wander down a cobblestone street.

Maybe they'd actually get there this year. Money was not an issue —they certainly could afford it. Traveling would be a great way to spend some of the grey-money he'd been accumulating.

"Earth to Vince—you okay over there?" His wife's voice brought him back to their kitchen. She was starting her nightly routine of going through emails over at the pantry desk.

"Yeah. Yes, I'm fine," he said. "I was just thinking about Mark—so terrible." He realized that in fact he hadn't thought about Mark Sonetto at all for several days. The poor dope. His murder had been a terrible shock though. Hell of a price to pay for that damn flashy watch. He had been a good team member, unlike most people.

"What do you think of actually doing the Italy trip this year?" he asked. "Maybe this fall. Let's really do it."

"Sure, we can talk about it," his wife said. "Didn't you tell me that Michael and Gloria are coming for your weekly tonight?"

"Yes, neither of them could do it tomorrow so we moved it up a day. I'm going over now to do some prep." He consulted his watch. "They should be here in forty minutes. They know to come right up to the office. I'll be back over by eight-thirty, nine at the latest."

"I'll be here," she said. "Tell them I said hi." She reached across the desk to a Bose Soundwave radio, switching it on and returning to her laptop. The kitchen and dining room filled with a soft guitar solo from her favorite Atlanta jazz station.

Vince raised his glass in a silent toast and opened the side kitchen door. Going through and out to the driveway, he thought for a moment of his two daughters, twenty and twenty-one, both in college in Atlanta. He wished they would come over to the house more often but they didn't have much of a relationship with Debbi. It bothered him, but he didn't know what to do about it. Charts and spreadsheets were so much easier to deal with than people. Well, he and his ex-wife had done what they could and his daughters would be able to take care of themselves.

He crossed over the corner of the driveway and opened the door to the garage. Stepping inside, he snapped up the light switch there at the bottom of the stairs and pulled the door closed behind him. He was now on a small landing, four feet square, just inside the door, with stairs leading up and towards the rear of the building directly in front of him. To the left was the large open space of the garage itself with another door to the side yard over past the cars on the far wall. Both his Mercedes and Debbi's BMW were fairly new, so neither of them was leaking automotive-bodily fluids onto his garage floor. The pleasant thought crossed his mind that his station in life at this point had freed him from having to deal with old cars leaking shit onto the floor. In the dim light of the tiny foyer he smiled in satisfaction. The last few years had been good. He had done well with the major reorganization of all the tech teams and had just been promoted to VP. His bonuses were equal to many people's annual salaries. He had made some tough decisions and they had worked out for the most part. He just needed to clean house a bit more and get the special activities all closed out. With Mark gone now, it had to be done.

Almost two years ago, he had spent a big chunk of money to finish the space above the garage as an office that could also serve in a pinch as guest lodging. There was a convertible sofa, a full bathroom, small fridge, and of course a serious desk, book shelf, double file cabinet, and a small storage closet. His home computer and the router setup for the whole house was there. He liked to think that it was the headquarters of the 'Gallo Empire'.

The remaining daylight was fading, though it wouldn't be fully dark for an hour. He started up the stairs.

58

V ince was a few minutes late and I was just starting to get concerned when I heard the door open.

The lights came on and right away I heard someone coming up the stairs. From just inside the small bathroom at the top of the stairs, I couldn't yet tell that it was Vince, but it sounded like a full-sized man.

I listened carefully as whoever it was reached the top of the stairs, turned, and took a few steps into the large open space of the office. As I heard him turn I stepped out silently, seeing immediately that it was him. He faced away from me and towards the front of the office and the windows that looked out onto the driveway.

As he started towards the desk, I moved forward quickly to close the distance between us. No doubt hearing a sound behind him, he started to turn to his left to look back, but it did him little good. I jabbed the Vipertek stun gun into his lower back, pressing the button that drove over a million volts into him.

The effect was instant and dramatic. Accompanied by the crackling of electricity, he spasmed immediately, bending backwards in a sort of frozen arc, arms jiggling at his sides, a loud moan came out of him and then he seemed to become jelly. He dropped to his knees, and then to flat on the floor. I followed him down and zapped him again for five seconds and pulled away, then five seconds again. A stun gun doesn't typically render a person unconscious, so I needed to work quickly. Jamming the unit into my right rear pocket, I dropped a knee with all my weight behind it onto his back, scooping up one of his wrists and then the other. Reaching into my jacket, I pulled out the cable-tie handcuffs that I had prepared. He was starting to regain muscle control but I was able to secure the ties around his wrists with minimal struggle. I stood up and stepped away.

"What the fuck!" he yelled. His words were garbled and he was clearly furious. He seemed to struggle with the realization that his hands were bound. "What is this? Who are you?"

Grabbing the Vipertek from my pocket I moved in and hit him with it again in his right side. A good five seconds. He yelled again and then went limp, panting.

I stood up, drew back my right leg, and kicked him in the side as hard as I could. He recoiled, thrashing on the floor and struggling for air. I knelt low beside him so he could see me, though my face was concealed by a lightweight balaclava-style face mask, revealing only a narrow strip across my eyes.

Holding the Vipertek a few inches from his face, I pressed the button. As the blue-white electrical arc jumped between the electrodes it let out a sharp crackling sound. He snapped his head away and let out a shriek.

"Quiet, Vince; take a minute and get it together. Be quiet and we can leave your wife out of this, got it? Debbi, isn't it? She seems very nice. It would be a shame for anything to happen to her."

I had planned to mention him and his wife by name very early in the process. I needed him to be terrified right away.

He was wide-eyed and breathing fast, but made an effort at control. "Okay, okay, what do you want? You are in such deep shit..."

I hit the button and showed him the electric arc again. "Quiet! We can talk for a while and like I said, keep it quiet and we'll leave the wife out of this. Sound good? Shall we leave her alone over next door?

Acknowledge!" I hit the button again and the electric arc hissed and crackled.

On his side now on the floor, he nodded quickly.

"Now, take a minute and move yourself over there," I said, pointing. "Sit against the file cabinet. Fucking do it!"

He dragged himself over that way, struggling with his hands tied behind him and cursing under his breath. While he did that I pulled my backpack out from behind an armchair and opened it. Stowing the Vipertek, I pulled out the big forty-five auto with the attached suppressor. As Vince managed to get himself reasonably upright against the cabinets, he saw the monstrous gun pointed at him and a look of terror flashed across his face.

"You really should have an alarm system for this place," I said.

His chin seemed to drop towards his chest and he shook his head before speaking.

"Come on now, you can't just come in here and do this. You'll never get away with all..."

I took three fast steps towards him and fired into the floor around his legs. Three shots, two seconds apart. The suppressor did a lot to muffle the blasts but still the fat bullets ripping into the hardwood floor and sending woodchips flying had the desired effect. His whole body flinched and he recoiled as though trying to melt back into the cabinets, letting out a small terrified yelp. He looked at me wide-eyed as I backed up a few steps and knelt down, gun leveled at him. The smell of burnt gunpowder and fresh oak was thick in the air.

"I hope that got your attention," I said.

He was scared, but working to remain calm.

"Are you insane?" he said. "You can't actually think you'll get away with this, can you? Take off that mask."

It was fair to say that he was a man who, in terms of looks, had been dealt an unfortunate hand. His facial features were not symmetrical at all; he had a large nose that bent to one side, a crooked mouth that seemed to bend in sympathy with the nose, and a high bald head above huge dark eyes. About my age I guessed, mid-fifties—but nature had not been as kind to him. Looking at these confusing features it was hard for me in that moment to discern his fear to anger ratio. Confusion also—yes, that was there too. As much as I hated him, I felt a touch of sympathy. Just a touch. Not enough to cut him any slack.

Being in a room with him, after all this time and after everything that had transpired in the past half-year, I felt my rage coming quickly to a boil. I worked to contain it.

"You idiot," I said, "don't you understand that if I take off my mask, I'll have to kill you? This mask is your ticket out of this. As long as the mask stays on and you give me what I want, you have a chance to buy your life. Get it?"

"Did you kill Mark?" he asked. He started to say something else before I cut him off.

"What? Who's Mark?" I said. I hoped that I was at least a little bit believable. "I don't know anything about any Mark. Just shut up and listen and we'll make this quick. I represent a group of people who are tired of you and John stealing from the company. All that BardLogic money going missing is very naughty of you."

I wouldn't have thought that his eyes could have gotten any wider at that point but they somehow did.

"Oh yeah," I continued. "I know about that and all about the money stashed in the Bahamas. I'm here to tell you that the whole thing is over. I don't know how you pulled it off and I don't care, but it's over now."

He puffed up, his face red, furious and indignant at the same time.

"Whoever you are, you're fucking crazy! I'm a VP, for Christ's sake. I don't need to steal. Look, I have some cash here. Let me get it for you. You can take it and just go!"

"Oh, you mean the safe in the closet there?" I said. "Yeah, I found that when I searched the place while you were having dinner. You'll give me the combination to that right now."

"People are coming," he said, "people are on their way. You better go—they'll be here soon. Just go."

I moved the gun so the muzzle was inches from his right kneecap. "Choose your words carefully. Don't bullshit me."

"Don't, don't! It's true. One works for me and the other used to.

Michael and Gloria. We have a regular meeting. Usually Thursday but it got moved this week. They're supposed to be here at seven-forty-five."

I looked down at my watch. Dammit! This was unexpected. It was a quarter after seven. I wasn't sure that I could do everything I needed to do and still get out in time. Well, I decided with a mental shrug, I'll just move forward and if I have to take care of those two also, so much the better.

I turned my attention back to Vince.

"Do they come together? Like in one car?"

"Usually one car."

"Okay then, here's what we're going to do. You give me what I want and I'll leave before they get here. I hate being in a room with you and I know you don't want me here, so let's get right to it, shall we?"

I didn't wait for any answer from him.

"The combination to the safe in the closet. Now."

One thing he had going for him was long legs, and I was taken by surprise when he kicked out at me. I jumped back fast enough that his right foot only hit me in the lower side. It wasn't any sort of deadly blow, but it was enough of a shock that I stumbled and fell. The gun fell out of my hand and skidded a few feet away. He struggled to sit up farther, trying to kick out at me again.

I couldn't quite reach the gun, but my backpack was closer and lay open on the floor. I could see the Vipertek and was able to reach in and grab it.

I spun around and jammed it into his leg, pressing the switch.

He jerked and kicked and tried to groan. I let him have two more good blasts.

While he was panting and recovering from that, I retrieved the pistol and composed myself, rubbing my side. I dropped the Vipertek back into the pocket of the backpack.

"Pretty good, Vince, that hurt. You got me there. I'll give you that one. But it won't change the equation for you. You've been stealing from the company and you've been a horrible prick to lots of people.

You've earned whatever pain comes your way and I brought a pile of it with me."

I knelt on the floor again, this time a little farther away. He worked to right himself against the cabinet.

"You can still get out of this," I said. "The combination to the safe, now. Don't make me ask you again."

"Just get out of here—come on. I'll write you a big check. They'll be here any minute. You better just run."

I looked down and shook my head, deliberately showing my exasperation.

I stood up and walked across the room to the little bathroom at the head of the stairs, returning with a hand towel.

"I'm thinking that you aren't quite taking me seriously yet, Vince. You need an attitude adjustment."

I roughly shoved the bunched towel into his mouth.

"Let's see now—which was it? Was it the right foot that you kicked me with?"

With that, I turned to point the big automatic towards his right foot, the end of the suppressor no more than a few inches from the top of his wingtip, and fired.

The big slug tore a jagged path through the bones and flesh of his foot, exited through the sole of his shoe, and smashed into the oak flooring. His whole body jerked and writhed as he struggled to scream with the towel in his mouth. His leg banged up and down a few times before he calmed a bit, chest heaving and eyes wide with terror.

I looked at his foot and saw that it was bleeding profusely, with a puddle starting to show under it. A shard of pinkish white bone, almost two inches long, protruded from the hole in the bottom of his shoe. I made a mental note that I had fired four shots. Four left.

He was panting and moaning. He looked like he might pass out. I tapped him sharply on the top of his head with the end of the suppressor to get his attention and yanked the towel out of his mouth.

"I hope you weren't planning to take ballet lessons, because that ship has sailed. You might have an hour before you bleed out. If you give me what I want I'll try to get out of here before your friends get here. They can call for help and you'll probably make it."

I pointed the gun at his other foot and his face filled with terror.

"The combination to that safe, right now."

He spat out three numbers. I repeated them back. He managed a nod.

I checked my watch. Twenty-five after. Cutting it close. I stood up and took a quick look through the windows above his desk, seeing nothing new in the driveway.

Grabbing my backpack, I went across the room to the open closet door and was able to open the safe on the first try. There were two shelves inside. The top shelf held mostly file folders and a few small booklets. I grabbed all of it and shoved it into my backpack in case it could be of some use in the future. What interested me a lot more were the contents of the larger bottom shelf. There were several stacks of banded bills, which I grabbed quickly and jammed into the backpack. Mostly bundles of US hundreds, there must have been seventy or eighty thousand or more. There were also a few bundles of euro bills, in hundred and fifty-euro denominations. Lastly, there were several rolls of what appeared to be gold bullion coins, Maple Leaves or Krugerrands, probably. I swept it all into my bag as quickly as possible, to be sorted out later. It was all gravy.

I carried the backpack over to be close to him again. He was looking worse still.

"You are one horrible piece of work. How many people did you fuck over to steal all that money?"

"It wasn't my idea. I had just gotten the college bills—one thing led to another. I'm not proud of it. Look, take that money and go. Call an ambulance, please. I'll tell them someone broke in to rob me."

He saw me look at my watch.

"Running out of time here," I said. "But I'm almost done. Here let me show you something fun." I pulled a small card from my back pocket. On the card, I'd written out 'Debbi Cha' in block letters, with the corresponding number—45229381 just below. I held it in front of his face so he could see it clearly. The look on his face confirmed what Sophia had already told me—that we had the right number.

"What is that?" he said. "How did you get that? What are you doing?"

"It doesn't matter how I got it," I said. "The important thing is that you just confirmed what it is."

I took out my phone and texted a quick message to Sophia. I told her to standby for the other information.

"Now," I said, "now that we're on the same page. What I need from you is the animal and the color. On the bright side, you'll still have your salary, your pension—all of that. All I want is the money you stole.

"What does that mean?" he said. "I don't know what that means."

He was close to hysterical, but I could tell from his tone that he wasn't quite ready to yield.

In a series of quick motions, I grabbed the small towel from the floor and shoved it roughly back into his mouth, and then blew a hole through his other foot.

He tried to scream as he thrashed around on the floor. Tears poured down his face. I didn't see any bone sticking out this time, but blood was flowing freely.

I tapped him across the forehead with the end of the suppressor to get his attention again, then rested the muzzle of the gun against his left kneecap.

"I bet your kneecap comes right off and smacks into that wall. Let's see. I need a color and an animal. If you make me wait any longer, I'll blow off both your kneecaps and then go downstairs for some gasoline. A color and an animal. Right now."

The few words he tried to yell came out more like croaks.

"Purple. Gazelle. Purple gazelle."

I held up my phone to him. "I'm going to know right away if that isn't it. Are you sure?"

He nodded up and down, fast, anxious to convince me.

I texted those two words to Sophia. Her confirmation came through in forty seconds.

I noted that it was now seven-thirty-four. There was a possibility I'd be able to get out before the others showed up.

"Good work, Vince," I said. We're almost done here and I'll leave you alone very soon. What do you think John does with his share of the money?"

He was panting and struggling to stay sitting upright.

"He has an offshore account like I do, but I don't know what he has there. His family—parents—has an old bar in New Jersey. He probably moves it through there. That's what I would do if I had a business. Look, you got what you wanted. Just take it and go. I'll tell the police I was robbed by a gang or something. Just go away."

"I will, Vince. I will. I'm going now. Only thing is—I didn't really come here for the money."

I pulled off the mask and shoved it into a pocket.

He looked at me blankly at first, recognition coming over him gradually.

"The name you're trying to come up with, Vince," I said, "is Boudreau. Dean Boudreau. And Mary and Evan Flores were good friends of mine. You stabbed them in the back, like you did to me. You should have seen Mark's face when I stabbed him in the back. Oh, it was priceless."

He was struggling to form speech but I stopped him.

"I just came to tell you something, Vince. I came to tell you that, effective immediately, your position has been eliminated."

He looked at me, eyes bulging as I stood over him.

The gun bucked three times in my hand, each time delivering a 230-grain full metal jacketed bullet into his broad and bony chest. His body jerked with each impact, a second apart, and then his whole frame slumped back against the cabinet and slid to one side. His head dropped to his shoulder. He let out just one raspy groan that became a quiet sigh as his last breath left him. He did me the final courtesy of closing his eyes as he died. His trip into Hell was a quick one, hurtling in on a hot river of lead. The whole thing had taken ten seconds at most.

I watched it all with a curious detachment, almost as though it was a scene in a play that I was viewing from the wings. I was a little shocked at how it had all looked, sounded, and smelled, but that passed quickly. It became to me more of a sense that a distasteful task, long planned and anticipated, had just been successfully completed. I also felt a distinct thrill at having just killed someone who badly needed killing. I looked down at him, slumped into his growing pool of blood, and smiled. I felt a weight lift off me and fly upwards and away. I felt good.

A stream of light reflecting off something in the room caught my attention. A quick glance out the window confirmed that a car was just pulling into the driveway. I realized that Vince's guests must be a few minutes early. Oh well, I thought, I would go with the moment and at least we wouldn't worry about those two as loose ends.

I shook myself, took a few deep breaths, and stretched my arms a few times to snap out of the moment. I had to move very quickly.

There was a throw rug in the middle of the room. I dragged it over to cover the bloody mess that was Vince. This way, I thought, as people came up the stairs and into the room, they wouldn't immediately see anything alarming. They would see a rug covering something where it shouldn't be. I just needed those few extra seconds of confusion.

I heard the sound of car doors closing. I did a quick look around the room and noticed Vince's little wine glass laying where he had dropped it, and kicked it into a corner. There was no time to do anything about the small puddle of wine.

I grabbed my backpack and ducked in to the bathroom, pulling the door halfway closed. I had just slapped a fresh eight-round magazine into the forty-five when I heard the door at the bottom of the stairs open.

"Hello! We're here," a woman's voice called out and I heard what sounded like two people coming up the stairs. Was that Gloria?

There was another hello from a voice that sounded like Michael's.

I listened to their footsteps as they climbed to the top of the stairs and entered the room. I heard a few more steps before they stopped.

"Vince—are you here?" Michael asked to the quiet space. Then more softly, he said to Gloria, "What the hell is that?"

I stepped quickly out of the bathroom, the gun just above my waist and leveled at them as they started to turn around towards me. They were not more than five feet away from me and less than that from each other.

"Michael, Gloria—long time no see." I smiled.

Confusion is what I saw in both of their faces. They saw me and may have recognized me, saw the gun, tried to process what they were seeing. They didn't make it to fear.

I shot them both in the belly. Gloria was first, on my left, then I swept the gun just a few feet right and put the second round into Michael. Two shots in three seconds and they were both down and on their backs. Despite the huge hot hole torn through their guts, neither died immediately. I had just enough room between them to kneel next to Gloria. She gurgled as if trying to speak, and looked up at me, confused and terrified. I briefly wondered if she was thinking that she had a chance to survive our encounter. After watching her face for a moment, I stood up and put two more slugs into the center of her chest. Her face went from shocked to blank in just a few seconds. The thought flashed through my mind that the world was instantly a better place.

I heard more gurgling sounds from Michael, who was clutching the hole in his stomach. He managed to get out a few words.

"Dean? Why?" And then something else that sounded like it might have been a request for an ambulance.

Well, I thought, it's important for one to have hope. But why does everybody ask 'why?' at the end?

I knelt beside him. "I came for Vince. You two fucks just have bad timing." I looked down at his belly, seeing the blood spreading under him, and shook my head. "That's gotta hurt. Tell you what, Michael, for old-time's sake. Because I knew you back before you were a pompous ass." His eyes opened wide, pleading, and he began to say something. I laid the pistol across his chest with the muzzle not more than an inch from the soft tissue under his chin, and fired. I saw a flap of skull and hair flip up as the bullet exited the top of his head. His eyes dilated and his face became an expressionless mask. Just like that, he became a memory. I heard some wood chips settle across the room where the bullet had landed in the floor molding. A piece of his skull, maybe three or four inches across and with thick, dark hair still attached, slid several feet across the floor and rested there, like some terrible, bloody spider.

I stood up just in time to avoid the blood spreading out from under both of them, merging into one puddle. I surveyed the mess all around the office and refocused on the task at hand.

The police would have plenty of bullets to dig out of bodies, so there was no point in bothering to collect my spent shell cases. They wouldn't need that to tell them what kind of gun had been used. I would dispose of the gun barrel later to prevent there ever being a ballistics match.

Open safe, that's good—looks like a robbery—what else? I crossed over to Vince and pulled the throw-rug aside enough to find his left arm and watch. A Bulgari—jackpot! I got that off him and dropped it into the backpack with the other booty. I went back to Michael and looked at his watch, nothing fancy, a Guess or some other designer. I started to move away but then had another idea. I took the watch off his wrist and dropped it a few feet away from his body. Maybe it would look like a thief had started to take it but then realized it wasn't valuable. Gloria wasn't wearing a watch or carrying a handbag. I didn't see any jewelry of note.

I shouldered the backpack at the top of the stairs and took a last look around the room. A bloodbath, but also a damn good day's work. Three pieces of shit with one stone. I silently apologized to Mrs. Gallo for the mess. I knew she'd be fine, and free now to find a better partner.

I set off down the stairs, the forty-five leading the way. I paused midway down to listen and heard nothing of concern. After breaking into the garage earlier, while the Gallos had been enjoying their dinner, I had pried open the gas tank door of the BMW that sat roughly below the center of the upstairs office. Kneeling down beside the car now, I located the cannon fuse and double-checked that one end was down inside the gas tank. After checking that the length of fuse wasn't doubled back on itself anywhere, I lit the far end with a disposable lighter. The fuse crackled away as it started to burn and I dropped the lighter onto the floor. I knew that the ten feet of fuse should give me close to five minutes. I set the bezel on my watch to time it. I walked carefully around the other car to the side door where I had broken in earlier, moving the rakes aside and slipping out to the narrow pathway. Closing the door behind me, I stepped around the remains of the two broken floodlights and started down the path towards the service alley. It was almost fully dark.

At the corner of the garage building where the side path met the alley, I paused to look around carefully. I saw nobody in the alley and no sign of people or traffic on Cutler Street. I took a moment to stow the automatic into my backpack, along with the latex gloves that I'd been wearing. I crossed the service alley, and went back the way I'd come earlier, passing along the side of the empty house and picking up the gym bag containing the pellet gun.

As the path along the house met the next street, I paused again to check for activity, waiting for a couple to pass, hand in hand. Stepping out to the sidewalk, I moved along casually but briskly, making it back to the Mercury within about two minutes. I paused and listened before starting the car and thought that I might have heard the muffled sound of an explosion.

Just before I put the car into gear I felt the phone vibrate in one of my cargo pockets. There was a message from Sophia in an informal code, indicating that the transfer had been completed successfully.

As I drove out of the neighborhood and along my planned route towards the interstate, I thought about how excited she must be. She probably just made a half-million dollars or more. A good day's work indeed.

I suddenly realized how hungry I was. I had missed dinner and was more than ready for the first drink of the day.

I reflected on the surprise of having Gloria and Michael show up. I would have been content with having those two live happily ever after, but the way it had all turned out had its advantages. No loose ends. Things were wrapped up quite neatly here, with just John to go now, up in New Jersey. I felt better this time than I had after Mark in Chicago. Some shaking came briefly and then faded as I drove. A slight nausea came over me also, but this time I was prepared. I popped the top on a ginger ale and sipped.

I drove north, possessed by thoughts of hot steaks and cold rocks glasses, but also thinking about justice done and payback delivered. I really did like it when accounts got settled.

Yeah, a damn good day's work.

59

After about twenty miles I stopped for gas, coffee, and communications. I sent Tommy a brief text indicating that all had gone well and that I was headed north. I would contact him within a few hours after I got further up the road and had secured dinner and a hotel for the night.

I found that I felt fine, apart from being dead tired.

It was almost ten before I, as David Somerset, checked into a hotel somewhere outside Chattanooga. It was late to eat much but I found a simple dinner at a mostly empty bar and grille near the hotel. After returning to my room, with a bottle of whiskey liberated from the trunk of the Mercury, I sat back to fire up the laptop and initiate a secure chat with Tommy.

D – Sorry for the delay. I wanted to get out of area ASAP. Outside Chattanooga now for the night.

T – Good. Everything go okay then?

D – Everything went well but not as planned. Major unexpected development. The other two showed up for a meeting while I was finishing up the main case. I had to go with the flow. We now do NOT have to worry about those two as loose ends.

T – Did they catch you off guard?

D – Just for a minute. He tried to scare me out by telling me they were coming over for a meeting. Said they usually met Thursdays but had been rescheduled to tonight. I hadn't known about any regular meeting but it all fits. I had a few seconds to get ready for them. Even with that, I was in and out pretty clean. Local police will now have a second case. Oh—he had a safe full of loot. Haven't counted yet. Maybe a hundred large or more.

T – Great—that will definitely make it look like a robbery. Good work. I'll keep on top of my source in the PD. Hopefully this will blow up in the press as a serial.

D – That would be good. Let's hope that Jersey doesn't freak. Also, got the needed info from him and techie said transfer successful, but I don't know details yet.

T – So you haven't looked at our drop box yet. She transferred just over 2 really large. He must have added more over the past few days. Rum and palm trees here we come!

D – Oh yeah—much better return than my 401K. Can you ask her to keep watch on anything of Jersey's that she can see? Money movements. Plane tickets charged, whatever. Might help us know how he reacts.

T – Will do. Also, you should get up there as soon as possible. If he still runs the bar on Fridays and Saturdays, can you be in place to watch by then? Maybe you can use the camera again.

D – Yes, I can be there to recon the perimeter by Friday after-noon. Let me know if techie sees anything. Going to sleep—exhausted. Long day.

T – The Seals say the only easy day was yesterday. You did well today double-oh. I know you must have a bottle of some-thing there. Have one on me.

D – Will do, thanks. Chat soon. Over and out.

60

Debbi Gallo and John Campbell had been on the phone for ten minutes. It was just after noon on Thursday, and Debbi had been up all night, with the police and fire crews back and forth and all over the property. She had done her best to fill him in on what she knew of the mayhem that had begun shortly after dinner the night before. She was still very shaken, and was completely exhausted.

"I can hardly believe it," she said. "It's like some sick dream. I thought it must have been some kind of accident, like with one of the cars catching fire for some reason. But then one of the firemen told me that someone had found something—bullet cases I think he said."

"Hmm, shell cases. That's not good," John said. "I can't help but think—with what happened to Mark just a few weeks ago, I wonder if there could be any connection. But, I don't know, that just seems so far-fetched."

"Well, I don't like it," she said, "but the fireman that talked to me told me something else. I got the feeling that he wasn't supposed to be saying anything but he was trying to help. He told me that he had heard something one of the detectives said after looking around last night. He said something like 'Well, it looks like we have another one'. So this fireman told me that's what he heard, and he thought that meant that this detective was thinking right off the bat that this was some kind of serial thing."

"That's interesting," John said. "Let me see if I can find out anything about that. I have some friends up here that might have connections in Atlanta. I'm sorry to put it this way, but that would be better than the alternative."

"You mean like, somebody after us?"

"Right, that's what I mean," he said. "I just don't see that though. It occurred to me for a minute after Mark, but that just doesn't add up. All the same, I plan to watch my back and keep an ear to the ground. You do the same, and I'll let you know if I can find out anything. Watch for emails and texts, in case I'm not able to call. Oh —what about the money? When was the last time you checked the bank?"

"A few days, I guess. I know Vince just moved some more there. I'll try to check tonight or tomorrow, after the circus around here dies down."

There was a long silence on the phone before Debbi spoke again.

"You know, I wanted him gone. I mean, I wanted to be free of him, but not like this, John. I didn't wish for anything like this."

"I know, Deb," he said. "I know you wouldn't even think like that. This is a terrible thing, but you'll be alright. Keep in touch over the weekend. I'll let you know whatever I find out about what the police are thinking. How are the girls doing?"

"They're stunned, of course, but they're tough. They were here earlier but there was nothing for them to do and we aren't close. They're with their mother now."

"Alright, well, try to get some sleep when you can," he said. "I'm glad you're okay."

Setting down the phone in Georgia, Debbi remembered the nightmare that Vince had told her about the week before. She remembered how much it had affected him. How much it had really scared him. Thinking about it now, a chill went through her body. After a moment she shook her head back and forth to get free of the image. Impossible, she thought to herself. There's just no way there could be anything there. But still, it gave her the creeps.

Campbell sat at his desk in New Jersey, thinking for several minutes, drumming his fingers on the leather pad. He had just lost his oldest and best friend. It was true that this BardLogic scam and then this entanglement with Debbi had affected the way he felt about Vince, but he still knew deep down that he had just lost a part of himself. Debbi would be fine. He needed to take care of himself. His thoughts turned to the two Tonys.

His friendship with Tony B. and Tony M. didn't go back as far as the one he had with Vince, but they still qualified as old friends from the neighborhood, and he trusted them. The two Tonys went way back themselves and were basically inseparable. Years before, to reduce confusion, John and other friends had taken to adding their last initial to their names, and the custom had stuck.

John dialed his phone and Tony Maranzano answered right away.

"Hey, Big J," Tony said. "What's up? You okay?"

"Yeah, Tone," John said. "I'm good, but I just got some bad news about a friend of mine down outside Atlanta. He was killed last night, looks like some kind of robbery. I just talked to his wife. I was hoping you could help me with something."

"Sure, John," Tony said. "What do you need? And I'm sorry about your friend. I hope the wife is alright."

John spent a few minutes filling Tony in on what little he knew about the events of the previous night. The fire, shell casings, and the comment that the detective supposedly had made.

"The thing is," he said, "and I'm just going to spit it out here, my friend and I had a little thing going on the side. Just a corporate thing, like some bills got paid and the money was misplaced, you know, that's all. No big deal. Obviously it's over now."

"There you go, that's the spirit," Tony said. "We're more alike than I thought. Hey, don't worry about it, Big J, you got your business and I've got mine. I'm not judging."

"Thanks," John said, "I really appreciate that. So, this all just happened last night, but what I've heard so far is that the locals are thinking it's part of some pattern—like maybe something like this happened before in the area. I just want to be really certain that it couldn't have anything to do with the other thing, the thing on the side. Seems to me the only people that would care about that anyway would be either the cops or my company. And neither would shoot people and burn down a building."

"Okay, I follow you so far," Tony said. "I think I probably have a friend who has a friend down there. I'll try to find out what the local cops are thinking."

"That would be great, Tony," John said. "Whatever you can find out would be a help. The second thing is related. Just because this whole thing makes me nervous, and probably there's nothing to be nervous about, do you think you have another friend who could hang out at the tavern for the nights I close down? Maybe sit outside somewhere for a few weeks? It's great when you and Tony hang out inside, but I wouldn't mind someone else outside for a little while."

"Yeah, I think I know someone," Tony said. "A guy I know, Angelo, good guy. He's laying low for a while and hasn't had much to do. He'll be good for that. I'll see if I can get him. We'll take care of you."

"Oh man, thanks, Tony," John said. "That means a lot. And I'll take care of you and Tony. And your friend Angelo. I'll take good care of you guys."

"We got you covered, John. I'll get back to you tomorrow with whatever I can find on the Atlanta thing."

61

After a long day's drive on Thursday capped by an overnight at a motel on Maryland's Eastern Shore, I made it to Paterson by mid-afternoon on Friday.

Though I was Jersey born and bred, I had never actually been to Paterson. It was in that eastern part of northern Jersey where one 'city' merged into the next, with spots of farmland and well-manicured neighborhoods in between. That part of New Jersey, along with parts of western Connecticut and Long Island, amounted essentially to a giant suburb of New York City.

I spent an hour driving around to familiarize myself with the area. I located the Campbell family's tavern without any trouble. It was on a corner of a largely retail block in a part of town where retail and corporate were just starting to give way to residential. There was a cleaners, a florist, a Chinese restaurant, and what looked like a thrift or consignment shop on the same block. It wasn't a run-down area but also didn't appear very upscale. There was an Italian restaurant across the street and down a few doors that looked like it would have a view of the front of the tavern and part of one side. There was a chain coffee shop a block off the main road that appeared to have a view of the small parking lot behind the tavern. I parked on the street and walked the area. I was pleasantly surprised to not find any sign of security cameras attached to the tavern or anywhere around the rear parking lot.

I decided that between a leisurely dinner at the Italian place and then sitting in the car, I could keep an eye on the joint for maybe two hours. Beyond that I would be in stakeout territory.

I was going to need to spend some time inside. I had met John Campbell on one occasion several years ago, and had spoken with him on the phone several times since then. Now I had a trim goatee, a suntan, and different hair. With a fake limp and some eyeglasses, I wasn't worried about being recognized, but it would nevertheless make sense to keep any contact with him to a minimum. With four of his accomplices dead in the past few weeks, he might very well be on high alert.

———

After getting settled into a hotel on the outskirts of town, I booted up the laptop and logged into the secure mailbox.

There was a message from Tommy with a summary of news coverage in Atlanta. It appeared that the second similar crime within a month had been enough for police agencies to go public and describe a related series of deadly home invasions. There were enough similarities that police were actively looking for the one group that was responsible. The most recent crime had occurred in a quiet neighborhood on Wednesday evening and had claimed the lives of three business people, including two from multi-national conglomerate BEQ. The news coverage asserted that valuables had been stolen, but details were unspecified.

There was more, but that was the gist of it. I hoped that news would make it to John Campbell quickly. The more I thought about it though, the more I thought that if I were him, I'd probably be watching my back, or at least feeling around back there to see if anyone had slapped a target on it.

There was a message from Sophia directed to both Tommy and me. She had been able to see that Campbell had moved almost two hundred thousand dollars into the Bahama bank account within the last twelve hours. I considered that for a while and I didn't like it. It might mean nothing at all. Vince Gallo had moved more money into his offshore account within the past week. Or, it might mean that John had sniffed the wind and was taking the first steps towards... what? Leaving the country? Of course I had no way of knowing, but this development was at least mildly alarming. On the other hand, it was nice of him to move more money to exactly where we hoped to steal it from. If we could come up with the right number and color.

More important than the money, I didn't want him to get away.

I texted Tommy to let him know that I was in Paterson. I told him I would be having drinks in the place later and would report soon.

62

T hat evening, I dined at the Italian place and took more time than I normally would have for dinner. I had been able to get a window seat with a good view of the Campbell tavern and wanted to make the most of it.

I observed people going in the bar's main street entrance. Some of them had found a parking spot on the street and some of them had appeared along the side of the building. I assumed that those people had either parked in the small lot behind the building or on some side street that was out of my view.

After dinner, I took a leisurely stroll around the block and up and down the street. During my walk, when the view allowed, I tried to keep an eye on who was parking in the area and who was going in or coming out of the tavern. As I came along the side street for the second time, I noticed a dark blue Cadillac parked against the building that hadn't been there before. I guessed that was Campbell's car and that he must have arrived to run the evening shift.

I killed a few hours back at the hotel, coming back to the tavern just before ten. The street was mostly empty at that time, though there were still several cars outside and a few people came and went through the front door.

I went in, exchanged hellos with a waitress walking by, and limped my way across the room to one of the closest stools. As I crossed the room, two beefy characters sitting together at the far end of the bar appeared to check me out closely. I gave them a friendly nod which one of them returned. It appeared that I wasn't interesting enough to hold their attention beyond the initial looks, and they went back to whatever they'd been talking about.

I was impressed with the bar's bourbon selection and ordered a double Blanton's on the rocks. As I savored the drink, I looked around casually to check the place out.

I sat at the end of the short segment of a standard L-shaped bar, which put me close to the center of the whole interior space. The two characters that had eyed me when I came in were almost to the far end of the long part of the bar. That put them roughly in the right rear corner of the building. If they were who I thought they were—Campbell's buddies—that would be a good spot for them to sit to check out whoever was coming in.

To my right, behind the bar and near the junction of the two segments, was a set of double doors that obviously led to the kitchen. The three waitresses came and went through them, including one who appeared to be doing double duty as the bartender.

To my left, just off the service bar, was the opening of a paneled hallway that I imagined must lead back to the restrooms and whatever storage or utility rooms might be back that way. Along the front of the building on either side of the entrance door and dotted around the main floor behind me, were round tables in various sizes. There was one pool table near the right front corner. Passers-by out on the street could look through the windows at the pool table and see the tavern as an inviting and comfortable neighborhood place.

As I nursed my drink and the one that followed it, I watched a few customers come and go. The waitresses picked up drinks at the service bar next to me and also gathered there to chat in their spare moments.

Halfway through my second drink, the kitchen doors to my right behind the bar swung open and a man came out. The combination of the shiny bald head and the dark goatee was hard to miss, and I immediately recognized John Campbell. He came over towards the service bar and gave me a quick nod and a hello before saying something to one of the waitresses. He then went past me again and down the long end of the bar, stopping there to talk with the two men for a few minutes. The three of them were clearly on very friendly terms and all laughed several times.

That clinches it, I thought to myself. *Those are his two buds from the neighborhood.* Mr. Barnes' file had noted that he thought they were mobbed up. I imagined that, if recent events had made Campbell nervous, he might have asked those guys to hang around the bar while he was there. Aside from that, nobody seemed to be overly on edge. I was sure they'd checked me out closely, but that could simply be their regular habit.

My thoughts were interrupted when I heard two of the waitresses talking to my left. I swirled the last of my drink and looked into my glass, feigning fascination with the amber liquid as I listened carefully to what they were saying. I dismissed most of their conversation as irrelevant but there was one interesting tidbit.

"Are you working Tuesday?"

"Not this week. I needed time off and John said he'd close for me."

"Really? I thought he didn't come in during the week."

"Yeah, usually just the weekend but he said his parents would be away and he was happy to do it. I mean, we close at ten, so it's not like some big deal…"

I motioned for my check and paid it. Getting up, I asked a waitress to point me towards the restrooms. As expected, she motioned down the hallway. "All the way down on the left," she said.

The hallway looked to be about thirty feet long and ended at a door clearly marked as an emergency exit.

On my left was a stretch of wall followed by a door marked 'Staff Only'—electrical or storage I guessed—then the two restrooms were after that. On the right was an unbroken expanse of wall, maybe twenty feet, on the other side of which I guessed had to be the kitchen. About ten feet short of the emergency door at the end of the hallway, the right wall opened up into a utility area with shelves holding what looked like bathroom, cleaning, and other supplies. A mop and bucket, a stack of extra chairs, and several large trash cans stood against the shelves.

That space appeared to be about ten feet square. Beyond it and towards the rear of the building, was a wall with a door marked 'Office'. It looked to me that this office probably occupied the left rear corner of the building. Though I couldn't see in, it made sense to me that the office would probably have a second door into the kitchen. If I had that right, then a person could travel in a rough circle, into the kitchen from the bar, through the kitchen and the office and out to the utility area; after that, past the restrooms and back down the hallway to the bar and dining room.

As I turned back towards the men's room across the hall, I was able to take a few seconds to inspect the emergency door. It had the standard push-bar, but there was no signage indicating that 'Alarm Will Sound', and there was no sign of any electronics.

Leaving the men's room and heading back down the hallway, I passed the ladies' room and the staff-only room again. From the end of the hallway, I gave a last friendly wave to the waitresses before limping across the main dining room to the exit. I was careful to not look across to John's two friends at the far end of the bar.

Before driving away, I took a pass through the rear parking lot. As I passed one dark sedan I caught the flicker of what looked like a cigarette lighter. Somebody was sitting in the driver's seat of that car. There had only been a handful of customers in the place when I'd left, and any customer who needed to smoke would certainly have done it while loitering around the front door. So the person in that car could be waiting to give someone else a ride home, or it could be that he was a third friend of John Campbell, helping the two guys inside to watch over him. Definitely something to keep in mind and to look for tomorrow night, I thought.

63

I didn't go into the tavern the next night.

I had an early dinner at the Italian restaurant, where the waiter that I had tipped so well the night before was happy to give me a window table. I watched the comings and goings across the street. I wasn't counting, but more just trying to get a general feel for the clientele and the level of activity.

After dinner, I moved to the coffee shop that afforded a view of the tavern's rear parking lot. From where I sat I could see the entire back wall of the building along with a triangular section of the rest of the parking lot. I nursed a latte and then another, pretending to do important work on my laptop.

It was six-thirty when a Buick sedan found a spot on the street along the side of the building. The two men I had seen the night before at the bar got out and went around to the main entrance in front. Ten minutes after that, the dark blue Cadillac pulled into the lot and parked nose-up to the rear wall of the building. John Campbell got out. He went right up to the rear door and banged on it. It was opened almost immediately by a figure in white kitchen clothes. Campbell went in and the door closed.

It was almost seven when the last guy showed up. I didn't know his face but the dark sedan—which I now realized was a Dodge Charger—registered as the one I had seen the night before. He pulled into the lot and parked in the middle row, facing the building. From where I sat in the coffee shop, I could only see the front half of the Charger and an occasional flash of movement from the driver.

There were now the two guys I had seen last night back inside the bar somewhere, along with John Campbell, and the third guy in the Charger. Presumably they would all be there until closing time, around one. The guy outside must have been able to go in now and then to use the facilities or to get a coffee, and I wanted to see how that worked. I wanted to see who went in and out of which door. I wanted to know who left last and what time that was.

I couldn't stay inside the coffee shop all night, but I had an alternate idea that I felt was worth a shot. The shop had a few tables just outside on the sidewalk, which were all unoccupied at the moment. The narrow seating area was cordoned off from the rest of the sidewalk by several wooden fence sections interspersed with long wooden planters full of a mixture of colorful flowers and ornamental grasses.

Before I left the shop, I went to the restroom. I took the little camera unit from my backpack and programmed it to take a picture every three seconds for a duration of eight hours. I set it to begin in ten minutes. On my way out I noted that everyone within potential sight of the outdoor seating area was occupied with laptops or books.

Outside on the sidewalk, I leaned against a section of fence while bracing myself on one of the flower boxes, as though adjusting my shoe or fixing my pant leg. Without too much trouble I was able to set the camera in amongst the plants. After a glance across the street towards the rear of the tavern, I did a last reach up to adjust the camera. With some luck, I hoped that I had positioned it properly to capture the tavern activity.

I drove back to the hotel and tried with mixed results to get a few hours of sleep.

64

I waited until two in morning to drive back over to the vicinity of the Campbell tavern. The building was closed up and dark and the area was mostly deserted. I had no trouble retrieving the camera from the flower box across the side street.

Back at the hotel, I wasted no time in downloading the image stream to my laptop and going through it carefully.

The camera had captured a view of the tavern and rear parking lot similar to what I had been able to see from the coffee shop. I couldn't see much of the Charger or its owner, but I could see the several times that he left the car to knock on the back door. In each case, based on the timing of the digital images, I could tell that the door was opened fairly quickly and he was admitted with no hesitation. In one case I could see enough of the person who opened the door to know that it was John Campbell himself.

Between ten and midnight, I saw an intermittent stream of staffers leaving through the back door. I gathered from who left when that the kitchen must have closed at ten. Four people who looked like kitchen crew left within forty minutes of that. I saw waitresses leave also, the last one at eleven-thirty. I concluded that Campbell was taking care of the few remaining customers himself at that point, with just his two buddies in the bar.

Not long after closing time, Campbell and his two friends left the bar via the back door. Campbell got in his car and drove away. The two other men walked over to near the front of the Charger, where they were joined by the driver of that car. The three men chatted for several minutes before getting into their respective cars and leaving. The man in the Charger drove away last. According to the camera's time display, that was all at about one-fifteen.

It was three in the morning in New Jersey and midnight in Seattle. Was it too late or early to contact Tommy? Tough shit if it was, he could take it.

I texted him. To my surprise, he responded promptly, suggesting that we start up the secure chat.

D – Glad to find you up. Working late?

T – At my desk, couldn't sleep. You know, visions of sugarplums. You're the one who's working late. What have you found out?

D – Watched the place last night and spent an hour inside. Actually said hello to him, so he is certainly there. And no, he didn't recognize me. Not with my brilliant disguise. Two shady looking friends hang out inside at the bar. They keep to themselves but looked to me like they were eyeing whoever came in. They fit the part. I didn't go in tonight but watched for a while from a coffee shop. Used your fancy camera after that. Just got done watching the movie.

T – Good. Glad you have it with you. Okay, so those are the two guys we read about in the file. We expected that.

D – Also, there's a third guy who waits outside in the rear parking lot. Sits in a car but goes inside every once in a while. Bathroom break I guess. I saw them all talking, so he's obviously part of it. Guessing he's probably extra help added in the past few days.

T – What about other staff? How busy is the area?

D – There is kitchen staff and looks like three waitresses. Kitchen left first, probably after they stopped food service. Then the waitresses drifted out over the two hours before closing. My guess is that it was just him and the two guys for maybe the last half hour before closing at one. Couldn't see the front door, so there could have been a few last customers too.

T – The neighborhood? What else is around?

D – Few restaurants, a coffee shop, not much else. Most everything would shut down much earlier than the bar. Street parking and a small rear lot behind. Residential is at least a few blocks away

T – Okay, sounds like a decent set up for a quick hit. We got another message from techie today—did you see it? He moved another hundred into Bahamas.

D – Shit! With that and now the third guy popping up, hard not to think he's planning a move. What do you think?

T – I don't like it and agree with your last. Feeling like my retirement plan is in jeopardy. It might all pass but I've got a bad feeling about it.

D – Almost forgot. When I was inside on Friday, I heard two waitresses talking. What I got was that he was going to be closing the bar this Tuesday. And I heard someone say they close at ten during the week. Maybe I should do something hard and fast.

T – Maybe, but wow, man. Four of them and at least three are probably armed. Might even know which end of a gun is the loud end. Tuesday though. You might be on to something. Let's sleep on this and reconvene in the morning. My brain is getting foggy. You've lulled me to sleep. Over and out.

It must have been almost four before I nodded off. About four hours after that I was awakened by the familiar sound of my phone receiving a text. It was from Tommy, telling me to check the secure mailbox.

I did so promptly and found a brief message from him.

"You're right. Hard and fast called for. Time for me to earn my check. I took time off so I can join you. Can't have you screwing this up by yourself. Pick me up tomorrow at Newark International. Will text a time and flight number later today."

Wow, I thought to myself, *Tommy flying in. That's serious stuff.* A team effort was in the works.

I texted him back.

"Message received. Will watch for further info later. See you tomorrow."

I had to laugh at the red hat.

I was pretty sure I recognized Tommy when he exited security the next afternoon at Newark International, but then I had known him all his life. As he got closer I could tell by the smile that it was him, but I was impressed with the effects of a few small changes.

He had the right build and height, but had longer and darker hair than I was expecting. He was moving a little differently also, not the loose athletic stride that I had been used to without knowing it. He moved as though wearing tight new shoes. As he came up to me, I realized that was exactly the case and they were brown wingtips. He had a few days growth of beard that looked like it had been darkened. The stranger started to pass but then stopped, turning to me.

"Got a match?"

"Just me and Gary Cooper," I replied.

"I brush my teeth with…?"

"Bombay Gin. Well, then, I guess that's you. Let's get out of here. I'm parked in short term. Good thing I have plenty of someone else's money. Oh, the car is silver now."

He nodded at that but didn't comment.

I relieved him of his garment bag, leaving him to carry his

casual backpack, and we walked to the car. Once in the car and driving out, he pulled off his hat and wig. He also pulled what looked like strips of plastic out of his mouth. I was unable to hide my curiosity.

"These are great. They fill out the shape of your face a little bit and also alter your voice slightly. More comfortable than you might think. It's the little things, you know."

He handed me a slip of paper with an address in Parsippany, about thirty miles away.

"Take me there first. I need to pick up a package from a work friend who owes me a favor. I've made a donation to his kid's college fund. It'll be a quick stop. After that you can show me the lay of the land in Paterson."

The stop at a house in Parsippany was as quick as Tommy had said it would be, and he loaded a small canvas bag into the trunk.

"It's polite of you to not ask," he said, "but I'll tell you anyway. It's a Heckler & Koch MP5 SD. We didn't have it yet when you were in. It's one of the Seal's main weapons for close-quarters assault. Thirty rounds of nine-millimeter and fully suppressed with a light amplifying 4-power scope. If I do my part, it should be balls-on accurate. Also a Beretta M9. You just can't carry guns on a plane like the old days. Before we leave the area we'll need to come back here and drop it all off again."

"Oh gee, Pops," I said, "can I play with the sub-gun?"

"Maybe another time," Tommy said, laughing. "We'll get you checked out on it for the next secret mission, I promise."

———

We made it into Paterson by late rush hour. I gave him a tour of the parts of town that I'd recently visited, focusing on the block with the Campbell tavern and the immediate vicinity.

Tommy checked into the hotel using his own alternate identity, and we met up in my room shortly after.

"I hear tell that you have a trunkful of good bourbon whiskey,"

Tommy said, looking around my room. "Who do I have to shoot to get a drink around here?"

I realized that it was cocktail hour, and needed no further prodding to switch into good host mode. I poured us each a stiff triple on the rocks and we took seats in the room's suite area.

"Our communications have been limited since Seattle, for obvious reasons," Tommy said. "But I'm here now. Take a few minutes and give me a blow-by-blow of what went down in Atlanta. All indications are that you did a fantastic job, but I want to hear it from you. Chicago also."

I was taken aback very briefly, but right away remembered that Tommy was a pro and this sort of thing was what he did. I had asked for his help and I had gotten him into this whole thing. I knew that it made sense to have an 'after action report'.

In about twenty minutes, I related to him the details of my assault on the Gallo garage office, and the demise of Vince Gallo along with his two associates. He asked pointed questions and I answered as accurately as possible. He nodded here and there throughout and I could tell that he was carefully digesting my story. He asked about my choice of weaponry and about the construction of the makeshift suppressor I had made for the pellet gun. He asked me how I had reacted to and processed the information that the other two people were about to arrive.

After talking about Atlanta, I backed up further and we went over the Chicago job. We spent another twenty minutes on that, with more questions and answers.

"My question right now is," Tommy said, "and I'm no Dr. Phil, but how do you feel? Are you ready for this last job?"

"I'm good, really, I'm good," I said. "I hated those people, especially Gallo. It felt good to send them to Hell. Like finally taking out a stinking bag of trash after letting it sit inside for too long. It bugged me to threaten Mrs. Gallo, but that was just part of the act, and it helped at the time. Yes, I'm all ready for Campbell."

"All right, good," Tommy said. "So you're still okay with this... this 'work' then. Nightmares lately?"

"A few," I said, "but nothing too bad and nothing recurring. It really hasn't bothered me very much."

"Fine then," Tommy said. "We can drop it, just so long as you remember that I've been through it myself and if you need to get drunk and blab about it, we can do that."

"Got ya," I said. "Thanks, and I mean it. I'm okay for now. If my evaluation is over, let's get some dinner and start talking about the job at hand."

―――――

The young lady at the front desk recommended a restaurant and gave us directions to a place a few blocks away from the hotel. It was one of those western-themed joints where, for some reason, it was normal and accepted practice to throw peanut shells all over the floor. The food was good and we were able to get a corner table with a degree of privacy.

Over dinner, we shared our impressions of the area and started to kick ideas around.

"Have you seen anything out here," Tommy asked, "that changes your mind about hitting him in the tavern?"

"No, not really," I said. "I've considered the office, his commute, home—all too complicated and too much room for collateral damage. I'm sure the tavern is the way to go."

"Yeah, I agree," Tommy said. "Just checking for new information. I think you've had it right all along. It's got to be the tavern at closing time. Too bad for those friends of his, but it looks like they're going to be in the wrong place at the wrong time when the lead starts flying."

"Right, yeah," I said, "that's too bad, but you know what? They're not our targets but those guys aren't innocent. They've made a choice to be on the field. Hey, I'd be thrilled if they walked out together and left Campbell alone, but that isn't going to happen. Those guys need to go. Let's not forget that they're likely criminal and, who knows, maybe even killers."

"Okay then," Tommy said, "that's settled. Closing time tomorrow night at the tavern. As soon as the customers are clear, we hit them hard and fast and blow outta there lickety split. We can spend a few minutes—ten maybe but no more—to try to make it look like a robbery and get the banking stuff out of Campbell."

"Right," I said, "as soon as the customers are clear and the block looks quiet. If there's too much going on inside or out, or if he's got other family members in there, we abort and re-assess."

We saw that the restaurant was closing down around us, so settled our check and reconvened the meeting back at the hotel. We picked up the conversation over fresh ice and whiskey.

"I don't know if we're going to get anywhere on the banking infor-mation this time," I said. "I mean, we'll give it a shot of course, but with Gallo in Atlanta, I was able to use the 'you can buy your way out of this' routine. This time, with John, if we get him alive and have time to talk to him, he'll probably know at that point that Vince was killed and he'll think we did it. Of course, he might blurt out information to try to save himself."

"Yeah, you're right," Tommy said. "What we've gotten so far might have to be enough. We'll try and see how it goes. I'll make sure Sophia's on alert just in case. Anyway, with luck and dry gunpowder, this will all be done by midnight tomorrow. Aside from the Heckler & Koch, I just have the M9 with me. It's got a laser but no suppressor. Do you still have that Walther P22?"

"Yeah." I said. "It's in the trunk. Haven't used it yet."

"Good," Tommy said. "Then I'll use that for my main piece tomorrow since it's small and quiet. The Beretta will be my backup. You keep your forty-five. Let's do what we can to keep the volume down."

I nodded my agreement with that.

"One thing," I said, "before I forget it. Since you're here now and we're going to work on this together, we should have a command structure. You okay with being in command?"

"That's fine," Tommy said. "Good idea to establish that. This is a small job but it's good to be clear. Don't hold back on your good instincts and your ideas."

We spent some time looking over my sketches and reviewing the footage from the little camera.

"So, it's Campbell and two friends inside," Tommy said. "And then…"

"Goons—let's agree to call those three guys goons," I said, interrupting. "Descriptive and also dehumanizing."

"Fine, I like it," Tommy said. He tapped one of my sketches. "So, it's Campbell and the two goons inside. You said they were camped out here at the long end of the bar when you were in there. Now we know we've got goon number three outside in the Charger. He's our first target. We pull up close and I'll use the MP5 to take him out."

"All right, good," I said. "I'll be driving. We'll pull in close to the rear door, and as long as the area is still quiet, you go in. Or do you think I should go in?"

"No," Tommy said. "You've been in once already and I don't want them seeing you again. I'll go in as an attorney who's been working late and needs a drink. I'll try to confirm as fast as possible that it's just him and the two bar goons. I'll see how it goes and if I have to, I'll bullshit my way into getting that drink. I have a few ideas in mind. As long as it's just them, we're on. I'll signal you at the right time and you'll come in the back door."

We covered more details of our plan until we noticed the lateness of the hour and how tired we both were. We agreed that, after a good night's sleep, we would check out of the hotel and find another place up over the border in New York State. Then, after a final plan review and weapons checks, it would be showtime at the Campbell Tavern.

66

Parked down the block from the tavern, we watched the front of the place for an hour and a half. It was a quiet night, there at the tavern and in the neighborhood as a whole.

By the time a group of four people came out at nine-thirty, we were reasonably confident that the place was free of customers. Part of our plan was to not harm any 'civilians'. We gave it another ten minutes before I started the car.

I drove up the street towards the bar ahead on the right and made the right turn just before it. Within half a block I slowed just opposite the rear parking lot, which had opened up to our left. We could see only four cars. There was Campbell's Cadillac, the Buick and the Charger belonging to the three goons, plus an old beater that had been there in the corner all weekend. I stopped the car, angled slightly, as though about to turn in. I leaned back in my seat as Tommy aimed the MP5 from the passenger seat beside me. Just as the guy in the Charger turned to look out his open window, probably wondering what we were doing, Tommy fired twice.

It looked to me like the first shot caused the guy to shake his head, as though feeling a raindrop or being bitten by a mosquito. The next shot, a second later, made him simply slouch back into the seat as if suddenly falling asleep. The shots had been almost silent.

Tommy set the gun down on the floor of the car and covered it with a dark towel as I pulled quickly into the lot, parking along the back wall of the tavern. I got out and went over to the charger to check the guy. He was as dead as it gets, with two neat holes just above his left ear. A little blood was starting to drip out and the man's eyes were closed. I gave his shoulder a quick shove to make him lie down across the seat.

I went back to the Mercury, meeting Tommy beside it. He was wearing a three-piece suit and carrying a brown leather folio bag. His tie had been carefully knotted and then pulled loose. The brown wingtips completed the picture of an attorney on his way home after a late night in the office. Not a high-powered corporate attorney, but more like one who spent his day handling divorces for regular working people. He was wearing wire-framed glasses that I knew to be of clear glass. He did a last check of the Walther and positioned it for a quick cross-draw from his left hip, tucked inside his belt. I knew that the much bigger Beretta M9 was in the leather bag.

"All right, it's on," he said. "I'll go in and start the play. I'll text you the signal when it's time. If it all goes south, or if I text you the abort signal, get out and meet right here. Let's set time."

We both reached to our watches and rotated the bezels to mark the minute hand. We could now count the minutes synchronously without any need for our watches to actually display the same time. My watch indicated that it was nine forty-six.

"And... set," I said. "I'll be ready. Let's do this. See you in a few."

Tommy disappeared around the corner towards the front of the building.

67

Rounding the corner onto the main street and approaching the door to the tavern, Tommy hit a few buttons on his phone to make sure the screen was fully illuminated. For the benefit of anybody inside who might be looking through the window out at the street, he held the phone up, pretending to make a call.

As he walked, he bent forward a bit and altered his stride, trying to look less like the toned and super-fit combat veteran that he was and more like the harried attorney, rushing always from one meeting to the next.

As he passed the windows and pretended to make a call, he stole several glances inside, glad to see that the place appeared empty. He pulled the door open and went in, leather bag under his left arm and appearing to concentrate on his phone.

Almost immediately a man called out to him from near dead ahead, behind what looked like the short end of an L-shaped bar, the long end of which extended against the back wall and off to the right.

"Sorry, man, I'm just closing up. I was just about to lock the door."

"Oh no," Tommy said. He held up his phone as if to show that he'd just made a call, "I just called for a car—be here in just a few minutes. One whiskey? Then I'll go."

Tommy held his hands with palms up in a comical plea. He knew that, based on Dean's description, the man that had spoken to him must be John Campbell. He had also noticed the two other men watching him from near the far end of the bar. He estimated that they were about twenty-five feet away.

"Take mercy on a thirsty traveler after a fifteen-hour day? The car should be here any minute. The driver will text me."

"Alright, buddy," Campbell said. "Because I'm very familiar with those fifteen-hour days. We have time for a quick one. What'll it be?"

"Thanks, I really appreciate it. I think I see a Blanton's bottle there, don't I? That'd be great, a few ice cubes."

He set the leather folio down on the first barstool and remained standing against the bar beside it. He laid a twenty on the bar to facilitate immediate payment. Campbell set the drink on the bar and made change.

Tommy raised his glass in a silent toast, took a deep drink, and then went back to making a show of fiddling with his phone. Campbell appeared to be checking or counting liquor bottles just a few feet to Tommy's right, halfway towards the kitchen doors. Tommy monitored the motion out of the corner of his eye.

Just then, one of the other men came away from his seat at the bar behind Tommy, crossed the room and rounded the end of the bar to say something to Campbell. They talked briefly before the man started to move back past Tommy as though to return to his seat and the other guy at the far end of the bar.

Several things happened within the next twenty seconds.

Campbell went through the doors off to the right and into the kitchen.

Tommy pressed the button on his phone to send the prepared one-word message to Dean, waiting outside the rear kitchen door.

Campbell's friend, perhaps remembering something, turned around and walked quickly back past the service bar and Tommy again, following Campbell into the kitchen.

Campbell came out of the kitchen and back towards Tommy and the service bar, stopping to do something at the cash register.

A series of loud crashes erupted from deep inside the kitchen, accompanied by a yell, and several loud popping sounds.

Campbell looked up sharply and started for the kitchen door, but then stopped to look across at the second man at the far end of the bar. That guy had jumped off his stool and was walking fast across towards the service bar, clearly intending to see what was going on inside the kitchen. He was starting to reach for something inside his jacket.

As the guy rounded the corner of the bar to get behind it, Tommy raised the Walther and fired into his chest six times fast, from two or three feet away. The guy fell to the floor.

There was another crash from the kitchen as Tommy turned towards Campbell, who just then managed to un-freeze himself from his position near the cash register, and run out from behind the bar, stumbling over the body of his friend. He was clearly in a state of shock as he staggered several feet out onto the main floor of the restaurant. He looked at Tommy and at the gun in his hand, horror filling his face.

Tommy shot him in the right thigh, careful to aim off-center to avoid hitting the femoral artery. As Campbell started to wail and grab at his upper leg, Tommy stepped forward and whacked him on the head above the right ear, knocking him out cold. Campbell collapsed to the ground, flat out on his back.

Tommy did a fast scan of the room, and then quickly took the few steps back to the end of the bar, stopping briefly to grab the Beretta from the leather bag on the bar stool. He hopped over the guy he'd already shot and ran to the kitchen door. With the Walther in his left hand and the Beretta in his right, he pushed the door open and went in.

Inside the brightly lit kitchen now, Tommy saw the door to the rear parking lot, closed tight, off to his right. Between where he stood and that door was a pile of pots and pans where a shelving unit had been knocked over, and a body. Stepping closer, he was relieved to see that the body was not Dean but was Campbell's second friend from inside. He had a bullet hole in his face that looked like it must have come from Dean's forty-five.

He spun, crouching low, as he heard a sound from the other side of the kitchen. He looked across and saw an open door. He thought fast, remembering Dean's sketch. That must be the office that would be on the far end of the building. Campbell was lying on the floor out there, out cold. The three goons were all dead as doornails. Should just be him and Dean at this point. They needed to be careful to not shoot each other. Unless—could there have been anyone else inside that they hadn't known about?

He took a moment to shove the Walther into his waistband, allowing him to take a two-handed grip on the Beretta. He pressed the button to test the laser sight, tracing the glowing red spot across the wall, and found it to be working as expected. He crossed the kitchen quickly but quietly, moving towards the open office door.

68

After Tommy rounded the corner of the building towards the front entrance, I pulled on a pair of latex gloves and waited outside the rear door, my body flat against the building.

The next six minutes seemed like six hours, but I finally got his text.

"Go."

I took a quick look around and saw nobody in the area. With my knuckles, I knocked firmly on the tavern's rear door, then stood to one side, the silenced forty-five up and ready.

The door opened halfway and light spilled out. I saw immediately that it wasn't John Campbell who had opened the door, but one of the two goons. He looked at me in surprise and reached towards what must have been a holster on his right hip, trying to sweep his sport coat aside in the process. I fired through the open doorway, hitting him in the abdomen. He stumbled back into the kitchen and I followed, stepping through the door. He managed to get out a yell before my second shot went through his left eye, instantly short circuiting his brain. He crashed into some stainless steel shelving and fell to the floor in a horrendous clatter of pots and pans. I walked up to him and put two more bullets into his chest.

I cursed to myself through gritted teeth. *That was a lot of noise!* I stepped back and pulled the rear door closed as I scanned the kitchen space, trying to relate it to what I had seen of the rest of the place a few nights before.

Across and to the left were the swinging double doors that would open out to behind the bar. From that direction I heard a yell and a crash and what sounded like a series of soft pops. I hoped that was the sound of Tommy doing his job with the Walther. *Who else was still out there?*

I sensed movement behind me and spun around to face the other side of the kitchen. I didn't see anyone there and I considered that it might have been nothing. I saw that there was a door to some other room and I ran to it, entering a small office. I realized that I was in the office I had noted the other night during my exploratory trip to the restroom. I heard another crash somewhere out in the dining room and decided that I'd better circle around down the hallway to help Tommy.

Leaving the office, I went through the utility area and started down the hallway. I made my way slowly along past the restrooms until the hallway opened up to the end of the bar and the dining room. I saw a pair of legs sticking out from just past the end of the bar and started towards them. I was glad to see that the feet weren't wearing brown wingtips.

The left side of the wall ended first, opening up to where the service bar was. I heard a sound and looked that way. *The other goon— shit*—I had dropped my guard! What was he doing there and where was Tommy? What happened next seemed to play out in slow motion, though really took no more than two or three seconds.

I turned towards him, trying to line up my gun, seeing that his was already lined up on me. It was something I knew well at the slightest glance—a government model forty-five automatic, and the hole in the end of it looked like the entrance to a huge dark cave. The realization that I was probably a dead man flashed through my mind.

My brain knew I didn't have time to bring my gun up enough, but my body still tried. As my arm rose, I fired into the floor, going for a ricochet up into his legs, or at least hoping to startle him.

I fired and then he fired.

My bullet didn't appear to hit him, but must have been sufficient to throw his aim off just enough that his bullet missed me by inches, tearing into the wood paneling behind me.

I fired again, still low, and grazed one of his legs. He screamed and grabbed at the wound with his left hand, involuntarily lowering his right gun hand at the same time. It was then that I saw a glowing red dot trace across the right side of his face. I heard a boom off to my left and saw most of his nose come off in a burst of red mist. Another boom caused his head to shake a few times and then he fell to the ground in a loose heap, like the skeleton had been yanked out of him.

I heard Tommy yell something and then appear to my left. I realized that he must have followed my own route through the kitchen, office, and then down the hallway to where we both now stood near the service bar.

"You okay?" Tommy asked. He looked me up and down quickly.

"Yeah, okay," I said. "I really thought he had me there for a second, but I guess my number wasn't up. And thanks, by the way. Good to see you."

Tommy stepped over the dead guy, looking down at him intently.

"I've killed this guy twice now, what gives?"

He knelt down and pulled at the man's shirt.

"Well, how 'bout that, guy's wearing a vest. Who wouldda thunk it? Here, let me borrow that a sec."

He gestured to my gun, which I handed to him. He checked the safety and then put a bullet point blank into the guy's face, making a neat hole through the bridge of his nose and causing his head to bounce once against the floor. He clicked the safety on and handed the gun back to me.

"That settles that."

Tommy checked his watch which moved me to check my own. We looked at each other and nodded together. He spoke first as I loaded a fresh magazine into the forty-five.

"It's been ten, maybe eleven minutes, and we've made a lot of noise. We can't spend much more time here. Like a few minutes at most."

He turned and pointed to Campbell, still flat out on the floor a few feet away.

"The three goons are down, so now let's get Campbell into the kitchen. Know what—I'll do that, you turn out the sign and make sure the door is locked." He waved me off towards the front door as he moved to Campbell.

I went first to the entrance door, found there to be a large deadbolt, and turned the knob to lock it tight. I wasted no time looking for the switch for the neon "OPEN" sign, opting to just trace the cord and yank it out of the wall instead. I also found a bank of switches by the door which I used to turn off the outside lights and most of the lights in the main dining area. I took a minute to look carefully out several of the windows and saw nothing going on outside.

I got back to the kitchen in time to see Tommy throwing water in Campbell's face.

69

The cold water snapped Campbell awake. He looked around as he came to his senses, gradually getting clear. Tommy had managed to prop him up into a seated position against some shelving, and his hands were now secured in front of him with a large plastic tie. At a certain point he must have remembered that he'd been shot. He moved his leg and winced in pain.

"It's only a twenty-two," Tommy said. "Don't worry about it too much, though you'll need to get that treated soon."

"You guys are so screwed, you have no idea…"

"Your three friends are dead," Tommy said. He gestured to the body on the floor across the room. "If that's what you mean."

Campbell dropped his head into his hands and seemed to shake all over.

"Oh shit. You can't do that. Those people were connected. You just can't do that."

"Well," I said, "they'll have to make some new connections on the other side of the pearly gates. On the bright side, you didn't kill them. And we all need to make new friends now and then."

"I know who you are—you guys killed Vince, didn't you. You killed all three of them."

"Yes, that's true," Tommy said. "But we didn't mean for it to turn out that way. We only meant to rob him but then those other two showed up. It was bad timing. What you need to ask yourself now is, are you going to have bad timing also. Are you going to have bad timing?"

"Come on now, there's no way you guys are going to let me go. You aren't even wearing masks. I'm no idiot."

Tommy made a show of looking at his watch.

"Look, we've already been here too long. Yes, you've seen our faces, but we also know all about you, your career at BEQ and all your friends there. We know where you live and all about your family. That's our insurance policy. At this point, why not give it a shot? All we want is the money in the Bahamian account. You and your family can keep everything else. What do you say? What do you have to lose?"

Campbell's face totally changed when Tommy mentioned the Bahamian account. Now it brightened some. I wondered if he was feeling hope.

"How did you know about that account? Who are you guys?"

I thought Tommy was doing a fine job so I let him keep talking.

"Oh, you mean the money that you and Vince embezzled from BEQ? Don't worry about that, let's just say we have some interested friends. They'll get a cut. Right about now, we figure you have a little over a million stashed there. We'll sell you your life for an even million and we'll go far away. How about if we do that and then don't bother each other again. That's kind of fair, right? How about it? Tick-tock, tick-tock."

"We need an eight-digit number and a color," I added.

Campbell had his head in his hands again.

"Fuck you guys. Won't make a difference if you get the money or not."

I motioned to Tommy and pointed at my watch. He frowned but nodded. Last ditch effort.

"Okay, John, time's up. We gotta go."

He made a show of putting a new magazine into the Walther and pulling back the slide to chamber the first round.

Campbell put his head down and started to say what sounded to me like a quiet prayer. I gave Tommy a 'this isn't going to work look' and he nodded.

With two squeezes of the trigger, I sent John Campbell into the arms of his ancestors. Remembering the earlier resurrection of his friend out in the bar, I put two more rounds into him as he fell. He died instantly and silently.

"Well," I said, "I guess that's the million that got away."

"You can't win them all," Tommy added. "Let's take five minutes to look around and then we've gotta make like horseshit and hit the trail. Five minutes max."

"Got it," I said. I was already kneeling to check Campbell's pockets, where I found no wallet. I stood up and motioned across the kitchen to the office.

"Nothing here, maybe it's in the office. Let's take a look."

Tommy followed me into the office. I went right to the desk while he went to a large corkboard on the opposite wall. I found Campbell's wallet in the top center drawer of the desk. It had nothing of interest other than several hundred-dollar bills, which I pocketed. No slips of paper with anything like an eight-digit number and a color. A very quick rifle through the other drawers yielded nothing. Nothing anyway that showed itself to be of use in the insufficient time we had to look around. There was a set of Cadillac keys and an iPhone that I guessed must be Campbell's. On a whim, I picked it up and browsed quickly through recent calls and texts.

"Hey, that's interesting," I said. "He's got Debbi Gallo programmed as a contact and they've had recent calls. And texts back and forth. What do you think of that?"

"I think that's very interesting. Do this—forward that text chain to your burner phone, then take out the SIM chip and the battery. We'll destroy the chip and dump the phone later on down the road. Now help me look for this damn number."

I joined Tommy to look at the corkboard, which was covered with pinned notes of various sizes, business cards, and a forest of curling sticky notes. I was briefly excited by the thought of a sticky note in a unique color with a number on it, but it looked like they were all the standard yellow and none appeared to have an eight-digit number.

There were a few photos pinned to the board, including one on the top right corner that showed some beautiful old car. A rare classic from a ritzy car show probably, something Campbell must have lusted after. I reached past Tommy for a picture of two blonde teenagers in ski gear. I remembered from Campbell's file that he had two daughters. Looking at the back I saw that there was a handwritten note.

"Amber and Sienna at Killington, Dec. 2012. Wonderful," I said. "Two daughters named after two colors. Shit. We're running out of time."

I stepped past him to look over a set of shelves on the other wall, not finding anything there.

"Man, what a car," Tommy said. "A Duesenberg I think. Beautiful."

I saw that Tommy had taken the car picture down and was admiring it. He turned it over to look at the back.

"Yo, bro—I think this might be it!" he said, motioning me over. "Look at the back, some kind of grid. A code maybe."

He held out the picture with the back to me. A large part of the space was covered by numbers in a neat square pattern. I quickly counted eight across and eight down, all single digits and with no zeros.

"That must be it," I said. "Sixty-four single-digit numbers. It could be the top row, or the top row backwards, or the fourth row down—something like that. Or one of the diagonals. If it's something that simple, I see thirty-six possibilities. If it's fancier than that, and needs some kind of key, then who knows."

"I'll send it to Sophia," Tommy said. He set the picture on the desk and started to frame a close-up with his phone camera. "She'll either figure it out or she won't."

While he texted to Sophia, I turned over the picture and looked at the car again.

"The car is red. Could it be that simple? A red car and the number on the back? We couldn't be so lucky."

"Well, we may or not be that," Tommy said, "but we are out of time. I don't see anything else jumping out at me as the color. Aside from Amber and Sienna in ski suits. And a red car."

We looked at each other, sharing our resignation. Tommy folded the car picture and put it into a pocket.

"You're wearing gloves, I'm not," Tommy said, gesturing to my hands. "I smeared the prints on the front door, so that's good. I'll go out to the bar and do my drink glass and grab my bag. I'll get the cash from the register too. You do the door knobs around here and the kitchen doors and meet me at the back in sixty. We can call Sophia from the car and brainstorm on the color."

70

O ur exit from the neighborhood was uneventful. After a few miles, we pulled off the main road onto what looked like some forgotten dirt lane. There, we did a quick check of ourselves and the car, moving most of the firearms to the hidden compartment in the trunk. The borrowed Heckler & Koch and the Beretta were back in their own bag, which was too big to go into the compartment. We would be rid of those items within the half hour once we returned them to Tommy's friend.

Tommy took off the suit jacket and the vest he'd been wearing and pulled a lightweight jacket on over his shirt. I swapped the hoodie I'd been wearing for a fresh one from a bag in the trunk. The clothes with potential blood spatter, along with my discarded gloves, went into a trash bag to be dealt with later.

After another ten minutes Tommy got a text from Sophia.

"Got the number, was the bottom right corner straight across backwards. Now just need a color. Have three tries only for that."

Tommy sent her a reply, telling her that we were working on the color and asking her to stand by.

"Alright," Tommy said. "We need to think of this damn color. What we have to go on so far looks like amber, sienna, or red."

"Yeah, agreed," I said. "But also, his car was dark blue and I noticed that the walls of his office were light blue, so there's blue as a possibility. I don't know if you noticed the sign on the front, but the name of the bar was actually 'The Red Pony'. Red Pony, red car in the picture, so maybe it's red."

We rode in silence for a few minutes as I took an exit and started down a different road.

"I just can't imagine," Tommy said, "that someone would have a secret bank account with a million dollars in it and use something like blue or red. Seems to me it should be something fancier, like mauve or fuchsia."

"That's funny," I said, "Gallo's color was purple. It's got to be something that he'd never forget, which makes the argument for something simple, like blue or red. I'm not vibing blue, because it just seems too dumb for someone to use what's obviously their favorite color. Guy buys himself a new Cadillac, that blue is probably his favorite color."

"What about purple for him too then?" Tommy asked. "Maybe these guys could be 'The Purple Gang' or something like that. Blue Cadillac, blue office walls, and the name of the joint is The Red Pony. Blue plus red equals purple. What do you think?"

"You know, that's not a crazy idea," I said. "Maybe that's what we need to think of—some function of this and that. I wish I knew what color you get if you mix amber and sienna."

"I don't know," Tommy said, "something really earthy and weird. Look, we get three tries. I get your point about blue being obvious, but I think it's worth one of our tries."

"Sure," I said. "What the hell. Have Sophia try blue."

Tommy texted to Sophia, who took less than a minute to respond. I could tell from his expression as he read that her response was negative.

"No, blue doesn't do it. Shit!"

"I didn't know the guy well enough to make guesses at how he would think," I said, "but I'm just thinking that if I were going to need some sort of secret word for whatever reason, it would be nice to have some kind of visual cue nearby. Something I see all the time. That's what keeps bringing me back to that picture of his daughters, Amber and Sienna. But which one? They're both warm earth tones. They're both famous actresses—Amber Heard and Sienna Miller. One is five letters and the other six. It's interesting that both the first and last name for each of them has the same number of letters—five for Amber and six for Sienna."

"Sure would be nice," Tommy said, "if we knew that the two of them were working together on a remake of 'A Clockwork Orange', or maybe 'Blue Velvet', but I doubt it."

"Yeah," I said, "I doubt it too. I think that's going off on a tangent anyway. We could go back and forth about colors all night. Honestly, my best guess is to try the daughters. Try Amber and then try Sienna. You cool with that?"

"Yes, let's do that," Tommy said. "I don't have any better ideas, unless you want to try red for this red car."

I looked over and saw that he was looking at the picture of the classic car again, and wasn't sure if he was kidding or not. He texted Sophia and again she replied within about a minute.

"Nope," he said, shaking his head. "She says it isn't Amber. One more try."

I realized that we were both hesitating to pull the trigger on the third and last color guess. I looked over and saw that Tommy was still lost in the photo.

"I was just thinking," he said, "how much this reminds me in a way of my first car. Do you remember that? That old Buick that my uncle handed down to me?"

"The Riviera?" I said. "What are you talking about? That beautiful old Duesenberg reminds you of a Buick Riviera? You've finally inhaled too much gunpowder."

"I know, right?" Tommy said, still admiring the car in the picture with a pocket flashlight. "I always loved sixties muscle cars, but never knew much about cars older than that. It's just the rear end of this thing that reminds me of the Riviera. Remember mine? In seventy-one they added that big bulge on the rear that came back to a point. You know—like the sixty-three Corvette split-window coupe. Almost like a boat."

"T," I said, "am I hearing you right? Seventies Riviera, sixty-three Corvette, and a boat?"

"Yeah, you got it," he said. "Anyway, I'll tell Sophia to try sienna."

"No!" I yelled, "Don't send that!" I checked my mirror and then braked hard to turn onto a side street and stop by the curb. We were just entering Parsippany, where we needed to drop off the bag of special armaments.

"Let me see that picture," I said. I snatched it out of his hand. I grabbed the flashlight from him also and examined the picture closely. Looking at the car carefully for the first time, I recognized it immediately. I had first seen one at an antique car show at the Jersey Shore. My father had pointed it out and explained what it was. It was amazing and beautiful. With the rear bodywork extending back and coming to a graceful point over the rear bumper, there was nothing else quite like it.

"T—this is no Duesenberg," I said. "The car in this picture was made in thirty-five or thirty-six and was called a Boattail Speedster. The company that made it went belly up a few years later. The cars were too fancy to sell during the depression."

"Oh, okay," Tommy said. "The suspense is killing me then. If it isn't a Duesenberg, what is it?"

"It's an Auburn. This car is an Auburn Boattail Speedster. Send that to Sophia. A-u-b-u-r-n."

71

I t was just after midnight by the time we got to our little motor lodge over the state line in New York, and we were tired. With the correct number and color in hand, Sophia had been able to transfer almost one-and-a-quarter million dollars out of John Campbell's Bahamian bank account. Tommy thanked her profusely from the car and asked her to summarize a final accounting and post it to our secure mailbox.

He made another call and asked one of his resourceful and confidential friends to pass on any information they could find over the next few days regarding recent violent crime in Paterson, New Jersey.

I sent a brief message to Elzey, telling him that the job had been completed. He replied that he would pass on the good news to Mr. Phillips, and that we could talk soon about money matters.

Before going to our separate rooms for some well-deserved sleep, we poured stiff bourbon nightcaps into plastic cups and sat up talking. While we still needed to collect our 'reward', and we still needed to split up all the incidental loot, our main objectives had been fulfilled. We agreed that the mission had been a resounding success.

"Oh hey," Tommy said, "you forwarded those messages from Campbell's phone, right? What do they say?"

"Ah—I almost forgot," I said. I dug out my phone and started going through it. "I have the main text chain, but I also noticed that they had a long call last Thursday morning, like twenty minutes."

"Ok, that makes sense," Tommy said, "probably the shocked widow crying on his shoulder—something like that. What do the texts say?"

"Oh this is nice, I can see the whole conversation." I scrolled through, reading the message exchange in chronological order.

"Interesting," I said. "Saturday through Monday—yesterday—he asks several times if she has 'checked the money'. Each time she answers that the bank website is down and she'll keep trying."

"So if they're talking about the Bahamas bank," Tommy said, "Mrs. Gallo isn't as innocent as we thought. It sounds like she not only knows about the money but has access to it. Wow—okay."

"Holy shit, T," I said. "The last text from her was just after eight tonight. If his phone was on the desk in his office, I'm guessing he never saw this. He must not have, because he would've freaked. Here —I'll read it to you."

"John—finally got in to our account and it's all gone. Over 2 million. Someone transferred it out just before the fire. Must have gotten it out of him somehow, then killed them all. I'm terrified that they were right over there next door when I was in the house. Got to be connected to Mark, but who? You better watch your back. Go hide somewhere. I'm going to a friend's place and then flying back to family in Seoul tomorrow. I have enough to start a small business there. It's been good. Be careful. I'll check with you if I'm ever back in the country. So sorry I got you both into this. Bye."

We looked at each other with stunned faces.

"That's it," I said. "And no reply from Campbell. She sent this and next thing you know we're in there shooting the place up. Sounds like it was her who started the whole thing—I didn't see that one coming. Debbi Gallo was the dragon lady after all. Does this mean we need to go after her?"

"I don't think so," Tommy said. "Seems to me like she's terrified and getting far away fast. All the way to Korea, it sounds like."

"Yeah, you're right," I said. "She may have somehow cooked the whole thing up, but she didn't work for either company. She's probably grabbing whatever money she can and bugging out for good. She's thinking she was spared for one reason or other but she's not pushing her luck."

"Good then, agreed," Tommy said. "Let's not worry about her anymore and we have a mission accomplished."

We tapped our plastic cups together.

"You have a few days, right?" I asked. "You know your deck is tops with me, but I think I know where we could find another set of Adirondack chairs not far from here."

"Will there be good food and can we have too much to drink?"

"I wouldn't have it any other way," I answered. "What do you think I am, a barbarian?"

72

When I contacted Kate early the next morning, I learned that she was with her husband in France and would not be able to join us on Block Island, though she would be thrilled to arrange lodging and have someone meet us at the ferry. We spoke only briefly and in general terms about completion of "the mission" and she thanked Tommy and me profusely for stepping in and helping her family. I was relieved during our call to not have the sense that we were tap-dancing around the ugly truth of all that Tommy and I had really done. It seemed to me that Kate did a superb job of conveying her family's thanks without any trace of regret or judgement hanging from her words.

Speaking with Tommy after the call, we agreed that it was good that we wouldn't all be getting together immediately. We both thought it would be helpful to put some time and distance between the actions of the past few weeks and our next reunion with Kate.

It was a mild day in the middle of June and the ferry ride over was a calm one. Tommy and I got cups of coffee at the snack bar and stood outside, enjoying the sun and the sea air as the island approached. We walked off the boat as soon as it docked, having left the Mercury in a secure parking lot on the mainland. I spotted what looked like the

Phillip's family Range Rover parked in the waiting area with a man beside it who appeared to be waving to us. As we approached, I realized that it was Damien, the bartender I had met during my last visit.

We shook hands and I introduced him to Tommy. He explained that he had taken a job with the Phillips family as the caretaker of their island properties. He maintained the houses, ran errands, and picked up friends at the ferry. We put our bags into the Range Rover and piled in. Damien drove us out of the ferry parking area and made the left onto Water Street.

"It's after noon," he said, "how does lunch on the Spring House porch sound?"

We both agreed to that idea and within three minutes we were parked beside the huge old hotel. As we walked through the parking area to the porch, Damien pointed out a Jeep Wrangler parked near the building. He held out his hand and gave me a set of keys.

"That's yours for as long as you're here. Also, the other key there is to the house, which is all ready for you. Do you know how long you'll be staying?"

Tommy and I looked at each other. We had already concluded that we could spend a well-earned few days on the island, but he would need to get back to a normal work schedule by the next week.

"Probably just the long weekend for me," Tommy said. "Dean can stay longer if he wants, but I need to get back to Seattle soon."

The staff had just finished setting up for lunch and we were able to get a table that was near the end of the long porch and had a great view of the sweeping lawn in front of the hotel and the ocean off to the right. We ordered lunch and sat talking over cold draught beers from the outdoor porch bar.

"It's good to see you again, Dean," Damien said. "Great that you could make it back. And what a small world. I hear you and Kate are old friends. I mean, the three of you, I guess. That's really cool. And you guys are both navy, right? Or were."

"Ancient history for me," I said, and then pointed to Tommy, "but this guy's a lifer."

"Well, you must eat lots of spinach," Damien said, "because you both look like you got out of Airborne school yesterday. Keep doing whatever you're doing."

Tommy and I shook our heads and laughed.

"Oh no, we're just a couple of old farts," Tommy said. "But thanks anyway."

Damien gave us directions to the house, along with several messages. Kate and her aunt Martha both sent their regrets but urged us to stay as long as we liked. They looked forward to seeing us another time. The second message was from Elzey, telling us that he would like to fly over tomorrow and have lunch with us. Damien had the good taste to not ask any questions.

As we were wrapping up lunch and paying the bill, Damien announced that he needed to go take care of some things but hoped that we could get together again for lunch or dinner in the next few days. After we exchanged phone numbers, he went off to the Range Rover and drove away.

Tommy and I got fresh pints of beer from the porch bar and went out onto the lawn, where we were able to claim two of the white Adirondack chairs that stretched in a long row across the grass. Nobody else was within earshot.

"Not bad. Not bad at all," Tommy said as we sat down. "I can see why you've always liked this place so much."

We were facing roughly east. The lawn curved down the hill to the road, and beyond that was a strip of marshy land and then the vast blue expanse of the Atlantic. If we could have seen for thousands of miles, we would have been looking at the west coast of Ireland.

We sat quietly for several minutes, just enjoying the air and the view. The push and pull of the warm sun and the cool sea air was both restful and invigorating.

"We haven't worked together in a long time," Tommy said. "It was good. I'd do it again."

"Yeah, I agree," I said. "It was good. I would do it again too."

"You know it's funny," Tommy said, "but this all reminds me of something. A year ago, maybe a year and a half, a couple of my higher-ups started talking about putting together some kind of special unit. I don't think the idea actually got off the ground, but I don't think it entirely died off either. They asked a few of us older guys what we thought of getting a few civilians to buy in. Like people with special skills."

"You mean like some kind of vigilante group?"

"Not vigilante really," he said. "More like for cases they want to stay off the record. Shit that needs to go away quietly. Not unlike what we just did, really, if you think about it. God knows there sure is a lot of terrible in the world. It makes my brain hurt just to think about how much there is that's just so wrong."

"You're right about that, T; there certainly is a lot of terrible evil out there. Wrongs just begging to be righted. I mean, think about it—you've got Crocs, man buns, cable companies. It's endless, man."

We laughed like two kids and clinked our glasses together.

"Anyway," Tommy said, "that's just something that had come up. I'll ask around and let you know if there's anything there."

"Sure, do that," I said. "No harm in getting information. You know what—just a thought—if there ever was anything to that, that guy we just met, or you just met, Damien. I can't say I know him really well, but I've been impressed with what I've seen so far. He's pretty solid. A veteran, a gun guy, seems to be open to flex work. I guess it's possible he could be overly burdened with morals though. Don't know if he's ever had to, you know. Well, anyway, just thinking out loud."

"Not a crazy idea," Tommy said. "Let's keep that in mind. Like a wise person said to me a minute ago, no harm in getting information."

We laughed again and sat in silence for a few minutes.

"What about that retirement anyway?" I asked. "Aren't you still thinking of a little beach house with a palm tree in the back yard and a shitload of rum?"

"Oh yeah, definitely," Tommy said. "I'm going to take this opportunity and do that. I'm thinking maybe St. Croix. You should too. We could get neighboring villas. I just figure I'll probably get bored after a while. I'll probably miss the adrenaline and the gun smoke. We'll see. So how about you? Are you going to drive back out west and switch cars? I'll buy you dinner at the Space Needle."

"Yes," I said, "I'll come out and give you the Mercury and become myself again. I've enjoyed driving it but it'll be good to get back into my car. On the way home after that, I think I've got some business to take care of in St. Louis. There's a... there's a book I picked up and looked at when I was headed towards Chicago. I'd like to read the first few chapters and see if the story takes off."

"A book, interesting," Tommy said. "Is this an adventure story?"

"I think so, though a little less adventurous than the past month would be cool with me."

"Does this book have a romantic twist to it?"

"I think it might, I hope so."

"Well then, after you read it, you'll have to give me a review."

"I will do that, T. I will do that."

We sat for a while, gazing at the fantastic hues of green lawn, blue sky, and darker-blue ocean. The colors seemed impossible, yet eternal at the same time. We sipped our beers, thinking our own thoughts.

"You know, T, what we just did, all that, I don't know if we can call it good or right, but I guess it doesn't matter at this point. I'm not going to lose sleep over any of it. The money will help a lot. But there's something I've been thinking of that I wanted to run by you."

"I bet I know what," Tommy asked. "Moving jobs offshore and all that? Corporate layoffs?"

"Yes," I said. "Precisely. I think it's about time."

And I told Tommy of my idea to strike back. To do something to help ordinary working people. We kicked the idea around until it started to form into a plan.

73

I t was a seasonably warm October evening in Beaufort, South Carolina, with a pleasant breeze coming across the marshes of the Beaufort River. I was in an exclusive community of wooded lanes and million-dollar homes. Within that neighborhood, I was inside one of those million-dollar homes, and a man sat across from me. He was secured to a heavy wood dining chair with numerous plastic ties. One of Tommy's associates had provided several high-tech toys that had helped me get inside the house quietly. The surprise had been complete.

Andrew Billings, Chairman and CEO of Benson, Ellis, and Quentin, was starting to shake off the effects of the tranquilizer dart I had fired into his neck about thirty minutes earlier. Tommy himself had helped me with getting the dosage at just the right level to knock someone out almost instantly, but such that they could wake up fairly quickly and interact at near normal capacity. I tossed a glass of cold water into his face.

He recoiled from the shock and his eyes opened wide. He tried to yell but the ball-gag in his mouth didn't let much sound out. He looked around in horror, testing his arms and legs and gradually coming to the realization that he was completely helpless. It sounded to me like he was trying to yell some combination of 'Why?' and 'What do you want?' to me. I slapped him across the face with my gloved hand. Not too hard—just enough to help focus his attention. I let him see the big silenced automatic in my other hand and his eyes bulged while he tried to yell again.

"Listen to me carefully, Mr. Billings. The tranquilizer should be mostly worn off by now and should have no lasting effects worse than a hangover. Let me know when you feel clear-headed enough to communicate. I can throw more cold water in your face, if you'd like."

He rolled his head back and forth and seemed to test his breathing around the ball-gag. It was a simple thing from one of those adult stores, slightly modified with Velcro for ease of use. He took a few breaths and then nodded to me.

"Good. Pay attention and cooperate completely and you'll get through this alive. I know that your wife is out on Hilton Head for the night at one of your friend's places, so she won't be interrupting us. Neither will anyone else. It's my plan to untie you and be gone within the hour but we have things to talk about first. Nod if you're with me so far."

He nodded vigorously.

"Good again. You're doing just fine. I'm sure you're still a bit groggy, but have you noticed the boxes under your wrists?"

He looked down at his arms and then back and forth several times from one to the other. A puzzled look came over his face as he tried to understand what he was looking at.

His arms, with shirtsleeves pushed up above the elbows, were tightly fastened to the wooden arms of the chair, but held slightly above them by virtue of the small boxes that were strapped independently under each wrist. Each rectangular box was about the size of a large and thick paperback and appeared to be made out of aluminum or some other light-colored metal. A set of Velcro straps extended from the end of each box nearest the elbow to wrap tightly around the thick part of his forearm. His gaze moved up towards his wrists where he saw what looked like a braided wire coming out of the box and describing a loose circle around the wrist.

I could see that he was confused and remembered that executives were frequently not very technical.

"Let me explain what you're looking at so we don't waste too much time. You can see that the box attached to each of your arms has a wire coming out of it that goes around the arm above the wrist. You can also see that both ends of that wire disappear into the box. I bet you're wondering what is inside the box, right? Is it an assortment of delicious chocolates? Is it a stash of love letters?"

The radio attached to my belt suddenly let out a squawk followed by some garbled speech.

"Excuse me just one moment please," I said. I walked over to the other side of the kitchen and spoke into the radio.

"Unit one here—report."

I held the device to my ear and listened to the static-punctuated response. I could hear brief references to units two, three, and four as they responded in turn. I transmitted again.

"On track here to complete in approximately forty minutes. Check in again at twenty-one hundred. Unit one out."

I replaced the radio onto the belt clip.

"I'm very sorry, Mr. Billings, just had to check in with the team there. Looks like a quiet night in this nice neighborhood of yours. Now, where were we? Oh yes—the boxes.

"Those boxes are really quite something. I got the idea from a movie, though I assume that in the movie it was all special effects. In any case I took the basic idea and designed the working model myself. I'm sure you'll be impressed. Nothing like American ingenuity, don't you agree?

"The cord around your wrist that looks like the cord you would use to hang a picture on your wall, is actually that serrated cord used in those emergency pocket saws. Normally a length of it would have a big ring at each end so you could pull it back and forth to cut through a log."

He was starting to look more and more terrified. He tried to give me some animated response but the ball-gag rendered his speech unintelligible.

"So inside each box, the ends of that cord are attached to two small servo-motors. They're AC powered."

I gestured to the power cords running from each box to an outlet strip under the chair. It was clear from his reaction that he'd just noticed them.

"I hope it's okay that I borrowed an extension cord from your garage. I'll put it back when I'm done. I always return tools."

I produced a small black object from my pocket and held it up for him to see.

"This is a remote control switch. There's a button for on and off, and then this small slider on the side that changes the code to control the box on either side—right arm, left arm. If and when I press this button, the two little servo motors will begin to reel in the cord. The motors aren't fast, but are geared for very high torque. When they sense a certain amount of resistance, the circuitry will begin to cycle power between the two motors. When that happens, the wire will go into a back and forth sawing motion. I tested it on a four-inch sapling and it works really well. Do I still have your attention?"

I thought he may have been starting to cry. He struggled in the chair and managed to stomp the wooden feet on the floor a few times.

"All right, so now that we have that understanding, let's get to the point.

"BEQ, like many US-based corporations, has for years been hiring more and more foreign workers in order to avoid paying the higher American salaries."

He groaned and rolled his head, trying to say something. I knew he was probably thinking that he now knew what this was all about—corporate terrorism. I backhanded him across the face and his eyes riveted on me again.

"But worse than that," I continued, "you've been engaged in an aggressive campaign to actually lay off thousands of American workers in good standing, so that you can then replace them with cheaper foreign labor!"

I was yelling at him now, finding myself getting genuinely enraged and with no need to try to put on a show.

"That is despicable, and you are a fucking disgrace! You and your corporate asshole friends are destroying lives so you can have a bigger bonus and inflate your stock options! When is it ever going to be enough for you?"

I made a show of calming down and lowering my voice.

"It's time for change. I represent a group of operatives who will be having quiet meetings like this with other corporate leaders over the next several weeks, tonight included. We plan to use various induce-ments to effect some changes. In your case, I know you aren't far from retirement. We want you to use your last year or two to begin a new life's purpose. We want you to become one of the leading corporate voices in the country for the cause of re-patriating jobs. Under your leadership, and with your directives, BEQ will freeze all foreign hiring and begin a full-speed-ahead effort to recruit and hire Americans. This process will begin immediately. I hope I make myself very clear."

He shook his head slowly, as though in resignation. I could tell that he sighed into the ball-gag.

I raised my arm quickly, holding up the little remote. The motion caught his attention and his eyes opened wide.

I pressed the button.

A slight hum started from within the box on his left arm. We both stared, he in horror, me in fascination, as the wire came taught against his wrist. A fine red line appeared under the wire, and soon became a substantial stream of blood as the cord buried itself into the meat of his lower arm. He jerked around in the chair, trying in vain to get free of it and to shake the box off his arm, but he was fastened too tightly. His face was running with sweat and tears and his ball-gag screams were as loud as he could make them.

The sound of the motors changed slightly as the cord hit bone. They began the back and forth cycling. About fifteen seconds after I had pressed the button, his left hand, severed above the wrist, flopped down to bounce off his knee and then to the floor with a wet thud. I watched as several of the fingers contracted, as though grasping at something just out of reach, before the hand was still.

"Well, I guess that's one hand that won't be in the cookie jar anymore," I said. I noticed that he gave no indication of appreciating my sense of humor, and he did not join me in my laughter.

With a final wide-eyed attempt to scream, he fainted. His head fell towards his chest. Thick, dark blood spewed out of the end of his lower arm. I noticed that the flow was pulsing in time to his heartbeats.

I checked my watch, then reached into one of the pockets of my backpack, retrieving several items I had brought for the occasion.

Moving quickly, and doing my best to stay clear of the blood flow, I released the Velcro strap holding the bloody box to the stump of his arm and set the box on the nearby counter. Holding the arm steady, I applied a combat tourniquet just below his elbow. Next, I wrapped the bloody stump tightly in a battle dressing impregnated with a clotting agent, securing it in place with several wraps of surgical tape. Lastly, I got out one of the pre-loaded morphine injectors that Tommy had given me months ago, and jammed it into his upper arm. I had prepared a dosage calibrated to diffuse the pain but not eliminate it. I wanted him to feel pain but also hope.

I pulled the kitchen trash can over to just in front of him as a makeshift table, and set the severed hand on it, positioning it so he would be able to see it clearly. At the kitchen sink, I washed my gloved hands with soap and water until they appeared free of blood.

I refilled the glass with cold water and tossed it in his face. He began to wake up. I slapped him a few times, lightly and back and forth. Clarity and understanding returned gradually to his eyes.

He looked at his bandaged arm in terror and then at the severed hand several feet away. Tears poured down his cheeks.

"Take a minute, Mr. Billings. You may feel a little strange because I've given you a small dose of morphine. Let me know when you're ready. Here, I'll give you something to look at for a few minutes."

I went to the far side of the kitchen and made some comments into the radio, getting several garbled responses. Coming back towards him, I grabbed a towel and a flat tray from the kitchen island. I laid the towel across his blood-spattered knees and set the tray on top of it. Pulling a small tablet from my backpack, I used the touch-screen to start a photographic slide show and set it on the tray so he could look down and watch the screen.

"One of our team took all the pictures. What do you think? I really like the new highlights in your daughter's hair. And she has such nice delicate hands."

More tears came as he watched. His wife and their daughter having coffee on some sunny terrace. His daughter serving a customer at the Hilton Head restaurant where she was a waitress. His son washing a late-model Mustang outside what looked like a college dorm. Son and daughter walking along a city street. The last picture was one of his wife together with both of the grown children, somewhere at the seashore.

I picked up the tablet and stowed it back in my bag.

"Wasn't that fun? I really like that last picture of the three of them. I'm going to loosen your gag now, but if you yell, or just piss me off..."

I held up the remote control and gestured to the box still on his right hand.

He recoiled and nodded vigorously up and down.

I pulled at the strap holding the gag and let it fall clear of his mouth. He worked his jaw back and forth and took several deep breaths.

"What do you want me to do?" His voice was strained and raspy. "Would you put my hand in the freezer please?"

Ever the executive.

I took a small envelope out of my back pocket and set it on the counter, making sure he saw it.

"Hold that thought about your hand. Here, I've written some instructions for you so you don't forget, but I'll go over them. Exactly how you do it is your business, but my organization wants to see a well-covered press release from BEQ within thirty days from today outlining your new direction to return jobs from overseas and to hire Americans. We have connections all over the corporate and legal world and we will be monitoring your progress carefully. We want to see fast results and we do not want to see delay in this effort. We expect actual hiring to begin within sixty days. My sources tell me that several board members will support you if you get the ball rolling. Use your powers of persuasion and sell it to the others. You can do it. Acknowledge your understanding please."

"Yes, yes, I get it," he said, nodding.

"I really hope you do. Would you like to see the slide show again?"

"No! I get it, I really do. What else?"

"I realize that when we leave here tonight, you may just decide to call the police and forget all about our understanding. That would be a grave error and they cannot protect you. If I have to come back to see you again, we won't have as much fun as we're having tonight. Do you want me to come back soon and see you again, Mr. Billings? Perhaps when your family is here?"

"No, no, just tell me what else!"

"Okay, we're almost done here. Within ten days, you will donate five-hundred thousand dollars of your own money to the ASPCA. Make sure it's covered by the press and make sure it's your personal money. We will be watching. That will be your good-faith gesture indicating that we still have an understanding and that your plans to comply are on track. Acknowledge."

"Sure, yes—I get it." He nodded quickly.

"Humor me. Repeat it all back to me to make sure we're clear." I held up the little remote for emphasis.

"Uh, ten days, five-hundred thousand to, ah, to the ASPCA. Press announcement about hiring by thirty days. And ninety, no, sixty days to start hiring."

"Bingo! You got it right! I guess you've been listening to me. As long as you hold up your side, you won't ever have to see me again. Now, my suggestion is that you tell the police that this was a robbery. Robberies of rich executives happen all the time. Do you have a safe? Seems like all you corporate types have safes."

"Yes, in my office, bottom of the desk. There's some cash in there." He tilted his head to gesture into the living room. "Office over there."

I fished a notepad and pen out of the backpack and got ready to write.

"Good work. Tell me the combination."

He dropped his head to his chest and cursed to himself. He looked back up at me and then over at the hand on top of the trash can.

"Oh, you are fucking kidding me. That is just too funny! You have a palm print safe? That's just too much. Well, I'll give it a try."

I grabbed another kitchen towel and wrapped it around the base of the hand. I went across to the office to find the safe.

It was easy enough to locate and I was able to use the severed hand to open it without any trouble. There was a pile of what looked like bonds, several envelopes, various documents, and a half-dozen bundles of bills, maybe forty or fifty thousand. I saw that his desk trash can was empty so I took the plastic bag from it and used it to wrap up all the papers and the money.

As I stood up beside the desk my eye went to a framed photo next to the phone. It looked like a fairly recent shot of Mr. and Mrs. Billings at some sunny beach bar, laughing, and with fruity drinks in hand. I knew that Sarah Billings was no longer with BEQ, but had been VP of Human Resources when the push to outsource jobs to India and the Philippines had begun.

You get a pass for the moment, lady, I said to myself, *but moments have a way of ending.*

I took the bundle into the kitchen where I shoved it all into the backpack. I set the hand on the counter.

My radio squawked and I spoke into it.

"Unit one—on my way out now."

I could see the relief on his face.

"That looked like enough money to cover the burglary story. No need to bother searching the house for jewelry or whatever. I suggest you think carefully about who to call after I leave. You want someone who will help you with some credible story. Whatever you do, remember my slide show and remember how that cord felt, cutting through your arm. I'm thinking it would cut through your daughter's wrist more quickly than it did yours. Food for thought."

I picked up the hand and walked out of his view to set it in the freezer. I came back up behind him as he was beginning to say something. Quickly reaching in front of him to cover his mouth with my left hand, I jabbed a small syringe into his neck with my right. I held his mouth while he struggled for a few seconds before surrendering to unconsciousness.

I found a trash bag under the sink and used it to pack up the two metal boxes and all the plastic ties. Thinking again about the hand, I found a gallon-size storage bag in one of the kitchen drawers and took it back from the freezer. Someone with his money and connections might hire the world's best surgeon to reattach it, and that just wouldn't do.

I left the house as I'd come in, through the garage. On my way out, I picked up the pre-programmed transmitter device that had sent all the fake transmissions to my own radio. I walked across the yard and dropped several cigarette butts gathered from a rest stop on the interstate earlier in the day. As I walked the few blocks to the rental car, I removed the colored contact lenses I'd been wearing and dropped them onto the road, grinding them a few times under my shoe. I pulled the plastic strips from my mouth and tossed them into a storm drain as I passed. I peeled off the stick-on treads from the bottom of my shoes and dropped them into the next storm drain.

As I approached the car, I pulled off the large overshirt I'd been wearing, stowing it along with my latex gloves into another plastic bag that was ready in the trunk, to be safely discarded or destroyed later. Washing out the temporary hair dye could wait till I was back in my hotel in Savannah.

As I crossed the bridge over the Broad River to the west of the city, I took advantage of a lull in traffic to pull over and toss out the hand, along with the two metal boxes from the first trash bag. I took a moment to wonder if gators came up this far north. If so, I thought, that bony old hand would be a disappointing snack.

74

As events unfolded, I did end up having to pay him a second visit after all. Chairman Billings had made the expected donation to the ASPCA within a week, but a full forty days on, I hadn't heard anything indicating a change in hiring direction at BEQ.

After my second visit, this time to a large house in Ridgewood, New Jersey, where I had to deal with an armed guard, things started to happen quickly. I heard indirectly from sources inside BEQ that there had been a major policy shift. There was a firm directive from the top that positions must be filled domestically whenever possible. Executives who were not on board with the new ideas were shown the door. The entire Human Resources organization was restructured. I saw an interview with one of the vice presidents where he insisted that hiring American was simply the right thing to do.

I heard about several people who had been laid off within the past year having been called back with job offers.

Within a month, it was announced that Billings would be stepping down to enjoy his retirement after thirty-six years with the company.

He and his wife moved to a gorgeous waterfront house in Florida, on Summerland Key, where they enjoyed a well-earned life of ease.

They had a lot in common and they enjoyed their time together. They were fabulously wealthy and their children were set for life. They loved to try new wines and cook together. They loved ballroom dancing and listening to light jazz. They liked to sail during the day and to walk on the beach at night.

And they were both learning to live with just one hand.

ACKNOWLEDGMENTS

The creation of this book would not have been possible without the assistance of several people.

First, I want to thank my wife and best friend, Bonnie. Particularly with her careful readings of the latter versions of the book, Bonnie helped me greatly to polish and refine the interactions of the characters. "If Person A did this, would it really make sense for Person B to do that?" Without her unwavering support and encouragement, I would probably still be living on 'Someday Isle'.

My good friend and next-door neighbor, Dr. Judy Ozment, served as my Alpha Reader, plowing through numerous versions of my manuscript as it evolved from rough ideas all the way through to the completed story. A teacher by nature and vocation, Judy always gave me patient and thoughtful feedback.

Another friend, also a teacher, Debbie Lavagnino, gave me a boost at the very beginning of my project. Her advice about story structure during our early discussions was very valuable to me as I moved forward into the crafting of the book.

All three of the ladies mentioned above helped me with how my few female characters might think, what they might say, or how they might react to a situation.

Lastly, many thanks to my editor, Alison Williams, of Alison Williams Writing in the UK. Alison's feedback was always professional and respectful, even when appropriately ruthless.

Made in the USA
Las Vegas, NV
19 July 2021

26717425R00194